MURDER IN THE ZOO

MURDER IN CHURCH

Babette Hughes

MURDER IN THE ZOO

MURDER IN CHURCH

Babette Hughes

COACHWHIP PUBLICATIONS
Greenville, Ohio

Murder in the Zoo / Murder in Church, by Babette Hughes
© 2022 Coachwhip Publications edition

Murder in the Zoo published 1932
Murder in Church published 1934
Babette Hughes, 1905-1982
CoachwhipBooks.com

ISBN 1-61646-522-0
ISBN-13 978-1-61646-522-3

Murder in the Zoo

For
GLENN HUGHES

Prologue

One evening not long ago Craig and I were sitting in his apartment, talking. We had just returned from one of the more gilded picture palaces—Craig's fondness for the talkies amounting almost to a passion—where we had seen William Powell in another of his very convincing variations on the theme of crime and punishment.

On the way home, I remember, Craig was particularly silent. The night itself was padded with fog through which the street lamps shone like yellow moons, and even the smallest neon sign glowed splendidly.

We had turned by tacit consent through the Spanish gates of the Eldorado Arms—as a matter of fact, I still have on my way home from a picture, a muscular impulse to enter that same gateway—and mounted to Craig's apartment before he gave me any clew to what he was thinking about.

"You know, Scott," he said, taking off his coat, "I once solved a murder case."

I didn't believe him, partly through inability to imagine a colleague of mine, a man I saw every day, in an heroic role, and partly because of the easy way in which he said it.

"Sit down," he said, amused by my incredulousness. "I'll tell you about it."

I sank into one of the two chromium and leather armchairs by the fireplace. On the table beside me was a gilt

Buddha—the only cheap object in Craig's rooms; on the wall just opposite me was a tenth-century Cambodian bas-relief of a procession—warriors with spears, prancing horses, et cetera—which I stared idly at, thinking what a curious fellow Craig was to bury himself in Oriental philosophy, to put up with a college professor's wages—in other words, to take for his profession what any other man would consider only as a hobby.

Let me explain myself: The average college professor is such for one of two reasons: either his desire to do research, to make contributions in his chosen field, is greater than his normal desire for wealth (as in my case), or else, having some sort of inferiority complex, he takes refuge in the academic life just as in the Middle Ages he would have entered a monastery.

Now, in Craig's case these two reasons for his career were obviously ridiculous; he had, so far as I know, made no contributions in the field of Oriental philosophy, nor did he contemplate any; as for needing a refuge—well, I personally can see no reason save laziness why a man with Craig's qualifications for a diplomatic or financial career should take refuge in a college.

Yet laziness was incompatible with him as was any physical or mental softness. In fact, his eyes, probably because of the blond, sharply arched eyebrows above them, had a sort of Spanish inquisition look that seemed the more diabolical because of the childish way his hair insisted on looping diagonally across his forehead and because of the cleft in his chin. No, Craig wasn't lazy, only too damned intolerant, I finally decided.

He handed me a Manila cigar and placed a bottle of Spanish brandy on the table between us. "'My damned Orientals,'" he quoted me good naturedly, "have an absolute genius for rum-running. And as for that!"—he indicated the Cambodian bas-relief—"without that, I might never have solved my mystery."

"What do you mean?" I asked, quite used to having my thoughts read and brilliantly argued by Craig before I had even got around to speaking them.

He had gone to get glasses—those large tulip-shaped glasses in which a drop of brandy can reveal itself; when he sat down opposite me, twisting the stem of his glass and scenting the brandy fumes that mounted from it, his eyes were intent and I could see that he was really serious.

"You know, Scott," he said. "I can't bear these fellows who make a fetish of cynicism. Oh, we all do, I suppose, at one time or another, generally when we're young—and afraid of being laughed at. That doesn't count, it's only bravado. But fellows who keep it up . . ." He paused and I wondered to whom he was alluding. In any college so large as ours there were bound to be all types, but I could think of no one the shoe particularly fitted. The academic type is, on the whole, rather naive—a trait at the opposite pole from cynicism.

"I'm thinking of a man at Earl College," Craig said. "If you don't mind I'd like to tell you about him."

"Mind!" I said.

"He was a psychologist and he was cynical. And by cynical I don't mean that harmless and decorative sort of cynicism that some men wear in their off hours as they would a *boutonnière;* I mean a devastating cynicism, the sort that aims at your appetites and capacities, that substitutes for the ordinary emotions, such as joy and sorrow, a feeling of superiority—rather monotonous in the long run I should think.

"I'm sure Brown found it so; he always looked as though he'd just eaten sawdust. What made his case the more pitiful was that, physically, he was magnificent. I don't mean to seem patronizing—it's easy enough to patronize a dead man—but I honestly did feel sorry for him; a handsome fellow with a first-rate mind that was rapidly going to seed. And I think he knew it, but he wouldn't retract. Perhaps he couldn't. God knows, enthusiasm is elusive enough to any one over twenty-one. Well, his enthusiasm for art, philosophy, literature and science was done for, eaten away by sheer cynicism. And, as he had to profess some interests, couldn't sit like a yogi contemplating his navel, he limited himself to the physical pleasures of life—eating and exercise. A magnificent gesture, of course—for a civilized man to turn primitive, not in the sensual way Gauguin did when he retreated to the South Seas, not even morally, but philosophically. I don't know if it's ever before been done. Oh, I know that plenty of men fully as cultivated as Brown have chosen to live a purely animal existence. And that's just where the difference lies: an animal existence is emotional; Brown's existence wasn't; it was, to be exact, the existence of a discriminating robot, a mechanical being to whom nothing mattered.

"I don't mean to imply Brown was inhuman; he wasn't. He had all the best qualities—charm, politeness and discrimination. He was a good friend and an amusing conversationalist on the trivia of life. Yet very few people liked him. They saw, I suppose, that his politeness was only a formula, that he considered none of them worth not being polite to. In the same way his cynicism accounted for his conversational wit. I wonder if you've ever noticed that people with strong convictions are very seldom witty. Brown had no convictions; he had no fear of misrepresenting himself because he was hollow—one of T. S. Eliot's "hollow men"; there was nothing to misrepresent. In other words, the identity of Courtney Brown was a rapid continuity of thousands of his actions and words, none of which in themselves ever represented him., The average man—John

Doe—is surprisingly sincere; almost any one of his states of mind is John Doe. Not so with Brown; only a movie of his thousands of different personalities could ever be his identity. That was why he was so generally misunderstood; and those who disliked him generally disliked, not Courtney Brown, but one of his discarded states of being."

Craig smiled. I think one of the most charming things about him was that sudden and ingenuous smile with which he punctuated a line of thought. "Tell me if I'm boring you," he said.

I shook my head. "Please go on."

"Well, I don't know that there's much more to tell about Brown, except perhaps a few important trifles. For instance, he had a genius for cooking. And it has occurred to me that those very characteristics that made his life a failure made his zabaglione and sauce Mornay and bisque Nantua a success. If you see what I mean."

"I think I do."

"Personally, I never cared for Brown's dishes; they were too oily; they lined the membrane of the stomach with a greasy film that retarded the absorption of this, for instance,"—indicating the brandy—"by the blood. But I don't deny his cooking was royal; it combined the techniques of France, Italy, Austria and the Orient."

He smiled again. "I wish you could have seen Brown's flower garden; he was inordinately fond of it. And I think I understand why. For one thing, of course, it gave him an outlet for his creative impulses, as did his cooking. But my theory is that he chose the botanical and culinary arts to the exclusion of all others simply as another means of confounding the layman and high-browing the artist and scholar. Any philosophical discussion he reduced to an anecdote about dahlias or soups."

He paused and for a moment neither of us spoke. I was profoundly stirred and for the moment life seemed worth living only to know more about this extraordinary man. "You say he's dead?"

Craig nodded. "Murdered!"

"Murdered!" I echoed.

"A suitable death for a cynic! I don't mean to be cynical," Craig added, "but when you know the circumstances you'll see I'm right: his was a suitable death. It's curious, you know," he said, lighting his cigar, "in almost all deaths the chief quality of the dying person is emphasized—as it was in Brown's case. Pepys died of indigestion; Molière died acting in his own ironic comedy, *Le Malade imaginaire;* Peter the Great died in bed, a reformed barbarian; Blake died seeing angels. It all comes down to the Confucian theory that life can be reduced to a series of patterns. I believed that theory; I'd seen it demonstrated in more than one man's life and that's why I felt that, knowing Brown, if I could get at the rhythm of his life, I'd probably be able by a process of deduction to put my hand on his murderer."

"And did you?" I asked.

Craig laughed at my eagerness. "Yes."

"But the bas-relief—what had that to do with it?"

There was a sculptured quality in Craig's face that ordinarily escaped me; now it was suddenly arresting. "You won't deny there's a palpable rhythm to those marching warriors," he said. "Well, the facts of Brown's murder placed in logical order had just as palpable a rhythm—something quite distinct from them. You felt it but couldn't place your hands on it. . . ."

"A sort of fourth dimension," I suggested.

"Precisely!" Craig relaxed. I saw he was tired, and got up to go. He followed me to the door, once more the weary dilettante.

"By the way," I asked, "who was the murderer?"

The shadow of a smile lighted Craig's face. A thousand revelations electrified the space between us. Then he said abruptly, "Wait!" He went to a camphor-wood chest, unlocked it, and returned to me with a red leather notebook which he placed in my hands. I opened it curiously. "My journal of the Courtney Brown case," he said. "It's all in there; do what you want with it; I don't want it back."

I didn't attempt to thank him; somehow, you never thanked Craig for favors; he followed his impulses and that was all there was to it. I took the journal home, read it, and—how futile words are as tributes. . . .

The Christmas holidays came; immediately after them I heard that Craig was leaving for Tokyo, where he had been invited to lecture at the Imperial University. It is now August; Craig is in Paris, lecturing in French at the Sorbonne. He plans, I think, to return home for the spring quarter. Should any one be surprised at my daring to publish this private journal without the author's consent, I can only say that I feel justified in giving to a jaded world so amazing a document.

1

It was approximately four-thirty Friday afternoon that Hulse appeared for the second time in the doorway of the departmental library. "Mr. Craig!" he said in a hoarse, unnatural voice. I looked quickly up. His face, ordinarily pale, was mottled and, in a flash, my brain reviewed the story of a man who choked to death on underdone liver.

In the same moment I had sense enough to go to him. "Dr. Brown!" he exclaimed in the same strangled manner. "Murdered!" I raced upstairs; I think Hulse recovered sufficiently to come directly behind me. Anyway, I know that a few minutes later he was standing beside me in the "zoo," the animal laboratory maintained by the psychology department.

As I looked at Brown, sprawling face up on the floor beside the animal maze, horror was not, strangely enough, my first emotion. Or rather, horror was there, dominated for the moment by one of my more heretical selves, summoned to the surface by this heretical sight, whose only reaction was that Brown would have hated, more than being murdered even, to be looked down on and pitied by myself, the janitor and two students. This illuminating thought, more than anything else, restored me to a balanced state of mind. Brown was murdered; there seemed to be no doubt of that. "Have you telephoned the police?"

I asked the boy and girl who were regarding me with that childish hopefulness that expects to see Humpty Dumpty put together again.

"I'll do it, Dr. Craig," the boy volunteered, eager to escape that ghastly sight.

"You can use the telephone in Brown's office," I said. "Don't forget to dial the outside."

The boy fled, and I was left alone with Hulse and the girl whom I recognized as one of Brown's student assistants. "Who found him?" I asked. Hulse, seemingly oblivious to my question, had stooped down to peer into the maze.

"He did," the girl said.

"What are you doing?" I asked Hulse. "You mustn't touch anything, you know."

"Listen!" he said, his head at the opening of the maze. From within came a muffled squawk. "There's a pigeon in there—poor thing!"

"Never mind!" I pulled him away. "We'll get it out later. The main thing now is to leave things as they are until the police have come. If you bother with that pigeon the police will find your fingerprints on the cage and think you killed Brown." As I said the words I couldn't help smiling at the absurdity of such a supposition: Hulse, frail, ignorant and timid—Brown's murderer!

Hulse straightened up under my grasp. "I didn't kill him, Mr. Craig. It wasn't meant for me to do it. But I knew it was coming. Every one of those poor little rabbits and pigeons, Mr. Craig—their lives count for as much as yours and mine, and they'd to be answered for."

The girl looked at me and I knew what was in her mind. "Be quiet, Hulse," I said. "That talk will land you in jail. You'd better go about your work now. We'll call you when the police come."

"All right, Mr. Craig," he said, instantly subsiding.

"Wait," I called after him on second thought, "you'd better not disturb anything on this floor. Have you done the downstairs?" He nodded. "Go and get a cup of coffee then; you'll feel better." He dragged himself out, still rather shaky.

"He didn't do it," I told the girl. "Don't let on to the police what he said; I know him well enough to know he's a perfectly harmless sort of modern Buddhist."

"Some one did it," she said, her eyes on Brown.

I looked her over: feet in calfskin oxfords wide apart, skirt, sweater, and small, sullen face. "You're pretty calm!"

Her gaze wandered from Brown to me. "I'm a behaviorist." I couldn't tell whether or not her tone was sarcastic.

The boy returned from Brown's office. "They'll be right up. I had a hell of a time getting them."

"Are you a behaviorist too?" I asked him.

He hesitated, wondering if I was baiting him, then turned to the girl. "What would you say, Miss Mullin?" She shrugged her shoulders. "Who do you think killed him, Mr. Craig?" he demanded of me.

"I've just been asking myself that," I replied, "and the obvious answer seems to be either the janitor or one of us."

He became instantly worried. "It couldn't have been us—Miss Mullin or me. We were in the lab."

I smiled. "Well, then, it must have been either Mr. Hulse or me; and since I can vouch for the innocence of Mr. Hulse. . . ."

The boy's tension passed and he broke into a smile, as did Miss Mullin. "No," I admitted, "I don't think it's as simple as all that—or perhaps it's simpler."

Waiting for the police, I took stock of the room, reflecting at the same time on the alacrity with which I had taken advantage of Brown's murder to step into a position of authority. And though I told myself I had only done what was necessary, I couldn't, looking at Brown's blood-less face, condone my attitude.

Miss Mullin was at a window staring idly across the campus. A crowd of students in bright slickers and berets appeared around the north corner of the forestry building. The boy, who was nervously pacing the room, stopped beside her. "They're coming from the basketball game. Gee! I wish I'd gone!"

The boy's honesty amused me; his regret was so patently not that Brown was killed but that he wasn't at the other end of the campus. He more or less echoed my own thoughts, and I wondered about Miss Mullin's. She had known Brown better than any of us. "It was quite obviously done with this." I pointed to the hammer beside Brown.

"I suppose so," she said, turning toward me. "At the base of the brain; you can see the blood came from there. If we dared lift his head. . . ."

"Better not," I advised. "Did Hulse touch him, do you know?"

"I don't know," she said. "Not after he called us anyway, and probably not before. I don't think he had sense enough to; he was too frightened. Jack and I felt his pulse and did all the usual things."

The boy had followed her over. He looked distastefully down at the corpse. "Did you ever hunt for the pulse of a dead man?" he demanded of me with a gesture of disgust. "Say!" He brightened up. "Do you suppose it's all right to smoke in here?"

"For all I care," I said, reaching for my cigarettes. Miss Mullin took one and the three of us lighted up.

"How long do you suppose he's been dead?"

I smiled at the excitement he was beginning to experience. It was, however, a sensible question and one I had asked myself. "He's cold."

Miss Mullin said, "He was cold when we came in. And the blood had dried on this. . . ." She touched the hammer beside him with her foot.

Jack turned to me, ingenuously curious. "Say! how do you suppose he was standing when that bird hit him? Do you suppose he just went plop on his back?"

The question bothered me. It was Miss Mullin who volunteered an answer. "He was probably bending over the maze."

"And fell on it, slid off onto the floor, rolling over onto his back," I supplemented. "I wonder."

"It sounds pretty fishy to me." Jack calculated. "Wait! I'll try it on this side. What do you want to bet I don't land like that!"

Miss Mullin stopped him. "Don't, Jack; you'll mess things up."

"When the police come we'll have a demonstration," I said. In the meantime I intended to pursue my inventory of the zoo. I hadn't realized the several times I had visited Brown or his colleague, Frampton, how fully the room justified its name. It was large—about thirty by forty feet, I should say—and permeated with an ammoniac odor that recalled vividly the indoor circuses in Paris, particularly the Cirque d'Hiver. The rat and guinea-pig cages were piled on one another in the northwest corner of the room. Some of them were empty and such specimens as there were seemed in a state of coma. In the northeast corner of the room, having access to the nearest window by a runway, was a pigeon cage, containing three fat pigeons. Halfway between the pigeon cage and vermin cages and set up against a locked door was a table holding the ant box, a wooden packing case containing dirt and rocks, its rim smeared with petroleum jelly to prevent the ants from escaping. In the long east end of the room were three large windows looking out on that section of the campus that runs, some five hundred yards farther on, into the lake. Directly in front of these windows were two long work-tables littered with wire, string, boxes, plates of glass, and so on. The hammer employed to kill Brown might easily have been taken from there. In the room's south wall were two more windows and a door leading out to a fire escape. The door to Brown's office was in the west wall, as was the hall door, the only other entrance to the room. A large wooden maze, as I have said, occupied the center of the floor. Other devices for testing animal intelligence—smaller mazes, problem boxes and ladders—were spaced about the floor, always at sufficiently large intervals to allow the experimenter plenty of leeway.

The room appeared to be, apart from its natural un-tidiness, in no particular disorder. I noticed that a drum on a small table near the maze, and connected by a tube with it, had not apparently been touched, although it was between the hall door and the maze, only a few feet north of Brown's head.

Looking again at Brown I wondered who could have wanted to kill him. He had irritated many people—that I could understand—but irritation is hardly a motivation for murder. What had he done in his urbane way, or said, that it should have been his last deed or word? In his face there was no clew, only the "smile of the dead"—an understatement of that same eternal verity so admirably overstated in primitive masks.

My philosophizing was interrupted by the police. Two detectives, Thompson and Andrews, took charge, stationing men at the various exits to the building—a measure I saw no use for—while the medical man they had brought along, Dr. Quigley, examined Brown. At the same time a fingerprint expert, Gottschalk, did his hocus-pocus with powder and a small blower. I looked on, amused by the dispatch shown by the rather ordinary looking Thompson and Andrews, who saw in Brown only another "stiff." Was it possible, I wondered, that they, incapable in their highest flights of understanding Brown, might be capable of understanding his death? If so, life was less orderly than I had dared suppose. To be interpreted when dead by intelligences we have spent our lives in denying is a fate even Brown must not have deserved. Not, I dare say, that I would have ranked any higher on his charts than Thompson or Andrews. We each were engaged in our own particular maze, and if I felt my maze to be the higher type, that feeling was probably as explicable as a superiority in any one of his white rats.

Nevertheless, as a man guided by instincts based on a lifelong study of the Baghavad-Gita, the works of Buddha, Confucius, Plotinus and Plato, I persist in thinking those instincts might be more relevant to this case than all the efficiency of Thompson and Andrews. If I fail I will have had my little fantasy; if I succeed I will have shown Oriental philosophy to be a practical science, I don't say I hope by finding Brown's murderer to do him a last good turn; he would have been the first to laugh at such a statement of sentimentality.

It was growing dark. Thompson had already ordered the shades pulled and lights turned on. I, and no doubt Jack Tobey and Miss Mullin, was wondering how soon we were to be allowed to go home, when suddenly the door opened—the hall door—and Mrs. Brown entered, perfectly furious, followed by two apologetic policemen.

"What does this mean?" she demanded of the room at large. Then she saw her husband's body, stretched on the floor. She stood quite still, seeming to rearrange the parts of the picture in her mind. We all watched her, quite obviously hoping for some revealing sign. When she did speak, her words fulfilled that hope to an unbelievable extent. I don't think I shall ever forget the look they produced on the faces of Thompson and Andrews.

"Frampton killed him," she said, and there was no uncertainty in her voice, no hysteria.

I think when our shock wore off we were more embarrassed than anything else. I know I was. Mrs. Brown showed no signs of grief for her husband. As a matter of fact the last hour had been characterized by an amazing lack of conventional grief. Except for Hulse we had all been from the first extremely calm, an observation that seems to argue that education tempers the emotions. I wouldn't say Miss Mullin felt no grief; Jack Tobey's was, apparently, for his own predicament; and as for my own, I might define it as grief at not being able to feel grief.

Mrs. Brown sat down in a chair Thompson fetched for her, and gently refused to answer his questions. Making a virtue of necessity, he decreed she needn't do so until the next morning. The rest of us and Hulse, who had timidly entered, he told to report back to the zoo at eight P.M.

I was tired and lost no time in leaving, stopping at my office for my hat. It was then I knew for certain that fortune favored me in my new role, and that, abetting mysticism with science, I decided to start this journal. For I found on the carpet of my office, ironic in its symbolism as Whistler's butterfly, a white handkerchief monogrammed with J.L.B.—Jennifer L. Brown.

2

After dinner I returned to the psychology department, Mrs. Brown's handkerchief, safe now in my desk drawer, having so successfully sharpened my suspicious as to make me anticipate rather than dread the forthcoming questionnaire. And my only fear now was that the police might refuse to let me participate in their findings. They were not, I felt, any too favorably inclined toward professors, judging us no doubt by our prototypes in motion pictures, where we are a necessary but unpleasant link in the plot.

My fears were justified. Messieurs Andrews and Thompson suspected me not only of pedagogism but also of having killed Courtney Brown. They were very frank. "Mr. Craig," Thompson said, having, with the aid of a policeman, assembled all four of us—Hulse, Tobey, Mullin and myself—in the zoo, from which the body had been removed, "where were you when the murder was committed?"

"If I knew when the murder was committed . . ." I suggested.

True to his calling of questioner he disliked questions. He did, however, answer mine: "Between three and four o'clock; that's the best Dr. Quigley could do."

Dr. Quigley spoke. "His blood clotted very quickly; there's no way of knowing more accurately what time he was killed."

"Thank you," I said. "I was in the philosophy library on the second floor between three and four. I arrived there about two, as a matter of fact, and didn't leave until the janitor came to tell me about Brown."

"Was any one else there with you?" Thompson growled.

"No!" I, too, was determined to be frank. "Mr. Hulse came in about four to sweep up, but except for that I was alone and had every opportunity to walk across the hall through my office to the fire escape, dash up it, kill Brown and return the same way to the library. You'll just have to take my word that I didn't."

"We don't take people's word!" I shrugged my shoulders. "Who found the body?" I indicated Hulse. "All right!" he said. "Miss Mullin, please!"

Miss Mullin stepped before the tribunal, still swearing the brown sweater and skirt and flat-heeled oxfords, her expression still enigmatical within a frame of clipped brown hair.

"Where were you when Brown was killed?" The words shot like bullets at her.

"In the laboratory."

"What do you mean, the laboratory? Isn't this a laboratory?"

"We call this the zoo," she said, appearing somehow slightly more human under pressure. "Of course, it is a laboratory, an animal laboratory, while the others are for human experiments."

Thompson frowned. He was of course smoking a cigar. "And what were you doing in this . . . human laboratory?"

"I was conducting an experiment on Mr. Tobey."

"And what was the experiment?"

"It was an experiment to determine the effect of attention or mental activity on the patellar tendon reflex or knee jerk," she replied gently as though to soften the blow.

Her voice was on a single pitch and so lacking in emphasis as to seem slightly foreign.

"Oh!" Thompson said. "Was any one with you?"

"Mr. Tobey was with me; I was experimenting on him."

"Oh, I see." He chewed the end of his cigar. "Well, how long had you been there when he called you?" He nodded toward Hulse, who was positively quivering with nervousness.

She debated a moment. "We started the experiment at a quarter of four; it took us about ten minutes to get ready for it; then the experiment took fifty minutes, counting the periods of passivity. We were just looking over the kymograph record when Mr. Hulse called us. That makes an hour in all, doesn't it?"

Thompson showed no approval of the accuracy of her statement; it seemed in fact to antagonize him. "When was the last time you saw Brown?"

"Why, just before we went to the lab about half-past three."

"He was alive at half-past three?"

For one brief second Miss Mullin's composure seemed strained; then she answered quietly. "Of course he was alive! If he was dead, I'd have told you."

"That'll do! Mr. Tobey!"

The boy stepped defiantly forward, his hands thrust into the pockets of his "cords"; his very red cheeks contrasted amusingly with the natural pallor of his skin and his blond, almost white, hair. "Mr. Tobey, do you subscribe to everything Miss Mullin has just said?"

"If you mean was she experimenting on me—yes, she was!"

"You're a student here?"

"A freshman."

"Was there any reason why she should have experimented on you instead of on one of the other freshmen?"

Thompson's suavity was, I noticed, in inverse ratio to the suavity of his victims.

"No, there wasn't."

"Being experimented on wasn't part of your class work?"

"Sure!"

"Thanks! Any other explanation why, out of all the students in the college, you should have been within a hundred feet of Professor Brown at the precise hour he was murdered?"

Tobey cocked his head to one side. "Say! let me get this straight! You don't think I murdered him!"

"I don't know," Thompson replied shortly.

Miss Mullin stepped forward. "Let me explain. This experiment I'm conducting is for my doctor's degree; it covers a period of several months and involves the cooperation of a number of untrained subjects. I naturally chose those subjects from my freshman psychology class. Jack was one of them. He agreed to come up to-day and let me experiment on him, probably because he thought it might get him a good grade. That's all there is to it."

"Is that right?" Thompson inquired.

Jack nodded vigorously. "Sure that's right."

"Do you always do your experimenting on Friday?"

"Yes. You see, it's the only day in the week I don't have to correct papers and prepare class work for the next day. Saturday would do just as well, but the students like it to themselves. Then, too, some of them work."

"All right!" Thompson grunted.

"Carl!" Thompson whispered hoarsely, "do you suppose we ought to tell them the murderer wore gloves?"

"Go on and tell them."

"The murderer wore gloves," Thompson announced. "Gottschalk looked for fingerprints on the hammer but there weren't any—just gloves. Couldn't find any fresh fingerprints anywhere, except the professor's."

"Mr. Hulse!" Thompson called in much the same way a train announcer calls ". . . and all points east!" Hulse had to be pushed forward. "How long have you been a janitor here?"

"Thirteen years in July. Yes, sir!"

"Married?"

"Yes, sir. . . . I mean, my wife's dead."

"Live alone?"

"Oh, no, sir. I keep pigeons, sir, and rats and guinea-pigs."

"Pigeons and rats and guinea-pigs?"

"Yes, sir. Dr. Brown gives them to me—when he's through with them, poor things! And sometimes he gives me the young—when they're not the right color. The bastards he called them, sir."

"Oh, I see." Thompson looked sternly at him. "You're sure you're not kidding us!"

"Kidding you, sir?"

His authentic bewilderment pacified Andrews. "Go on, Hulse, tell us how you found the body!"

The janitor cleared his throat. "Well, sir, I washed the stairs like I always do Fridays so they'll be clean for Monday."

"What time did you start?"

"Right after lunch."

"At one o'clock?"

"Yes, sir."

"All right, go on. And think carefully. We've got to have things right."

"Yes, sir." Hulse commenced again. "Well, sir, I washed the stairs—right after lunch, that is. Then I did the rooms on the first floor."

"What time?"

"After two o'clock. There aren't any classes after two o'clock Fridays or I couldn't do them so soon, sir. Most days I wait till nearer four. Then I did the rooms on the second floor.

"Did you see Mr. Craig?"

"Yes, sir. He was the only one I did see; they'd all gone home but him. Then I went to ask Dr. Brown if I might do the third floor. . . ."

"Yes!"

"And he was dead. I called those two then, and Mr. Craig, and he sent me out for a cup of coffee."

Andrews rubbed his hand over his beard. "Why didn't you just clean the third floor? Why did you go ask Dr. Brown? Did you think something might be wrong?"

"Oh, no, sir. I always ask Dr. Brown before I clean the third floor. If there's people in the laboratories I shouldn't bother, he tells me."

"What happens then—do you wait until later to clean them?"

"I don't clean them at all. Sometimes three days go by that I don't clean a laboratory."

"Hmm!" Thompson reflected. It seemed to me that considering his fright Hulse had made a very creditable showing—almost too creditable. Could his hysteria have been faked, I wondered—and for what reason? Thompson again whispered.

"Wait!" Andrews blared out. "While you were washing the stairs did any one go up them?"

The janitor's answer was prompt. "Dr. Brown and Mrs. Brown went up them—Mrs. Brown said hello to me. And Miss Mullin went up them. And, oh, yes, Mr. Craig went up them."

"Thank you, Hulse," I murmured.

Thompson spoke to Hulse, glaring at me. "You're sure no one else went up. How about him?" He pointed to Tobey, who was beginning to be anxious.

"Not while I was washing the stairs, sir. He might have gone up while I was doing the first-floor rooms or the men's lavatory."

A faint smile passed over the faces of Andrews and Thompson. Evidently a sample of the only humor they could appreciate! Thompson mastered his amusement. "What time did you enter the building?" he demanded of Tobey.

"Three-thirty! That was the time Miss Mullin told me to come," was the prompt answer.

"Then," Thompson deduced, "if any one else had entered the building about that time you wouldn't have seen them."

Hulse considered. "Yes, sir . . . I mean, no, sir."

Thompson scratched his head. "What time did you enter the building, Miss Mullin?"

"About two-thirty."

"Then," to Hulse, "you were washing the stairs between one and sometime after two-thirty and all that time there was no one in the building that we haven't accounted for and no one new entered."

Hulse nodded. "That's right. But later, while I was working on the second floor, sweeping up the hall, that is, a man went downstairs past me."

"What!"

"A man went downstairs past me, I said, sir."

"Why didn't you say so?" Thompson exclaimed, jarred from his Olympic calm.

"You didn't ask me."

"I'm asking you now." Thompson pointed out. "Was he one of the professors?"

"No, sir, I'd never seen him before that I remember. He was a dark man."

"Was he short or tall?"

"He wasn't short and he wasn't tall—about my size."
Hulse is about five feet three.

"What did he wear?"

"I think he wore a hat and coat. I'm sure he wore a
coat—it seemed big for him. I was busy and I didn't notice
about the hat."

"Well," Thompson commented dryly, "I suppose we
ought to be glad you noticed about the coat. Anything
else about him?"

"No, sir, except he seemed a funny person to be around
the college."

"Oh, he did?" As Thompson was about to dismiss him
Andrews again leaned forward. "Just a minute, Mr. Hulse.
No one here saw Dr. Brown after three-thirty. Was there
anything to prevent your killing him between three-thirty
and four-thirty and later raising an alarm?"

Hulse seemed for a minute stunned. "Why, yes, sir," he
said finally in a startled voice, "I was working."

"He came into the philosophy library sometime during
that period," I said.

"You couldn't say what time, though."

"Around four—not very long before he came the second
time to say Brown was dead."

His look stated clearly that he thought I was shielding the janitor. "You say you didn't see Brown alive at
any time this afternoon!" I shook my head. "Did you ever
quarrel with Brown?"

I smiled. "Whenever we met. Brown, you see, is a behaviorist while I am a mystic. Shall I explain the terms?"
Taking silence for consent, I proceeded. "The behaviorist
considers man a machine; he is interested only in what man
does; he takes into account only man's bodily changes. Emotional experiences such as anger, fear, pleasure, sorrow,
anticipation and dreams don't exist for the behaviorist;

he refuses to take any notice of them. For instance, I place my hand on this table. The behaviorist sticks a pin in it. My hand is promptly withdrawn. The behaviorist sees my hand withdrawn, therefore he believes it. He cannot see the pain I say I feel, therefore he ignores it. He reduces everything to behavior, even thinking—which he claims to be concealed speech—a result of having been told as children to keep quiet. Have I stated your case accurately, Miss Mullin?"

"Very," she said, smiling, and it suddenly occurred to me that she must be beginning to like me. I think, being a quiet little thing and used to Brown's cavalier treatment, she was flattered by even my cursory attention.

"A mystic," I continued, ". . . well, it's very much easier to define any one else's beliefs. Shall we let it go at this: a mystic places logic above behavior and intuition above everything. The average person is apt to think of mystics as vague—if he thinks of them at all. A mystic is not vague; he is logical about large and therefore vague subjects such as earth and heaven."

"Do you think all this has anything to do with Brown's murder?" Thompson demanded crisply.

"Everything to do with it," I said. "I expect to prove that to you."

"Oh, you do! Well, in the meantime, how about giving Mr. Tobey a chance to answer some questions? There are still a few matters I want cleared up." Tobey stepped forward. "You say you came up to this room at three-fifteen to-day. Who was here when you got here?"

"Miss Mullin. I told you she'd said to meet her here."

"There wasn't any one else in the room? Brown wasn't here?"

Tobey considered. "No, just Miss Mullin and me. Dr. Brown was in his office, I think. I remember hearing voices in there."

Thompson rubbed his hands together. "Voices! Well, well, this is interesting. Who would you say the voices belonged to?"

Miss Mullin interrupted. "I know who Dr. Brown was talking to; it was a young reporter who comes here quite often to get feature stories for the *Sun.*"

Thompson questioned her savagely. "Why didn't you tell us before?"

"Maybe she thought we wouldn't be interested," said Andrews.

"No, no! It was only that he's a nice young fellow with no possible reason for having committed this crime and I thought as long as no one else had seen him here I might do him a favor by not implicating him. That was my only idea, really."

Though I thought it rather foolish of her, my opinion of Miss Mullin went up considerably. Not so with Andrews. "Do you know his name?"

"No, but it would be quite easy to find out. He's been here often. I think he's the regular reporter on this beat."

"Well," Thompson said, "if there's anything else you're keeping to yourself you'd better tell it. We'll get it sooner or later." He brought down his fist on the table. "And that applies to all of you!" Did my dramatic instinct play me false or did I see Hulse start?

"Did this reporter get here before or after you did?" Thompson asked Miss Mullin.

"Quite a while after. He came to the zoo and then Dr. Brown took him into his office. Just a few minutes after that Jack came and we went to the lab to start our experiment. That was at three-thirty; I guess the reporter came about three-fifteen."

"And you never saw the reporter again—you don't know what time he left?" She shook her head. "Could he have been the short, dark man the janitor saw go downstairs?"

"Oh, no. He isn't dark or short. In fact he's quite tall and I think his hair is brown."

"I see. Now, Mr. Hulse, at what time did you say this dark, short man went downstairs?"

"While I was sweeping the second-floor hall, sir. That was right after I cleaned the men's lavatory and just a little bit before I cleaned the second-floor rooms and saw Mr. Craig."

"How long before you saw Mr., Craig? Make a guess."

"Ten minutes or so."

Andrews referred to the chart he was keeping. "That would make it three-fifty when the man left the building. Craig said it was about four when Hulse came into the library the first time."

"All right," Thompson said. "I don't think of anything more. Read them the chart, Andrews, we'll let them check up on it." He addressed us: "Now remember this is important. Think hard and tell us if anything's not O.K. Go on."

This is what Andrews read:

"Courtney Brown:—Entered building at 2 p.m.—last seen with reporter at 3:30—found dead at 4:30 by Hulse.

"Mrs. Courtney Brown:—Entered building at 2 p.m. with Brown. . . ."

"Just a minute!" Andrews' voice broke the pall of concentration that had fallen on the room. "We know Mrs. Brown entered the building, but did any one see her leave?"

"Yes!" Miss Mullin again in her regular tones volunteered. "She went down the fire escape; she quite often does because, as her car is parked at the foot of it, it's quicker. She went down about 2:30—just after I came."

Andrews continued:

"Mrs. Brown:—Entered building at 2 p.m. with Brown—left by fire escape at 2:30.

"Grace Mullin:—Entered building at 2:30—was in laboratory with Tobey from 3:30 to 4:30.

"Jack Tobey:—Entered building at 3:30—was in laboratory with Mullin from 3:30 to 4:30.

"Ian Craig:—Entered building at 2—was in philosophy library on second floor from 2 to 4:30.

"Axel Hulse:—Washed stairs from 1 to 3—cleaned first-floor offices from 3 to 3:30—washed men's lavatory from 3:30 to 4—cleaned rooms on second floor from 4 to 4:30—found Brown dead at 4:30.

"Reporter:—With Brown in office at 3:30.

"Short, dark man:—Seen by Hulse to leave building at 3:50."

He stopped. "Is that all?" Thompson asked. "Now then, any corrections?" He looked from one to the other of us. "No corrections!"

Hulse raised his hand. "Please, may I speak?" Thompson nodded.

"It's just come to me that the middle of the afternoon—while I was working on the first floor that is—Mr. Frampton went upstairs. I remember now he said, 'Fine day!' just like that: 'Fine day!' and I said 'Yes, sir.' I guess I didn't remember it before because I'm so used to Mr. Frampton going upstairs."

Thompson for the first time smiled. "What time would that have been, Brick?"

"Between three and three-thirty if he was working on the first floor," Andrews replied after puzzling over his chart.

"So Mr. Frampton went upstairs!" Thompson repeated. He darted a menacing glance at Hulse. "You didn't see him come down!"

"No, sir!"

I had never liked Frampton, but now, as I watched the glances Andrews and Thompson exchanged, I felt sorry for him.

3

Leaving Science Hall, I hurried home across the campus, anticipating the delights of a drink, a hot bath and Jean Giraudoux' latest play, which had arrived from Paris only that morning. Two of these simple pleasures were denied me by a note tucked in my mail box which informed me that Mrs. Wayne Grinnell had left a telephone message to the effect that I should call at her home immediately, no matter how late the hour. Dr. Wayne Grinnell being president of Earl College, his divine right to order members of the faculty about was reflected in his wife, leaving me little doubt as to whether I would now forego the diverting Jean Giraudoux or the less diverting Mrs. Wayne Grinnell. I did manage a drink of Jamaica rum before retracing my steps to the campus, where the president's house—as white colonial as his point of view—is set in a park of evergreens about fifty yards southeast of Science Hall.

The night was crisp and starless, and as I walked over the wet lawns my weariness was gradually dissipated by the amusing prospect of a conversation with the first lady of Earl College, who regards us, I know, as a flock of sheep to be led through green pastures by her husband. He being absent on one of his interminable trips—a sort of academic traveling salesman—she, I assumed, was acting in the role of shepherdess.

A Swedish maid answered the door and led me into the drawing-room. As I sat there, on a carved rosewood sofa upholstered with brocade, facing a marble mantel bearing a gilt clock, two gilt candlesticks and three miniatures in gilt frames, there came to my mind, like the angel into Abou Ben Adhem's room, Corbusier's famous statement, *La maison est une machine à habiter*. And while there is much to be said against machines, there is equally much to be said against the average house. This one, for instance, was designed to meet every contingency but the very actual contingency of habitation; it was designed to be dusted, swept, arranged, admired and treasured—but not to be lived in; luxury was admitted, even a cold beauty, but comfort was the prodigal son for whom we of this century have killed the fatted calf.

This brief reaction to the stimulus of a hard sofa was consummated before Mrs. Grinnell entered the room. "I'm sorry I was so long," she said. "I was rubbing goose grease on Junior's chest; he has a cough."

I expressed my regrets.

She sat down in a replica of a Belter chair—a type I find very ugly—clasping her hands. "I'm so worried, Mr. Craig. Otherwise I wouldn't have sent for you at this time of night. This terrible crime . . . I don't want it to get to the newspapers!"

"I don't see how that's to be prevented," I said. "After all, a murder is public property."

"I know." She really was upset. "If Dr. Grinnell were only here! He'd know what to do." I rather doubted that. "But he's in Tampa, Florida—attending a convention—and I can't have him bothered."

"How about the trustees?" I asked.

She threw up her hands. "It's for their sake I want to keep it out of the papers; one or two of them are quite old, especially Mrs. Otto B. Wister, who gave us the money last year to build the library, and Mr. Kronberg, who built Kronberg Hall for us—they wouldn't like it at all. I think it might kill them—Mr. Kronberg is ninety-one, you know—to have their names involved in a public scandal."

"But I don't really see how it affects them," I said. "Brown wasn't murdered in the library or in Kronberg Hall . . ."

"No. . . ." Her tone was dubious. "But then, old people are so peculiar; you never can tell what they might take exception to. Besides, their children wouldn't like it. Miss Thelma Wister manages her mother's affairs, and I'm sure she'd think it was vulgar and . . ."

"Unnecessary?" I supplied.

"Yes, unnecessary! After all, affairs have been hushed up."

"Yes," I admitted, "they have. And since Dr. Brown's murder will have only a sensational interest for the public, I personally am in favor of keeping it quiet. But what if we did try to hush it up—the press, thinking we weren't playing fair with them, would become the more voracious; whereas, if we treat the whole matter in a frank and dignified way . . ."

Mrs. Grinnell shook her head. "I'm sure you're wrong, Mr. Craig, and if Dr. Grinnell were here I'm sure he'd think so. I wonder if you remember the time four sophomores—from very good families too—thrashed a faculty member. Not a word of that got to the papers. Dr. Grinnell saw to it."

"But, Mrs. Grinnell," I pointed out, "that was what the headlines might call 'a boyish prank'; this is a murder!"

"Of course," she said. "I was only illustrating Dr. Grinnell's attitude toward notoriety. And while that, as you say, was a boyish prank, I insist that this case demands, if anything, stronger use of the same tactics."

My patience was exhausted. "If you'll pardon me, Mrs. Grinnell, why did you ask me to come here this evening? I have no power with the press."

"No," she said, "but then, by being in Science Hall at the time of the murder you became more or less involved in it, so I thought . . . well, frankly, Mr. Craig, I thought you would be interested in keeping it quiet." I smiled. Seeing my smile, she added. "And I know Dr. Grinnell thinks very highly of your work."

Then if ever I was tempted to have what Groucho Marx calls "a strange interlude." Yes, I thought, by refusing me a raise and once a year standing me to a cup of tea and two macaroons, Dr. Grinnell has shown me how highly he thinks of my work. "It's very kind of you to say so," I said. And then, because there wasn't any use in antagonizing her, I suggested, "Why don't you call the editor of the *Sun?* And the district attorney might be able to do something. District attorneys come up for election so often they're inclined to do favors when they can."

"I might try the district attorney," she said slowly, "but I hoped you'd fix it with the *Sun.* You see, Dr. Grinnell isn't on very good terms with the editor."

"Well," I said, attempting to keep a straight face, "that does make it more difficult. But how about your trustees? They're the logical intermediaries. Isn't there one of them you can go to?"

She shook her head. "One of them is abroad and two are in Southern California. Mrs. Wister and Mr. Kronberg are too old to be bothered, Mr. Adams has just resigned, and as for Mr. Gaffner—well, I'm sure Dr. Grinnell wouldn't want me to ask favors of him. He's been trying to put his son-in-law in Dr. Grinnell's place as president of Earl— another reason why this affair must be handled as tactfully as possible. If the trustees . . ."

"Yes, of course." I felt genuinely sorry for her. Her predicament was no easy one, and, for the first time looking closely at her, I realized she was a pretty woman gotten up, like the heroine in act one of a play who is to emerge as a butterfly in act two, to look as plain as possible. I also realized that for Mrs. Grinnell there was to be no second act, and it was perhaps that realization that disposed me more kindly toward her. I stood up. "I'll do what I can, Mrs. Grinnell, and let you know how much or how little that is."

"Just a minute, Mr. Craig," she said hurriedly. "There's one more question."

I wondered what it could be to rob her voice of its former dignity, leaving it so breathless. "Yes?" I said, sitting down again.

"Mr. Craig. Who do you think killed Dr. Brown?"

So that was it! I concealed my annoyance. "It's rather soon to say, isn't it?"

"Yes. Yes, it is," she repeated. "But . . ." she leaned eagerly forward, "have you no suspicions?"

In that second I realized why she'd gotten me there. The other had been a side issue. "None, Mrs. Grinnell." I was now frankly curious. "Is there anything you'd like to tell me?"

For a moment she seemed about to withdraw. Then, apparently reconsidering, she spoke. "Yes, Mr. Craig, there is something. It concerns Mrs. Brown."

Seeing that she expected me to be startled, I assumed the proper attitude, wondering what more she could know about Jennifer than the gossip any plain woman knows about any pretty one. I also wondered if she could tell me the one thing I wanted to know how Jennifer's handkerchief got in my office.

"It's something I've kept secret now for two years," she continued with an importance that was amusing and at the same time pitiful. "My husband knows it and he agrees it is best forgotten."

I didn't feel up to any embarrassing confidences. "Do you think it's wise to tell me?" I suggested.

"You must know," she said. "It won't do any harm to tell you—only it mustn't go any farther. The general public must never know."

"What mustn't the general public know?" I asked.

She pulled her chair across the polished floor toward me. "That Dr. Brown and his wife lived together six months before their marriage!"

I raised my eyebrows significantly, a response which evidently satisfied her.

"Dr. Brown should have been discharged," she said, "would have been were it not that Dr. Grinnell found it impossible to fill his place for the same money—and wished to avoid a scandal. I thought at the time he did wrong; now I know it."

"Indeed!"

She settled righteously back in her chair. "And that isn't all. Mr. Craig, that woman has a lover."

I had been right about the embarrassing confidences. "Who is he?" I asked.

She shook her head. "I don't know. There may be more than one. I only know that every afternoon for the last month she has been seen driving with the same man."

"That hardly constitutes a moral offense," I said, not thinking how my levity might affect her.

She seized on my words, disregarding their meaning. "A moral offense! Mr. Craig, that woman committed her first moral offense in living with Brown. Heaven knows how many since then! What is more, she is impudent and shameless—as she has often shown in her attitude toward other faculty wives. She actually seems to feel proud of her iniquity."

"You wouldn't want her to apologize," I felt impelled to say.

"That's not it. I'm merely leading up to the fact that I feel that woman to be capable of anything."

"Murder?"

"Yes," she repeated defiantly. "Murder! One crime leads to another."

I had never calculated the lengths to which jealousy and futility could drive a respectable, middle-aged woman. The charge itself I didn't take very seriously. "But, Mrs. Grinnell," I argued, "that's rather a serious implication. Are you sure it's justified—that you're not exaggerating her delinquency? Granting she is a fallen woman"—even as I used that quaint term I had to smile at it—"it wouldn't necessarily make her a criminal."

My defense antagonized her, as I had known it would. "I see that you share my husband's theory that a pretty woman is incapable of wrong. I'll put the same question to you that you put to me, Mr. Craig: are you sure you're justified?"

"Yes," I replied. "The law backs me up in believing any person innocent until proved guilty."

"And if I were to say I knew for certain that she and her lover drove toward the campus this afternoon at about a quarter of four?"

This was interesting. "Did you see her?" I asked.

"My second maid's brother runs a filling station on Chestnut, halfway between down town and here."

I marveled at her own shamelessness. "And I, Mrs. Grinnell, was only a few yards from Brown at three o'clock. Am I therefore guilty?"

Her reversion to amiability was as sudden as her *bouleversement* had been. "I only told you my suspicions to relieve my mind of them—and because, Dr. Grinnell being away, you are in a way acting for Earl College. You may act on them or not as you please."

I arose. "I will at least give them my fullest consideration."

"And you won't forget to call the editor of the *Sun?*"

I reassured her on that point and, more amused than impressed by that unpredictable conversation, walked once more back across the campus toward my apartment.

4

Mrs. Brown was to appear before Andrews and Thompson in the zoo at eight Saturday morning. I awoke, shaved, dressed and hurried there, preferring to miss breakfast to missing a word of her testimony. I hadn't yet got in touch with the editor of the *Sun;* it is an evening paper or I should have called him late Friday night. As a matter of fact I very much wanted to get it over with and made up my mind to do so not later than noon Saturday.

Jennifer arrived at the zoo shortly after I did. She was not in mourning; on the contrary she looked very *sportive* in a polo coat and beret. I remember when Brown married her and the sensation he caused. There had really been nothing very surprising in it; in attractiveness, sophistication and family—in everything that is, save age—they were on equal planes, and were it not that a world bereft of miracles craves a seven-days' wonder, I believe their marriage might have passed unnoticed. The prediction was of course it wouldn't last; I liked Brown and approved his taste enough to hope it would. There was no denying Jennifer was chic and her very chicness was perhaps an added fillip to public malice. She was also at times very amusing in a self-conscious way and, while I had never cause to like or dislike her, I could see that whatever reaction she did create would be a strong one; she would never be, as so

many women are, merely accepted. They had gone to the
Riviera on their honeymoon—she and Brown. It amused
Brown to do the conventional thing—raise flowers, keep
dogs, play golf, go to Deauville—knowing in that way he
could annoy the greatest number of people. And when they
returned to Brown's bachelor quarters—the most minute
of houses with a large garden—Jennifer did what she liked,
went where she liked, whether to Victoria or Hollywood,
and had continued to do so during the two years culminat-
ed by Brown's murder.

Thompson was suspicious of her as he would have been
of any sophisticated person and particularly of a woman.
Jennifer, for her part, was her most disquieting, and, to
be perfectly fair to Andrews, had I been in his place, I too
might have been driven to blustering by the casualness
expressed by her eyes and crossed legs and her hands, from
which she declined to remove the pigskin gloves.

"Where were you Friday afternoon?" he demanded after
disposing of the perfunctory details.

"I was down town shopping," she replied.

"Shopping!"

"Yes, I bought three pair of golf stockings . . . this is
one of them." She glanced down at one ankle. "Neat . . .
don't you think?"

"Mrs. Brown!" Thompson's contempt was searing.
"Will you please try to remember your husband has been
murdered!"

"Mr. Thompson, will you please try to remember to
whom you are speaking."

Thompson calmed down. "I didn't get you here to talk
about stockings. What I want to know is where were you
between three-thirty and four-thirty yesterday afternoon?"

"Oh, I see. You want to know if I murdered my husband."

"Will you answer my question?"

"Yes. Let me see! After lunch I drove Courtney here, then I drove down town and parked my car."

"You came upstairs to this room with your husband, didn't you?"

"Why, yes, I did. But I didn't think you cared to hear about my actions that early in the afternoon."

"We care about everything."

She shrugged her shoulders and proceeded. "I went to the shops I always go to. If you like I'll make a list of them for you. Then, since it was too early to call for my husband I had tea at The Blue Boar."

"Alone?"

"Certainly."

Andrews leaned forward to whisper. Thompson nodded. "Just where did you park your car, Mrs. Brown?"

"While I was shopping, you mean?" She hesitated. "I don't remember the exact spot; it was quite far up on Chestnut, about Sixth."

"Then you didn't put your car in a parking station."

She smiled engagingly. "No, Mr. Thompson, I didn't. It's a shame to deprive you of the pleasure of checking up on me. If I'd only known!"

Thompson frowned. "You needn't worry, Mrs. Brown," he said; "there'll be other ways to check up on you."

"I suppose there are other questions too?" she looked at her wrist watch. "I have a golf appointment at ten."

She might just as well have waved a red flag before a bull, I thought, but I was mistaken. "Well, well, a golf appointment at ten. We'll see you don't miss it." What subtle plot could, I wondered, underlie his suavity?

Jennifer too, I think, was puzzled. "Thank you," she said.

"And now, Mrs. Brown, what explanation can you give us of your words when you entered this room last night? You said, 'Frampton killed him'!"

Jennifer showed no concern, having of course anticipated that question. "I'd rather Dr. Frampton himself
answered that."

"You refuse an explanation!"

"Of course not. I'm not that silly. Where, by the way,
is Frampton?"

"On a fishing trip," Thompson growled. "We were going to post a man at his house but his mother promised to
send him around to-day whenever he got in."

"Well!" Under four disapproving eyes Jennifer opened a
shagreen cigarette case. "He'll have plenty of time to think
up a good story."

"What the devil!" exclaimed Thompson.

"What have you got on him anyway?" Andrews demanded.

"I'll tell you if you let me smoke." Inserting the cigarette between lips that were deliberately insolent, she
lighted it from a monogrammed lighter. "I saw Frampton
turn off Chestnut onto the campus a little after three yesterday. He was in his car."

So the brother of Mrs. Grinnell's second maid had the
right dope! Thompson's next question was the one on my
mind: "What were *you* doing around here a little after
three yesterday afternoon?"

Jennifer was nonchalant. "I knew you'd ask that. Well,
the explanation is very simple, so simple you won't believe
it. After driving my husband here to the lab, I drove home
to change my clothes before I went down town. It was on
the way down town that I saw Dr. Frampton."

It was a good story, though it contradicted the second
maid's brother's. He said she was driving up town, and he
also had said a quarter to four. There was, in other words,
a discrepancy of forty-five minutes between the two stories.

Andrews was, I think, inclined to believe her. It was
Thompson who finally spoke. "How are you going to

prove you went home and changed your clothes? Got any witnesses?"

"No. I don't keep a maid. The house is too small. That's why I said you wouldn't believe me."

"And how are you going to prove, even if you did go home as you say, that you didn't stop at the college on your way down town?"

Jennifer shrugged her shoulders. "The easiest thing," she said, "would be to find my husband's murderer, thus eliminating any necessity of accounting for my actions. It really would simplify things a lot for you if you took my word that I didn't kill him."

"My God!" Thompson exclaimed.

"Say!" Andrews demanded. "Where would we get if we took everybody's word. Who's going to say they did kill him?"

"I can see your point," Jennifer admitted. "But still, there's no reason why my word isn't as good or better than any one else's. My record's clean; I've never been in jail—except on a traffic charge." She got up. "Now that I've answered your questions may I go?"

"No!" Andrews bellowed.

"Shut up!" Thompson ordered, then turned to Jennifer. "Go right ahead, Mrs. Brown." She lost no time in leaving, giving me a smile on the way out. "Have Jennings follow her," Thompson ordered the policeman at the door. "And tell him to report back here with the name of her golf partner."

"So that's your game!" Andrews' admiration was apparent.

Thompson turned on him. "Do you think I wanted her around when Frampton testified! You are a dumb cluck!"

"Oh, yeah?"

"Oh, yeah! I want Frampton's story pure and simple. It'll be time enough then to plug holes in it. O'Brien!" The policeman appeared in the doorway. "Has Frampton showed up yet?"

"Sure thing, chief! We've been holding him below like you said."

"Show him up! And now, Mr. Craig!" Thompson leveled his glance at me. "Who told you to hang around to-day?"

I had been surprised to be unmolested so far. "Sorry if I'm not wanted, Mr. Thompson," I said. "But since I'm here can't I be of some use?"

"Use!" he roared. "What use can you be? When we want you we'll let you know!"

For a moment I was more or less at a loss; to be turned out now would ruin my scheme, making this journal worthless. Determined to hang on, I used the one ruse that came to my mind. "Then, you don't know I'm handling this case for the *Sun.*"

"No, I don't know it! Do you?"

"I'm not a reporter," I said. "But I have had some journalistic experience."

"We don't want your life story," Andrews cut in.

"Mrs. Grinnell—wife of the president of this college— wanted the case handled discreetly; she asked the editor to let me handle it."

"Where are your credentials?" Thompson demanded. "And why didn't you tell us sooner?"

"The editor notified me this morning by telephone; I haven't had time yet to get a card." A policeman appeared in the doorway.

Thompson nodded to him. "All right," he said grudgingly to me. "Have it your own way. But I want to see that card, see!"

Frampton was led into the room. Never prepossessing, he seemed to me this morning and must have seemed to the two detectives, a strange specimen. He is very narrow, very stiff and very pale. But it is not his narrowness, paleness, nor stiffness which annoy me, although they might possibly be corrected with mineral or cod-liver oil. It is

his rimless glasses, detachable, striped collar and high
shoes I object to; not on principle—so great a mystic even
as George Russell wears high shoes—but on Frampton. To
put the case briefly, he represents what I at every turn am
flayed with: the public conception of a college professor.
He lives alone with his mother. I think he would like to
bicycle to school but, yielding to convention, he drives;
and both his house and the catboat on which he spends
hours cruising the lake he has turned into laboratories. I
remember that one story made the rounds of the campus
to the effect that Frampton was carrying on an experiment on his boat to determine the sexual energy of white
rats deprived of vitamin C. Like all the best stories it
turned out to be true. Another experiment of his, one for
which he was later well paid by a tobacco company—he
always had an eye for the main chance—had to do with the
effects of nicotine on the nervous system of guinea-pigs.
His reports, whether or not he jockeyed them, turned out
to be just what the tobacco company wanted. I remember Courtney Brown had been quite bitter about that. He
went so far as to discuss it at a dinner given by the Dean—
rather bad taste on his part, I thought.

"Now!" Thompson metaphorically rolled up his sleeves.
"Your name!"

"Charles Frampton." One curious phenomenon of
Frampton's that worried most people without their being
able to place it was that he seldom blinked; it made his
glance inhuman and birdlike.

"Age!"

"Thirty-four." I looked at him with some surprise—
barely older than myself!

"Never mind the address," Thompson said. "We've got
that. How long have you been at Earl College, Mr. Frampton?"

"Four years this past September."

"Did Dr. Brown bring you here?"

"Yes. I took my doctor's degree at Columbia. The head of the psychology department there was a very good friend of Dr. Brown and he suggested to me that I apply for this position. Up to then the work had been mostly with undergraduates; now we have quite a large graduate department which Dr. Brown handles, or did handle, leaving me and Miss Mullin to manage the elementary courses. It worked out very well."

"So you and Brown got on fine, did you?" said Thompson. "No quarrels—nothing like that!"

"Why, no!" For the moment Frampton's glibness deserted him. "We didn't quarrel. We had professional differences, of course, but personally we were very friendly. Has any one told you we quarreled?"

"No!" Andrews outdid himself in heartiness. "Just one of those questions we ask every one."

Frampton appeared relieved. "I admired Dr. Brown very much," he said. "His death will be a great loss to both our department and the entire field of behavioristic psychology."

Andrews consulted his notes. "Now, Mr. Frampton, get ready for another question we ask every one. Where were you yesterday afternoon between two and four?"

"Your mother has already told us," Thompson interposed. "But we must have the data from your own lips."

"I was on my boat. That is what my mother, told you, is it not? My classes here are over at twelve on Fridays. I went home to lunch as usual and after lunch—about one-thirty, I think, drove down to Thirty-first and Lockart Drive, where my boat is anchored. I stopped on the way at a delicatessen—Sweeney's, to be exact."

"Just what we wanted, Mr. Frampton." Andrews wrote busily. "You were on your boat then all yesterday afternoon from about two o'clock on and all last night?"

"Not last night. I very seldom sleep on my boat. I stayed on it until about midnight and then drove straight home. My mother waited up for me—there hadn't been any way to get hold of me sooner or she would have—and said you wanted me here early this morning. When I did get here—about nine—your men wouldn't let me come up; they kept me downstairs."

Thompson nodded. "That's right. There's just one thing more, Mr. Frampton, and then you can go. If you were as you say on your boat all yesterday afternoon how is it that you were seen on this campus at three-fifteen?"

It is always interesting, if only for scientific reasons, to see a man trapped. Frampton's response to this trap was quick and cold-blooded, a little too quick and cold for his own good. He smiled carefully. "I was on this campus at three-fifteen yesterday. I also went down to my boat, as I said, about two. The discord of facts is due not to a lie but to an omission."

"Oh!" Thompson's voice was thick with sarcasm. "I see!"

Frampton was not disturbed. "When I got down to my boat at about two-thirty I pulled up anchor and started for Piers Point. Halfway there I remembered that I'd forgotten to change the diet of the rats in the dark room. No one ever enters that room but me, and though the rats wouldn't starve in my absence—there was plenty of cornflakes for them to eat—it was absolutely necessary that I go back and give one group one gram of dried brain tissue and the second group an equal amount of dried anterior pituitary extract. You see, I've been asked by a meat-packing company to make this experiment, the success of which depends on absolute accuracy."

"Why a meat-packing company?" asked Thompson.

"They want to increase the sale of their byproducts. For some time now they've put up thyroid and ovary gland for human consumption. These experiments I am now making on white rats are intended to test the efficacy of dried brain tissue and anterior pituitary extract in treating stunted development."

"Why keep them in a dark room?"

"To stunt them," Frampton answered, now in his element. "There are of course other ways, some of which we employ. In the experiment previous to this one by a special diet I developed rickets in twenty white rats. Rickets, as we know, stunts mental as well as physical growth. I then tested the intelligence of the rats with rickets before and after two weeks feeding of dried brain tissue mixed with bread and milk. The results were highly satisfactory." He indicated the wooden box beside which Brown was found dead. "The maze I used to test them! This dark-room experiment I started just one month ago on newborn rats; they have never been exposed to light and are now sufficiently stunted so I can go ahead with the diet of brain tissue and pituitary extract. The packing company hopes to prove that children living in sunless and crowded cities may by this same means be raised to the health of their country cousins."

"Very interesting," said Thompson. "And now, Mr. Frampton, how are you going to prove to us that this isn't just a cock-and-bull story?"

"Why, by showing you the rats. It will ruin my experiment to expose them to light, but if you wish . . ."

"We do wish," Thompson replied. "That's the door to the dark room, is it?" He pointed to the locked door behind the ant box in the north wall.

"It would be better to enter from the hall," Frampton said, "since that door is very seldom—almost never opened."

"Just a minute," interpolated Andrews. "Why mess up Mr. Frampton's experiment. I don't doubt there are rats in the room; I don't even doubt that they're eating minced brains on toast, as the gentleman said. And even if we did bust in and discover it was sweetbreads instead of brains, what would that prove?"

"Listen, you wisecracker!" Thompson said. "Frampton admits no one goes in that dark room but him."

"Not even the janitor?" demanded Andrews.

Frampton shook his head. "Not during experiments. I tell him when he can clean up in there. The rest of the time I just manage as best I can."

"When was the last time he cleaned up?"

"A month ago. Just before I started this experiment. When I work in the dark room I deal with as few subjects as possible—I have ten rats this time—which makes it possible for me to tend to everything. I'll admit I don't keep their cages as clean as Hulse keeps these." He glanced at the animal cages in the northwest corner. "But they're clean enough for my purposes. You're quite welcome to look in there if you like, you know. My experiment isn't so important to me that I'd want it to interfere with your investigations. I can always start over."

"Well, I'll tell you," Thompson said. "It's not that we don't believe your story, Mr. Frampton, but the truth is I would like to have a look around there. It's one of the first places I'd have looked into if the key had been handy. But Miss Mullin didn't have it and the janitor didn't have it and it wasn't on Dr. Brown's key ring."

"No," Frampton said. "No one has a key to the dark room but me. I've discovered it's the only way to carry on an experiment—to keep every one else out. Of course when any one else wants to experiment in there I keep out. But that hasn't happened lately, not all this year."

"And no one ever enters the dark room from this room?" Thompson asked.

"No. Of that I'm absolutely certain. The door, you see, is not only locked and more or less barred from this side by the ant box, but quite obviously, if you look at the dust and cobwebs that have accumulated on the other side of it, has not been opened recently."

"That's interesting," Andrews said.

"You were thinking I might have slipped from the dark room into this room to kill Brown," Frampton's small, blue eyes darted from one to the other of the two detectives. "I couldn't possibly have, as you can see for yourselves when you come in there. But," and now he looked at me, "if you're looking for clews—why, that fire escape leads directly into Craig's office."

"As I have already pointed out," I informed him, more amused than angered by his naive desire to acquit himself by involving me.

Thompson watched us narrowly. "We'll leave the fire escape out of this," he said. "Mr. Frampton! the key to the dark room, please."

Frampton took it from his pocket.

"O'Brien!" Thompson called. "Has Gottschalk showed up yet?"

"Sure thing, chief." O'Brien vanished and in a moment Gottschalk, short, rosy and near-sighted, took his place in the doorway.

"Mr. Gottschalk," Thompson said, "I want you to go with Mr. Frampton into the dark room. He will show you everything he touched yesterday afternoon. By the way, Mr. Frampton, was three-fifteen the first time you were in the dark room yesterday?"

"I was in there for a moment at a quarter of nine in the morning."

"Don't bother about the old fingerprints," Thompson directed Gottschalk. "Just the fresh ones—anything since yesterday noon. Mr. Frampton will give you all the light you need."

The two men walked out into the hall. "How about it?" asked Andrews, *sotto voce.*

"I don't know. He looks pretty slick to me." Thompson turned to me. "What do you know about him, Craig?"

At the point of replying that I knew nothing whatsoever of Frampton, I was saved the trouble by the informal entrance of a tall, good-looking boy. "Sic your bloodhounds off me, will you!" he demanded.

"Who the devil are you?" asked Thompson.

"I'm Dick Sterling, reporter for the *Sun*. For the last half hour I've been trying to convince that squad of half-wits downstairs that I'm not after a story. Do you think they'd believe me!"

"It's all right, Kennedy," Thompson said, and the two policemen who had followed on Sterling's heels departed. "What's your story, kid?"

"Say!" Andrews sputtered. "Are you the reporter that was with Brown. . . ?"

The kid dug his hands into his pockets. "You've heard about me already? The hell. . . ."

Thompson glared at his subordinate. "What does it matter?" inquired Andrews peevishly. "Out with it, kid!"

"First!" said Sterling, "do I get exclusive rights to this story?"

"How many exclusive rights are there to one case?" Thompson looked at me.

"Sure, kid!" said Andrews genially. "You'll get everything that's coming to you. Why, you may even get arrested for the murder of Courtney Brown."

"Not me!" Sterling grinned. "I didn't kill him. But I can tell you who did."

"The hell you can!"

"Well, hold it!" Thompson nodded toward Gottschalk and Frampton, who had just entered. "Well, Gottschalk?"

Mr. Gottschalk looked troubled. "Sorry to be so long, Mr. Andrews. I knew you'd want me to look over everything. I tried all the cage doors and the table and the door handles. But no one but Mr. Frampton has been there since yesterday noon. At least, there weren't any fingerprints but his. And to tell the truth, Mr. Andrews, there weren't even his fingerprints because he wore gloves."

Andrews whistled. "Well, well!" Thompson exclaimed. "So you wore gloves, Mr. Frampton. Is that a habit of yours?"

"Yes," Frampton answered, seemingly unconcerned. "I carry an old pair in my portfolio to slip on when I'm around the animals. It's a dirty business, you know."

"I know. A very dirty business. And there's another thing I know, Mr. Frampton, and that is . . . Brown's murderer wore gloves!"

5

As soon as Frampton had left, swinging his shoulders in his prim way, Thompson once more directed his attention toward Sterling. "Your turn, Mr. Sterling. Do you still know who killed Brown?"

"Sure I do," the boy replied. "I suppose you think Frampton did it. Well, take my word he didn't. That guy's no killer." He smiled contemptuously.

"He wears gloves," said Andrews smoothly.

"Circumstantial evidence! How far's that going to get you. This fingerprint stuff is all boloney and you know it. You work with me; I'll hand you plenty of good publicity and between us we'll crack the case. I've already got a pretty good line on the bird that did it."

"How about letting us in on the secret?" demanded Andrews. Thompson's mouth was curved with silent disdain.

"It's this way," said Sterling. "I saw Brown alive and kicking about three-forty-five, see! Then I beat it and on my way out a guy passes me on the stairs, see! A greasy-looking guy—a dago maybe. Find him and you've got Brown's murderer."

"Honest?" said Andrews.

Thompson looked him over. "How do we know this isn't a plant, that you haven't invented the dago? It's just

as easy for me to suppose you killed Brown as it is to suppose you passed a dago on the stairs."

"Aw hell!" The boy's disgust seemed genuine enough.
"Why would I kill the only live subject on my beat. There
isn't any news in the rest of these college deadheads. Brown
was good for a couple of columns a week. He gave me a
swell pigeon feature yesterday. It made the peach edition
and then the make-up man cut it out."

"What did this dago look like?" Thompson asked.

"I don't know. He was hot-footing it up the stairs. Sort
of dark, I guess, and short."

Andrews nudged Thompson. "That's the fellow Hulse
was talking about."

"Shut up!" Thompson growled.

"Did some one else see him?" Sterling demanded excit-
edly. "Why didn't you tell me? Why did you let me think
I was seeing things?"

"We want your story," drawled Thompson. "I know
witnesses. Let them hear every one else's testimony and
pretty soon they have a story that sounds like a hop-head's
dream."

"Not me!" said Sterling. "I'm a newspaper man and we
deal in facts."

"Oh, yeah?"

"What did you do in Brown's office?" Thompson asked.

"We had a couple of drinks and he gave me the dope on
this pigeon experiment. That's all. Oh, yeah, then we came
in here and took a squint at the maze."

"I suppose you know he was found dead beside that,"
said Thompson calmly.

The boy started, then controlled himself. "I didn't
know that. Honest, you don't think I did it, do you?" He
wiped his forehead.

"I don't know," said Thompson. "Let's see your gloves."

In spite of his nervousness the boy grinned. "Never wear them. That's a break."

"Oh, I don't know." Thompson looked at his watch. "Time for Jennings to report back. O'Brien!"

"Yes, sir!"

"Jennings back?"

O'Brien advanced a few steps. "He telephoned, sir, to say the lady drove to the Hillcrest Links and was taking a lesson from the pro there." He referred to a card. "The pro's name is Jimmy. No one seemed to know his last name."

Every one but Thompson smiled. "When Jennings gets back," he said, "send him in! You can go," he told Sterling. "And for God's sake stick to pigeon stories for a day or two. I don't want this case smeared all over the front page."

"How am I to find the dago without publicity?" Sterling's tone was aggrieved.

"We'll find him," said Andrews.

"And, by the way!" Thompson nodded grimly toward me. "Here's competition. Fight it out, you two! And remember, whichever one of you gets the assignment, we don't want two-inch headlines."

"Well, if you don't," said Sterling, now thoroughly recovered, "you're the first guy that ever didn't!"

"I'll come with you," I said, following him past the faithful O'Brien.

"O.K." We tramped down the worn wooden stairs and out onto the campus, white with the petals from dogwood trees. "Say! what'd he mean by competition? I've seen you before some place, haven't I?"

"On the second floor of Science Hall perhaps."

"Oh! You're a prof!" He looked curiously at me. "Got anything to do with this business?"

"Just another suspect," I said.

He laughed. "You and me both! Poor old Brown! I guess I was the last person to see him alive. Looks bad for me, doesn't it?"

"I don't think it does," I said.

"Yeah. But it's what Thompson thinks that counts and he's a mean baby. When did you see Brown?"

"I didn't see him at all Friday but I had the misfortune to be practically the only person in the building at the time he was murdered. That is, except for you and the janitor and the dago and a couple of students," I added.

"Quite a little crowd," he commented cheerfully, turning down a path that ran from the campus into Chestnut Street. "Well, I'll be seeing you."

I turned down the same path. "If you don't mind; I'll come along . . . if you're on your way to the office."

He stopped. "Then that was all on the level, about your wanting to handle this story, I mean! The editor never said anything to me about it."

"He didn't know about it," I said. "And I won't have to tell him if you can get me a reporter's card to let me in on this case."

"What for?"

"First," I said, "because I was a friend of Brown's and I don't want his murderer to escape. Second, because I want to try out a system I believe in and have never before had the occasion to try out."

"A system! Like they use at Monte Carlo?"

"Yes. Only there it's applied to numbers instead of people. I mean to keep a record of the persons involved in this crime—putting down not only everything they say and do, but everything suggested to me by their actions and words. That is, I mean to employ a form of intuition based on actual observation and acquaintance with Brown and his circle."

"Pretty neat!"

"My theory," I continued, "is that the police not only proceed in too haphazard a way, but being unacquainted with the murdered man, have no clew to the psychological reasons for his murder. After all, the murderer always has a motive, sometimes tangible like money or revenge, and sometimes not tangible. The police as a machine for tracing down physical clews are highly efficient, but as a machine to trace down psychological clews they are blind and powerless. That is where I hope to come in. The very pieces that are missing from the puzzle I expect my intuition to supply. But intuition must be based on a real knowledge of the persons connected with Brown. And that is where you come in."

"How's that?"

"By supplying the reporter's card to get me past Andrews. He let me in to-day after I told him I was handling the story for the *Sun*. To-morrow I've got to produce a card."

Sterling nodded. "I might be able to fix you up."

"It might turn out to be rather a scoop."

"I get first shot at everything?"

"Righto!" I agreed.

"You'll get the card!"

"In that case," I said, "I won't see the editor. Come up to my apartment instead and I'll buy you a drink."

He grinned. "Sure thing! I don't have to report back to the office until noon. I can interview Frampton this afternoon."

"How about the fellow you passed on the stairs?" I asked. "Is there any way to trace him?"

He frowned. "I might go through the morgue and the rogues' gallery. And I can feature him in my stories if you don't think that'll do more harm than good. Those are the only ways I know of."

Shortly before noon I called Mrs. Grinnell. "This is Ian Craig," I said.

"Have you seen the editor of the *Sun?*"

"Better than that! I've spent the morning with the reporter who's covering the case. He's promised to let me O.K. his stories before they go to press!"

"Mr. Craig, you're marvelous. But then I knew you would be. Come to Sunday supper. I'll ask Dr. Frampton and his mother."

"I'd like to," I said. "But. . . ."

"No buts! Seven o'clock then. A very simple meal! Good-by."

6

With Sterling gone and my duty to Earl College in the person of Mrs. Grinnell fulfilled, I suddenly realized the noon whistle had blown and I'd as yet had no breakfast. I went into the kitchen, put on the coffee pot and was in the act of making an omelet according to a very simple recipe given me by a Frenchman—two eggs and two eggshells full of water—when the doorbell rang. Cursing my luck, I turned off the electricity under the frying pan and went to the door.

Mrs. Frampton, whom I had last met at the president's reception, was in the hallway and as I greeted her it occurred to me that it was at least twelve years since I had seen a hat adorned with celluloid cherries. Their brightness was not reflected in her face. She entered and closed the door behind her. "Mr. Craig, I'm Mrs. Frampton."

"I remember you very well," I said.

"I had to come and see you. I'm so worried and Mrs. Grinnell said you were the person to come to."

"Won't you sit down?" I said. "And if you don't mind I'll finish cooking my breakfast. Perhaps you'll have a cup of coffee with me?"

"Did you just get up?" she asked, her gaze wandering about the room and lighting as I knew it would on the glasses and bottles on the bookcase.

I laughed and left her to her illusions. When I returned with two cups of coffee, having decided to forego the omelet until later, she was exactly as I had left her, cotton gloves, red cherries and all.

"Now!" I said, placing one cup beside her, "I am all attention. Is it about your son you're worried?"

"Yes. And Mr. Craig, Charles is worried too."

"He didn't seem so," I said. "I saw him only this morning and he seemed quite—well, happy."

She clasped her hands together, a gesture that, however well meant, never loses for me its Delsartean flavor. "Charles hasn't been happy for the last two years. Oh, Mr. Craig, if you only knew what it was to work day and night with Courtney Brown!" She shook her head. "But that's not what I've come to talk to you about." I waited and sipped my coffee. "Mr. Craig, I'm willing to swear to you that my son didn't kill Brown—although he had provocations."

I felt inclined to warn her her statement was far more likely to convict her son than to acquit him. "What provocations?" I asked.

Her face beneath the comedy hat was tragic. "Courtney Brown was a devil! A smiling devil! He believed in nothing, and everything Charles holds dear he laughed at. Yes, even psychology. It was all right for those who could laugh back at him—as his wife does. But Charles couldn't. Charles is religious and psychology is his religion. Surely, Mr. Craig, you can understand that—you who study the mystics of the Orient."

I nodded. This case, if it revealed nothing else to me, had at least showed me what possibilities for melodrama underlay respectability. "But," I said, "was there never anything more tangible than that? Didn't their antagonism ever break out in some definite quarrel?"

"Not until recently. And that is partly why I'm so worried. You see they did quarrel only a week ago, and Mrs. Brown knows that."

"But the rest of the department and the students? Surely they know there was something wrong."

"Not the students. I'm sure they have no idea of it. Charles is very reserved. For a long time he didn't even tell me how miserable he was. And Courtney Brown—well, you know what he was like, his indifference. As for the assistants, Miss Clare has been at Cologne on a leave of absence all this fall and Miss Mullin is very discreet. She, of course, knows how things were, but has promised me to say absolutely nothing."

"Do you think you are wise in telling me?" I asked.

"Oh, I didn't mean to tell you this," she said, dropping her eyes. "I came to swear to you that Charles didn't kill him, and now. . ."

"Don't worry! You are quite right to tell me everything and you can rely on my discretion too."

"Oh, thank you," she murmured.

"And now, it might help a lot if I knew what their quarrel was about."

"What are any quarrels about!" she said despairingly. "Just an accumulation of little things. For instance, Dr. Brown always resented it when Charles made any money from his experiments, although he scarcely paid him enough to live on. He never said anything to Charles, but we felt it, and then we heard he was talking to other people about it and laughing behind Charles' back. I was furious and I knew Charles was, but I never thought anything would come of it. Charles was trying all the time to find another position, and I thought before long we'd move away from here."

"Has he another job yet?"

"No. Of course, he wouldn't accept anything under an assistant professorship, and then most colleges seem to be so conservative. They don't want behaviorists, although behaviorism is the modern trend of psychology. If only we had moved from here—if only we'd never come at all!"

"Tell me," I said, "why are you so sure your son didn't kill Brown. You admit he was justified."

"No, no. Charles didn't kill him." She covered her face with her hands. "He didn't, Mr. Craig, he didn't."

I waited and in a moment she looked up. "Charles has never been willful, never excitable, even when he was a child. Most boys are cruel at one time or another, but Charles wasn't. He wouldn't do anything that might hurt me or reflect on me. I know it. Why, Mr. Craig, in all his life he's never spoken any way but sweetly to me. Do you wonder that I'm sure he couldn't kill a man?"

"No, Mrs. Frampton, I don't," I said. "Unfortunately, however, my opinion carries no weight. And, as a matter of fact, though my quarrels with Brown were limited to metaphysical problems, I was in Science Hall at the time he was murdered, which places me with your son on the wrong side of the fence."

"They suspect you too?" she demanded.

"Yes," I replied. "Along with a number of others—so you see your son isn't so much worse off than the rest of us."

She seemed greatly relieved, as people always are to learn of the hard luck of their friends. "I didn't know that," she said, "Mrs. Grinnell didn't tell me you were suspected. Otherwise I wouldn't have bothered you with my troubles."

"I'm very glad you did. I know I'm not guilty and you know Dr. Frampton is innocent so we can now join forces in finding the criminal. That will demand absolute frankness and fearlessness of all of us. So if there is anything else that might help. . . ."

"There is!" Her anxiety fell from her. "I was hesitating whether or not to tell you. But I feel as you do that it's the only way out of all this—absolute frankness. And besides, I must do what I can to shift some of the suspicion from you and my son to some one else—some one who deserves it far more."

"Mrs. Brown?" I asked.

"How did you know?"

On the point of some generalization with which to answer her wonder, I was restrained by the memory of Yang Hsiung's words, "Ordinary people are concerned with the particular; it is impossible to make them understand a generalization."

My silence suited her better. "Yes! Mrs. Brown!" Above the wrath of her face the red cherries were now oddly incongruous. "Mr. Craig, I know—in my own heart I know—that either that woman or her lover killed Courtney Brown." She relaxed in much the same way Mrs. Grinnell had relaxed after those words.

"Who is her lover?" I asked.

"His name is Elliott Randall and he has an office in the Securities Building. That's all I know," she replied. "I've never seen him and I don't know what he's like."

"Yet you accuse him of murder!"

She looked startled as though my conclusion had been in the nature of a revelation—as indeed I think it was. I am often astonished that the simplest logic, the mere labor of following an idea through, should be so foreign to the average person. Her surprise very quickly turned to defiance. "I haven't accused him of murder. But it seems to me very likely that when a man is murdered his wife's lover should be suspected."

I shook my head. "I disagree. Now if it were the lover who was murdered I should be the first to suspect Brown. But judging from the largely vicarious experience I have

had in such matters the lover is the last person to wish to
do away with his lady's husband. It would only mean an
end to romance and illicit love. And if he should escape the
electric chair the chances are he would be forced to marry
his former mistress and see his place as lover usurped by
another. No, I don't believe Brown was killed by Jennifer's
lover, providing, of course, she has one."

Mrs. Frampton's voice was icy—the voice of enraged
virtue. "That's ridiculous. You mean to say immorality
doesn't lead to crime!"

I'm afraid I smiled. Perhaps Yang Hsiung was wrong. At
any rate here was a generalization that left me speechless.
In my younger days I would no doubt have answered it
condescendingly, but now, condescension being the *cheval
de bataille* that it is, I avoid it. "After all," I said, "the only
thing that matters to us is whether Jennifer's immorality
led to Brown's murder. I don't think so. We'll assume Randall is her lover."

"In my day we would have called that a crime," Mrs.
Frampton exclaimed. And once more I read in the eyes of
a plain woman, morbid jealousy.

I glossed over the extenuating circumstances of such a
crime. "I'd like to have a talk with Randall. But," I added,
"I think you're wrong in assuming that Brown's murder is
the climax of a *drame passionel.* Contrary to the prevalent
belief, the husband is the last person to be killed in such
a case. Happy lovers thrive on secrecy; unhappy lovers kill
one another. The husband's is generally the safest side of
the triangle—though not the most enviable."

"How can you talk that way!" Her face flamed with
embarrassment.

"I'm sorry," I said. "I was only being logical. It was
stupid of me."

She arose, still angry. "I think you actually sympathize
with Mrs. Brown."

"All the world loves a lover," I said, never having been able to resist taunting the bourgeois with their own by-words. "However, no one is more anxious than I am to find Brown's murderer, no matter who he is."

"Or she?"

"Or who she is. Tell me," I asked, "why do you dislike Mrs. Brown?"

She stood at the door, her hand on the knob, "I don't dislike her; I only suspect her."

"It is much more Christian," I said, "to do as I do and suspect every one."

Soon my omelet was for its brief moment on the stove, a plate of buttered toast beside it, and coffee bubbled once more in the percolator. But, distracting as were sound, fragrance and sight, I was not nearly so hungry as when Mrs. Frampton inadvertently interrupted my breakfast. Then I had seen myself like Tantale in Daumier's famous cartoon. Now, with breakfast in the offing, my mind insisted on dwelling on that least interesting of women, Mrs. Frampton. How unpredictable are the orthodox! It is only the irrationalist and the sinner who never surprise us! I, who have discarded Aristotelianism in favor of a religion that admits no limit to consciousness, found my mind stimulated by contact with a mind incapable even of logical reason.

Mrs. Frampton, if anything, interested me more than Mrs. Grinnell, for I wondered what more her son found in her than any son finds in any mother. He was absolutely devoted to her, never going anywhere but to college without her and even bringing her name constantly into conversations. Obviously some stronger tie than ordinary mother love or admiration existed between the two. And no one could help but marvel that Frampton, whose one outstanding quality is intelligence, should choose the constant companionship of a rather stupid middle-aged woman no more prepossessing in appearance than in mind.

The answer to that riddle, much as I disliked it, persisted in my mind: the mother complex is often a corollary of the criminal type. I have talked often enough, not only during my days as a reporter with criminals, but also with psychiatrists, to know that. Here was a distinct case of a mother-complex which, though it didn't prove Frampton to be a criminal, might well be the result or accompaniment to criminal instincts. The criminal instinct in a great many men of Frampton's type is due to a sense of inferiority, an acknowledged weakness which develops in them a hatred of society, thus turning them sooner or later into criminals. Frampton is a weak type and undoubtedly a non-social type whose reliance on his mother has strengthened rather than weakened, as is normal, with the years. Whether or not he has any defined prejudices against society I don't know, but his friends are, I should say, nil, and whatever emotions are awakened in man by friendship and love must long ago in his case have been diverted to his work or stifled.

I finished my breakfast—how right Dumas was in saying "An omelet is to cookery what a sonnet is to poetry"—I dressed and started down town, wondering more and more about Frampton's past. He had, I know, come here from Columbia, but his speech and his mother's had the nasal quality of the Middle West.

I arrived at the Securities Building about two o'clock and was admitted almost immediately to Elliott Randall's sanctum sanctorum. The first thing that impressed me was a Rockwell Kent woodcut in his usual dazzling style; I am not used to finding modern art in lawyers' offices. The second thing was the astounding attractiveness of Randall himself. He might have been a northern Italian. He was blond as Venetians are sometimes blond, with that same quality of slumbering perversion that distinguishes them. It is a more interesting blondness because rarer than the Nordic and reminiscent, not of Roman Italy, but of that later, lighter civilization characterized by the *commedia dell' arte.*

I sat down at his request across the magnificent mahogany desk from him. "I'm not a client," I warned him. "And my business is unpleasantly personal."

"From Scotland Yard?" he asked, smiling.

"From Earl College." I handed him my card.

The name sobered him. "I half thought of coming out there," he said, leaning across the desk. "God! what a rotten business! If I thought there was anything I could do. . . ."

"There is," I said. "I'm investigating this for the college and for my personal satisfaction as a former colleague of Brown's. I have nothing to do with the police. But if you would answer some questions. . . ."

"Certainly. Anything."

"Did you know Dr. Brown?" I asked.

"Only slightly. I've been to his house several times for dinner. But it was Jennifer I knew first. We met last year at Agua Caliente." He hesitated. "Oh, hell! there's no reason why I shouldn't tell you, and otherwise you might think there was something up. I'm in love with Jennifer," he said. "You might as well know that right now."

"And this leaves you free to marry her."

He shook his head. "Yes. Poor old Brown!" He stared into the burnished depths of a paperweight. "Damn it, you know. I didn't like him! That makes it all the worse."

I liked Randall. He was intelligent and apparently sensitive. What fools women like Mrs. Grinnell and Mrs. Frampton are! "You'll be married, I suppose? You and Mrs. Brown?"

"I suppose so," he said gloomily. "And move to San Francisco. I never have liked it here. But . . ." he looked up, "I don't suppose that's what you wanted to know. Go on—ask me anything you like. I don't care."

I agreed. "But you needn't answer unless you want to. . . . How did Jennifer get on with Brown?"

"She didn't have much to do with him." He smiled. "He wanted her to divorce him and so did I. She wouldn't though."

"Why not?" I asked.

"She's a Catholic and doesn't believe in divorce. It's been hell!" He offered me a cigarette. "Brown was decent enough. He's been through hell too. You see, he loved her—and living in the same house and all. . . ." He gave me a light. "It's sort of a relief to tell you this. Let me know if I sound like a gossiping old woman."

I smiled. "This is one of the strangest layouts I know of. She must be a very strict Catholic."

"She is. Goes to Mass, confession and all that. It's not her fault. Her mother was Swiss and she had that training. But in every other way she's A-1."

I nodded. "I like her very much. How did she feel about Brown's death?"

"On the whole, glad. I wouldn't tell the police that; they'd be stupid enough to misconstrue it. But it was the only way out for her. Why shouldn't she be glad? Of course she was shocked. You know," he added, "Brown wouldn't have minded. You don't think he'd expect her to go into deep mourning for him!"

"I hadn't thought of that," I said. "For that matter, would he have minded being killed—except for the instinct of self-preservation, I mean? Any man resents death, but as for giving up life—well, he never seemed to particularly enjoy it, and from what you say I infer that he enjoyed it even less than he seemed to."

"Now that you mention it, I can't think of any man who would have feared death less than Brown. I remember Jennifer had a dog, a wire-haired terrier—this was when

I first knew them. It got sick. I forget what was wrong with it, but anyway Brown's attitude—he was damned cold-blooded about it—burnt Jennifer up. He would have taken if to the laboratory if she'd let him. And he was the same way with human beings. No sympathy."

"The scientist's attitude," I said. "Brown went further than most scientists in that he applied it to himself and his friends as well as to his subjects. I think you're right about his not fearing death. It's a good thing, I guess, but not common. You know what Shaw says: 'Mankind won't get anywhere until it ceases to fear death'—or approximately that."

"God!" Randall exclaimed. "Imagine killing a man like Brown! What sort of a maniac could have done it?"

"A maniac!" I repeated. "What makes you think so?"

"Why, I took it for granted. No one had any reason to kill Brown."

"You think that!" I looked at his Italian renaissance head above the white collar and gray suit of an American business man—the Duke Ercole d'Este in modern dress. "You want me to be perfectly frank."

"By all means."

"Well then! Two women I scarcely know have already informed me they're sure either Mrs. Brown or her lover killed Brown."

I was rather curious to see how he'd take it. His reaction was not as strong as I should have expected. "Good God!" he said. "The fools! I wondered how you found out about me. So that was it—gossiping old women! Well, it's only natural."

This, I thought, wasn't the speech of a guilty man. "It doesn't matter what they think," I said. "They probably won't go to the police with it."

"To hell with them! Let them think what they want so long as . . ." Randall stopped. Jennifer stood in the doorway, her eyes fixed savagely on me.

"What the devil!" she exclaimed, stamping her foot. "Spying on me!"

Randall stood up. "Jennifer! Please!"

I had also arisen. Jennifer advanced, trembling with rage. Her lips were a tight line of rouge. "Oh, leave me alone. Let me say what I want. I'm sick of all this hypocrisy, sick of it! And you!" She was now within a foot of me. "You're spying on me, aren't you!"

I nodded. I suppose I was. "For God's sake!" exclaimed Randall. "Don't! You'll queer everything."

Even during that tense moment I wondered what he meant by queer everything! What was there to queer?

Jennifer quieted down and I saw by the half-amused, half-impatient look she flashed at him that she was really fond of him. "Oh, all right. But why shouldn't I be a hell-cat for one hour out of twenty-four. Give me a cigarette, some one, will you?" She ripped off a glove and pulled a cigarette from my package with insolent fingers, tanned and blunted with sport. "I've been attending to Courtney's funeral. Whew!"

Randall laughed, shaking his head. She turned again to me. "So the vultures out at the college put you on to him," she said. "I knew they would. Well, they might have done worse; you're not so bad."

"Thanks," I said.

"Don't mind her," said Randall.

"No, don't mind me." She smiled. "I've been interviewing first and second grave-diggers all morning—in my golf clothes—it burned them up. What a boot Courtney would have gotten out of that, rest his soul!" She crossed herself. "How about some lunch, Elliott? You eaten yet?" she asked me.

"Breakfast an hour ago. I'm going now."

She leaned against the side of the desk. "So long."

"How about lunch one day?" asked Randall.

"Any time. Call me at my apartment." As I turned to leave I noticed in Jennifer's purse, which she had tossed open on the desk while she powdered, a crumpled white handkerchief like the one in my desk. "Make it soon," I said.

It had been a strange scene and a paradoxical one. Randall's frankness and friendliness seemed to me, although at variance with his Borgia profile, very convincing. I liked him and I liked Jennifer, although it was impossible to be sure of her. Each of her swift moods during that dynamic five or ten minutes had been consistent enough with her character, and yet, I wondered about the sudden emotional drop that had followed Randall's warning: "You'll queer everything." Were they shielding each other or was Randall possibly shielding her? I hadn't much faith in Jennifer's alibi for Friday afternoon and it was only her sudden entrance that had prevented me from questioning Randall about it. There'd be another opportunity.

The monogrammed handkerchief took on more and more significance as I walked leisurely up town, turning over in my mind the possible explanations for its presence on the floor of my office. It hadn't, I knew, been there before lunch, and according to her own testimony she had been in Science Hall only twice Friday, once when she entered with her husband at two P.M., the second time at five p.m. when she called for him.

One explanation was that while descending the fire escape to her car, as she admitted having done, her handkerchief had blown in the doorway to my office. But the door was closed—I kept it always closed in my absence as a precaution against having my papers blown about the campus—and the window giving on the same side was screened. The door to the fire escape, though closed, was not locked, Hulse locking it always when he locked the rest of the building, and my only theory was that Jennifer

for some reason on her way down the fire escape from the
zoo must have stopped for a moment in my office. I had
no idea why.

Suddenly I realized why, or a possible why. It was so
simple as to have until now escaped me. I determined after
that, whenever I knew of a person's action, to let my mind
dwell on the reverse action. Jennifer came down the fire
escape, at least as far as my office. There was nothing to
prevent her waiting there a while until the coast was clear,
then running swiftly back up to the zoo.

The theory didn't really convince me; I hadn't as yet
given it sufficient thought, but with Jennifer's alibi as
flimsy as it was, the theory was a perfectly good one and I
was proud of it.

The next step, I saw, was to determine whether or not
Jennifer had the capabilities and motives for killing her
husband. She was fairly cool, of course, and no doubt the
sort of good Catholic who washes his hands in the Blood
of the Lamb. I wondered how recently she had confessed.

That stopped me. There was probably no reason why
a priest should refuse to supply that information. It was
a rather good bet, I thought, and even though it proved
nothing at all, it would be the starting point which was
now lacking.

The Cathedral was only a few blocks away; I turned
toward it, remembering the Christmas two years before
when I had last been there. I wondered just how right I
was in doing this. False clews were my greatest fear. Brown
himself, I thought, had based his philosophy of life on
false logic, and not he alone. In this day of blind devotion
to science and scientific methods, numbers of clever men
have based their seemingly impregnable systems on false
evidence or no evidence at all. That is the great danger
of all research, whether in mathematics or murders, and
one which Groucho Marx in *Animal Crackers* summed up

nicely: "It's easy to be right when you ask questions and answer them yourself." Meanwhile: I walked toward the Cathedral. Luckily there didn't seem to be much going on at that time of day—it was just two-fifteen—and I had the good luck to find a priest on his way out, no doubt to lunch. I put my case to him and he promised to see what he could do. He said some years before he had attended a summer course at Earl College and had known Brown. I dropped quarters in three collection boxes and presently he returned.

"I am permitted to tell you this, Mr. Craig," he said, his round face and blue eyes very grave: "Mrs. Brown confessed before the six-thirty Mass this morning."

"Thank you," I said. "That's all I wanted to know."

He stopped me. "But, surely you don't think . . ."

I shook my head. "I haven't yet made up my mind what I think."

7

An *impasse?* It seemed so. All very well for Foch in a like situation to say grandly, *"Mon centre cède, ma droite recule; situation excellente. J'attaque!"* For me the issues were not quite so clean cut. My center gave way, my right fell back; for me also the situation was, strategically, excellent. But whom should I attack?

Jennifer Brown? Having just returned from the Cathedral her name leapt first to my mind. Though, quite frankly and for wholly masculine reasons, I hoped her to be innocent, I took a perverse delight in piecing together the evidences of her possible guilt: the handkerchief which, since it could not possibly have blown into my office, proved that she was in my office sometime between two-fifteen when the handkerchief was not there and five o'clock when it was; the discrepancy in time and direction between Jennifer's account of her actions of Friday afternoon and the testimony of the Chestnut Street filling station operator reported to me by Mrs. Grinnell; the fact that she not only did not love Brown but did love Elliott Randall; the motive provided by the irreconcilability of Catholicism and divorce; Jennifer's confession at the Cathedral immediately following the murder; and lastly, her temperament—willful, defiant, proud and passionate!

I looked over the list—all very substantial and inter-locking parts of a picture puzzle which, if ever complet-ed, would portray the murder of Courtney Brown by his wife.

And yet, how ridiculous! The lovely, gay, irresponsi-ble Jennifer as a murderer, a religious fanatic, a desperate and grimly passionate woman. Ridiculous and yet, item by item of evidence, all true enough! There was nothing in that stack of details that was wrong or perverted except the conclusion. Would a jury see that? Would they see the fallacy, the subtle fallacy, of a case that could attribute the qualities of murder to a girl so patently innocuous as Jennifer? Why, her very surface irreverence and frivolity should prove her innocence. Comparing the real Jenni-fer with the portrait that circumstantial evidence would enable a district attorney to draw of her before a jury, I recalled the couplet of Leonidas of Alexandria:

Menoditis' portrait here is kept; most odd it is
How very like to all the world, except Menoditis.

Applying myself to arguments against Jennifer's guilt, I found only one that was real and convenient: Framp-ton. However many suspects there may be, however many plausible motives, only one person committed the murder. To convict Frampton would be to clear Jennifer! And yet, much as I disliked Frampton, perhaps because I did so dislike him, I found myself no more able to believe in his guilt than in Jennifer's. My convictions betrayed me; they refused to function, and in the words of the inscription on the bathtub of King Tching-thang I cried to them, "Reno-vate, dod gast you, renovate!"

There was so little direct evidence against Frampton. Beyond the fact that he quarreled with Brown, that he lied regarding his actions Friday afternoon, that he admitted

being on the third floor of Science Hall sometime after
three p.m., that both he and the murderer wore gloves,
that he was devoted to his mother and wore high shoes,
what did we know? No one of those details was especially
incriminating; judged together, and for want of better
evidence against some one else, there was a fifty-fifty
chance he would be convicted on the strength of them.

Yet this was the paradox: were one of those facts—
the fact that he admitted having been on the third floor
of Science Hall after three Friday afternoon—taken away,
none of the remaining facts could possibly incriminate
him. What if he wore gloves, disliked Brown, adored his
mother—harmless enough details! And yet the very circumstance he shared with six other persons, Grace Mullin, Jack Tobey, Axel Hulse, Dick Sterling, the dago and
myself—the circumstance of being on the premises at the
approximate time of the murder—was what, if he were to
be hanged at all, would hang him.

That is why I was not thoroughly convinced of Charles
Frampton's guilt; the argument against him hinged not on
a fallacy, but on a commonplace; on an insignificance, on
peu de chose. It would have been, as a matter of fact, quite
easy to build up a convincing case against any of the rest
of us, Mullin, Tobey, Hulse, myself, or the unknown dago,
starting always, of course, with the known elements of
proximity and opportunity, conceiving a motive and, by
the alchemy of suspicion, turning irrelevancies into rele-
vancies. Take Hulse, for example: he had every opportunity to kill Brown and later, to allay suspicion, discover the
body. Motive: love of animals and almost fanatic hatred of
their exploitation. Irrelevancies which become relevant:
he lives alone, therefore probably broods; the Scandinavians are a race given to insanity and brutality; he was in
a position to know that no one would be apt to enter the
zoo for an hour or so; et cetera.

A good case, but probably wrong! And yet— No! Reason was the wrong approach to this puzzle. The mind, jumping to wrong conclusions, does more harm than good. Reason must be discarded!

O soul repressless, I with thee and thou with me,
Thy circumnavigation of the world begin;
Of man, the voyage of his mind's return,
To reason's early paradise,
Back, back to wisdom's birth, to innocent intuitions,
Again with fair Creation.

At that moment the doorbell punctuated my thoughts. It was rung by Sterling. "I took a chance on finding you home," he said. "Mind if I come in? I've got some pretty important dope."

"I'm glad to see you," I said.

He sat down, took a cigarette and sighed. "It's been a hard day. I've been at Police Headquarters ever since eleven, trying to locate that dago in the rogues' gallery. No go! But I did happen in on a conference—thought I'd telephone you about it but then I had a hunch to interview Frampton at home; he lives just the other side of the college."

"You haven't yet seen Frampton?" I asked.

He shook his head. "I'm hot from Headquarters. Listen! They're planning to arrest Frampton to-night at his house, hold him twenty-four hours on an open charge and then if he won't come clean, book him for Brown's murder."

"Arrest Frampton!" I repeated. "I see! So he's to be the decoy!"

Sterling leaned forward, his long legs stretched out before him. "Say! I hadn't thought of that. So that's the game! A decoy—hm!"

"Only a guess," I added, "but, for the moment I'm inclined not to question my guesses. Just before you came in I decided that; I decided to apply the doctrine of Prince Hui's cook to Brown's murder. This is what Prince Hui's cook said." I went to the bookcase, took down the book and, so often had it been opened at that page, it fell naturally open.

"'What your servant loves is the method of the Tao. When I first began to cut up an ox I saw nothing but the whole carcass. After three years I ceased to see it as a whole. Now I deal with it intellectually and never use my eyes. I discard the use of my senses, I work by eternal principles. Observing the natural lines, my knife slips through the great crevices and slides through the great cavities, taking advantage of natural openings. So my art avoids membranous ligatures and much more the large bones.'"

I closed the book and replaced it. "This is my first application of the method of the Tao, or law. If it hasn't failed me I shall continue to apply it."

"What are you going to do?" asked the boy.

"Telephone Thompson to find out if Frampton is being held as a decoy."

"They won't tell you," said Sterling incredulously.

"They won't have to."

I called the police station. After a wait of ten minutes, during which I was shuttled from one sphinx to another, a distant roar which, since we were one hundred and fifty miles from the surf, must have been Thompson, assailed my eardrums. "This is Craig. Could you come closer to the telephone and not shout?"

"Craig, you say?"

"Ian Craig of Earl College. And could you come a little closer to the telephone and not shout?"

"Ian Craig—yes, yes. Sorry I can't hear you. Go on."

"Listen!" I shouted. "I have some new evidence on the Brown case."

He heard that and let out his breath. "Against Frampton?"

I winked at Sterling. "No. Not Frampton! You'd better come around and look it over."

"Wait a minute!" I heard him mumble something to Andrews. Andrews' reply was slower and more distinct. "Tell the bastard he'll find us here."

Thompson's roar had subsided. "Where do you live?"

I told him. "See you around seven?"

"Seven—O.K."

I hung up. "'So my art avoids membranous ligatures and much more the large bones.'"

Sterling beamed. "Meaning Thompson and Andrews? Pretty good—I hand it to you. But, say! what is this new evidence?"

I went to the bookcase and took a quart of Buchanan's Black Label from behind the *Arabian Nights* (unexpurgated). "I don't know yet." I held it up to the light—only a quarter full and this was Saturday. "There isn't a boat in from China until Monday. Where can I get some Scotch for to-night? Or would they rather have gin?"

"You're not kidding me?" demanded Sterling.

"Better stay around."

He fell back onto the sofa. "You couldn't pry me loose, except"—he stood up—"to interview Frampton. I got to have a story for the peach in case the big news doesn't make it. I'll be back!" He stopped at the door. "Honest to God! haven't they anything on Frampton?"

I smiled. "You heard my conversation with Thompson. What do you think?"

His head almost touched the lintel. "I think they haven't a damned thing on him."

"I think you're right. And, by the way, if I'm not here, just walk in. There are still a couple of drinks in the bottle."

"Where are you going?"

I laughed at his fear that he would miss something. "Me? Oh, I'm going after that evidence I promised Thompson."

"Can I come along? It'll only taken ten minutes to interview Frampton. Let me meet you."

Since I had at the moment no idea where I was going and since he was so very eager, I nodded. "'You, sir, I entertain for one of my hundred; only I do not like the fashion of your garments. You will say they are Persian attire; but let them be changed.'"

"You mean I can come?"

"I mean I'll walk over to the college with you."

8

To the patrolman outside the zoo I offered a cigar which he refused; he did, however, accept a cigarette and, producing a match, gave me a light. Observing he was both lonely and an Irishman, I remarked that he agreed with Oscar Wilde that a cigarette is the perfect type of a perfect pleasure. It is exquisite and it leaves one unsatisfied.

I like the Irish because they never disappoint me. An Englishman, at the name, Wilde, would have leered; an American have looked blank; a Scotchman have told a joke. The patrolman broke into a bitter harangue against the English who, it seems, had not only killed Wilde and oppressed Ireland, but caused the cows on his brother-in-law's farm just outside Dublin to stop giving milk.

I interrupted him to ask if any one else had been around since he came on duty.

"The janitor," he said, "was wanting to clean the animal cages. I wouldn't let him. It was against my orders. My orders was to let no one touch nothing. I let him feed the guinea pigs though and watched him doing it."

"No one else?"

"A young lady—the same young lady what was fussing around up here when the professor was murdered. She's in one of them rooms; she wanted to work, she said, and I didn't think it'd hurt none. And the professor—the one

that wasn't murdered—he went into the dark room a little while back. That's all that's been here and me on duty
steady, lunch box and all."

"And, if I promise not to touch anything?" I asked.

"Sure! Go on in!" He stretched himself, drew a key
from his pocket and unlocked the door. "Any one who's a
judge of human nature knows it's the funny guys like you
a man can trust."

The least I could do was slip him a dollar. "I suppose
they've frisked Brown's office."

His eyes twinkled. "And what did they find: booze! Say!
professor or no professor he wasn't no better than the rest
of us."

The fastidious Courtney Brown! I crushed my cigarette.
"The sweet war-man is dead and rotten; sweet chucks, beat
not the bones of the buried; when he breathed he was a
man." "I won't be long," I said, entering the zoo.

That gaseous compound of hydrogen and nitrogen
called ammonia drove me out almost as soon as I entered,
but before I went into Brown's office I had a brief look
around, half-hoping for signs that the murderer, in obedi-
ence to the myth, had returned to the scene of his crime.
I found none, only remnants of the cornflakes Hulse had
fed the guinea pigs.

The offices in Science Hall were designed *en gros,* and
I knew in advance that Brown's, occupying as it did a
position on the third floor identical with mine, on the
second floor, was quite likely to measure eight by fourteen
feet, have a window in the south wall and the usual desk,
bookcase and *armoire*. There was one difference: my office
gave onto the fire escape which, being diagonal, ended in
the south wall of the zoo rather than of Brown's office—
an important detail in that it was responsible for the one
substantial clew: the handkerchief.

The drawers to the desk contained only old class books and themes. On top were a few textbooks, a calendar and telephone. The bookcase was filled with psychology journals and references, and the *armoire* contained on one side a number of lantern slides and on the other the "booze" of which my friend had spoken: two full quarts of "moon," three empties and several glasses—the same, doubtless, from which Sterling and Brown had drunk shortly before the murder. I inspected them, one by one. They had all been carefully rinsed out, probably under the tap in the zoo, that being the most available.

Uncorking a bottle, I smelled the contents, a fairly low grade of corn whisky. How characteristic of Brown to thus intimate that bonded liquor had become under the eighteenth amendment too bourgeois a commodity. How characteristic that moonshine should be for him just another pose, another illustration of his theory that simple pleasures are the last refuge of the complex.

And how diabolically characteristic that he should outrage the already inflamed dogmatism of Frampton, not only by keeping liquor in his office, but probably by offering him from time to time a drink. A motive for murder there!

"You ain't touched nothing?" demanded the patrolman, putting his head in the door.

I reassured him, contemplating once more the five bottles. What if this was the earthquake at my feet of which the Book of Verses speaks! "The person who patiently awaits a sign from the clouds for many years and yet fails to notice the earthquake at his feet is devoid of intellect."

By the "earthquake" I refer of course to the two full quarts which might possibly have not been in the cupboard at the time Brown and Sterling had a drink. In any case they emptied one of the other bottles, my supposition being

that the two full quarts were brought later by a bootlegger—by the man Sterling passed on the stairs, the dago!

I closed the *armoire,* my mind still on the identity of
the dago and, instinctively, for thoroughness happens to
be instinctive to me, opened the door leading to the laboratories. This first one, except for the usual screen, time-
clock and table containing odds and ends of mechanical
apparatus, was empty. Miss Mullin must, since the officer
hadn't seen her leave, be in the adjoining laboratory, no
doubt at work on an experiment. I rather wanted to talk
with her and I had a feeling that she might want a talk
with me. She was shy; she suffered the combined inhibitions of the pre-war maiden and the post-war professional
woman and I knew that, either through an aversion to
taking up my time or making advances, she wouldn't demand a conference with me. Not least of all, she seemed
acutely aware of that barrier of resentful disdain that psychologists, behavioristic psychologists in particular, have
erected between themselves and the rest of humanity.

I listened a moment at the door to the second laboratory; it was fairly solid but I could hear voices and get the
tempo of the conversation though not the content. Could
it be Frampton with her, I wondered. Though he had entered the dark room, he might, I supposed, have come
through the little-used door in the north wall into the zoo
and through Brown's office, here. Whoever it was, the conversation was serious and subdued with very few breaks;
too subdued and too continuous, it seemed to me, to be
casual. There was a tenseness to it, just audible though it
was, that held me.

I quietly opened the door.

". . . you can do. Nothing!" At the sound of the door
Frampton turned. Startled as he was, there was nothing in
his face to give him away. My eyes flashed to Grace Mullin
who was leaning against one arm of the dentist's chair.

She smiled sardonically. "Mr. Craig!"

"I'm sorry," I said. "I had no idea . . ."

Frampton buttoned up his overcoat. "I was just leaving." He took his hat from a chair. "Good-by, Grace." He walked by me. "Good afternoon, Mr. Craig."

"You're going home?" I asked.

"Yes. Why?" He demanded, instantly on the defensive.

"I happen to know that Sterling is waiting for you there."

"Dr. Frampton is always glad to see reporters." Grace Mullin's tone was gently sarcastic.

Frampton turned on her. "You're right. I am. Perhaps it's because I have no reason to fear publicity. Good-by." He closed the door behind him.

Miss Mullin sighed. "Poor Dr. Frampton."

"Poor! Why?"

She shrugged her shoulders. "He's so sure of himself. It must be nice. Still. . . ."

"Wasn't Brown?" I asked.

"Dr. Brown?" She considered. "Yes. But he was different. Oh, he was conceited all right. But why not?"

"He was very handsome."

She nodded. "Very. And clever."

I climbed onto a tall stool, facing her. "Too bad he was so lazy."

"Lazy? Wouldn't you say it was more a *laissez-faire* attitude? Boredom? You know."

I smiled. "I know that boredom sounds better than laziness but I've always thought they amounted to the same thing. Either one gets you out of work. Have you ever heard of a bored ditch-digger? Or a bored hobo? They're just lazy. You've got to have two or three degrees before you're entitled to boredom. Well, small matter! At any rate, Frampton will never be accused of either. By the way, is there anything wrong between you and him?"

"Lots." She examined her hands. "He thinks I killed Dr. Brown."

I lighted a cigarette. "Did you?"

"Dr. Frampton is very convincing." She lifted her eyes to my face. "But, on the whole, I think not."

"I'm beginning to see why you said 'poor Dr. Frampton?'"

"He's a very good psychologist."

"More of a psychologist than he is a man. It's a pity that any one who knows so much about rats should know so little about human beings. It's a pity and yet rather encouraging."

She laughed. "They haven't much in common besides their reactions to vitamins and cigarette smoke. Do you remember that experiment Dr. Frampton made for a cigarette company? He devised a system for blowing cigarette smoke at regular intervals into one of the rat cages. It didn't harm the rats in the least. They grew as well and had just as much energy as non-smoking rats."

"I don't know that I like having my vices tampered with." I pulled at my cigarette, tossed it on the floor and stepped on it. "Do you suppose Frampton had any idea of beating you to the draw; that is, of accusing you of Brown's murder before you or any one else accused him?"

She shook her head. "I don't think so. As I said, he's rather sure of himself."

"True. And yet, the police are on the verge of accusing him."

"What?"

"Are you surprised?" I asked.

"Yes." She hesitated, then climbed slowly into the chair she had been leaning against since I entered. "Yes, I am."

"Why?"

"I don't know. I just don't think he did it. It's so definite: the killing of any one." She smiled. "Anything definite is surprising to a psychologist. But how do you know the police suspect him? Are they going to arrest him?"

"No doubt. They won't be satisfied until they arrest some one. It doesn't mean much, only that Frampton is at the moment the most interesting factor. If there was any reason—can you think of any reason why he shouldn't be arrested?"

She considered. "I'm not sure. I didn't hear all the testimony."

"You do know that he was in the dark room at about three-fifteen."

She nodded. "He said so. Of course, I was with Dr. Brown until after that, until about three-thirty and Mr. Sterling was with him after I left. I don't know for exactly how long."

"Fifteen minutes or so, I think. He says that he left the building at about a quarter to four. Did Frampton tell you how long he stayed in the dark room?"

"No, he didn't. Didn't that come out at the investigation? Whether or not Dr. Brown was seen alive after Dr. Frampton left?"

"Unless he left almost immediately there'd have been no one around to see Brown alive," I said. "That is, after Sterling left at three-forty-five there was no one but the mythical dark man. And who knows when he'll turn up. However, the police must have gone into all that with Frampton. They certainly would have questioned him as to how long he stayed in the building. Feeding the rats doesn't take long, does it?"

"Not if that's all he did."

I reached for my cigarette case. "Cigarette?" She shook her head. "Strange," I said, "how murders and fires and such things lead to friendships. We might have gone on for years without being even acquaintances."

"Are we friends?"

"I think so. If we're not enemies. We might be either according to a statement of Wilde's: 'I choose my friends for their good looks, my acquaintances for their good characters, and my enemies for their good intellects.'"

She smiled. "You're right. My character isn't good."

"All the better! I couldn't help wondering. You're extremely industrious."

"Only so I won't have to be industrious." For the first time since I'd become aware of her she was animated; her eyes brightened. "I've promised myself that after I get my Ph.D., I'll take a vacation. Russia probably. I have a little money. Enough for a year anyway. That's why I'm working so hard for my degree. If I can make it by next spring I'll leave right afterwards."

"I wish you luck. What are you working on for your degree?"

She was instantly serious. "The effect of mental activity on the patellar tendon reflex or knee jerk."

"Oh!" I said. "It was that you were working on with Tobey."

"You mean when . . . ?" I nodded. "Yes. Except for teaching a couple of freshman classes, that takes up all my time. But what about you? So far we've talked nothing but psychology. What do you do?"

"Me? Oh, I spend my time in looking for the Sacred Emperor in the low-class tea-shops. To be more explicit, I lead a strange life, not so aimless as it may seem but aimless enough." I arose.

"Must you go?"

I nodded. "By the way, was Frampton's accusation purely a flight of fancy or was it based on one of his many illusions?"

She smiled. "I wouldn't care to build up too careful a case against myself. But the fact is, Dr. Frampton implies that Dr. Brown was a Don Juan, that he continued to make advances to me and that I killed him in self-defense. An utterly ridiculous theory as I was trying to point out when you entered. In the first place Dr. Brown would never in a thousand years have made advances to any one but his wife, whom he was intensely in love with. Even though she didn't love him. But I suppose you know that. Secondly, he was the most courteous man alive. Thirdly—well, I was with Jack in the laboratory. Fourth . . . It's too ridiculous."

"I agree with you. It sounds like Frampton."

"Dr. Frampton has been devoting so much study to the sexual life of rats."

I laughed. "It's bound to get one." I opened the door. "Back to the low-class tea-shops! *Au revoir.*"

"Au revoir."

Her eyes followed me through the door, farther than that I should say. Back in Brown's office I looked around for the telephone book; it was hanging under the window between the desk and west wall. Stupid of me not to have thought sooner of it. Another earthquake at my feet! I took down in my notebook, as a precaution, the entire list of names in the front of the book, faculty members and all.

"Thought you was never coming out," remarked the patrolman as I closed the door behind me. "Now there's only the girl left. And the reptiles in there." He pointed to the zoo. "This is the first time I was ever in the halls of higher learning and I don't know that I like them."

I laughed, slipped him another dollar, and proceeded downstairs. Then, instead of returning straight to my apartment, I started across the campus in a different direction, in the direction of Frampton's house, half thinking to meet Sterling and with more than a vague desire to talk with Frampton, with whom I'd had few words at any time; fewer since the murder.

The bungalow where he lived with his mother was of red brick surrounded by a neat lawn and shrubbery. There were no flowers, Frampton having neither the time nor inclination for gardening. Now, for the first time, often as I had passed by there, I turned up the brick walk and rang the doorbell.

Mrs. Frampton opened the door. She didn't seem particularly glad to see me, our previous conversation still, no doubt, rankling in her mind. "How do you do?" she said. "Do you want to see me or Charles?"

"Is Dr. Frampton home?" I asked. "I would rather like to see him."

Her reply was curt. "He's gone out. He's gone for a walk."

"Alone?"

"She regarded me suspiciously. "No. With a young man. They just left—not more than ten minutes ago. They were walking slowly."

"I don't think I'll bother to try to catch up with them," I said after a moment. "May I come in instead?"

She remained motionless. "I don't know how long they'll be gone."

I smiled. "It doesn't matter. I won't wait for them. But I would like a few words with you."

Silent and still antagonistic, she led the way into the sitting room, seated herself in a rocking-chair beside the empty fireplace, folded her hands and regarded me with stern and unwavering attention.

"You're very comfortable here," I said, looking about the room which with its golden oak furniture, flowered walls and carpet, cushions, tidies and photographs seemed in this day of whitewash and chromium as naive as a room painted by Matisse. Mrs. Frampton made no answer. I strolled over to the mantel. "What a charming photograph of Raquel Meller! And autographed!"

"She sent it to Charles. You've never been here before, have you?"

"No," I said. "And I had no idea you had such a collection of celebrities: Yvette Guilbert, Mary Lewis, Jeritza,

Pavlova, Karsavina, La Argentina, Mary Wigman, Mary
Garden, Melba, Ruth St. Denis . . ." I rattled off the names
of those that caught my glance. "And even my old friend,
Isadora Duncan!"

Mrs. Frampton's iciness melted visibly. "They all belong to Charles and they're all autographed. He has ever
so many more but only the autographed ones are framed.
Would you like to walk around and look at them?"

"Indeed I would," I replied, starting on a slow circuit of
the room. The walls from a height of five feet on upwards
were literally plastered with pictures of women, some of
whom I could identify and many of whom I couldn't.

"I can't say who they all are, myself," said Mrs. Frampton. "I don't pay much attention to them beyond dusting
them. But Charles can tell you the name of every one and
how old she is and just where she's appeared. She's his
favorite." She pointed to the large Raquel Meller. "Charles
met her when she was here. He thinks she had the greatest possibilities of them all but that circumstances were
against her."

I proceeded on my tour. "Your son has many interests."

"Oh, yes. He wouldn't be happy just sitting still; he's
got to be up to something." So patent an understatement
made me look around. The only evidence of her gratified
pride was a slight smirk. "Are you interested in singers and
dancers, Mr. Craig?"

"Very much."

"Then you'd like his albums. It's too bad he's not here
to show them to you. He's got one completely filled with
women who sang and danced in California at the time of
the Gold Rush. He went to a lot of trouble to collect those."

"I don't doubt it." I paused. "Tell me, Mrs. Frampton—I'm very much interested—how did Dr. Frampton
happen to get started collecting these photographs?"

She frowned. "I don't remember. He's been at it so long
now; ever since he was a little boy. I think at first he

did it for fun—the way children collect stamps. Then he
thought they might be valuable so he kept on. He's very
much attached to them now. Of course it's only a hobby;
he doesn't allow it to interfere with his experiments."

"Very wise." I sat down beside the center table and
absently examined the leaves of the potted fern on it. "By
the way, Mrs. Frampton, is your mind any easier than it
was this morning?"

"What do you mean?"

"You seem less concerned. I wondered if you'd had a
talk since then with your son."

She drew herself up. "Charles and I have no secrets
from each other."

"No?" I inquired gently. "Then he knows you suspect
Mrs. Brown of being an accomplice, if not the actual murderer?"

She turned white. "How dare you!"

"But surely, Mrs. Frampton, nothing I said could have
changed your views on that subject. So if no more influ-
ential person has argued them with you why should you
be *en garde?*"

Her eyes slowly shifted to meet mine. "What is it, Mr.
Craig?"

"Just this, Mrs. Frampton: you say you and your son
have no secrets from each other, yet I doubt very much if
he knows that you suspect Mrs. Brown, and I doubt likewise if you know that he has indulged in equally absurd
accusations of Miss Mullin."

Her face relaxed; her eyes, in that brief second following my words, told me what I wanted to know. Distress,
I think she might have concealed, but not relief. "Why
aren't you frank, with me, Mrs. Frampton?" I asked. "It's
not Mrs. Brown you suspect of having killed her husband;
it never really has been. What's more you haven't talked
this thing over with your son; you've wanted to, perhaps,

and he's refused. However it is, you've done your best to put me off the track; you've done your best to mask your fears. But it's all very obvious."

"I don't understand you."

"Oh, yes, you do. This morning you told me you were sure he didn't commit the murder. That's not true. You're desperately afraid that he did."

There was a pause, the quiet after lightning. Her lips parted for a denial; then she said simply, "Well?"

"Your son is a very complex person." I leaned forward. "Has he been so different the last day or two?"

She nodded. "I love him, Mr. Craig. He's all I have. If only he weren't so . . ."

"Eccentric?"

"He's too clever. He's always been too clever. He's never liked people, only ideas. I'm the only one—the only person on earth he feels any affection for. I don't know why. I'm not clever; I don't know anything about his work. But he's always been so sweet; he's always said he'd rather be with me than any one. I wanted him to go out with young people, with girls. I've tried not to be selfish; I wouldn't have minded being lonely. I wanted him to enjoy himself like other boys. But he wouldn't; he said he'd rather be with me. And now. . . ."

I felt strangely touched. I say strangely because mother love in all its manifestations has usually left me cold; too many journalists, too many vulgarians have played on it. "Don't worry, Mrs. Frampton," I said. "You mustn't. I want to help you—if you'll let me."

Her face softened. "Mr. Craig, you don't think . . . ?"

"Have you asked him?" I inquired.

"He won't come straight out. And I can't say, 'Charles, are you a murderer?' I can't say that. He'd never forgive me if he thought that was in my mind. Don't you see?"

"Yes." My eyes drifted over the pictures: Raquel Meller, Isadora Duncan, Mary Garden. . . . High priestesses of romance. "Has it ever occurred to you," I asked, "that these are your son's only outlet for his emotions?"

"You mean . . . ?"

"I mean he has nothing to do with flesh and blood women. And that the mere fact that he collects these photographs shows that he isn't lacking in a natural interest in and appreciation of beautiful women. These are a very poor substitute for love. He's tried to put his physical needs on a mental basis, to suppress them, to satisfy them with ideas, photographs, words. And it hasn't worked."

Mrs. Frampton looked perplexed. "Then, he should have been like other boys. Even if he didn't want to he should have gone to dances and parties. If I'd only made him! I could have. I was selfish. I didn't insist enough. I thought if he didn't want to, if he was happier this way, perhaps it was just as well."

"Perhaps it was," I said. "I don't know. I don't pretend to know. But it's quite obvious that your son isn't entirely normal, especially in his attitude toward women. First, his statement to Miss Mullin, and now these." I indicated the pictures.

"What did Charles say to Grace Mullin? He's often told me how efficient she was; what a splendid worker. Far better than Miss Clare—she's the other assistant. He likes efficient women. Of course, Grace is very plain."

I nodded. "Exactly! Yet he suggested to her—suggested is hardly a strong enough word—that Dr. Brown had made advances to her and she in self-defense had—"

"Had killed him?" She took the words from my mouth. "Oh! How could he have!" Her voice, her eyes were indignant. "How could he say that. It's not like him, Mr. Craig. He's not himself or he couldn't say that to a nice girl, a girl he's known and worked with so long. Oh, I knew he

wasn't himself." She arose and walked agitatedly past me
to the window. "He was so patient. If you'd only seen how
he put up with Dr. Brown. I knew what he endured. Day
after day he'd never show a bit of resentment, he'd go back
there, to Science Hall to be sneered at and insulted, but
never a word from him. He was thoughtful, Mr. Craig, and
self-controlled. He wouldn't have hurt any one's feelings
no matter what he thought."

"I've always thought him extremely tactful," I said.

"He always said it never did any good to say malicious
things and sneer at people the way Dr. Brown did. He said
that slander was a boomerang; it came back at you. Even
in his letters, when people attacked him unjustly, he always answered politely. Oh, I don't understand!"

I too arose. "If anything at all comes up, Mrs. Frampton, you have my telephone number. I've an appointment
now; I'll have to leave." She said nothing but her eyes were
heavy. "And don't worry. Please."

She followed me to the door. "Thank you, Mr. Craig."

I walked down the red bricks to the sidewalk and back
to my apartment. Sterling was waiting there for me. "So
you took a stroll with Frampton," I said.

"Yeah. I'll tell you about it. But what about you? Any
luck?"

"'Observing the natural lines, my knife slips through
the great crevices and slides through the great cavities,
taking advantage, of natural openings.'"

"Yeah? And what about that evidence you promised the
chief?"

"It won't be long now."

He looked at his watch. "It had better not be. What
time did you tell them to come? Seven? Well, it's way after
four now. Three hours to do your stuff!"

I lighted a cigarette. "What did Frampton say for pub-
lication?"

"A lot of hooey, if you ask me! but it makes a good story. That bird has plenty of crust—you don't ever need to feel sorry for him!" Sterling laughed. "And does he like publicity? Say! he eats it up! Spread himself like a prima donna—and when I mentioned the police just to take the wind out of his sails what do you think he said?"

"No idea!"

Drawing himself up, Sterling delivered in the manner of a Charles Rann Kennedy, "'Let them arrest me! I have done no wrong. My heart shall not reproach me so long as I live. And when they come to arrest me—then! and not until then shall I play my ace!'" Sterling looked at me. "What do you think of that! Nothing but a plant to make the front page is the way I figure it."

"I wonder."

"You don't think he has an ace!"

"It may look like an ace to him," I suggested. "What it actually is we'll find out to-night."

"That's right. And what do you want to bet it's a phony?"

"You mean you think he killed Brown?"

Sterling drew a greenback from his pocket. "I'll risk this on it."

"Only five?"

"Frampton's a tricky devil; five's enough on him."

I smiled. "You're on. My convictions are worth five dollars, if only to me. And if I lose—well, there's a Chinese proverb: 'Without error there could be no such thing as truth.'"

9

Back at my apartment I took out the list copied from the front of Brown's telephone book and studied it while Sterling poured a couple of drinks. It wasn't that I didn't know which name represented the bootlegger—out of a dozen or so names it isn't very difficult to select "Nick" as belonging to that celebrated class. My problem was rather to convince a bootlegger, suspicious normally as a mother jaguar, that it wasn't to arrest him either for the murder of his client or the peddling of moonshine that I wanted him to visit my apartment, but merely for the purchase of his wares.

"What's the name of your sports editor?" I asked Sterling, whose curiosity was fairly apparent.

"Bill Kelly. Why?"

I gave Nick's number to Central. After a long wait a woman answered the telephone. "Is Nick there?" I asked.

"I'll see," she replied.

After two or three minutes a guarded "hello" came over the line.

"Nick?"

"Who is it?"

"Ian Craig—from the *Sun*. Bill Kelly, the sports editor, gave me your name."

"Bill Kelly?"

"Yes," I insisted. "He said one of the boys gave him your name—said your stuff was O.K." I waited for his answer.

"I don't know what you're talking about."

"Sure you do. I'm throwing a party to-night—for the boys on the *Sun*. Don't hold out on me."

Nick hesitated. Then softly, "What do you want?"

"Make it a couple. And the number is 24, Roosevelt Apartments, at the corner of Spruce and Fourteenth. Got it? Make it soon," I pleaded, but Nick had already rung off.

I turned to Sterling. "'Are these the breed of wits so wondered at?'"

His disgust was unbounded. "All that fuss about a couple of quarts for to-night. Jees'!" He swallowed his liquor and stood up. "Got to get back to the office."

"Frampton's story? Use my typewriter."

"Thanks." He went over to my desk and commenced hammering away with two fingers on my portable while I paced the floor, wondering whether or not Nick would come and if, after all, he was the man Sterling passed on the stairs. If neither of those two hopes was fulfilled I had still a third piece of evidence for the police—one which for various reasons I would give them only as a last resort: the handkerchief.

A thousand tributaries of thought branched from that clew, all of which my mind traced and retraced: the priest's admission, Catholicism, behaviorism, their incompatibility and, therefore, the incompatibility of their disciples. . . . At last, tired of pacing the floor, I dropped into an armchair and contemplated the perfect tranquility of my Buddha, its youthful erectness and its wisdom, symbolized by the moonstone in its forehead.

Practically twenty-five minutes after my telephone call the doorbell rang. "Don't look around until I say to," I told Sterling as I answered the door. The bootlegger was short and dark and wearing the same enormous overcoat Hulse had alluded to; a brown felt was pulled down over his eyes. "You Mr. Craig?"

"Come in," I said.

He advanced warily, taking note of the various doors and places of concealment, with a furtive frown for Sterling's back. I nodded reassuringly and, drawing two quarts out from under his coat, he set them on the table. "That'll be five bucks."

I took out my wallet, looked through it and extracted a ten-dollar bill. "The smallest I have. Sorry!"

"I got change." Taking a greasy coin purse from his pocket, he handed me silently five dollars. At the door he turned and faced me. "Your number's seventy-six. Next time you want something don't ask for me; I'm liable to be out making deliveries. Just tell the dame your number and what you want and I'll bring it around. See?"

I nodded. "You were wrong, Sterling," I said. "He's a Greek!"

Sterling swung around. "That's the bird all right. Close that door!"

Nick closed the door and leaned menacingly against it, his jaws and neck-muscles bulging. "Trying to frame me?"

I sat down. "Nick what?"

"Fransioli."

"I took him for a dago," said Sterling.

"Open one of those quarts, and get another glass. We'll have a drink. Cigarette?" I offered Nick my case.

He only swore.

"Of course you know if you try to get away I can telephone down and have you stopped before you're out of the building." Sterling brought an extra glass. "I hope you don't mind drinking your own liquor. Skoal!"

"That was a fast one," said Sterling. "I never tumbled to it till he was making change; then I caught him out of

the corner of my eye. And me looking through the rogues'
gallery! The chief's going to be knocked for a loop."

I nodded. "Yes. I know. And now"—I glanced at my
watch. "I think we owe Mr. Fransioli an explanation."
Nick's belligerence was equaled only by his bewilderment.
"First! Your name and telephone number—where do you
suppose I got them?"

"Bill Kelly?"

"I said Bill Kelly. That was so you'd come. Would you
have come if I'd said I found them in Courtney Brown's
telephone book?"

It takes a thoroughly fearless man to be thoroughly
cowed. "Jesus Christ!" issued in a whisper from his teeth.

"Drink your whisky; you'll feel better," I said. "Now,
sit down."

Sterling's eye was on the telephone; it had been on it
for rather a long time. Now he asked casually, "Mind if I
use it?"

I crushed my cigarette in the ash tray. "'When the
hunter sets traps only for rabbits, tigers and dragons are
left uncaught.'"

Sterling thrust his hands in his trousers pockets. "Oh,
all right!"

His disappointment was very boyish. "What time does
the home edition go to press?" I asked.

"Around midnight."

"Telephone in your Frampton feature and tell them to
save another column in the home edition."

"Swell!" Sterling's eyes sparkled. "Say! how about a picture. Well . . . no hurry about that." He raced to the telephone.

I filled our glasses, then turned to the quiescent Nick.
"Married? Better telephone your wife you won't be home
to dinner. 'We'll drink away the woes of ten thousand
generations' and, of course, eat." Drawing my notebook

and pencil from my pocket I scribbled down a number of items and, when Sterling hung up, handed him the list together with five dollars. He took one look at it, laughed and departed.

"Now! Friday afternoon . . . concentrate on it. What time did Brown call you?"

Nick's answer was prompt enough to leave no doubt as to what had been on his mind the last twenty-four hours. "My wife took the message. I was out. It was before lunch—around eleven, I guess." He wet his lips. "Yeh! around eleven."

"What time did you make the delivery?"

"After lunch."

"After lunch," I meditated. "You wouldn't care to say how long after?"

"Sure!" Nick scratched his head. "Around two, or maybe it was later. I don't know."

"And you don't care?"

"Say!" Nick set his glass on the table. "Who are you anyway? And what's it to you what time I took Brown his liquor? I didn't croak him. You can't hang that on me."

I laughed. "I'm not hanging anything on you. I'm trying, as a matter of fact, to keep you from being hanged."

"Yeah? Well, who are you?"

"Who am I? Only 'a madman of Chu singing the phoenix-bird song and laughing at the sage Confucius. At dawn a green jade staff in my hand, I leave the yellow crane house and go, seeking genii among the five mountains, forgetting the distance. All my life I've loved to visit the mountains of renown.'"

Nick shook his head. "Well, whoever you are, you're a new one on me! Go on and ask your questions; I'll answer them."

"Excellent!" I said. "What time yesterday afternoon did you last see Brown?"

Nick frowned. "Honest to God! I don't know. I had a watch on me but I never looked at it." He grinned. "It don't take you long to get down to business. I never saw a bird like you. One minute it's nut-stuff and the next it's 'what time did you see Brown?' I hand it to you for a quick change!"

"Thanks! I'd rather you'd looked at your watch yesterday afternoon. Go on! What did you do with the liquor?"

"I took it up to Brown's office like always. And, about the time . . . I've been thinking . . . I made a couple of deliveries before Brown's, one in the city and one about thirty miles west of here."

"That helps. Well, you took the liquor to Brown's office. . . ."

"That's right. And pretty soon he comes in and pays me and I beat it . . . just like always. And say! when my wife wakes me next morning with the paper in her hand, she says, 'Nick! you lost a customer!' You could have knocked me over with a feather!"

"Yes. It must have been a shock. So Brown wasn't in his office when you first arrived."

"Nope!"

"Where was he?"

"He was in the room next door. That's all I know. See?"

"You're not sure if he was alone in there? No voices?"

"I wasn't glued to the keyhole. What do you take me for? All I wanted with Brown was to deliver the goods C.O.D. I ain't—wasn't interested in his private life."

"How long did he keep you waiting?"

"He kept me waiting until I knocked on the door; then he comes in and pays me and I beat it like I told you."

"You didn't see any one else all the time you were in the building."

Nick looked accusingly at me. "I never said that."

"Then you did see some one."

"Sure I did. What's so funny about that? It's a public building, ain't it. I saw that guy that was in here now. Say! I spotted him for a news hound right off the bat. He looked kind of fresh."

"Any one else?"

"Yeah! Just as I ducked into Brown's office a guy came down the hall. He was a funny looking guy; skinny; and he walked like this." Nick proceeded to give a heavyweight's interpretation of Frampton's walk.

"You couldn't say what door he came out of?"

"No. But it was past the place there where the hall turns. I heard him coming before I saw him."

"He went down the stairs?"

Nick stopped before my Buddha, picked it up, looked at the bottom of it and set it down. "Yeah! down the stairs. If you had some stairs handy I'd show you how he took them."

"You can show that to the police."

"Police!"

I nodded. "It's all right. They won't arrest you. I've asked them around after dinner."

Nick looked longingly at the door. "Anything you say. But the police ain't my idea of a party. They'll drink your liquor and then pinch you. That's them!"

"This time they'll just drink your liquor." I looked at my watch. "It's getting late. Do you want to telephone your wife while I prepare the salad?" I left the room, carefully closing the door after me and, while I sliced tomatoes, listened to Nick's conversation which, with the cupboard doors open, was perfectly audible.

"Hello. Babe? This is me, Nick! Yeah! No, nothing wrong but I ain't coming for dinner. No, don't hold it. I'm tied up. No, it's O.K. I tell you—just business. I don't know his name. Naw! says he's a madman of Chu or something. Forget it. I was kidding. Any one called? Tell them

I'll be around first thing in the morning. O.K. Well, I'll be seeing you."

The bootlegger's wife! What was the tune it made me think of? And then I remembered: "Who takes care of the caretaker's daughter when the caretaker's busy taking care?" I dropped a couple of eggs into boiling water. When I opened the door Nick was examining the Buddha. He turned around. "Funny little fellow. Seems to me I seen one like him somewhere. Wonder where it could have been. A chink, ain't he?"

"No. Indian. Sixth century. This man," I indicated my portrait of Li Po, "was a chink. You'd have got on with him."

Nick looked doubtful. "I never was one to pal around with foreigners."

"He'd have been one of your best customers."

"Say! I got a picked clientele; it wouldn't look good to take on chinks. No, sir! When you got Lions and Kiwanians on your books you got to look smart—turn the scum over to your friends. That's what I do. That way you don't get in wrong with no one." He added pacifically: "Course if he's a friend of yours. . . ."

I nodded. "A very good friend of mine. However, I won't ask any favors for him."

"You ain't sore? You get the layout, don't you?"

"The layout! Yes, Nick, I think I do." With an effort, I recalled my mind to the present. "Set the table, Nick, will you. You'll find everything in the cupboard. I've got the coffee to make. That is," I added, noting the gathering rebellion on his face, "if you want to eat before the police come."

"Say! no cops is going to take away my appetite." He grinned, and commenced painstakingly to select cutlery from the drawer.

I retired to the kitchen and very shortly afterward heard the door slam and Sterling inquire, "Well, big boy? And, where's the boss?"

"In there. Say!" Nick's voice dropped. "Who the hell is he anyway?"

"Why don't you ask him?"

"I did. Said he was the madman of Wu."

Sterling laughed. "Not so far off at that. The madman of Wu, eh?"

"Give a guy a break," Nick pleaded. "I've come through, ain't I? Who is he? A plain-clothes dick? Then, what's he doing butting in on Brown's murder if he ain't a dick?"

I thought it time to open the door. Nick, putting up his hands as though to ward off a blow, retreated and Sterling, his arms full of groceries, winked and hurried past me to the kitchen. "I'm disappointed in you, Nick," I said. "You've no more poetry in you than a policeman. Why, you're not worthy of your profession. Do you realize that the sale of alcohol, the most idealistic if not the oldest profession in the world, has now the added fillip of being the most dangerous—melodrama added to poetry! Yours is a pedigree written in the *De Tranquillitate* of Seneca, in the Letters of Pliny, in Plato's Symposium, in the ecclesiastical history of Constantine, St. Gregory Nazianzen and St. Augustine, in the adages of Erasmus, the epitaph of Darius of Persia, in the treatise of the German, Vincentius Opsopoeus, in the sonnets of François de Montcorbier, *dit* Villon, in the *chansons à boire* of every language and most perfectly, by"—I indicated the portrait of Li Po—"the first madman of Chu!"

Nick's eyes narrowed belligerently. "Yeah! that part's O.K., but what do you mean: you're disappointed in me. What've I done?"

"What have you done? My dear fellow, you've simply revealed a complete lack of imagination. You asked me who I was. Instead of replying 'Ian Craig,' a reply which though it told you nothing about me, would have satisfied you, I flattered you by answering 'a madman of Chu

singing the phoenix-bird song, and laughing at the sage
Confucius.' I won't bore you with the rest. In that answer
I told you much more than my name; I told you all about
myself—my philosophy, my interests, everything about me
that matters. Because you're a bootlegger, because you deal
in that commodity of which Li Po said: 'Three cups, and
one can perfectly understand the great Tao; a gallon, and
one is in accord with all nature . . .'"

Nick's mouth fell open. "A gallon? Gawd!"

"Because of that I revealed myself to you," I continued.
"Stupid of me, wasn't it. I might have known you'd ask
Sterling first chance you got what my name was."

"Aw! Forget it! I didn't mean nothing."

"In fact I hoped you would; I rather wanted to see if,
even in the minutiae, Sterling was playing square."

Sterling grinned. "Lucky for me I was. Say! you're pretty slick, aren't you? I suppose you're all set to tell Andrews
and Thompson just who did kill Brown."

"Honest?" demanded Nick.

"I'm half inclined to," I admitted, "if it's only to *épater
les bourgeois*. But I shall restrain myself. The ambition to
impress is after all a cheap one—better to leave that to the
press. No, I shan't be precipitous but, discarding the use
of my senses, work by eternal principles. You know the
rest."

"By Jove!" exclaimed Sterling. "I believe the devil has a
clew. What's on your mind, Craig? Out with it!"

I smiled. *"Andromaque, je pense à vous."*

Sterling frowned, started to speak, then rushed to my
desk. In a moment with a triumphant smile he looked up.
"Andromaque—the goddess of conjugal love." His smile
faded. "Craig?" I made no answer. "That's a fast one!"

10

Thompson stood in the doorway; he sniffed. "Onions! I like 'em—fried!"

Andrews exhaled a cloud of smoke. "Me too!"

I handed him a Havana cigar. "If you don't mind." He took it, held it to his nose, then tossed his cigar in an ash tray. "The onion," I observed, "is a favorite of mine. It has had a part in most of the really purple moments of my life." Sterling took their coats and hats. "There's a café in Versailles—La Boule d'Or—very small, even *gemütlich,* but the *soupe à l'oignon!* I must ask them next time if there isn't ripe Camembert in it. Take this chair, Andrews; it's more comfortable. Then, there's a claret, *pelure d'oignon*—I shall never forget it: 1869. I was younger then. Now I think I should prefer a Lafite—less obvious. And, do you know, there's only one passage I remember from the Nineteenth Odyssey and that's the one in which Odysseus' tunic was said to glisten like the sheen on the skin of a dried onion. Amusing, isn't it?"

"Yeah!" said Thompson. "And now for the evidence!"

Andrews rubbed his hands together. "We didn't come here to talk about onions. No, sir."

"No?" I asked. "What did you come to talk about?"

"We came to talk about Frampton. Come on—no stalling now! What's on your mind?"

"You know," I said, "my mind isn't quite the clear and limpid reservoir you make it out, and if you expect from it, as I see you do, undiluted jets of wisdom, you're going to be frightfully disappointed and even more frightfully bored. 'The poets have muddied all the little fountains,' and so you'll have to put up with the fragments of Orientalism that muddy my logic."

Andrews yawned. "O.K. with me."

"Just the same, you got something up your sleeve."

I lighted a cigarette. "Just why were you going to arrest Frampton? Why not me—or Sterling?"

"It took guts," said Andrews. "You guys ain't got the guts."

Sterling sat up. "Yeah? You'd be surprised."

"Shall I tell you why you're arresting Frampton?"

"We're arresting him 'cause we've got a case against him."

I leaned back. "Oh, no. Not a case; only the beginnings of a case. What you lack is the one irrefutable argument—the keystone—to support and crown your arch of circumstantial evidence. That you haven't got. What you have got against Frampton is this: First, he lied concerning his whereabouts at the time of the murder; second, he confessed to proximity to the zoo at the approximate time of the murder; third, both he and the murderer wore gloves; fourth, he and Brown are known to have quarreled on several occasions." I paused. "There gentlemen, stands your case to date—a weak enough rope!"

"It'll hang Frampton," insisted Andrews.

Thompson drummed on the table. "He's right. There's no conviction there. But that don't matter. If he's guilty we'll get it out of him before the case gets to court; if he ain't, let him prove it to a jury."

"And the prosecuting attorney?" I asked.

"O.K. with him; he's looking for a set-up."

"A set-up. Rather minor, isn't it, compared with the set-ups arranged by Alexander, Charlemagne, Kublai Khan, Napoleon and Wilhelm II . . . but then, the prosecuting attorney is, no doubt, a man of modest tastes. And this set-up—what if it should turn into a backslide. They sometimes do."

"I don't follow you," growled Andrews.

Thompson, still chewing at his cigar, demanded from the corner of his mouth, "What are you driving at?"

"Only this: If, when you have spent several months, a vast amount of money and the combined mental and physical energy of the law on convicting Frampton—if then he slipped through your fingers it might prove—well, embarrassing. You see that."

Sterling grinned. Andrews, after a glance at the immobile face of his chief, blustered: "Trying to scare us out! What's it to you who we arrest? If you weren't cuckoo you'd take time off to thank your lucky stars it ain't your neck we're wringing."

"Go on," said Thompson crisply. "But let me tell you before you do Frampton any good turns, he ain't no friend of yours. I shouldn't be telling you this and if I do it's only because"—a cloud of smoke obscured his face—"I believe in giving you literary fellows a break. We had Frampton on the rack this morning and he gave you one of the sweetest black eyes I've seen for a long time."

"What!" I said. "Has Frampton's tact deserted him? I fear that his nerves, under stress, are fraying a bit. Well, that shan't prevent me from doing him a good turn, if it's only to spite you gentlemen."

"Well?" demanded Thompson. Andrews eyed me defiantly.

"I happen to know," I explained briefly, "that Brown was alive after Frampton left Science Hall yesterday—Friday afternoon at approximately three-forty-five."

"You 'happen to know'! What does that mean?"

"It means that I can produce a witness who saw and talked with Brown after that time, after he saw Frampton leave—go down the stairs."

"Holy smoke!" Sterling's voice was awed. "You sure chiseled plenty out of that baby."

"Who is he?" Thompson demanded. "Get him here. I want to get this straight."

"Yeh," drawled Andrews. "He sounds to me like a wild woman's dream."

"Nick!" I called. He entered from the kitchen—dark, stocky, with the face of a prize fighter and the rolling gait of a Gilbert and Sullivan sailor: to all appearances a tough customer.

I was amused by the reaction apparent on the policemen's faces. For my shadowy witness to turn out to be such a formidable flesh-and-blood specimen for a moment floored them. Thompson recovered first. "You pick 'em pretty, Craig. Come here, young fellow. What's your name?"

"Fransioli," said Nick in a tone that implied, "What's it to you?"

Andrews drew forth his notebook. "Occupation?"

Nick thrust his fists in his pockets, spit out, "Capitalist!" and shot an imploring glance at me.

Andrews shook his head. "That don't go."

"Put it down," roared Thompson. "Put down everything. It ain't for you to decide what's true and what's not. This isn't the judgment day and you're not Saint Peter—not yet."

Andrews put it down, grumbling as he wrote, "And if he ain't a capitalist it'll be just too bad."

"So you're the bird Sterling passed on the stairs," said Thompson, subjecting him to a cold and careful appraisal. "What's your story?"

"Go on," Nick," I directed. "Just as you told me."

"Just as you told him would be more like it," Andrews muttered, scrawling in his notebook.

"But first," I suggested, "how about a drink? I had Nick bring along a bottle as exhibit A."

Thompson nodded and Sterling went after glasses. Andrews beamed. "I spotted him for a bootlegger all along."

"You dumb cluck!" growled Thompson. Andrews added to his notes. "What are you writing now? Cross it out, whatever it is."

Andrews crossed it out. "You said to put down everything."

"Yeah? Well, we weren't drinking then. Me drinking in front of a bootlegger—that'd sound swell in court, wouldn't it?"

"How about me?" Andrews protested mildly.

"How about you?" Thompson turned to Nick. "So you sold Brown the raw liquor we found in his office!"

"Pretty bad." Andrews shook his head. "I hope what you got there is better."

Sterling handed him a glass. "Try it."

"Don't mind if I do."

Thompson, with a deprecating glance at his subordinate, demanded of Nick, "Why didn't you come around before this? You knew we were looking for you. And next time you've got evidence you can bring it to Police Headquarters. See? Go on with your story now—and be careful."

Nick told them the facts much as he had told them to me, interrupted occasionally by questions. When he had finished, Andrews sighed. "Well, that hits the Frampton deal on the head. We'll never get that tight a case against nobody else. The way we had that baby tied up! and now—gone! This business is sure a bunch of grief."

Thompson took a drink and set his glass on the table. "I'm not through with Frampton."

"What do you mean, you're not through with Frampton?"

"Well, you blockhead, he could have sneaked back up the fire escape, couldn't he?"

Andrews' eyes bulged. "After the Greek left. Yeah!"

Thompson nodded crisply. "After the Greek left."

"Golly!" Sterling grinned. "Things are looking up."

"Possible," I admitted, "but not probable. For one thing, since he didn't know Nick was waiting, there would have been no point in his leaving the building. He might just as well have killed Brown at the time, rather than take the added risk of being seen on the fire escape."

"There's something in that."

"He knew some one would be around to see him go down the stairs," Thompson objected.

"But no one was," I pointed out. "No one, that is, except Nick, who doesn't count, since Frampton was unaware of his presence. If Frampton had really desired an alibi he would have taken the trouble to see Hulse on the way out."

"Well, maybe he did. That Swede's too dumb to say."

"I wonder. Anyway," I continued, "unless Brown had been seen alive after Frampton left the building, Frampton's alibi—being seen descending the stairs—would have been useless, worse than useless: incriminating."

"That's right," said Sterling. "No one but a chump would risk going down stairs and then back up the fire escape."

"And how do you know he ain't a chump?" Andrews looked witheringly at me. "Being a professor don't cut no ice; they're dumber in some things than the rest of us."

"How about it, Craig?" asked Thompson. "You know Frampton. Mightn't, he, after he got out of the building, have decided to go back up and kill Brown?"

"No. I'd accuse Frampton of anything but impulsiveness or stupidity. Your theory imputes both to him. Not

that I think the murder was committed by an impulsive or
stupid person. No, it was coldly and methodically preconceived—but not by Frampton. Frampton, you see, would
have arranged his alibi as carefully as he arranged the murder; it's the very sketchiness of his alibi that saves him—in
my eyes."

"Yeah?" said Andrews. "Well, it wouldn't have saved
him in mine."

"It's not difficult, using true evidence, to build up a
fallacious case against a man. After all, so hasty an act as
a murder must be solved at leisure. As the fourteenth-cen-
tury Japanese monk, Kenko, said about football: 'Mistakes
always happen when an easy place is reached. It is when a
difficult kick has been made and the next appears easy that
one is sure to miss.'"

"Football!" exclaimed Sterling. "I'll be darned."

"What's the dope on Saturday's game?" Thompson
asked him.

Nick leaned forward. "I got some money on the Bears."

The telephone rang. "Thompson wanted," I announced.

He left the discussion unwillingly. "Hello. Yes—
Thompson speaking. What's that?"

"Can I go now?" Nick whispered to me.

I referred him to Andrews. He nodded. "Beat it! But we
got your number and don't forget it!"

Thompson hung up the receiver and turned from the
telephone. "Frampton's murdered. His mother called up
Headquarters. They're over in his office. Get the coats,
Andrews!"

Andrews moved mechanically toward the closet. Sterling
was the first to speak; his eyes sparkled. "Mind if I use the
phone?" I nodded consent; he darted to the telephone and
gave the number in a tense voice. The rest of us silently
followed Thompson into the night.

11

"Speak, ye that ride on white asses, ye that sit in judgment, and walk by the way."

"Well," said Andrews cheerfully, his eyes traveling from the bullet wound in Frampton's head to the pool of blood on the floor, "it looks like the Doc was right: a clear case of suicide."

Thompson cut him short. "Don't let his old lady hear you saying that. She's touchy on that point, swears it's murder. And around her it is murder. See?"

"I get you. Guess you can't blame the old girl—only son and all that. I'll feed her all the soft soap she wants."

Thompson straightened. "You keep your mouth shut; that's all I'm asking you. About time for the coroner to show up. He would kick off when there wasn't any one at the switchboard."

Sterling burst in. "The coroner'll be along. Golly! I'm winded—ran all the way. Called the paper while I was at it and told them suicide, not murder. And say! I got an idea."

"Save it."

"No wisecracks. This is a birdy." Sterling turned to me. "You know that ace Frampton said this afternoon he was saving up to play?"

I nodded. "What's that?" said Thompson sharply. "You saw him this afternoon?"

"I got a story out of him," Sterling explained. "Nothing wrong in that, is there? So while I was pumping him I says sort of casually, 'What if they arrest you?' I didn't say, 'they're figuring on arresting you,' understand! I just said, 'What if they arrest you?'"

Andrews looked at him with disgust. "You would!"

"Yes," said Thompson. "Go on. What did he say?"

"Wait a minute." Sterling reached for his notes. "He said, 'Let them arrest me! I have done no wrong. *My heart shall not reproach me so long as I live.* And when they come to arrest me—then! and not until then shall I play my ace!'" He replaced his notes. "That's what he said."

Thompson puffed at his cigar, then solemnly removed it. "There's the solution all right. He murdered Brown and that"—he pointed to the pistol beneath Frampton's, dangling fingers—"is his ace!"

"Hell!" said Sterling, acute disappointment on his face. "That was my idea. Give a fellow a chance, will you?"

"You'll get credit for it," Thompson's voice was frigid. "And what's more you'll get credit for robbing the state of a boarder."

Sterling started. "You mean he took what I said as a warning and—"

"And played his ace! That's what I mean. Think it over."

Andrews shivered. "Think I'll take a stroll down the hall; I never did get on well with stiffs. Want to come, Sterling?"

Sterling nodded dumbly. "Send the doctor in here," directed Thompson. "You and Sterling stay with Mrs. Frampton. Remember, it's murder. Stay around, Craig."

"Have a heart," pleaded Andrews.

Thompson turned his back. I walked to the side of the desk nearest the window and scanned the papers on it. Fortunately, Frampton, though he faced the desk, had slumped back in his chair, so there was not even any blood on the broad oak surface. "Well, Craig." Thompson's tone was barely sarcastic. "Still think he was innocent?"

I took time to light a cigarette before answering. "I'll let you know if I change my mind; I don't think I shall, though. You see, my theory was based on Frampton's character as I knew it and on the physical facts of Brown's murder. Well, I don't see that this or anything else can alter them."

"Fair enough." Thompson looked at me as though it were for the first time. "Fair enough," he repeated, this time absently. "You know, Craig . . . Hello, Doctor. Come in, won't you. How's Mrs. Frampton?"

Dr. Hall, wearing *pince-nez* and the capable yet weak look of the family physician, entered, shook hands and seated himself in a chair by the door facing the window beside which both Thompson and I were standing. "Mrs. Frampton is, I am glad to say, quite calm. Of course I gave her a sedative and advised that she go home to bed. Mr. Sterling offered, as a matter of fact, to drive her home, but she refuses to leave while her son's body is still in the building. Obviously, I couldn't insist. I don't think, though, if she isn't excited, that she'll cause you any trouble. I have attended both her and her son for several years now and I can assure you she is a very sensible woman."

"She seems so," replied Thompson abruptly. It was quite apparent from his tone that he had very little interest in either Mrs. Frampton or the doctor. "Now, Doctor, I wonder if you'd give us your account of the last hour—in detail, please."

"Certainly." His courtesy was so professional as to be annoying. "I was fortunately at home when Mrs. Frampton telephoned—at dinner, to be exact. I kept no office hours this afternoon, it being Saturday, but I had a number of calls to make and didn't reach home until nearly seven. As soon as I heard what it was I left the house and drove to the drugstore down here on Campus Avenue to pick her up. In the meantime I believe she telephoned you, did she not? I found her sitting at a table, really quite calm; she got into my car with me and we drove here to Science Hall. The downstairs lights were on, but the stairs were dark, and I didn't at the time stop to look for the switch, but came straight up here. This light was on and Frampton was there as you see him now; I ascertained he was dead and since Mrs. Frampton had already sent for you, and since I thought it better not to leave her alone, I didn't go call the coroner as I should otherwise have done. Then a curious thing happened." The doctor paused but Thompson's broad back remaining immobile, he continued. "I went to turn on the lights. Mrs. Frampton stayed here; she was, as I said, quite calm and promised to touch nothing so I thought it safe to leave her for a moment. This floor was pitch dark and as I felt my way along the hall, hoping to come on the light switch, I thought I heard music. For a moment I'd have sworn it was an hallucination—brought on by shock; then I realized it was nothing of the sort, but actual music being played quite close to me. I didn't bother to find the lights first but struck a match and groped my way toward the music. And as I came closer I realized it was a harmonica. It led me to the door of that large room at the turn in the hall—I believe you call it the zoo. I opened the door and saw—well, a most surprising picture. For one thing, all the animals had been let out of their cages and were scampering and flying about, so I had to close the door very quickly to keep them from escaping to the hall. The musician, of course, had stopped playing when I entered, and stood up so that, although the room was lighted only by one light—and that shaded by a paper—I had a pretty good chance to examine him. He told me he was the janitor, and when I had explained what I was doing there he offered to light up for me. He said it wouldn't hurt to leave the animals loose until later when he had time to lock them up. Then I returned to this room where I had left Mrs. Frampton and shortly after, you arrived." The doctor finished, removed his *pince-nez* and polished them with a clean handkerchief.

Thompson turned. "How long would you say he's been dead?"

The doctor replaced his glasses. "It's difficult to say exactly." He consulted his watch. "About three hours—not more. It's now eight-forty; I'd say death occurred not earlier than five-thirty and not later than six-fifteen." He walked over to the body. "When I first arrived—about half an hour ago—I made a cursory examination to determine that very thing. The body temperature then was 77°F. It cools very slowly, you see. But if death had occurred more than two or three hours ago it would have been lower than 77°F.—74°F. or thereabouts. Also, the muscles still retained some muscular irritability; that is, by repeated blows of the hand they could still be made to contract. On the other hand, if you'll come closer you'll see that rigidity has already affected certain muscles, particularly the eyelids and lower jaw."

Thompson nodded. "Instantaneous death?"

"Yes. The bullet entered the parietal bone—took a piece with it, in fact." He pointed to a blood-stained fragment of bone on the floor a short distance from the desk. "There's no doubt that death was instantaneous."

"O.K., Doctor!" Thompson turned wearily to me. "Any questions, Craig?"

I had been gazing at the bullet imbedded in the wall on my right, almost parallel with Frampton's head. "Thanks," I said. "But though one drinks at a river, one cannot drink more than a bellyful."

"All right, Doctor. Send in Hulse, will you? And when the coroner comes you'll take Mrs. Frampton home. I

won't question her further now. If anything comes up I'll
see her in the morning."

The doctor arose. "Very well. Good evening." He bowed
slightly to each of us. "If you need me again, I'm at your
service."

Thompson nodded. "At the inquest. We'll notify you."

"If you don't mind, Doctor," I said, "I think I'll come
along and say a few words to Mrs. Frampton—nothing to
upset her, of course."

We strolled down the hall past the zoo. "Hulse is probably in there," suggested the doctor. "I'll stop in and tell
him he's wanted." I continued down the hall to the laboratory in which Mrs. Frampton was waiting. Sterling and
Andrews stood disconsolately in the doorway.

"Funny the coroner don't come," Andrews grumbled.

"I'll stay here if you want to watch for him."

Sterling's eyes brightened. "Think I'll take a look at
that apple machine; they may have overlooked one."

I laughed and went in. Mrs. Frampton was sitting in a
student armchair, her eyes fixed on one black-gloved hand
resting on the broad arm of the chair and of which, every
now and then, she tapped the fingers. Her face, beneath
the cherry-trimmed hat, had relaxed into definite folds;
its expression was indeed so vacant as to seem inhuman.

"Mrs. Frampton," I said gently, "would you answer a
question or two?"

She looked up, her eyes dry. "You don't think it's suicide." Her lips scarcely moved.

"No, I don't. That's what I'm about to prove to the police—if you'll help me: that it couldn't have been suicide."

"If they only knew him they'd know it wasn't suicide."
Looking straight ahead, her hands clasped, she spoke rem-
iniscently but in a flat, unemotional voice. "They asked
me if that was his pistol on the floor. I said it was; he kept

it in his desk; he had to on account of the animals, but he never used it; he hated firearms. He wouldn't even go to plays where pistols were fired. I remember when the war came he said he wouldn't go; nothing could persuade him to go. He hated everything about it—the excitement and lies, but most of all, the violence. All he wanted was to go on with his experiments—work: that was all he cared about. That's why it's so silly to think he could have committed suicide. Oh, I know what they say: that it was because he killed Courtney Brown. Well, it doesn't matter now, does it? It won't bother him any more; it won't interfere with his work to know they're saying that. That was silly too, but this is worse; if Charles had killed Courtney Brown— if he had, he wouldn't have acted this way. He would have told me. It's true. He would have told me. No matter what it was. And I wouldn't have minded. Some mothers would mind. A murderer for a son! But what does it matter—if they never find out. But shoot himself, leave me alone— Charles wouldn't do that. I know. Even if there hadn't been his experiments—and who's going to care about them now; even if he wasn't too proud, too ambitious to want to die, why—there was still me." She paused. "Charles loved me."

"I believe you, Mrs. Frampton," I said. "And soon every one will."

For the first time there was interest in her face. "Then— you really—there's some way you can prove. . . ."

"I think there is. And it depends entirely on one question." I leaned forward as did she. "Tell me, Mrs. Frampton was your son left-handed?"

She half-arose from her chair; her lips forming the single syllable: "Yes."

"Then," I said, "he was murdered by a person who either did not know he was left-handed or else carelessly forgot it."

"But . . . how did you know?"

"That he was left-handed? I didn't know. I thought in the first place, as you did, that a man of his nature never would have shot himself. Then I observed that the bullet with which he was shot was imbedded in the wall at a spot on an almost direct horizontal plane with the wound in his head. That alone was enough to make suicide most improbable. A man, shooting himself, naturally points the pistol upward, causing the bullet to take a perpendicular course. It would be extremely difficult to shoot oneself holding the pistol at a right angle to the head. Last, your son's handwriting inclining to the right, I suspected he was left-handed. In that case he would certainly not have shot himself with his right hand. *Voilà tout!*"

"All!" she repeated. "You call that 'all'!"

I shook my head. "Not by any means all! Your son was shot; it still remains to discover who shot him—and why!"

Mrs. Frampton spoke slowly as though reading my thoughts word by word. "The same person who killed Courtney Brown?"

"Perhaps." A thousand masked revelations crowded my mind. *"Qui sait?"*

12

Before going to sleep I left word at the desk I wasn't to be disturbed. I was awakened by the telephone and, looking in the dim light at my watch, discovered it was a quarter to six. My voice as I said "hello" was none too dulcet.

No more so was the voice that came back; it belonged as a matter of fact to Mrs. Grinnell. "Mr. Craig! I'd like to know what they mean by waking me up at five-thirty in the morning!"

"So you were awakened too," I sympathized. "But to just whom do you refer as 'they'?"

"The reporter, of course. Did you put him onto me? What did he want?"

I cursed Sterling. "I assure you I had nothing to do with it. And I haven't the slightest idea what he wanted. Didn't he tell you?"

"I didn't give him a chance. I was so angry at being awakened, and by a reporter, that I hung up."

It was only then that my mind, numbed by sleep, remembered the events of the night before. "I'm sorry," I said. "I was wrong when I said I had no idea what he wanted. I have: he wanted probably to get your reactions to Frampton's murder."

"Frampton's murder!"

131

"Yes. He was murdered in his office sometime around five-thirty yesterday. It should be in the morning paper."

"But . . . who murdered him?"

"That," I confessed, "is problematical." Then, as she groped for a proper expression for her mingled excitement, anger and regret, I added, "Suppose I call the police to see if anything new has turned up. I promise to keep you posted and, if you like, I'll tell the newspaper to get in touch with you again. You may want to give out an official statement for the college."

"Of course! Of course! Oh! How I wish Dr. Grinnell were here! Two murders! First Dr. Brown, and now. . . . It's terrible! Terrible! What shall we do to stop it? Poor Mrs. Frampton! And to think that to-night they were coming to dinner. . . ."

"I'll call you back," I said, "in a very few minutes. And when the reporter telephones, just a brief statement: We shall spare no effort to apprehend the criminal, or to that effect. You understand."

"I think I ought to wire for Dr. Grinnell to come home. What do you think?"

"I'd wait a day or so." I shivered as a breeze from the open window enveloped me. "I'll get in touch with you again. Good-by." Swinging my legs over the side of the bed, I reached for my dressing gown, got my arms into it and still reviewing last night's events, went to close the window.

I didn't close it and I don't know how long I stood there, seeing for the first time in many years the early morning and hearing Li Po describe the City of Po Chu-i:

> Hundreds of houses, thousands of houses—
>   like a chessboard
> The twelve streets like a field planted with
>   rows of cabbage.

In the distance perceptible, dim, dim—the
fire of approaching dawn;
And a single row of stars lying to the west of
the Five gates.

Only such a rare experience as dawn could at such a
time have taken complete possession of me and I have
only pity for those persons who, through continued early
rising or continued late retirement, have become *blasé* toward it. I don't know when I should have been restored to
the world of ideas if it hadn't been for the ringing of the
telephone.

This time it was Sterling. "Craig! Listen! I've got a
scoop!" Even if he had allowed me a moment for com-
plaint the tense sincerity of his voice would have made me
refrain. "They're holding Hulse for Frampton's murder—
been putting him through his paces—locked him up a couple of hours ago and went home to bed. They wouldn't
give me a break on it; they knew the Sunday paper was off
the press; said they'd see I got the story in time for Monday's peach. But listen! I was hanging around outside and
saw them hop into Thompson's car. The guard in here's a
friend of mine, see! I put him in a story once. He gave me
the dope on Hulse and said he'd fix things so I could see
him. But he goes off duty at seven. Can you make it by
then?"

I looked at my watch. Six-ten!

"I'll be down by six-thirty." I rang off, called a cab and
proceeded to dress.

Eighteen minutes later my cab drew up before the entrance to the Public Safety Building. Sterling was waiting
at the curb. He rushed me through corridors and down
stairways which were waiting, virginal from the char-
women's mops, for the footprints of the civil service. We
stopped before an office marked *Private;* Sterling knocked,

stuck in his head, said, "O.K.," withdrew his head and strode down the hall some twenty yards. He threw open a door. "They'll send him in. Pretty soft, eh?"

The room was small and apparently more of a sitting room than office, though in one corner was a typewriter desk. That, three straight-backed chairs, a washbasin and hatrack were the only furniture. Sterling washed his hands and dried them on his handkerchief. "If Thompson knew I'd crashed the gate he'd blow up. Try to put one over on me, will he!" He placed his handkerchief, pulled down his cuffs and took a couple of chocolate bars from his pocket. "Nourishment? Golly! I'm starved."

I shook my head. "Any other time. By the way, doesn't it seem a bit strange that Thompson and Andrews should have been in such a rush to examine Hulse? To have arrested him, to have let him languish in prison a day or so— that seems natural enough, though a bit ridiculous under the circumstances. But to have devoted the small hours of Sunday morning to a Spanish inquisition of a Scandinavian vegetarian—how do you explain it?"

Sterling, hampered as he was by a mouthful of caramel and nuts, grinned. "Looks to me like they've got an eye on you. You cramped them on the Frampton deal; this time they're not giving you a chance."

"You know," I said, "that occurred to me and I dismissed it as egomania."

"They waited till you'd gone home, didn't they, and then put the irons on Hulse. And I'll bet it's because they've got us spotted for a team that they wanted to keep me in the dark. Well, I fooled them! I beat it over here just as soon as we'd put the paper to bed. Telephoned back the story just in time." He unwrapped the foil from the second bar. "What do you bet it's marshmallow." He sank his teeth into the center of it, chewed seriously, then considered the cross section. "Naw! coconut! Not bad."

The door opened and Hulse was pushed in by a uniformed guard; his hair was disheveled and he was extremely pale. "He was taking his beauty nap," said the guard.

Sterling slipped him a bill. "It's all right. I'll let you know when we're through with him."

The guard jerked his thumb toward a bell just below the light switch. "You can ring for me. If I'm eating my breakfast one of the others'll come."

Hulse stood still, his face blank, quite as though we were strangers to him. "Sit down," said Sterling. "Been pretty tough, has it? What all did they do to you?"

He sat down, a smile slowly widening his lips. "He said I was asleep. Asleep! What does he know of Nirvana! Nirvana—Buddha's gift to his children. And at last I am one of his children. He came to me—that night in the zoo he came to me."

"What night?" I asked.

"The night of his vengeance on Dr. Brown. He came to me in the zoo. I knew right away who he was on account of his looking just like his pictures in books and he said, 'Now, you are one of my chosen people. Verily, I love you. You have followed the Way. And your reward is Nirvana.' He kissed my forehead. But when my Nirvana was over he'd gone and he's never come back. Every night at the same time I play to the animals but he hasn't come back."

Sterling sniffed. "What the hell is Nirvana?"

"It's being in tune with the infinite," answered Hulse blissfully. "And it's only for his children. No one who isn't in tune with the infinite can hear him when he talks to us and teaches us his Way. That's what it's for—so we'll be listening with pure hearts when he talks. And if we've eaten meat or drunk intoxicating liquors or destroyed innocent life or not suppressed our sinful desires we can't enter into Nirvana. And then we don't hear him when he talks."

Sterling winked at me. "Funny you never heard him, Craig; I'd have thought he'd be a pal of yours, the way you spout Chinese poetry."

"Oh, no, sir," Hulse corrected him patiently. "It's not book-learning that counts with Buddha; he doesn't care if you can't read or write so long as you're pure of heart and don't drink or smoke or eat meat or destroy innocent life. If you'd heard everything he said to me that night in the zoo you'd know that."

"Well," said Sterling impatiently, lighting a cigarette, "I don't see that this is getting us very far. By the way, as a representative of Buddha, you won't kick at a cigarette?"

"Oh, no, sir. It's only when he tells me to that I lift my hand against his enemies. I wouldn't take it on myself."

"Thanks."

"You know," I said to Sterling, "I disagree with you; this is getting us farther than I'd dared hope. Go on, Hulse, what did he say to you that night in the zoo? More than you told us?"

"Oh, yes, sir, much more. The trouble is"—he pressed his hand to his forehead—"I can't remember it all—not very well. I could until those policemen kept at me; it was their questions—you don't know all the questions they asked, and so fast. One after the other just like that!"

I nodded. "Do the best you can. No hurry." Sterling, from force of habit, took out his notebook; I signaled him to replace it.

"He said first of all that he'd had his eye on me for a long time." Hulse spoke slowly and there was a rapt expression on his face. "He said people had to show him they could go in his Way before he'd have anything to do with them and that even then if their characters weren't strong they couldn't be in the chosen few. He said he thought for a long time my character wasn't strong and that was why he didn't come to me sooner. It isn't enough for people not to drink or eat meat or suppress their sinful desires.

They have to do that too but that isn't enough. If it was enough there'd be too many chosen few. So he makes it harder; he says a person has to prove himself before they can see him."

"Sort of a Holy Grail proposition," interposed Sterling.

Hulse was wholly oblivious of the interruption. "You've got to prove you love Buddha more than earthly riches, you've got to gird yourself with his sword. Yea, even though you be slain in the combat. You've got to show him that you're no longer a coward and a sinner and he'll love you for it—and take you unto his bosom—and put you in tune with the infinite so you can talk to flowers and stones and trees and birds and animals, and you'll never be lonesome again or hungry or tired because Buddha is a friend and lover and husband and wife and brother and sister and mother and father." I suppressed Sterling's exclamation of approval. "And he said because I'd girded on my sword in his cause maybe some day he would make me a Bodhisattva and I would live with the other Bodhisattvas in a palace with a garden with peacocks in it and beautiful girls to wait on us and sing and dance for us and wine to drink. But first I must suffer and go through fire and water like the other Bodhisattvas did."

Sterling frowned. "What the hell are—"

"First," I interrupted, my eyes on Hulse's drawn face, "what exactly was it you did? You say you girded on your sword . . ."

"I didn't know what I'd done at first," Hulse admitted. "I didn't know why Buddha came or kissed me on the forehead. But now I know—it came to me: I avenged the poor little animals. I killed Dr. Brown."

Sterling jumped to his feet. "You killed Brown?"

Hulse nodded. "Yes. I remember it all now. I had to. If I hadn't some one else would have. There were the lives of the little animals to answer for; they count for as much as we do in Buddha's eyes. It was my duty. Buddha will reward me; he told me so. I'll live in the palace—they're waiting for me—the beautiful girls . . ." He stood up. "Beautiful girls—I feel dizzy . . ."

I caught him. "Ring the bell," I told Sterling.

Sterling rang, then returned, wide-eyed. "Golly! Want to loosen his collar?"

"No. He'll be all right when he's had some sleep. Too much excitement." I glanced from his hollow cheeks to his bony hands. "Half-starved too . . . a fairly popular inducement of Nirvana."

Sterling clasped his hands behind his back; his tone was aggrieved. "You don't seem exactly bowled over. I suppose you've had all this doped out for several weeks."

I laughed. The guard entered, took a look at Hulse and nodded knowingly. "That's swell! You lay 'em out and I bring 'em to. The third one this week! Might as well be a hospital." He bent over him. "Come out of it there!"

"We'll carry him back," I said, "if you show us where he goes. I have an idea he fainted from lack of food. Has he had breakfast?"

"Wouldn't eat it., Another hunger-striker!" He picked up Hulse. "Forget it! He ain't so heavy. I wouldn't have lighted into you but I get sort of sick of seeing the poor devils put through their paces and then we got to get 'em ready for more. It ain't fair."

"I'm sorry." I slipped him a couple of dollars.

"O.K., chief!"

"Well?" said Sterling.

I took my hat and coat from the rack. "Breakfast?"

Sterling stared at me. "You're the damnedest man. Don't you ever spill anything?"

I opened the door. "'He who knows the way cares not to speak of it. He who is ever ready to discuss it does not know it.' Come on to breakfast."

13

We walked up the street to the Roosevelt coffee shop. It was about half-past seven when the waitress finally set two pots of coffee, toast and bacon and eggs on the table between us. Until then I had been thinking almost uninterruptedly about the proportions of the case—its rhythm, one might say. Sterling had kept a sullen but gratifying silence which now, encouraged by the sight and odor of food, he broke. "Why all the reverie anyway? It looks to me like the armistice was signed."

I poured a cup of coffee. "I may be making a mistake."

"You said a mouthful! Sure you're making a mistake if you think Hulse didn't turn the job. He killed Brown all right; Frampton too maybe." He emptied a jug of cream into his coffee. "Too hot. Mind if I use yours? You don't take it, do you?" I passed him the cream. "The trouble with you is you don't know when to stop. The case is over and you won't admit it. Sure it was fun while it lasted. You beat Thompson at his own game and I hand it to you, but there's no point in prolonging the thing, in making it out so damned subtle. When a man confesses he's a murderer, take his word for it; that's my policy."

"You know," I said, more amused by his straight-from-the-shoulder talk than I would have been before breakfast, "I'm afraid you misunderstood me. When I said I may be making a mistake I didn't refer to Hulse's confession. I don't for a minute believe he killed Brown. I merely wondered if I ought to disillusion Messieurs Thompson and Andrews—shatter their hopes, you know, and all that."

Sterling's fork was poised in mid-air, globules of egg-yolk suspended from its prongs. "You mean you don't think he's guilty but you're thinking of letting them hang him anyway?"

I'm afraid I smiled. "I never cease to marvel at the fantastic logic of the human race. You're extraordinarily warm-hearted, sentimental even. Oh, yes, you've just shown it. And yet the one word 'guilty,' little or much as it may mean, stimulates you to cry, 'Hang him! Hang him!' It's all because you're so ignorant of the physical facts of hanging. To you—oh, I don't mean you personally—it's only a word, a synonym for punishment. You must feel some way about it; I dare say any one knows whether or not he favors it, but how many know anything at all about it—its history, for instance. It has a fascinating history. Gala, you know, in Anglo-Saxon meant gallows. I don't suppose you even know the hangman's formula—or that he has a formula. It's rather clever—invented by a Yorkshireman: you divide 412 by twice the weight of the body—in stones, of course—to get the length of drop in feet." The globules of egg-yolk on his fork had congealed; they fascinated me. "Go on and eat," I said. "I don't mean to take away your appetite."

Sterling thrust the fork viciously into his mouth. "Oh, shut up!" I commenced to eat. Sterling stared at me. "Honestly, Craig, don't you think Hulse killed Brown?"

"Honestly."

"Why?"

I leaned back. "If Hulse announced a thousand times that he was innocent he wouldn't be believed. He announces once that he's guilty—that he killed Brown. There are any number of reasons why he couldn't have. First, his mind wasn't definitely unhinged until after Brown's murder. He was always, or at least since I've known him, a border-line case—a prey to inhibitions, grievances, morbidities. Granted that he may have, probably did harbor a grudge against Brown, an impulse to kill him even. But then, so do multitudes of respectable people harbor impulses to throw themselves from high places, to cry out in public, to inflict pain, to play practical jokes. Almost always they resist those impulses; it's only those who don't resist them that we hear about. Well, to get back to Hulse: I believe that his impulses, whatever they were, were not irresistible. That is, up until the time of Brown's death he continued to be a border-line case; there was needed just that one shock to make him dangerous, unable to resist his criminal impulses, I mean. Now I can't prove to you that that's so, but there it is."

"That's all?"

"All? Oh, no. The rest, though, is fairly obvious: Hulse frankly admitted that it wasn't until the night following Brown's murder that he conceived the idea that he might have committed it; in other words, like his vision of the beautiful girls it's an illusion, not so patently Freudian, of course. Next, supposing Hulse did kill Brown; his discovery of the murder and his actions during the several hours following the murder would take on a new significances— the significance of cleverness, of feigned stupidity. Some fanatics are extremely clever, far cleverer than they ever were as sane men. But I don't think Hulse is; I'm sure he isn't. He's ingenious—yes. But not clever enough to give the convincing portrait of stupidity which he has given all along since the murder, not clever enough, in the state of fatigue and starvation in which he now is, to never once slip up, not clever enough to suppose that his ridiculous confession of Brown's murder would be ridiculous in the eyes of the law." I paused. "Enough?"

Sterling grinned. "You've got me down. But I don't know that Thompson and Andrews will say the same."

"Precisely why I've entertained the idea of not telling them. Who was that poor devil—mythological, of course—who was made to clean out a stable. All his cleaning never had the slightest effect since it turned out the gods were playing a joke on him. Well, it's worth thinking about."

"You really think if you don't butt in they'll hang him?"

I erased the gallows I had drawn on the tablecloth. "He'll hang himself, given half a chance. The idea of a persistent Nirvana—women, wine and song—is a most appealing one. What's more he'll be, for a brief moment, a hero—his picture in the papers, syndicated interviews, his name on every one's lips—the halo of notoriety—you surely appreciate the desirability of all that to the starved soul of a middle-aged janitor. What right have we to take it from him—to destroy his dreams, his future, his heroism?"

Sterling nodded. "I get your point; it's taking dope from a hop-head."

"Exactly!"

"Poor devil!"

"The Scandinavians," I said, "are given to insanity; half the insane asylums in the country are peopled with them. Curious, isn't it? There's an excuse for volubility—not that I shall ever forgive the Italians theirs, especially when it takes machine-gun form."

"Golly!" said Sterling, still wrapped in meditation. "If Thompson got a conviction, if he got Hulse hung and then if the bird turned up—the bird who killed Brown! Some one must have killed him."

"Undoubtedly. And thereby hangs a tale! Suppose, at some future date, he should turn up, as I expect he would; and suppose I didn't like him. Then, in spite of my satisfaction at having restored Hulse to his perpetual Nirvana and having played a most excellent joke on the Law, I

should feel perfectly rotten, and there'd be nothing whatever to do about it."

"Nothing?"

"Well, I don't know what the law would say to hanging
two men for the same murder but it would seem going a
bit far. Besides, I don't mean to sacrifice all my leisure to
the cause of justice or injustice. As a matter of fact I'm
thinking of going soon to some place where neither of
them exist— Marseilles, perhaps."

Sterling wrinkled his nose; he has a nose that wrinkles
very easily. "You're a card. I never can tell how serious you
are about anything."

I poured the last of the coffee. "Serious! My dear fellow, it's just because I am and have been so serious about
these murders that I feel it can't last much longer. Brown
was, in a way, my friend, you know."

"I know." Sterling nodded. "But all joking aside—if
you were joking—what if the murderer turns out to be a
woman?"

"Yes," I said. "There's that. She's charming, isn't she?"

"I'll tell the world!" His enthusiasm was unquestion-
able. "Gee! Craig, she's a peach too. You know, Friday
night—I didn't tell you about this—I was hanging around
her house sort of wondering if I couldn't get hold of some
pictures. You know how it is; people are pretty touchy
sometimes and you got to go easy. Well, I guess she saw
me from the window because she called me—she'd seen
me in Brown's office plenty of times—and said she'd let
me in. She looked swell too, had on green pajamas. We
had a drink of real Scotch—none of Nick's stuff for her—
and she gave me the picture we used in to-day's paper.
Seen it yet? She said she'd kept it around in case she ever
got a divorce. She wanted to have a decent picture in the
paper instead of the lousy one they usually dig up from the
morgue. There's something in that."

I agreed. "And when you left she said to come back any time?"

"That's right. She was damned decent—said she liked reporters. And she asked me not to let the sob-story writers get busy on her."

"So you haven't."

"A guy's got some consideration."

"You know," I said, reaching for the check, "I'd rather like to see a paper."

We left the coffee shop, buying on the way out a copy of the *Sun;* I removed the news section which carried a large banner on Frampton's murder. "She's on page two," said Sterling. "The Frampton stuff crowded her out. Not hard to look at, is she?"

I glanced at the photograph; it was signed Edward Steichen. Jennifer's elbows were resting on a table and both arms were covered from elbow to wrist with loose, wide bracelets; her face, supported by her hands, was small and hard and clear against a dark background. "It might be called *cannibale mais ingenue,*" I said, handing it back to Sterling.

He stuck it in his coat pocket. "I'm going home to bed. What are you going to do about Hulse?"

"Nothing." I buttoned my coat.

"Poor devil! A hell of a hole to be stuck in when you haven't done a damned thing. Well, see you later."

"Just a minute."

Sterling turned. "What is it?"

"I shouldn't feel too sorry for Hulse. After all, he is a bit mad, even dangerously so. And though I'm certain he didn't murder Brown I'm not at all certain he didn't murder Frampton."

"Craig. . . ."

I hailed a taxi. "You're to telephone Mrs. Grinnell. She won't hang up on you this time."

14

On the way up to my apartment I stopped at the desk. "Any calls?"

The clerk passed three slips over the counter. "Up early, Mr. Craig!"

"That's right. I did leave word I wasn't to be disturbed before ten. I don't suppose you know anything about those two calls that got to me around six."

"No, sir, I don't. I came on at seven. It must've been the night clerk."

"Yes. Well, it's of no consequence. I'll be in for a while now." I stepped into the elevator and on the way up glanced at the slips: Mrs. Brown had called at seven-twenty-one; Miss Mullin at seven forty-five and Mrs. Grinnell at eight-three.

When I opened the door to my apartment my clock was just striking eight-thirty. The maid had not yet been in and the sight of the empty bottles, highball glasses and ash trays filled with cigar and cigarette stubs recalled vividly to me last night's *cénacle*.

After taking off my coat I was making a hasty disposition of them when there was a knock at the door. "Come in," I called supposing it to be the maid.

"I expected you'd receive me in bed," said Jennifer, closing the door behind her. "I'm frightfully disappointed. When I telephoned they led me to believe you were asleep."

"Just a ruse to get you here," I explained.

"I hope they all work as well." She sat down in an arm-chair, crossed her legs and surveyed my room mockingly. "It is early."

"Cigarette?" I offered her my case and then a light. "You know, this scene might be from any one of fifty plays. It's a pity you didn't wear a veil—the Iris March sort, not the Madame X."

"So I might lift it, you mean?"

"If you would."

"You may count it lifted."

I smiled. "Then, this is a friendly visit?"

"You're thinking of that time in Elliott's office," She laughed. "I was pretty bad. Well, this is by way of contrast."

"Of course," I said, sitting down, "I'm grateful for this—peace pact; I've even been looking forward to it. But, like the parties to other peace pacts I shall be skepti-cal. I hope you don't mind."

"So long as you're not really antagonistic, I don't."

I looked at her. Steichen had most certainly "gotten her." Her arms were not of course covered with bracelets and the collar to her polo coat and beret contributed con-siderably to an *air gentil,* but aside from that there was in her face the same tenacity and sophisticated barbarity that I had been aware of in the photograph. There she was *can-nibale mais ingenue;* now the order was reversed.

"Well?" I asked.

"Well, I've come to make a confession."

"You've seen the paper?"

"To-day's? No. Is my picture in it?" I nodded. "And do they say I killed my husband? I often thought of it. But it seemed too . . ."

"*Gauche?*"

She flashed me a look of gratitude. "Yes, *gauche.* Be-sides, I should never have used brute force."

"I can stand brute force," I quoted, "but brute reason is quite unbearable. There is something unfair about its use. It is hitting below the intellect."

"Oscar Wilde?"

I nodded. "And now for the confession. I suppose it has something to do with a handkerchief you dropped in my office?"

"Did I? I didn't know it. Have you got it here?"

I went to my desk and took the handkerchief from the drawer. Jennifer watched me silently. I handed it to her. "J.L.B. It is mine. Here—you can keep it. I'm changing my initials anyway."

"Thank you." I replaced it in the drawer.

"I'll be glad to explain how it got there," she said, unfastening the buckle of her coat. "It isn't what I came about but that's all the better. You may believe me. I'm sure I couldn't think up a lie so quickly—not a good one."

I smiled. "Does it matter whether I believe you or not?"

"No. . . ."

"But you like to think you're convincing."

"Yes. It was Friday, wasn't it, when you found the hand-kerchief? Of course; that was the day Courtney was done in. Well, I took him to the zoo after lunch—you heard all that though; you were there, weren't you, when I told the police."

"I was there."

"I didn't tell them Courtney and I had been quarreling. I forget what I did tell them but it wasn't that. You know, I think I'm the only person Courtney ever quarreled with; that shows he loved me. Well, I was feeling pretty low—I may as well tell you it was about Elliott—and like a fool I went and got myself looking like a John Held, Junior, of the drunkard's wife; in other words, I cried. Thank God! Grace Mullin walked in then; there's nothing that restores one's self-control quicker than the sight of another female;

and I did my disappearing act down the fire escape." She paused, extinguished her cigarette and, in her usual enigmatical way, looked at me. "End of Chapter One! Halfway down the fire escape I paused, acutely conscious—that's the way they put it, isn't it?" I nodded. "Acutely conscious that I looked like hell; eyes red, nose shiny—you know! And there, walking across the campus were some students. Only one course was possible: I fled into your office—if you will have an office on a fire escape!—bathed my eyes with cold water, powdered, rouged my lips, and descended the fire escape to my car. And, oh, yes! dropped my handkerchief." She lifted her hands in a gesture of finality. "Do you believe me?"

"Next time," I said, "you must call when I'm in."

"I have."

"With a complete stock of ulterior motives. Well, out with them."

"I lied to the police."

"Oh?" I said.

"I thought you'd have found out by now or I wouldn't have come." She regarded me closely. "Have you found out?"

"I suppose if I haven't found out you don't intend telling me."

"Why should I? If you were really clever. . . ."

I stopped her. "Please! My cleverness isn't involved; only your—how shall we put it—stupidity?"

The mockery vanished from Jennifer's lips. "What do you mean?"

"It was stupid to lie to the police; it was stupid to assume you could keep Randall's name out of your testimony; it was stupid to accuse Frampton of murdering your husband; it was stupid to try shocking the public by playing golf Saturday morning; it was stupid—"

"To come here."

"No, that was charming."

Jennifer smiled. "I think you like me. Is it because I'm stupid or because you're sure I killed Courtney?"

"I'm not sure. . . ." She laughed. "I'm not sure," I repeated, "that you didn't kill him. That's quite different. Cigarette?"

"That's something." The cigarette between her lips as I lighted it was almost too motionless.

I pocketed my lighter. "You told the police that after leaving Science Hall at about two o'clock you drove home, changed your dress and then drove back down town where you shopped and had tea. You didn't shop. Instead you picked up Randall at the Securities Building, drove out Chestnut Avenue sometime around three-thirty and—do you care to supply the rest?"

"We drove around the lake." Her tone was antagonistic.

"A nice drive."

"I shan't try to convince you. We drove around the lake."

"What time did you end up at the Securities Building?"

"At quarter to five."

For a moment we were silent and at the end of that moment my telephone rang. Jennifer, from habit, started to her feet; she hesitated, then as I made for it, intercepted me. "Hello." She flashed me a glance of amusement; I shrugged my shoulders. "Yes, this is Mr. Craig's apartment. . . . Well, I'll see. Just a minute." She half-turned toward me. "Darling, can you come? It's Mrs. Grinnell."

I went to the telephone; Jennifer sauntered to the window and stood, with her back to me, looking out of it. I took up the receiver. "Yes, Mrs. Grinnell."

"Oh! Mr. Craig. I telephoned to say that I've talked with the reporter."

"That's splendid."

"And I was going to ask you to come to supper to-night as we'd planned . . ."

"Yes."

"But—now—" She plunged in. "Excuse me for asking, Mr. Craig, but—you haven't been married?"

My voice was as decorous as I could make it. "No indeed."

"No, I—thought not. Good-by."

I hung up. Jennifer hadn't turned around so I felt free to indulge my desire to smile; my voice however was serious. "I don't suppose you'd like to be called a good woman."

"Good?"

"We were quoting Oscar Wilde a while back; do you mind if I quote him again?"

Jennifer turned around. "Have I lost you your job?"

"Probably. But that's not what's important."

"What is?"

"That, at last, you've done one thing that's more than stupid. It's, thoroughly stupid."

She was outlined against the window-drapes. Nonchalant, silly, charming—whatever one chose to call her—stupid and good seemed the least applicable. "I'm waiting for the quotation."

"Here it is then: 'It takes a thoroughly good woman to do a thoroughly stupid thing.'"

Jennifer laughed.

"You know," I said, "I'm sorry I haven't a copy of the *Sun* to show you. There's something in it—something besides your picture, I mean, that may interest you: Hulse, the janitor, was arrested last night and is being held for your husband's murder."

Jennifer frowned. "The damned fools! The *damned* fools!"

15

I lunched in my apartment with Grace Mullin. It was a clear day—like spring is the accepted analogy—and I had opened the French windows and placed the coffee table beside them. Our luncheon was sandwiches sent up from Schmidt's delicatessen across the street, fruit, and iced lager made for me as a special favor by Mrs. Schmidt.

I emptied a bottle of beer into two tall glasses. *"Mademoiselle est servie."*

"Oh!" she came to the table, sat down silently and took a ham sandwich.

"Enough mustard?" I inquired, amused by her faintly antagonistic silence.

She took another bite and put down her sandwich. "I suppose you have women to lunch all the time."

I shook my head. "Only when they telephone me at noon that they must see me."

"I could have come after lunch."

I laughed. She finished her sandwich; then she drank some beer. "I telephoned early and you were asleep; I didn't know what time you'd get up." She looked at me. "This is the first time I've ever had lunch with a man in his apartment."

I ate an olive. "It's pleasant enough but it doesn't compare with breakfast."

"I don't eat breakfast."

"A cheese sandwich?" I suggested. "There's Swiss and Gorgonzola." She took one silently. I peeled an apple. "The psychology department has been rather depleted. It must have shocked you—hearing of Dr. Frampton's death."

"I suppose I'll be the next."

"I disagree with you there," I said. "I have an idea it's over, that there won't be any more killings."

"What's to stop it?"

"Hulse's arrest may."

She looked sharply at me, then continued to eat. "What do you think about it?" I asked. "Did he kill Brown, or Frampton or both of them?"

"How should I know?"

"You might hazard a guess; you're among friends."

"Well, then," she raised her eyes, "he didn't kill any one."

I smiled. "Fine. That makes two of us."

"Two of us?"

"Who think Hulse is innocent."

"Oh." She took a banana from the fruit bowl and slowly skinned it. "I didn't know you thought he was innocent."

"Oh, yes. I've thought so all along. And you?"

"I haven't thought much about it. He doesn't look like a murderer. And he seems so gentle. There are other people I'd suspect quicker."

I lighted a cigarette. "Let's be scientific. First we'll check off the various possibilities: either the same person killed Brown and Frampton or one person killed Brown and another killed Frampton or else Frampton killed Brown and was killed by a third person."

Holding the banana in one hand, the peel falling back from it, Miss Mullin bit off a piece. "I don't see why any one killed Dr. Frampton."

"Our one loophole! No one could possibly have want-ed to kill Frampton; in order to want to murder a man

you've got to take him seriously. And who could have tak-
en Frampton seriously? A moron perhaps, but that murder
wasn't planned by a moron."

Miss Mullin pushed back her chair from the table and
crossed her legs. "I hadn't thought of that."

"The doctor called it suicide; the police were within
an ace of calling it suicide and the coroner's verdict would
most certainly have been suicide. That wasn't mere chance;
it was cleverness on the part of the murderer. And, as
I've said, a clever person might be annoyed by Frampton's
eccentricities but never to the extent of actually murdering
him. Murder—preconceived murder as this was—involves
deeper emotions than could be possible where Frampton
was concerned. Do you see?"

She nodded soberly.

"So that hits one of our theories on the head: the theory that Frampton was killed by a different murderer than
Brown was. A ridiculous theory anyway!"

"I think so too."

"For the same reasons I also suspect that the man who
killed Brown and later Frampton—a supposition—didn't
kill them for the same reason." I paused long enough to
drink some beer. "He killed Brown because of some griev-
ance—plausible, isn't it?"

"You mean were there people with grievances against
him? You don't have to ask me that."

I smiled. "Well, my point is, if we stick to the theory
that a third party killed both Brown and Frampton, he
killed Brown for personal reasons and later killed Frampton for reasons which were born of Brown's murder. The
most logical is that Frampton knew too much and threatened to tell."

"And if Frampton killed Brown?"

"Brown is avenged. Too fine a gesture for my taste—
but worth considering."

She examined her finger nails. "If Frampton did kill Dr. Brown and if I'd known about it I wouldn't have killed Frampton; I'd have let the state hang him."

"*'Va, cours, vole, et nous venge!'*"

"What's that?" Her tone was sharp.

"A line from Corneille. His most famous. 'Go, run, fly, and avenge us!' As opposed to 'Let the state hang him.'"

She balanced her chin on her palm. "I still say let the state hang him."

I smiled. "And so do I and so would have Don Diégue if he'd had any confidence in the state."

Her antagonism passed. "You like to argue, don't you?"

I nodded. "My life should be comparatively safe since most people manage not to take me too seriously."

I stood up to stretch myself. "You knew Brown as well as any one did," I commenced abruptly, hesitated and then faced her, my hands in my pockets. "If I'm impertinent tell me."

"Ask anything you like. I don't care."

"You are charitable. Then, to start with, how long have you known Brown?"

"Exactly?"

"Certainly not," I said carelessly. "That question was borrowed from Thompson's tactics anyway. I thought it sounded businesslike."

"I came here as a graduate student. I've known him ever since I came. That's three years."

"Three years," I repeated. "That's right; you came while I was in the Orient."

She nodded. "I remember you were away."

"Go on," I said. "Anything at all about Brown. You worked with him quite a lot, didn't you?"

"When I wasn't teaching. I came here to work with him. Dr. Terry of Columbia sent me; he wasn't a behaviorist himself but he said if that was what I was interested in I should come here, that Courtney Brown was the best man in the field."

"That's interesting," I said. "You know, I've often wondered how Brown was rated by his brother psychologists."

"By behaviorists he's rated next to Watson. By nonbehaviorists he's not accepted at all."

"That's clear enough. Then, I take it, you're heart and soul a behaviorist."

Miss Mullin regarded me coolly. "Yes. It's the only philosophy of life possible to a rational person."

I laughed. "I long ago learned the futility of arguing with a behaviorist. But I will show you that behaviorism isn't as new as you psychologists make it out. You used, in eighth-century China, to be known as Monists and your leader was Chuang-Tzu." I took my copy of Li Po from the bookcase.

> "Chuang Tzu levels all things
> And reduces them to the same monad.
> But I say that even in their sameness
> Differences may be found.
> Although in following the promptings of their
>   nature
> They display the same tendency,
> Yet it seems to me that in some ways
> A phoenix is superior to a reptile!"

Miss Mullin's smile was faintly superior. "We're the Monists and you're Li Po. Is that it?"

"Professionally, yes. Or, if you'd rather, the idealist versus the materialists. However you put it, it's an old story."

"That's no argument against behaviorism."

"Rather not," I agreed. "Nor is newness any argument for it. It's not your fault if so many converts to behaviorism have been converted for the wrong reasons: because they think it's new or simple or a short-cut to science, because they think, based as it is on observation of mere physical phenomena, it nullifies the research of two thousand years, because it satisfies a characteristic American need for a science that is purely American and can be learned by the unsophisticated in ten lessons. You don't deny that to the uninitiated it presents all that."

She considered a moment. "I don't think that matters."

The telephone rang. I answered it.

"Hello, Mr. Craig? This is Nick."

"Yes."

"Say! You know that little fellow you got at your place—the chink?"

I laughed. "The Buddha?"

"Yeh! Well, you remember I said I seen one like him somewhere. I passed him this morning; in the window right near the joint where I live. He's a beauty too."

"I'd like to see it," I said. "Perhaps this next week."

"Aw hell! Come to-day!"

I smiled at his impatience. "No. Sorry. Besides, to-day's Sunday."

"That don't cut no ice. I know the dame that lives there. She'll let us in."

I remained firm. "Not to-day."

"Some one'll buy him. And he's a knockout—all gold. He beats the one you got all hollow."

"Yes?" I said. "Well, I'll do my best to get down to-morrow. If I can make it I'll call you first."

"O.K." His voice was disappointed. "And, say! if you change your mind. . . ."

"Yes?"

"I'm not working to-day. I'll be around. You got the number."

I hung up. My visitor, during the conversation, had arisen and was looking out the window. For the first time

I noticed she had discarded the sweater and skirt and oxfords she habitually wore at college for a brown silk dress
and slippers. The beads around her neck seemed oddly
pathetic and I remembered that Mrs. Frampton had described her as "plain."

"Why don't you go?"

I returned to the windows. "It's nothing important."

"I wish you would go."

"Why?" I was amused by her insistence.

"Because you're staying here with me out of pure convention. I don't believe in being conventional about such
matters."

"I'm staying because I want to stay; because at the moment I don't feel the slightest desire to go on a wild-goose
chase to the lower end of town."

She shrugged her shoulders.

"Shall we sit down?" I suggested. "What were we talking
about? Behaviorism? Or were we off that?"

She had sunk into a chair and was staring moodily
through the window. I was puzzled and amused by her
sulkiness. Was she offended that I refused to treat her cav-
alierly? Did she take my gesture as a formality of which
there was no need between friends? Evidently. My eyes
followed hers to the range of snow-capped peaks parallel
with the windows. "'The mountains of renown.'"

"I wish you'd go."

"Very well." I stood up. "I will go."

"Because I want you to?"

"Partly." I laughed.

She turned quickly toward me. "Don't go unless you
want to. Don't go on my account. I just don't want to
stand in your way. Do whatever you like."

"That, after a time, loses its novelty." I picked up my hat.

"But you mustn't go to satisfy me. Are you? I wish
you'd tell me."

I looked at her and she was forced to smile. "I'm going for a thousand reasons, none of them worth mentioning. However, to set your soul at rest, I will mention them. First, to please Nick who seemed disappointed when I turned him down; second, to get a breath of fresh air which the sight of those mountains and that sunlight has suddenly filled me with a longing for; third, if I stayed we would discuss, the rest of the afternoon, why I had stayed; fourth—"

"That's enough."

"Will you come with me?"

She shook her head and arose, reluctantly. "I'll go home."

"Then," I sat down, "I shan't go."

"But . . ."

"I wouldn't think of it. Unless you stay here to keep the home-fires burning until I return and we can resume our arguments I shall stay here and sulk, and you—well, you will be conscience-stricken for the rest of the afternoon."

She smiled and resumed her seat. "I'll stay."

"Excellent. I'll send up the maid to clear away. It's a quarter of two. I'll be back by three." At the door I turned. "You'd better come."

She shook her head.

"Auf wedersehen, then."

16

I walked leisurely to the cab-stand, cursing myself, cursing Nick, cursing the perversity of Grace Mullin, all having combined to start me off on what I had described as, and knew to be, a wild-goose chase.

Not only was I annoyed by this waste of time, this ridiculous interlude to see an object I had very little interest in, but I felt that my train of thought had been rudely interrupted. For the first time since I had set my mind on solving Brown's murder and then Frampton's, I felt restless, jarred from my concentration, and all to no purpose.

Well, this thing had to be gone through and then, perhaps, I could return, refreshed, to a contemplation of the various characters and motives involved in this complex and gruesome puzzle.

Nick's address was in that section of town which used in more Puritanical days to be called the "red light" district. Now, localization being a thing of the past, it is known simply as Harding Avenue. We passed the courthouse and county jail, drove a few blocks farther and drew up in front of a small grocery store. As I paid the driver a patrol wagon shot past us on its way to the jail which shadowed the entire district, reminding me of a passage from the Tao Hio: "The people like to live within a radius of an hundred leagues from the royal dwelling."

I entered the grocery store, bought a cigar and inquired for Mr. Fransioli. A stairway was pointed out to me which I mounted. The door at the top was opened by Nick. "Come in, Mr. Craig. Glad to see you." He closed the door after me. "Well, I see they nabbed the murderer. Takes a big load off my mind, I tell you."

"I'm not surprised," I said, sitting down in an over-stuffed armchair under a piano lamp. "Cigar?"

"Thanks." Nick bit off the end, lighted it and called, "Babe!" A tall girl with yellow hair reaching to her shoulders appeared in the doorway. "Meet the wife!"

She smiled. "Hello. Nick's told me all about you."

"That I showed him plenty of excitement?"

"I'll tell the world. I told her what a cook you was, too. Well, Babe, how about a snifter?"

"Sure. What'll it be?"

"Gin or Scotch, Mr. Craig?" asked Nick. "Babe shakes a mean gin fizz."

"I'd like to try it."

Babe disappeared into the kitchen.

"What do you think of her?" asked Nick. "Got class, ain't she?"

"She's very attractive."

"Her old man was a pal of mine. When he got bumped off down in L.A. I took Babe out of the joint where he boarded her and we was married. She's a lot better off and it ain't too hard on me."

"Have you been married long?" I asked.

"Going on a year. I'm aiming to take her to Hollywood soon as I've saved the dough. She ain't never been in Hollywood and her Pop's buried there." I nodded understandingly. "That's why we're living in this dump: to save coin. But Babe don't mix with the other tramps around here; I don't let her."

"Doesn't she get lonely?"

"Lonely? Hell, no! She takes singing lessons three times a week and French twice. And I'm here off and on."

Babe reappeared with a tray holding glasses and a frosted cocktail shaker. She poured two drinks and handed them to us. "Won't you?" I asked.

"Babe don't drink. Well! here's mud in your eye."

"It's excellent," I said. "Egg and gin and lemon?"

"That's all," Babe replied. "Want another?"

"Thanks, but I'm rather anxious to see that Buddha."

Nick arose. "O.K. Come on." Babe leaned against the wall, smiling at us; at the door Nick turned. "Stand by! That's a good kid."

"Good-by," I said.

I followed Nick downstairs, through the grocery store and around the corner; he stopped before the window of a second-hand shop. "See him?"

For a moment I could see nothing for the maze of musical instruments, old silver, field glasses, clocks, pictures and jewelry. Then my eyes focused on the Buddha. It was a small figure of gilded wood, undraped and seated cross-legged in the characteristic Hindu manner. Its hands were folded in its lap and its eyes downcast, presumably on a glass ruby set in its navel.

My first impulse was to laugh and inform Nick that his Buddha was one of thousands imported annually from China. But when I saw how eagerly he was watching me I restrained myself. "All right, Nick. Let's see how much she wants for it."

"I thought it'd make a hit with you."

He knocked on the door and presently we heard footsteps within the shop and a light was turned on. An old woman wearing a new set of false teeth opened the door. "Hello, Mrs. Judd," said Nick. "My friend wants to price some of your window display. How about it?"

"Why, yes. Come right in. Is there anything special?" While Nick pointed out the Buddha to the old lady I prowled around the dusty interior of the shop, fascinated by the maze of useless objects. In a minute Nick came to me, beaming. "It's yours; the old girl's wrapping it."

"What?" I said.

"I said it's yours. I bought it for you."

"But, Nick . . ." I remonstrated.

"Now, don't be ritzy! It only set me back ten bucks and I can make that in a morning. See! I owe it to you for the way you squared me with the cops."

I laughed. "You don't owe it to me, but thanks anyway."

"Forget it!" The old lady brought the Buddha, laboriously wrapped in newspapers; I put it under my arm and we left the shop. "Come up to the apartment," Nick said. "I'll buy you a drink."

I shook my head. "I've got to get back. There's a taxi stand by the courthouse, isn't there?"

"Sure! Well, so long! Say!" Nick thrust out his elbow toward my parcel. "He'll sure make that old one of yours look sick!"

"I'm afraid he will," I agreed.

The streets were practically deserted with the exception of the square beside the courthouse and one corner where a crowd of derelicts paid tribute to the eloquence of a barefoot swami. As I passed them I recalled Sunday in Paris, the races, the parks, the suburban cafés filled with workmen and their families, none of them without the price of a glass of beer.

At the courthouse I hailed a taxi, gave my address and got in, my Buddha, by now escaping from its wrappings, under my arm. All my attempts to cover its rotundity failing, I threw the newspaper, now reduced to its original pulp, out of the window and set the Buddha beside me on the seat. While it was wrapped I had thought of it only as an example of decadence in art. Now, placed beside me, it recovered a semblance of its significance and I realized that, sentimental and inefficiently realistic as it was, there was in its design a remnant of the grace and compelling repose of its Hindu forbears, of the colossal seventh century Buddha of Ceylon or of those charming Buddhas set among blossoming tulip-trees which I saw on my last visit to Leyden. None of those, of course, had the jeweled navel nor even the more common forehead jewel—the third eye of spiritual wisdom. And there occurred to me as I looked at the chip of red glass a poem by Arno Holz—one of his *Phantasus,* only a few lines of which I remembered:

Auf einem roten Thron aus Lack
Sitz ich im Allerheiligsten.

Ich sitze
mit untergeschlagnen Beinen,
denke mir dies . . . denke mir das,
fuhl es, wie Wolken, mir durch mein Hirn ziehn,
und bespiegle mich in meinem Nabel.

Der ist ein blutender Rubin
in einem nacketen Bauch aus Gold!

"On a red lacquer throne I sit in the Holy of Holies. . . . I shall sit with my legs crossed under me, thinking of this, thinking of that, feel how the clouds travel through my brain, and mirror myself in my navel. This is a bleeding ruby in a naked belly of gold!"

Der ist ein blutender Rubin—Ich sitze—denke mir dies . . . denke mir das . . . The lines crossed and crisscrossed in my mind; lines I hadn't thought of for years, now become suddenly, and for no apparent reason, tenacious.

This is nonsense, I thought. Sheer nonsense. To be so stirred by a silly toy, a silly gilt toy. I looked once more at the little figure, I took it in my hands, amused and rather surprised by my sentimentalizing over an object that meant nothing to me, nor to any one else for that matter. I looked into his chubby face. Well, little fellow, we've been tossed together. What shall we do about it? You don't mean anything to me, yet I shan't probably throw you away as I have half a mind to. I haven't the heart.

His ridiculously devout expression reproached me. Nothing to say, eh? No regrets for having disrupted my afternoon, not to mention my peace of mind. Why have you come into my life anyway? Why out of a junk shop on Harding Avenue?

I put him down on the seat. This is nonsense, I thought again. I'm becoming too damned imaginative. But is it nonsense? Wait! Buddha—contemplation—*denke mir dies*. Might it, could it have anything to do with . . . ?

Something within my brain clicked. The answer! I leaned forward. "Driver! Stop at the next drugstore. Please!"

The driver drew up at the corner. "Wait," I said, getting out. I went into the drugstore and straight to the telephone booth at the back where I looked up Jack Tobey's address in the directory. Then I returned to my taxi. "509 North Broadway. Never mind the other address I gave you."

"Yes, sir."

509 North Broadway was a small, shingled house about a mile from the campus. I told the driver to wait and proceeded to ring the doorbell. A middle-aged woman wearing an apron answered the door and I immediately realized that I had arrived at the Sunday dinner hour. "Is Jack Tobey home?" I inquired.

"Yes. Come in," she led me into the living room which was filled with radio music and the odors of vegetables.

Then she went into the dining room and in a moment the boy entered.

"Mr. Craig!"

I laughed. "In person. I'm sorry to interrupt your dinner."

"That's all right. Gee! I was surprised to see you here. Something about the murder?"

"Nothing specific."

His face fell. "I thought maybe you wanted me for a witness or something. Say! I saw where Frampton was killed and they arrested Hulse. Do they think he killed them both? I always knew he was cracked."

"How did you know he was cracked?"

"Oh, I don't know. He was always mooning around the zoo, talking to the animals . . ."

"You've seen him there quite a lot?" I asked.

"It depends on what you call a lot. A couple of times anyway. I've just been around there this quarter myself."

"That's right," I said. "You're a first-quarter freshman, aren't you?"

"Yep."

"And you take psychology I from Miss Mullin."

"It's a snap, too. All you have to do is to take tests to see if you're color blind or got an ear for music or a good memory or a knee jerk. And the rest of the time you make charts with colored ink. And 'yes and no' exams! Gee! I like it."

"Rather different from most requirements."

"I'll tell the world! You ought to see how they work you in sociology and French."

I lighted a cigarette. "This knee-jerk test you took had nothing to do with the intelligence test they give all the freshmen?"

"No. The intelligence test was last month; I took that, too. We had to take that. Gee! there was a mob—about six hundred. But this knee-jerk test was different; Miss

Mullin asked our class which ones would take it; she just wanted about ten of us. So I volunteered. I didn't mind the first time; it was sort of fun."

"The first time? Then, there was a second time?"

He scratched his head. "She lost my paper so I had to take it again—and miss the basket-ball game. That's what burned me up! But I guess I was pretty lucky at that—getting a look-in at the murder like I did. The first murder I ever saw! Golly!"

The jazz coming over the radio had by now given way to a sermon. I turned it off. "Do you mind?"

Tobey grinned. "You and me both!"

"Now," I said, "would you mind telling me just what this knee-jerk test is—not from the scientific viewpoint but from your own. I haven't a very clear idea of what goes on."

"There's not much to it. You just get in this dentist chair and she gives you a puzzle to work on. Then the hammer keeps tapping your knee and makes it jerk and there's a wire attached to your heel so that every time you kick it makes a line on a piece of paper and the harder you kick the bigger the line is. When you're through with the puzzle she gives you something to read, first something exciting and then something dull and after that you sit there and don't do anything. See?"

"I see. I suppose your knee jerk is stronger when you're working."

"That's the idea. For instance, when I was reading Lincoln's Gettysburg speech I didn't kick hardly at all, just little short lines but when I was reading a gangster story I sure kicked like the devil."

"And the puzzle?" I inquired.

"That was swell. I always was strong for puzzles, crossword or any other kind."

"What kind was this one?"

"It was a maze. You know! there's a square all full of tracks and you got to start at one corner and follow through to the other without taking your pencil from the paper if you can help it. Golly! it's tricky; if you aren't careful you get going wrong and have to back up. I guess you kick harder for that than for anything, especially when you get almost to the end."

"It sounds fascinating," I agreed. "I'd like to try my hand at one."

Tobey jumped up. "I've got one upstairs now. I'll get it. They gave them out in class and I brought one home to show my sister. She didn't fall for it though, said it was too hard on the eyes. It is too. They make them awfully close. It'll just take me a minute." He dashed into the hall and while he was gone I took the opportunity to tune in on the Boston Symphony. In a minute he returned holding a mimeographed sheet in his hand. "Here she is."

"Thanks a lot." I folded it and placed it in my vest-pocket. "I'll have a try at it later."

The dining-room door opened and Mrs. Tobey entered. "Jack."

The boy turned. "Say, Mom! This is Mr. Craig; I told you about him. Remember?"

She smiled and her smile was typical of a thousand other middle-aged women whom an introduction—to me, at least—seems to tie in knots of embarrassment, affectation and naivete. "How do you do," I said. "I'm afraid I'm disrupting your dinner hour. Dreadfully thoughtless of me."

"Now you're not doing anything of the sort, Mr. Craig. I only came in to ask if you wouldn't take a bite of dessert with us. I knew Jack wouldn't ask you."

Jack scowled. "I'd be delighted," I said, "if I hadn't a taxi at the door waiting to take me to an appointment. As a matter of fact I was at the point of asking Jack to accompany me."

Jack beamed. "Sure. Where are you going?"

"Just a wee bite of dessert," pleaded Mrs. Tobey. "It's lemon chiffon pie; Jack's favorite."

"Cut it, Mom! We're in a hurry."

I laughed. "My favorite, too, when I have time for it. Ready, Jack? I won't keep him long, Mrs. Tobey."

"I know he's in good hands. Good-by, Mr. Craig. And that piece of lemon chiffon pie will be waiting for you whenever you want it."

"I won't forget. Good-by." We left the house, I gave my address to the driver and we climbed into the taxi. Jack picked up my gilt Buddha. "What's this doing here?"

"Do you take German at college?" I asked.

"No. French."

"How much have you had?"

"Two years in high school."

"All right. We'll see how much you know." I took the Buddha. "This is what Buddha said when asked to preach the law: *Je médite l'idée merveilleuse du Nirvana, l'oeil de la vraie loi, et je vais maintenant te la transmettre.*' Get it?"

Jack shook his head.

"This is the translation: 'I meditate on the marvelous idea of Nirvana, the eye of the true law, and now I am going to transmit it to you.'"

"I don't see what that's got to do with us."

I laughed. "You will."

17

I stood outside the door of my apartment for a moment, then opened the door. Tobey followed me in, carrying the Buddha. Sterling and Miss Mullin looked up from a game of checkers.

"You know, Sterling," I said, "I had an idea you'd be here. It's splendid knowing some one so dependable. This is Mr. Tobey, Mr. Sterling."

"We've met." Sterling took a drink. "I helped myself to your Scotch. O.K?"

"Of course. Pour me a drink, will you." I sat down. "How are you, Miss Mullin? Not bored?"

"No." She looked from me to young Tobey. "What are you doing here?"

"Sit down, Jack," I said. "I'll explain in just a moment." I followed Sterling to the kitchen where he was getting ice. "How about dashing to the grocery?" I asked.

"What for?"

"Ginger ale."

"There are three bottles left in the case."

"White Rock then. And take your time."

He looked at me. "You're on."

I carried my drink back to the other room. Sterling followed with the ice and a couple more glasses. He rolled down his sleeves. "Be back in a jiffy."

"A drink, Miss Mullin?" I asked. She shook her head. "Yours will be waiting for you, Jack; I want your head clear for the next few minutes." I took the Buddha from the table and placed it beside its sixth-century brother, then I took the mimeographed sheet Jack gave me from my pocket. "I've changed my mind about this; instead of tasking my own mind with it I'm going to do as you psychologists do—task Jack's. How about it, Jack?"

"Sure. I like puzzles."

I turned to Miss Mullin. "You won't object to my applying your methods to my own problems?"

"Have you problems?"

I laughed. "You've got me there. Problems hardly go with my role of madman of Chu, do they? Well, I expect five minutes from now I'll be singing the phoenix-bird song again; that is, if I have any luck. All right, Jack, sit here, will you?" I indicated a rather high chair at the side of the main door. "Get your pencil ready. I want you to see how quickly you can get through that maze. I'll be timing you." I handed him the paper and took out my watch. "Here's a book to work on. All right, start!"

Except for the ticking of the clock the room was perfectly still. I leaned against the wall beside the kitchen door and Miss Mullin sat a few feet from me, her hands folded in her lap, her face expressionless. When five minutes were up, during which Jack had worked steadily, his eyes within a foot of the paper, I walked quietly to Miss Mullin's side, touched her on the shoulder and, with my finger to my lips, motioned her to follow me to the kitchen, the door to which I had left slightly ajar. I looked back, observed that Jack was undisturbed, and signaled to her to sit down at the breakfast nook. She did so and I returned to my position opposite Jack.

All this, I noticed, occupied a few seconds over a minute. Six minutes later Jack, for the first time, looked up, a broad smile on his face. "Finished! How long did I take?"

"Twelve minutes and twenty seconds."

"Not bad. Gee! I was careful. You do better when you're careful and don't get in any blind alleys like when you try to go fast. I've learned that. It's going back that eats up the time."

"That's right," I agreed. "By the way, would you say I'd been here the last twelve minutes?"

"Sure! you were timing me, weren't you?"

I nodded. "And Miss Mullin?"

His eyes traveled around the room. "Where is she? I'd forgotten all about her. Gee! I got so interested. She was here when I started."

"She went to get a glass of water."

Jack grinned. "And I never noticed. Can you beat it?"

"You'd call that concentration, wouldn't you?" I asked. "Well, concentration is very closely allied to meditation— transitive meditation or meditation with an object, that is. Exactly what you've been indulging in the last twelve minutes." I indicated the Buddha. "Now do you see what he's got to do with us?"

His face brightened. "Yeh! That thing you said in French; it meant he was meditating."

I laughed. "Good boy! Fix yourself a drink. I'll be right with you."

Miss Mullin had left the breakfast table and was standing at the kitchen sink, her back to me, rinsing out a glass. She set down the glass and turned, her hand to her throat, her face extremely pale. Her voice was weak and she spoke quickly. "I've taken hydrocyanic acid. There's no antidote, so don't try to do anything. Come here."

I went quickly to her and put my arm around her waist to support her. She leaned against me. "That's right." She swallowed convulsively. "My throat!" Her sentences were spasmodic and interrupted by agonized attempts to swallow. "I lied to you. No, don't interrupt me! No time! I told you Dr. Frampton thought I killed Courtney. He did. He heard me, he told me he heard me Friday afternoon in the zoo. It was after Mrs. Brown left. I told Courtney I loved him, that I knew his wife hated him. She'd never divorce him. I wanted him to take me. I begged him to. I'd begged him before and he'd always laughed at me." Her voice grew fainter. "Water!"

I gave her a drink.

"He said I was a fool. I said his sophistication was a pose, that he was puritanical, he was moral; that was why he wouldn't take me. He laughed; he called me plain, ugly, uninteresting. He said if I was beautiful and wanted to give myself to him he wouldn't hesitate a minute, that there was no such thing as sin where a beautiful woman was concerned. I hated him then. God! I hated him. I told him so. I threatened him and he laughed. All he did was laugh."

She leaned more heavily against me, clutching at her throat as she spoke. Her swift inspirations and long, slow expirations of breath fixed the tempo of her sentences and I could feel the hard rapid beat of her heart against my arm.

"Dr. Frampton was in the dark room. He heard me. He told me—yesterday, when you came in and interrupted he was telling me he heard everything I said to Courtney. He said he'd go to the police. Then you said they were going to arrest him and I knew he'd tell—so I shot him. I got the pistol from his desk right after you left. I thought maybe— it was all I could do. Courtney was dead. Now—me . . ."

She was unconscious. As I started to pick her up to carry her to the sofa she stiffened suddenly, her hands clenched and her eyes opened wide, the pupils horribly prominent. "Tobey!" I called, "Tobey! quick!"

He came to the doorway. "Help me carry her," I directed. He obeyed me in a hypnotic condition. We half carried, half dragged her to the sofa where she lay, her convulsions over, but her face still covered with sweat, her eyes glassy and a white foam on her lips. She scarcely breathed.

Tobey stared at her, fascinated, his face white. "Sit down," I said, and poured him a drink.

He took it in his hand and slowly moved his eyes, almost as glassy as hers, to my face. "Shall I call a doctor?"

I shook my head. The door opened and Sterling burst in, a paper bag in his hand. He stopped short. "Good God, Craig! What happened?"

"Poison."

Sterling came slowly forward and bent over her. "Dead! Then . . ." he looked at me. "She—killed . . . ?"

I nodded, poured a pony of Scotch and swallowed it. "Telephone the coroner, will you, Sterling?"

"Dead," Tobey repeated.

Sterling slowly recovered his nerve. He set the paper bag on the table, thrust his hands in his pockets and smiled. "Well, Craig? All over but the shouting!"

I walked to the sofa, closed her eyes and wiped the foam and sweat from her face with my handkerchief. *"Baissez le rideau! La pièce est jouée."*

18

Grace Mullin's drama ended Sunday. Monday morning Dr. Grinnell returned from Florida. As I walked back from my interview with him the phoenix-bird song was very real to me, more real than the chatter of the campus sparrows—and my laughter at the sage Confucius more sincere than for many days.

Thirty-six hours, not more, had elapsed since I had last walked on this clipped lawn, circumscribed by these Gothic buildings and shadowed by these dogwood trees. Was it possible the petals on the grass were the same that lay here yesterday? Was it possible that a climactic day takes up no more space in time than a day? An inch, an hour—there are, besides our emotions, no adequate measurements. Only another old theme newly arrived at.

I reached the edge of the campus. A news stand—headlines in nine-line type: *Murderess Confesses—Takes Poison.* How anticlimactic!

I entered the lobby of my apartments, stopping at the desk for mail. The clerk addressed me with new respect as had the elevator boy. It's fortunate I'm leaving, I thought. To be a hero to one's valet might be paradoxical enough to be pleasant; but to be a hero to the employees of an apartment hotel equipped with frigidaire and shower baths. . . .

175

As I started toward the elevator I heard my name called; Jennifer caught up with me. "Mr. Craig! May I have your autograph?"

"Blood or ink?"

She laughed. "Elliott and I have come to pay our respects. And to get the lowdown. Will you give it to us?"

"Delighted. Come up to my apartment." She motioned to Randall and the three of us entered the elevator.

"Hello, Craig," said Randall. "I hope you don't mind our busting in on you like this."

"Of course, he doesn't mind; he's simply longing for an appreciative audience. Aren't you, Mr. Craig?"

"Not too appreciative. And not misguided appreciation! I had enough of that last night. Just as the poor girl was being carted downstairs Thompson paid me his tribute. 'We could use men like you on the Force,' he said. 'You don't have to go after criminals; you whistle and they come to you.'"

Jennifer looked up at me. "It sounds like Thompson, and yet—there's something in that."

I unlocked the door to my apartment. "I may be optimistic; but I still hope to convince you to the contrary. You, at least, Randall."

Jennifer shook her head. "You're too attractive for me to believe anything else. If I were a criminal and if you whistled . . ." She sank into an armchair, looked around and pointed to the sofa. "Exhibit A?" I nodded. "Was it pretty awful?"

"Have you ever seen any one die?"

"No."

I looked at Randall. "You were in the army, weren't you? So was I. And saw them die by the hundreds—in every way imaginable. No reason why either. Yes, this was pretty bad."

Jennifer stared ahead of her. "It's unbelievable! A girl you know—knew; that you've talked to. . . . She was in love with Courtney; isn't that it?" I nodded. "Funny, isn't it? I told Courtney he oughtn't to laugh at people."

"Three of them," said Randall.

"I know. One of them my husband. Whenever I think of it, it seems fantastic. That's all; just fantastic. Why, I never even thought of her; she was so—insignificant. And there was all that going on in her mind. She must have hated me. I suppose she even thought of killing me too."

"No doubt."

She took Randall's hand. "I'm glad she didn't. I'm even glad I can't seem to take all this as I ought to. Oh, dear; Elliott, let's go away to-morrow—somewhere where I shan't be expected to take life—or death seriously."

He leaned over the back of her chair. "We are, soon."

"To-morrow! Away from the ghosts, poor things! Oh! I hate feeling sorry for people—even dead people. Mr. Craig, is her ghost here? On that sofa?"

"I think it is."

"Don't you mind?"

"I'm leaving."

"You're leaving!" exclaimed Randall. "Earl College?" I nodded. "Why?"

Jennifer's eyes shone. "I'm glad."

"Did you ever read a novel of Victor Hugo's?" I asked, "in which a sailor, by accident, lets loose a cannon on one of the decks; there's a rough sea and with the rolling of the ship the cannon rolls, endangering everybody's life. Well, the sailor secures the cannon at the risk of his own life. The ship's captain decorates him for his bravery and then orders him shot for carelessness. That, though it doesn't parallel my case, comes close enough to it."

"You've been decorated and shot?" demanded Jennifer. "By whom?"

"Dr. Grinnell."

"Is he back?"

"I've just talked with him at his office. The poor man returned by airplane from some delightful convention in Florida to find he needn't have come after all; the sword of Damocles had already fallen. He was in a very bad humor. The decoration was administered none too gracefully."

"I can see why you'd be decorated," said Jennifer, wrinkling up her nose, "but I can't see why you should be shot."

"No? Why, for leading a life of debauchery, of course; drinking, keeping women in my rooms, being generally a bad influence."

Jennifer gasped. "Oh!"

Randall leaned forward. "What's the matter?"

"Oh, my dear! What have I done? I'll go tell him."

"Tell him what?"

"I was up here yesterday morning to talk to Mr. Craig; it was quite early—I hadn't even seen the morning paper or I mightn't have come. Yes, I might. Anyway, he annoyed me—I forget how—and to get even I answered his telephone and then. . . ."

"And then?"

"I called—well, loudly enough, 'Darling, you're wanted on the telephone' or some such rot. It was Mrs. Grinnell."

"Jennifer!"

She looked penitently up at him. "Oh, I know. I'm a fool!"

I laughed. "After all, if any one minds it should be me."

"And don't you?"

"Do I look it?" She gazed dubiously at me. "You're thinking that my smiling face is but a mask, that I'm another Pagliacci, another He-who-gets-slapped. Aren't you?"

Jennifer covered her face. "I'm so ashamed; that's exactly what I was thinking."

Randall laughed and patted her shoulder. She looked up. "Where do you think you'll go?"

"From here? I hadn't thought. Wait!" I walked over to my desk, opened my letter-file and extracted from it a letter. "I received this in June; I never answered it." I handed the letter to Jennifer.

She read it, then handed it to Randall. "Two years. It does seem frightfully long and Tokyo's so far—the ends of the earth. Don't go."

I smiled. "I can't stay here."

"Why not?"

"I should be afraid of becoming a hero."

Randall handed back the letter. "The Imperial University. It sounds very imposing."

I placed it on my desk. "That cinches it. I'll go—"

"Don't go," repeated Jennifer. "If you want a job Thompson will give you one."

"I don't know how often my theory would work. This time it did." I lighted a cigarette. "But out of a hundred cases there would surely be twenty-five or more where it wouldn't work—the conditions might be wrong; there'd be a flaw somewhere. That wouldn't bother me; I'd consider seventy-five out of a hundred a rather decent score, but would the police department?"

Jennifer smiled. "Did you take me seriously?"

"I take my theory seriously."

"What is it?" asked Randall. "I'd like to know."

"Merely an extension of Oriental mysticism—a sort of forced sensitivity—training the mind to register shocks and impressions as a seismograph registers an earthquake. I always think of Chang Heng's in that connection; it was constructed of eight copper dragons on springs sitting around a bowl. Each dragon had in his mouth a copper ball. In the middle of the bowl squatted a toad with

a wide-open mouth. When there was an earthquake the
dragon nearest the shock dropped his ball into the toad's
mouth. Simple, you see, but effective."

Randall nodded.

Jennifer smiled. "I'm sure it's not that simple."

"I'll give you an example or two," I said. "Of course, I
followed up intuition with reasoning; that's necessary. But
the intuition generally gave me a start. For instance: Tobey
swore that Grace Mullin hadn't left the laboratory while
he was taking the test. There was no reason to doubt him
and the police didn't doubt him. I believed he was telling the truth yet I was almost certain by yesterday morning that neither Hulse nor you nor Frampton had killed
your husband. I won't go into that now beyond saying that
the crime was done by a logical and cold-blooded person.
Well, sure as I was that Grace Mullin had committed one,
if not both of the murders, I could find no loophole in her
alibi—that is, not until it occurred to me that there was
such a thing, even among Occidentals, as profound concentration. I followed the idea through, talked with Tobey
and found that on the afternoon of the murder he had tak-
en the reflex test for the second time, Miss Mullin having
lost the results of his first test. That coincided with my
theory that, having found him capable of deep concentration, she used him to establish an alibi. The rest was easy;
I brought him to the apartment, restaged the reflex test
in her presence and proved to myself that it was possible
for her to have left the laboratory, killed Dr. Brown and
reentered without Tobey being aware that she was gone."

"How did you get her here?" asked Randall.

"She telephoned she wanted to see me. Curiosity, I suppose; perhaps anxiety combined with an abnormal desire
for masculine company. There are plenty like her."

"Dangerous, you mean?"

"Well, I should say that a behavioristic philosophy of life might serve to make them dangerous. It hardens, breaks down barriers. Oh, it's well enough for a balanced person. But the unbalanced, the neurotic need a few barriers, a few illusions and repressions to keep them within the confines of decency."

Jennifer was looking past me. "Yes. Illusions."

"Buck up, darling," said Randall. "We have a golf date at eleven; it's almost that now."

She smiled at him. "Golf—of course."

"I'll see you before you leave," I said.

"It won't be until we've seen this thing through."

Jennifer stood up; she drew on her gloves. "Mr. Craig, I think you're marvelous. No matter what else I've said, or say, that stands."

They left. I walked through the French windows onto the balcony. Any emotions I may have had deserted me and, looking down at Earl College, the lake beyond it, and the town where I had now lived several years of my life I saw it as I would see it five or twenty-five years later.

I saw it as . . . I smiled, thinking of a line of François Villon's: *Angers, basse ville et haults clochers, riches putains, povres escholiers . . .* and spoke it aloud in English—a curse? a benediction? What does it matter! "Angers, low town and high steeples, rich harlots and poor scholars."

Murder in Church

1

Ian Craig had a hundred reasons for attending Sunday morning mass at St. Barnabas, all of them insignificant beside the fact that he did attend Sunday morning mass. With him was Thomas Follett ("T. F.") Blake, professor of mathematics at Western Institute of Technology, who had no reasons at all and didn't hesitate to say so.

"I was raised on hymns and oatmeal," he complained as the two men walked the short distance from the faculty club to the church. "And one's as bad as the other. Oh, call them Gregorian chants if you want to," he added, anticipating Craig's reply. "They're hymns to me. 'Will there be any stars, any stars in my crown?'" he caroled loudly.

Craig laughed. "T. F., you're a living argument against a religious childhood."

"And proud of it. Bring your brats up as atheists, I tell my friends. An unsound soul in a sound body; that's the recipe for happiness."

"Have you tried telling that to Radford?" inquired Craig, a twinkle in his eye.

Blake grinned. "I did suggest though that now the news is out that God's a mathematician, my salary ought to be raised. By Jove!" Blake's eyes brightened and he increased the length of his stride. "Seeing me in church may convince the old boy I'm a genius. Geniuses," he explained, "get as high as ten thousand a year. Full professors stop at six."

"Where does Quinn come in on that salary scale?" asked Craig. "Super-genius?"

Blake shook his head. "Big business. Sir Arthur is paid off by the Chamber of Commerce."

The two men, both of medium height and in their late thirties, though one was dour and gray-haired, the other broad-shouldered and blond, arrived at the church at the precise moment that President Radford's limousine drew up at the curb. They hurried up the steps and were already seated in one of the side pews when Radford and his two guests walked down the aisle.

All three were scientists and celebrities; all three wore frock coats, but there the similarity stopped. Physically and mentally they were of different breeds.

President Radford, the most imposing, was short and thickset. His massive face, lined in reality by a lifelong attempt to reconcile science with religion, was falsely suggestive of a strong character. He was an unproductive, jealous and disillusioned man.

Yozan Saijo, youngest of the three, had secured premature distinction by being the outstanding physicist of a country not generally prolific in physicists. A small, slender man with the somnolent face that is typically Japanese, he created in some indefinable way an air of arrogance.

But it was the third and most famous of the group who interested Craig. Sir Arthur Quinn, tall, well-built, with the small neat head of a British clerk, had not at all the cachet of a great scientist. The theories that had undermined the whole structure of applied reason had left few lines on his face; he might to the casual observer have spent his life selling haberdashery rather than substituting a universe of caprice for the old universe of law and order.

The faint, almost negligible smile he wore as he took his place between Saijo and Radford, Craig well understood. No man belonged less in church than Quinn. In his picture of the universe there was no Divine Plan and no Creator. A metaphysical Houdini, he had showed the theologians to be charlatans, religions to be apologies, and his more cautious confrères to be opportunists.

The church had reason to hate and fear him; whereas other physicists, either because they believed in free will or because they did not, inferred a God, Quinn had broken down their pronouncements into fallacious and sentimental arguments. He had not left the theologians a leg to stand on. And yet, with the courtesy for which the English are notorious, he had this morning consented to be led by his host into the enemy camp.

"Papa Radford reminds me of van Maanen's star," whispered Blake.

"How so?" Craig asked with the amusement that T. F.'s succinct and generally illuminating comments never failed to provoke in him.

"Ten thousand times as dense as any known substance. He'd bring the devil to church."

At that moment the congregation in a body slipped down on its knees. Blake did likewise. "Always bobbing up and down," he grumbled.

President Radford and his two companions, Craig observed, simply bowed their heads. And though not a flicker of Quinn's regular features suggested that he was not a confirmed worshiper, Craig was delighted to catch him half-way through the prayer in a characteristic gesture: he slipped between his lips one of the fruit lozenges that a press, whose pleasure it is to humanize genius, had made famous.

Quinn's third law of thermodynamics might be Greek to the public; his universe might be as unintelligible as

Einstein's; but the entire English-reading world knew that Sir Arthur Quinn had an extraordinary fondness for mushrooms and a habit, deplorable according to dentists, of continually sucking a fruit lozenge.

He had succeeded in keeping his private life out of the newspapers; very few people even knew there was a Lady Quinn; but the fruit lozenge and the mushroom had become to the Quinn myth what the apple is to the Newton myth.

Typical, thought Craig, and somehow pathetic that the public should find it necessary to offset the incredible figures in which Quinn dealt. But, after all, only three hundred years ago Giordano Bruno was burned at the stake for his statement that the earth was not the center of the universe. Was it any wonder that modern scientists, able to weigh, measure and classify stars, the nearest being twenty-five million million miles distant, should be compelled to manifest their *Genus homo* by sucking lozenges, reading the Bible, and drawing absurd models in which the solar system becomes nine specks of dust revolving around a pea?

The prayer ended. The congregation slipped back into the pews. "Back on our tails like good monkeys," said Blake with a sigh of relief. A moment later he gripped Craig's arm. "Radford's pew," he whispered. "There's something up!"

Craig's eyes switched back to the three scientists. He nodded. "It's Quinn! He's ill."

At that moment Radford turned. His frantic glance met Blake's. Blake arose. "Come on!" he whispered. "He must want to get Quinn out."

The choir continued to sing joyously as the two men, followed by Saijo and the President, supported Quinn down the aisle to the vestry. He seemed very ill indeed. His face was gray and covered with a cold sweat; he was exhausted to the point of paralysis; and yet, while Blake loosened his tie and collar, he apologized between parox-ysms of pain for the trouble he was causing.

Radford, greatly perturbed, paced the floor. "Can't imagine why Byrne doesn't come. I saw him get up. Blake! Would you mind seeing what's . . ." His words were inter-rupted by the arrival of the doctor. "Byrne!" An expression of vast relief lighted the President's face. "Thought you were never coming."

"I went for my bag. I'd left it in the car," explained the doctor.

The four men watched with apprehension as he applied the stethoscope to Quinn's chest, felt his pulse, determined the exact region of his pain. The case was apparently an obvi-ous one. Byrne nodded several times during the examination.

"Coronary thrombosis," he announced briefly in reply to the question in Radford's eyes. "A block in the heart vessels. I can't tell how complete. The main thing is to ease the pain. I've just given him half a grain of morphia." He turned to Quinn. "Any better?"

"Confound it, no!" Quinn's agony was appalling to see. Gradually, however, under the influence of repeated doses of morphia, he relaxed. "Never knew I had a heart," he murmured.

The four men standing like a Greek chorus in the back-ground relaxed with him. Dr. Byrne turned. "Better get him to a hospital," he commented impersonally.

"Blake, will you call an ambulance? The Columbia." President Radford, reacting against twenty minutes of futility, spoke with authority.

Blake and Ian Craig left the vestry-room in search of a telephone. When they returned, only a few minutes later, Quinn was dead. Beside him, with bowed head, stood the President. Dr. Byrne was occupied in replacing his instru-ments in his bag; Saijo had not moved from his position beside the farthest wall.

"Most tragic," said Radford solemnly. "Most tragic. The papers must be notified at once."

"And Lady Quinn?" inquired the doctor with professional dispatch. "The disposal of the body is of course up to her."

"Of course." The President frowned. "Lady Quinn is in San Francisco. I shall send for her."

The faculty club at Western Tech, like all well-designed clubs, has an atmosphere of expensive repose. The air is always faintly blue, there is just enough light to read by; and the solid oak furniture gives promise of finding its way, in a century or two, into antique shops. There is practically always a log fire in the fireplace.

Perhaps because of the seclusion, thought Craig, perhaps because they were capable of a scientific attitude, the group of men who happened to be in the clubhouse on Sunday afternoon discussed Quinn's death with a curious detachment—a detachment that might to a non-scientific mind seem almost repugnant. Craig was amused and interested by it; for he was sufficiently well-acquainted with two of the men to know at what point their scientific abstraction failed them. Wechsel, for instance, in most of his contacts as cold-blooded as a frog, where his wife was concerned was a bundle of emotions. Blake's entire life was a network of prejudices, of completely unreasonable likes and dislikes; and yet in dealing with the most abstract of sciences, mathematics, his mind was as regular and precise as a machine. The rest of the scientists were, to Craig, unknown quantities. As for the only foreigner there—Yozan Saijo—Craig, studying his flat disciplined face, wondered if it were ever possible to destroy the inherent whimsicality of a Japanese.

One of the men, arriving only a few minutes earlier, had brought with him a copy of an extra issued by the

Pasadena *Morning Dispatch* to announce Quinn's death. It lay on the table.

"Leave it to an atheist to kick off in church," gloated Blake.

"Look out, T. F.," Wechsel warned him. "You'll be telling us next there's a divine justice, 'a divinity that shapes our ends, rough-hew them how we will.'"

"A divine sense of humor comes closer."

Wechsel leaned back, a twinkle in his Teutonic eye. "No use hedging. I've never yet seen a mathematician who wasn't a moralist."

"Me a moralist!"

"Exactly." Inspired by the appreciative grins of his audience, Wechsel elaborated his theme. "You can't help yourself. You translate human relationships into mathematical terms and what do you get? A neat little set of morals: Two and two make four, virtue is rewarded, thou shalt not commit adultery."

A burst of laughter greeted his argument.

Blake clenched his teeth. "You damned astrophysicist! Where would you be without mathematics? Groveling in the dust where you belong!"

"Oh, I don't deny that you're of some use when it comes to measuring the distance between stars. I only say that your philosophy of life is bound to be naive."

"Naive!" repeated Blake helplessly. "Naive! By God, I'd like to be Voltaire for just long enough to make you eat those words."

Craig came to his defense. "I'm under the impression," he said, "that naiveté consists largely in a desire to give external existence to our thoughts. The child, told that two plus two equals four, thinks of four apples; you and I, being more sophisticated, substitute a philosophical analogy—virtue is rewarded—for the apples. T. F. and his fellow-mathematicians need no illustration. They have reached the height of sophistication—pure abstraction."

Blake's eyes lighted up. "By heaven!" he cried with a fervor that brought a laugh. "Why didn't I think of that?"

"You Scotch aren't quick on the draw," said Wechsel.

Craig shook his head. "It was too easy. In the words of the sage, Ti Li: 'He who listens for the intricate melodies of the court musicians hears not the call of the cuckoo.'"

Wechsel's thin mouth widened to a grin. A number of the other men smiled appreciatively.

Blake's bony forefinger shot out at Wechsel. "The call of the cuckoo! By God, Fritz, that's your sophistry to a *T!*"

With a laugh Craig turned to Saijo. "I'm afraid the scientific mind is too crude for Oriental subtleties."

Mr. Saijo smiled a polite and unconvincing smile of concurrence.

A few moments later the telephone rang. The call was for Bernie Webster, a young botanist who lived at the club and was a permanent member of the silent, though amused, majority. He came back into the room, his pipe in his hand, and a compelling look on his young face.

"Quinn didn't die of heart failure," he said briefly. "He died from eating poisoned mushrooms for breakfast. Radford remembered I did some work on mycology and sent for me. I'll bring back the lowdown."

The door closed behind Webster and for a moment there was silence. Blake as usual was the first to voice a general reaction. "A swell boost for Pasadena," he said dryly. "We bring a man six thousand miles, ballyhoo him to the skies and then feed him poison in his morning mushrooms."

"What the hell!" argued Wechsel. "Quinn was a fiend for mushrooms. He was bound to draw a poison one sooner or later."

"There's something in that," agreed a less talkative scientist.

"The Japanese are authorities on mushrooms," said Craig. "What do you think, Mr. Saijo, are the odds against being poisoned?"

"I have eaten many varieties of mushrooms. I am still alive."

"I still maintain," said Blake indolently, "that Western Tech will get the credit for ridding the world of a first-rate atheist. And while we're on the subject, Fritz, you're no loser by Quinn's death."

Several of the more conservative men looked shocked by Blake's statement.

"Can it till after the funeral, T. F.," advised one of the bacteriologists.

"Blake's right," said Wechsel bluntly. "If we're scientists, for God's sake, let's take a scientific view. Quinn's dead and I don't mind admitting that I'm not shedding any tears over his decease."

"You take a scientific view!" protested the bacteriologist. "I'll hang on to my job."

"Radford may be God Almighty," retorted Wechsel with a sarcastic smile. "But, as far as I know, he's not all-seeing and all-hearing. Not yet."

"Now, now, gentlemen!" interrupted Blake. "Let's not forget that we're just a little band of Sir Galahads out to get the cosmic ray. *Lux sit!*"

"I should say there was more heat than light in your arguments," laughed Craig, getting to his feet. "Come on. We're going for a walk."

The two men left the clubhouse and strolled down the campus path, past the aerodynamics laboratory, to the sidewalk. The air was crisp; the January sun had almost completed its short arc; and in the blue eastern sky a full moon was visible.

Craig had seen Western Tech on a summer day, its white stucco units deflecting sunlight onto the tiled paths and precious squares and circles of grass that were already drowned in brilliance.

He had stood on the patio of the physics building on a spring night that was steeped in the fragrance of orange blossoms and the sibilance of a dozen fountains, and watched an evening star set behind the gnarled branches of an olive tree that was rooted formerly in the sandy soil of a hill overlooking Athens.

But he had never seen Western Tech so compellingly lovely as it was on this January afternoon, its contrasts of line and color subdued and coordinated by an atmosphere of evaporated snow straight off the peaks of the coast range.

"At any rate Quinn got to the promised land before he died," said Blake with unexpected seriousness.

Craig regarded him quizzically.

"No kidding, if it wasn't for the sunshine and flowers I'd have left this palace of culture long ago. Radford and his damned fool attempts to prove that the universe is being reborn! When every physicist worth his salt knows it's running down!" Blake stalked ferociously forward. "Cosmic rays the birth cries of raw matter being born! Cosmic rays experimental evidence that there is a Creator!" He stopped short and demanded querulously, "Did you ever hear such rot? Did you?"

Craig shook his head. There was a preoccupied look in his eyes.

"You're going to break out with another Chinese proverb," Blake accused him.

"I'm going to buy some candy," said Craig, leading the way into a drugstore.

"You didn't buy this candy because you liked it," Blake reasoned when they came out into the street. "That much is obvious. Whose address did you look up?"

"Dr. Byrne's."

Forty minutes later, after waiting half that time in the sitting room, the two men entered Dr. Byrne's office. His professional manner admitted no surprise at their appearance there.

Craig casually explained his errand.

"You know, Craig," Blake complimented him as they left the doctor's office, "for an Orientalist you think damned straight."

"It's not so much a matter of thinking straight as of not thinking crooked," argued Craig with a smile. "'He who can resist the lure of by-paths seldom loses his way.' The aphorism is Ti Li's."

President Radford's appearance at eleven o'clock that evening at the faculty club was unexpected and almost unprecedented. He was not on friendly terms with his faculty; pompous and ill-at-ease in their presence, he seemed to sense their disrespect. He got on much better with the general public with whom he could play the great man. It was therefore on very rare occasions that he came to the faculty club.

Tonight he asked to see Ian Craig. That in itself would have caused comment, for it was difficult to imagine what the President of Western Tech could want with a Stanford professor. Blake and Craig came downstairs together; and after a moment's conversation the three men returned upstairs to Blake's room where they remained for over an hour.

The President departed shortly after midnight; his car was waiting outside; and Blake and Craig, who had accompanied him to the door, were immediately besieged by questions.

There were a dozen or more scientists in the room, all of whom stayed at the club. They had waited up in order to learn the reason for Radford's mysterious visit, and they were determined to know.

Blake, very much flattered by their interest, demand-ed silence. "Well, gentlemen," he announced importantly, facing them, "I have just witnessed a little drama entitled 'Telling It to the President.'"

A good many eyes were turned on Craig who, having settled down modestly into an arm-chair, was laughing at Blake.

"What did he tell the President?" demanded Bernie Webster.

Blake raised a silencing hand. "I'm coming to that. He told the President"—hesitating impressively, he frowned at his audience—"that Quinn didn't die of heart failure. . . ."

"We know that," announced one of the scientists.

"Shut up!" ordered Blake. "He didn't die from eating poisoned mushrooms . . ."

"Are you sure he died?" demanded a geologist.

"He died all right," said Blake. "He was murdered."

There was a moment of silence.

"He was murdered," repeated Blake, annoyed by the number of skeptical glances that flashed between his lis-teners. "It's a fact. Tomorrow the papers will have it."

"Just the same there was mushroom poison in his guts," stated Webster.

"Sure there was," agreed Blake quickly.

"What the hell then?"

"The mushroom poison in his guts wasn't from the mushrooms he ate for breakfast." Ignoring the rather dis-couraging attitude of his audience, he continued gravely, "It was fed to him in a fruit lozenge. Here!" Taking from his pocket a handful of the square fruit lozenges Craig had bought that afternoon, he tossed them to several of the men. "Have one!"

"You wouldn't kid us?" said the geologist.

Blake threw up his hands in despair. "Craig! You tell them," he suggested. "The damned fools won't believe me."

"It's true," said Craig in reply to the inquiring glances shot at him. "Mushroom poison, technically known as muscarin, was administered to Quinn on a fruit lozenge. There were four lozenges in his pocket at the time of his death; one of them was coated with the poison."

"Pretty slick," commented one of the men.

"But who the hell—"

"Listen!" said Blake. "The police are getting busy on that now. The police and my friend, Craig. What do you think Radford wanted with him? Why do you think the old frog came here?" Blake's voice was charged with superiority and he looked with more or less scorn on his fellow scientists. "Why," he replied to his own question, "to ask Craig to lend a hand in the investigation."

"I don't get the point of dragging in a Stanford man," objected the geologist.

"A lot of good you dead-heads would be," retorted Blake. "Craig's had experience in such matters. Did you ever hear of that Earl College murder?"

"A psychologist, wasn't it?" questioned Webster.

Blake nodded. "Craig solved that."

Craig smiled and got to his feet. "That doesn't mean I'll solve Quinn's murder," he protested.

"If it hadn't been for you they'd never have known it was a murder," argued Blake. "The poor saps never thought of analyzing the lozenges in Quinn's pocket; not until Craig suggested it, and even then they thought he was screwy."

"Finding the poison in his guts, and all . . . I'd have sworn it was a plain case of mushroom poisoning," admitted Webster with reluctant admiration.

"They all thought that," said Blake. "Death by accident. Pretty soft for the murderer if it had stuck."

"The murderer, whoever he was," said the geologist thoughtfully. "What made you think of the lozenges?" he asked Craig.

Craig shrugged his shoulders.

"Leave him alone," ordered Blake petulantly. "Don't nag at him."

"That's all right," said Craig with a laugh. "I don't quite know myself what made me think of the lozenges. I remembered seeing Quinn eat one in church. . . ."

"Radford was sitting on one side of him," announced Blake.

Saijo suddenly arose. "I was on his other side," he said, and walked over to the window.

No one commented; an expression of embarrassment circled the small group.

"Anyway," Webster broke the silence, "it's damned ironic that he should have died in church."

"Even if it can't any longer be blamed on fate."

"I don't know, T. F.," said Craig with the casualness that was so characteristic of him and that distinguished him so abruptly from the other men. "The murderer probably had no idea where Quinn would be when he ate the poisoned lozenge."

"By God!" exclaimed the geologist, rising impatiently, "It's—it's unbelievable!" He joined Saijo at the window.

"It is," said Webster, half to himself. "The great man murdered. Here, of all places. By someone we know probably."

No one elaborated on the implications he had suggested. The scientists were silent as through the mind of each one of them passed the same questions and suspicions.

"It's too much for me," announced Webster shortly.

"Murdered in church! What a finish for the world's greatest atheist!" Blake repeated his theme.

The geologist turned and regarded him sarcastically. "You'll never get over that, will you?"

"No." Blake shook his head defiantly. "I won't. If he'd died in church from eating a mushroom omelet, that would

have been good. This is even better. Maybe he was murdered because he was an atheist."

"Rot!" Webster condemned the idea.

"What do you think, Craig?" Blake appealed to his
friend.

Craig's rather indolent features were crossed by a smile.
He thrust a lock of hair back from his forehead. "The motives for murder are always disappointing," he said. "At
least I've found them so. There are ten good ways of killing a man to one good reason for killing him."

"That's a damned arbitrary statement for a philosopher," argued Blake. "I can . . ."

"A shooting star!" interrupted the geologist who was
still standing by the window. "A beauty too. Too late," he
told the men who started toward him.

"A shooting star," repeated Saijo, speaking for the second time. His face was turned toward the heavens; his
voice was pregnant with irony: "'When beggars die there
are no comets seen; the heavens themselves blaze forth the
death of princes.'"

2

Craig had arrived in Pasadena on Saturday afternoon. It was not his first visit. During the two years of his association with the Oriental literature department at Stanford he had often come down for a week-end with Blake.

On this occasion he had been particularly glad to have an entrée to Western Tech. Sir Arthur Quinn's appearance there had focused the attention of the entire West on the college and faculty. And invitations to the banquet that climaxed Quinn's week of lectures, though they were not for sale, had brought from the public bids as high as fifty dollars.

A number of celebrity hunters and many internationally famous scientists had already met Quinn in the East, where he had lectured at three other institutions. The rest flocked to Pasadena where, from Monday on, he was involved in one form after another of social activity.

By the end of the week the ovation had spent itself: the flowers on the lamp-posts of Euclid Avenue faded and were taken down; the telephone wires had been cleared of ticker tape; the Elks put away their uniforms; and the author of the third law of thermodynamics, by this time in a very bad humor, had attended the banquet which was to wind up his stay in America.

It had fulfilled its purpose, thought Craig who, now that Quinn was murdered and he himself curiously involved in the solution of that murder, looked back on that boring and conventional affair as a treasure mine of emotions and relationships, a treasure mine whose ore, if sifted and resifted through his memory, might yield one or two valuable clues.

Accordingly, having pieced together from Blake's thrifty comments the outline of Quinn's stay in Pasadena, Craig set about to fill in from memory the suddenly vital details of Saturday evening, the only and very brief period of the dead man's entire life that was included in Craig's personal experience.

The banquet, unfortunately, was not as brilliant and delightful an affair as the public was led to suppose. And it was preceded by an embarrassing scene of which Blake, with the best intentions in the world, was the sponsor. Early in the week he had promised Polly Wechsel to sound out Quinn in regard to her husband's major project: namely, that the predominance of red in starlight is caused by a gravitational drag on the light waves rather than by the recession of the stars themselves. A number of men had already worked on that hypothesis but none had offered data sufficiently compelling to divert attention from Lemaitre's theory of a rapidly expanding universe. Wechsel, working alone and quietly, had almost completed the paper with which he hoped to electrify the entire scientific world. No one, up to the present, had been able to reconcile the size, age, and rate of expansion of the universe. Eddington's universe, with its radius of three thousand million light years, allowed for an age of only two thousand million years, a ridiculously brief period according to geologists, who claim to have the evidence of radioactive rocks that the earth is at least that old and the sun millions of millions of years older. Wechsel's concept, by allowing for a less fantastic rate of expansion than that of his predecessors, would, he believed, dislodge Lemaitre's and Eddington's bubble universe and restore faith in the more conservative cosmologies of de Sitter and Einstein.

It was this theory on which Blake was awaiting an opportunity to sound out Quinn. The opportunity came Saturday evening, before the banquet. Blake and Ian Craig, arriving at the hotel, went directly to the mezzanine. A number of guests, among them Quinn, who was staying at the hotel, were already assembled in the small lounge just outside the banquet hall. The dignitaries, President Radford, the Mayor and the regents, were still to arrive.

Quinn, obviously, was not encouraging conversation. He stood beside a window, smoking one of the extra-length Virginia cigarettes that were made to his order in London, and replying curtly when he was spoken to.

"Here's my chance," said Blake. And with a wink at Craig and a warning to "Stand by," he approached Quinn.

Sir Arthur listened with a supercilious smile as Blake outlined his friend's project. More guests were arriving each moment. Several of them, after they had checked their coats, joined the two scientists by the window. Sir Arthur paid no attention to any of them. Enough taller so that the smoke from his cigarette drifted over their heads, he leaned back against the window, his eyes half-closed. Blake didn't waste any words. But his taciturn face was alight with enthusiasm and his nervous right hand, when it was not engaged in emphasizing a point, twisted a button on his waistcoat, or flashed in and out of his pocket. Craig was amused to see Blake looking so decorous; he had even forsaken the pungent tobacco he bought in ten-pound lots for a cigarette. It was true he rarely puffed at it, and then cautiously, with a dubious expression on his face. It wasn't that he disliked the taste of cigarettes, he had frankly admitted to Craig at one time; but there was nothing to them and they were socially *comme il faut,* two qualifications highly distasteful to his rebellious Scotch soul.

For much the same reasons he disliked the popular conception of good food. Tea-room stuff he termed it. Salads and desserts filled him with contempt, his idea of something first-rate being a sirloin steak, burned on the outside and rare inside, and French-fried potatoes. These he ate daily, contrary to the advice of his doctor, who had also warned him against strong tobacco and numberless cups of black coffee. But Blake was stubborn. He didn't give a damn about his constitution, he claimed; mathematicians were no good anyway after they reached fifty; he'd just as soon kick off. The one dissipation he had condescended to give up was liquor, and that only because it interfered with his work.

He was equally stubborn in regard to his appearance. His neckties were chosen without any regard for sensitivity and, when he could not find riotous enough patterns, he had them made to order of silks bought in Chinatown. His pajamas and smoking jackets were unrestrained and, if he had had his way, his suits and the walls of his room would as well have blazed with color.

The oddest part about his mania for strength in color, tobacco, language and drink was that it was not an affectation. His system needed it; it provided the vitality necessary to his work. Without it he was listless and irritable. This he explained by the fact that as a boy he had been raised on a farm in Scotland where the only food was potatoes and oatmeal and the people and physical surroundings were as drab as the food.

Craig, though he hated to see T. F. burn himself out with bad living, knew that nothing less than serious illness would persuade him to change his habits. And in the meantime he was enjoying life, he was productive, and his work ranked A-1 in the scientific world.

Blake's right hand, the little finger of which was adorned by a blue scarab and a nail that he wore, in the Chinese manner, a half-inch long, dropped to his side.

"Well, Sir Arthur," he concluded his brief statement of Wechsel's case and qualifications, "what do you think? You didn't get around to the red shift in your lectures."

"No," said Quinn promptly, and in a more distinct voice than Blake's, "I didn't. But you can tell your friend, Mr. Wechsel, that the red shift is very much on my mind. So much so that my paper for the May meeting of the Royal Astronomical Society will be on that very subject."

"Is that so?" said Blake.

"When I return to London," continued Quinn, "I intend to compute from atomic theory what the rate of cosmic expansion should be. If the figure I arrive at checks up with my former observations, as I am convinced it will, the red shift will be interpreted beyond doubt."

"And Wechsel's theory?" persisted Blake.

Sir Arthur shrugged his shoulders. "You may tell Mr. Wechsel that only a miracle can save his theory from being still-born."

"Still-born?" Wechsel, apparently just arrived, for he was wearing his overcoat, repeated Quinn's phrase with quiet sarcasm. "That's very interesting."

Sir Arthur raised his eyebrows. Blake turned guiltily. "Oh! hello, Fritz," he said.

"Hello," said Wechsel from the outskirts of the small group that had heard Quinn's ultimatum. "And thanks." He turned and walked toward the checkroom.

Fortunately, the arrival of President Radford and the Mayor prevented further discussion of the incident. The scientists, many of them in borrowed dinner jackets, were herded into the banquet hall.

The dinner progressed slowly and without brilliance. Blake dismissed the food as "bellywash," and commented succinctly to Craig that "the better the scientists, the worse the table talk."

Craig, at the time, had agreed with him. These men were, all of them, of major importance in the scientific world. Their names would read like a *Who's Who;* their distinctions included honorary degrees, medals and royal gifts. Bernie Webster, the botanist on Craig's right, had only a short time before been a recipient of a gold watch emblazoned with the Swedish royal coat of arms. But his table talk was apparently limited to a dissertation on his scottie, Bridget, who was being treated for mange.

Craig had listened perfunctorily. On his other side Blake was occupied in telling his own left-hand neighbor the proper method of cooking steak, while directly across the table and almost concealed from Craig's vision by a bowl of roses and maidenhair fern, Wechsel ate his dinner with military dispatch. If, after the first course, he spoke at all Craig wasn't conscious of it. His dinner companions, a bacteriologist and an astronomer, after several attempts to break his contemptuous silence, directed their attention elsewhere, leaving Wechsel to an isolated and sullen absorption in his food.

Put a monocle on that irascible face, Craig remembered thinking as he peered adroitly through the greenery; shave that bristle of pale hair; and in place of an American scientist sits a Prussian officer.

But it was not Wechsel's bad temper that stood out as most significant in Craig's recollection of the banquet. He remembered with far greater interest an incident which, coming with the charlotte russe, climaxed five courses of labored conversation and banquet food.

With every course the faces of the fifty-odd scientists had grown uniformly blanker and their conversation more sparse. When the charlotte russe was set before him Blake, removing the maraschino cherry from it with his prong-like fingers, announced to Craig, "Would I like to aim this at Radford's right eye! Look at the old poop."

Craig glanced down the long table at the dignitaries clustered around the end of it. Sir Arthur and the Mayor had by this time lapsed into a moody silence from which Radford, with the persistence of a mosquito, sought to rouse them. His florid face was set in a smile as he leaned first to right and then to left.

"You'd think he was watching a tennis game," said Blake.

Then, suddenly, the silence which, for the last twenty minutes had been threatening the banquet, came. The conversation had spent itself; there was not even a subdued hum; only the tinkle of spoons against glass. Blake, with a wink at Craig, followed the example of his fellow-scientists and thoughtfully sipped his coffee.

The silence endured; even the rattle of spoons ceased; and the longer it lasted the more reluctant was any one person to break it with an inconsequential statement.

President Radford, conscious of the burden imposed on him by his faculty, was obviously racking his brain for conversational bait. He looked nervously about him. Suddenly, his eyes fell on the Japanese scientist, Yozan Saijo, who was seated on the Mayor's left. His face lighted, and he inquired triumphantly of Quinn, "Well, Sir Arthur, I suppose you're looking forward to making use of the new two-hundred-and-fifty-inch telescope at Tokio."

Sir Arthur, impervious to the attention of the fifty or so men within earshot, nodded and lighted a cigarette. "Yes, I am," he replied negligently. "Although I consider the whole thing a mistake; a waste of equipment. The atmospheric conditions aren't right and the Japanese are, after all, third-rate scientists."

Instantly, the attention of everyone was riveted on
Saijo. His inscrutable face betrayed no notice of Quinn's
remark. Quinn, himself, seemingly unaware of the furor
he had caused, casually drank his coffee.

The speeches that followed were on the whole brief and
uninspired. The Mayor spoke; Quinn bade Western Tech
a formal farewell; and lastly Radford paid his customary
tribute to his own efforts in the wedding of science to religion.

His speech was consistent enough: it expressed an attitude for which he was noted; nevertheless it lingered in
Craig's memory as unpleasant and curiously sincere. Its
effect on the other listeners, if less marked, was much the
same; they appeared to be, not so much bored, as faintly
uncomfortable. Why was that, Craig wondered. Not a man
there paid Radford the compliment of taking him seriously;
ordinarily they laughed at his pompous fence-straddling.
Why then, on this occasion, should their faces betray a
definite distaste? Why should he himself, Craig wondered,
resent and analyze the effect of so typical a speech. Was
it because Radford, excited by the presence of a famous
atheist, was unduly eloquent? For years he had preached
the union of science and religion. A convenient and popular attitude, it conciliated the layman without harming
the scientist. But now, suddenly, it seemed to Craig, there
crept into Radford's gospel a touch of fanaticism, a sincerity alarming in that it transformed a popular scientist
into an evangelist.

Radford started out, naturally enough, with a eulogy of
Quinn. "In the past," he said, by way of conclusion, "when
a group of scientists have gathered together as we are gathered together here"—the pompous paternalism with which
he surveyed his listeners caused Blake to snicker—"there
has been some feeling on the part of the layman that science is taking to itself undue importance, and that among

so many scientists there must be some whose work constitutes a mysterious and—if I may put it so strongly—an
irreligious force."

Quinn's expression, Craig noted, was faintly derisive.
Adroitly, almost absently, he slipped a lozenge between his
thin lips.

"Little by little," continued Radford feelingly, "thanks
to the unceasing and enlightened leadership of a few,
that antagonism toward science is being supplanted by a
healthier attitude."

"How's that for patting yourself on the back?" whispered Blake.

"Little by little the layman is learning that science and
religion are one and the same thing, that God is truth, and
that we of the laboratory, in as full a sense as the mission-
ary or the churchman, are His workers."

"He's got nerve getting off that sort of drivel to us," observed Blake under cover of polite applause. "Why doesn't
he save it for his radio talks!"

The banquet broke up almost immediately. Blake and
Craig were among the first to get their coats. As they were
leaving, Wechsel hurried up to them. "Hold on," he said.
"Quinn's coming to the house for a drink. Want to come
along?"

"Do we!" exclaimed Blake. "But what's the idea? Are
you and Quinn going to get together on the red shift? Just
a couple of pals?"

Wechsel smiled strangely. "Something like that," he retorted, turning on his heel. "Wait here. I'll round up the
rest of the party."

A few minutes later, in the company of Wechsel, Sir
Arthur and two astronomers, Craig and Blake descended
to the lobby.

On their way out Sir Arthur stopped to speak with a
woman whom Craig recognized at once, in spite of certain

points of dissimilarity between herself and her pictures, as the German dancer Lona Lang. The shoulder-length aura of chestnut hair, so vital a part of her personality, was not in evidence, and she was older and more haggard than seemed possible for the owner of so glamorous a name and reputation; but, to Craig at least, the heart-shaped face and deep-set eyes, at moments so strangely blue, was unmistakable. Once in New York and again in a Berlin theater, he had watched it through opera-glasses, watched that body grapple with moods that were listed on the program as spring, nocturne, or Chopin Rondeau XVI.

It pleased him now to observe her close up. In the theater it had been her personality rather than her dancing that interested him. Would it continue to interest him? Or, robbed of its margin of darkness, would it, like so many stage personalities, fade into mediocrity?

Craig wondered and was not sure. If Lona Lang, projected across footlights and audience, had been brilliant or beautiful he might have expected to find her proportionately shallow. And not have condemned her. For work in Oriental philosophy had mellowed him and taught him the uses of illusion. Consequently he loved the theater in all its forms and believed that if bombast can be staged so as to pass for wit and beauty, so much the better.

But Lona Lang in the theater had not been brilliant or beautiful. Her virtues were negative, her triumph a denunciation of the spring, nocturne and Chopin Rondeau XVI of her predecessors. Music and make-up she dispensed with; her movements were harsh, her interpretations grotesque and often venomous. She was inelegant, and the critics called her significant; she was perverse, and they called her sincere; she was inconsistent, and they called her original. The debt she owed the Oriental, the Spaniard, the Negro and American Indian had, of course, been pointed out; and the public, reassured by suggestion of an historic background, ceased to be shocked. By 1918 they ceased

to be shocked; post-war psychology had something to do
with it. They never ceased to take Lona Lang seriously.
And by 1930 instructors of esthetic dancing were teaching
growing girls that, contrary to prewar belief, the Greeks
did not have a monopoly on barefoot dancing. Lona Lang's
influence, described alternately as German and modern,
was foreordained to popularity: the pre-Raphaelite passion for flowing lines had worn out its welcome; it is easier
for growing girls to be emphatic than graceful; and once
the first shock was over, it was with obvious relief that
dancing instructors accepted an art whose major premises
were discord and emphasis rather than grace and harmony.
Probably none of them guessed that the interpretations
they so sedulously imitated were evolved out of contempt,
not love, for spring, nocturne, and Chopin Rondeau XVI.

Craig had been amused by Lona Lang's dancing; he had
been aware of her influence, now he was curious as to her
personality.

"Who's the muted gong?" asked Blake.

Craig explained that, since she happened to be a dancer
whose ultramodernism consisted partly in a preference for
barbaric music, the name was more applicable than Blake
had guessed.

"Her music may be barbaric," said Blake with another
glance at Lona Lang, who was talking with Quinn while
her escort waited a few steps away, "but her men aren't."

Wechsel and the two astronomers laughed. Craig, struck
by the truth of the statement, considered the two men
more carefully. The dancer's escort was as typically American as Quinn was typically British. Gray-haired, distinguished but not intellectual, he was, Craig concluded, like
so many citizens of Pasadena, a retired banker or broker,
into whose regulated and luxurious life Lona Lang had
by accident entered. For it was not conceivable that she
should normally be in the life of so substantial and recog-
nizable a type. That shrewd, kindly face, heavy set but not

flabby, florid but not dissipated, was the face of a man
whose pleasures and investments would be chosen with the
same foresight and care for consequences. He would never
be credulous. If Lona Lang were his mistress she would be
his mistress in name only. Actually she would be his wife,
treated with the selective and disciplined indulgence of
which such men are capable. They are employers, habit-
ual commanders, and their indulgences are commands to
enjoyment, to extravagance and frivolity.

It was quite possible, of course, that Lona Lang's escort
had a family. Craig imagined him as a young man reasoning that his bank account was large enough to support
a wife, that it was time to multiply. There was a look of
domesticity about him which suggested that between business conferences and golf games he had carved prime rib
roasts, taken the children on picnics and to movies, weed-
ed and watered the lawn, paid doctors' and dentists' bills.

Then what was Lona Lang doing with him? And the
familiar, even possessive patience with which he waited
while she chatted with Quinn: how was that to be accounted for? Were they old friends, he and the dancer? That, of
all the explanations that occurred to Craig, seemed least
remote. And yet, the average American banker would no
more include in his portfolio a foreign dancer of question-
able reputation than a bond of the same class. He might be
liberal to the extent of liking her: he probably liked to be
seen with her, but he would never approve of her.

And, for that matter, what did Lona Lang want with a
conservative and dispassionate American? Her publicized
liaisons had been with celebrities—writers, artists, politicians, all of them richer or younger or unhappier men than
her present escort. Solidity, moderate success and normal-
cy had never been in her line. Craig was frankly mystified.

A moment later, with apologies for having detained
them, Quinn rejoined the five men. It was at once

apparent that his humor had changed. Outwardly he was still the reserved, civilized *homme du monde,* impeccable of manner, and handsome in a rather inbred way; but the irritability and antagonism, so easy to mistake for arrogance, had vanished. Suddenly agreeable, almost apologetically so, he confided in his companions that if there was one thing he abhorred it was a banquet without wine.

"Wine wouldn't have saved that banquet," remarked Blake.

Quinn laughed.

"At any rate, it's your last formal appearance in Pasadena," observed one of the astronomers. "We're not so lucky."

"That's where you're wrong." Quinn shook his head. "I promised your President tonight that I'd go to church with him in the morning. You see," he added with a twinkle in his eye, "as a conscientious man I intend to really earn my wages."

"In your place I'm damned if I'd do it," said Wechsel bluntly. "Well, let's get going. I don't know about the rest of you but I could do with a stiff drink."

The six men left the hotel. Quinn, Wechsel, and the astronomers walked on ahead.

"Fritz always bites the hand that feeds him, and vice versa," Blake commented on Wechsel's unaccountable amiability. "He's a perverse devil. I thought he'd burn up over that crack about his theory being still-born. Polly will. That's a cinch!"

"He didn't look any too cheerful at dinner," observed Craig.

"Look at him now!" Blake shook his head wonderingly. "Playing up to Quinn for all he's worth. If Quinn had done him a favor, or was apt to, Fritz would be growling at him."

"You know Wechsel better than I do. But I'd say he was putting it on."

"Why the devil should he?"

Craig regarded his companion quizzically. "Because his great grandfather was a drunkard maybe. Or because he found a worm in an apple at the age of four. How should I know? That's the sort of question only a mathematician would ask."

"Is that so?" rejoined Blake complacently. "Well, knowing the workings of the philosophical mind the way I do, I'm willing to bet dollars to doughnuts you're asking yourself a couple of questions right this minute."

"Of course I am," admitted Craig. "Unanswerable questions like yours. But I don't ask you to answer them."

"You introverts!" sighed Blake. "Some day when you're off guard I'm going to catch you asking what time it is or who played guard for Navy in 1906. By the way," he added, his dour Scotch countenance lighted by a gleam of sarcasm, "I'm only a poor bastard of a mathematician but if you ever want to know anything about the physical constant or the recurrent decimal . . ."

Craig shook his head. "Thanks, but I want to keep my mind."

"What for?"

"Among other things, to account for Quinn's change of heart."

Blake studied the four men strolling ahead of him. Quinn was talking; the other three, abreast of him on the wide sidewalk, listened.

"It must be love," said Blake. "That dancer. He may like them weather-beaten. Personally . . ."

It was a cold, moonless night, dark except for a pink glow over the business district. Because of the clearness of the atmosphere the stars seemed extraordinarily sharp and distant. The sky was thick with them—golden clusters thinning at the horizon to icy points, but Craig observed that the four astronomers kept their eyes on the ground. Their conversation, he later discovered, concerned the advantages of American football over Rugby.

It was but a few blocks to Wechsel's house. Polly Wechsel met them at the door. In contrast with the formal dress of the men, she wore sneakers and a skirt and sweater. The red sweater clearly defined her firm, pointed breasts, her lips were rouged and she had faintly shadowed her eyes with blue. Framed in thick layers of black hair cut in a Dutch bob—the bangs reached almost to her eyebrows—her face, without losing its human quality, had the picturesque values of a mask.

Wechsel took his guests' coats and piled them on chairs in the hallway. Blake led Sir Arthur into the living room.

"Go wash your face!" Wechsel ordered his wife roughly. "What do you mean by getting yourself up like that!"

With a contemptuous glance over her shoulder at him Polly followed the men into the living-room. Taking a cigarette from a box, she lit it, and then went over to the mantel. The men sat down. Polly, having adopted an entirely relaxed pose, stood watching them with eyes that were sullen beneath wax-blue lids. Voluptuous in a peasant way, she had the mind and exhibitionist instincts of an adolescent, thought Craig—a dangerous combination. A combination especially dangerous to the peace of mind of a small-boned and repressed scientist. To tantalize or excite him was her sole object. Wechsel should have a comfortable wife, a wife he could with impunity kick around. There was no doubt that he kicked Paula around, or that he answered for it.

Wechsel's reprimand had put her in a very bad humor which she made no effort to conceal. Ignoring her guests she continued to lean against the mantel until Wechsel remarked to her impersonally as one does to a servant, "Drinks, Polly?'

Obediently she started toward the kitchen. At the door she stopped and looked back at Blake. "T. F.!" she said, and beckoned him to follow her.

"She wants to know what Quinn said about the red shift," grumbled Blake softly. "Now there'll be hell to pay."

"Don't tell her," suggested Craig.

"Keep anything from her? Fat chance!" Reluctantly Blake got to his feet.

It was a good quarter of an hour before they returned from the kitchen. Blake came first with a whisky bottle and a soda-water siphon. Polly followed him carrying a tray which she set down on the table before taking her position by the mantel. Her expression was unchanged.

"It's about time," said Wechsel. "Here, I'll fix them." He dropped a cube of ice into each glass. "Oh! I forgot. You English don't take ice."

Quinn laughed. "That's right."

One of the astronomers began an account of his attempts to get an iced drink in London.

Polly lighted a cigarette. In doing so she dropped her handkerchief. Quinn promptly sprang to pick it up for her. As he stooped over, three lozenges fell from his vest pocket onto the hearth. Two of them broke to pieces. He straightened up with a laugh. "That's what I get for being gallant. Your handkerchief, Mrs. Wechsel."

Polly took it without thanks.

"How are you going to get through the rest of the evening, Sir Arthur?" inquired Blake with a twinkle in his eye.

"Without my lozenges, you mean?" Quinn laughed. "Oh, I'm prepared for such emergencies. I always carry a reserve supply in my overcoat pocket."

Wechsel handed around the highballs. A few minutes later Polly left the room. Once the constraint imposed by her presence was lifted, the conversation, at first spasmodic and forced, grew more spontaneous. The time passed quickly as the quart of Scotch diminished.

Quinn became exceedingly voluble. Sitting back in an arm-chair, a glass in his hand, legs crossed and his long left leg swinging like a pendulum, he discussed recent experiments and inventions in a soft voice that seemed at times to retire into his throat. His voice was not only surprisingly gentle for so tall and dignified a man; it was also rather high; and contrasted with the aggressive, unrestricted speech of the Americans, Quinn's was uneven and whimsical and difficult at times to catch. Craig for days afterwards could hear that cramped, modulated voice and see Quinn's well-bred face with its long, almost motionless upper lip.

It was several hours later that Polly entered the room to tell Sir Arthur he was wanted on the telephone. She showed him where it was and then returned to the living-room.

"I thought you'd gone to bed," remarked Wechsel.

Polly regarded him with a not unfriendly sarcasm. "And I suppose you could hardly wait to come to me."

Blake laughed; the two astronomers, Craig observed, looked uncomfortable.

"You see!" Wechsel addressed the four men. "At heart they're all prostitutes."

"You're drunk," said Polly calmly, and held the whisky bottle up to the light; it contained but a few drops.

"Not drunk." Blake rather uncertainly shook his head. "Fritz isn't ever drunk. He's just intellectually alone."

"Mind your own business, T. F.," suggested Polly, emptying the bottle into a glass.

"That happens to be my glass," said Blake.

"What of it?"

"Why did you ever marry her, Fritz?" demanded Blake.

"I had my reasons," replied Wechsel shortly, and surveyed his wife with hard, calculating eyes.

Disregarding his stare, she sipped the Scotch.

Quinn's reappearance in the room eased the tension. "I'm afraid I must go," he said.

Neither Wechsel nor his wife made any attempt to detain him. The two astronomers, with obvious relief, arose.

Blake went over to the piano and started to play the love song from the second act of "Tristan and Isolde."

"Time to go, T. F.," suggested Craig.

Blake paid no attention.

Polly sighed. "My God! He'll be here all night." Quinn and the astronomers left and Wechsel, having taken them to the door, returned.

Craig and Polly were standing; Blake continued to play passionately.

"He never leaves until he's put out," said Wechsel. He went over and laid a hand on Blake's shoulder.

Blake shook it off. "Go away," he said without interrupting his playing. "Haven't you any reverence?"

"Where's his overcoat?" asked Craig. "I'll get him out."

Polly started toward the hall.

"Wait!" ordered her husband. "Never mind. Let him stay all night if he wants to. We'll go for a walk."

Polly's face brightened instantly. "Where to?" she demanded.

"Anywhere. Hollywood, if you want."

"I do." She seized her husband's arm with a sudden and spontaneous show of affection. "Oh, Fritz! That will be fun. We'll have breakfast at The Brown Derby. I'll get my coat."

"You don't mind staying here with that lunatic, do you?" Wechsel inquired of Craig.

Craig laughed. "I'd just as soon do that as start out on a twelve-mile walk."

"Oh, we often walk all night. To clear our heads," explained Wechsel. "Well, so long."

Blake took no notice of their departure. An hour or so later he suddenly ceased playing and turned to Craig, who was reading. "I'm never called away from anywhere," he said plaintively. "It's discouraging. If I thought there was any chance of being called away I'd go out more."

"Careful, T. F.," laughed Craig. "You're getting wistful?"

"Wistful?" Blake arose unsteadily. "Hell! I'm cockeyed!" He stretched himself slowly and with animal enjoyment. "Let's go out and eat!"

Craig was silent. His head thrown back and his eyes closed, he methodically tapped the arm of his chair with his long, slender fingers.

"I never felt more like an oyster stew," said Blake.

Craig opened his eyes and raised his head. "You told Polly what Quinn said about Wechsel's experiment?" he asked.

Blake nodded. "She'd have found out sooner or later. Plenty of people heard him say it."

"How did she take it?"

"She cursed Quinn up one side and down the other. Luckily I'd closed the doors." Blake grinned. "If I hadn't . . ."

"She's a strange woman."

"A strange woman? She's a wild woman! Speaking of wild women"—Blake's eyes were sardonic—"who do you suppose telephoned Quinn?"

Craig shrugged his shoulders. "You're not suggesting Lona Lang?"

"Damned right I am! Polly told me it was a woman."

"She did?" asked Craig with interest.

"A telephone call from a woman at midnight." Blake groaned enviously. "Nothing like that ever happens to me."

"Mr. Ian Craig?" inquired a voice over the telephone. It was three a.m. Monday morning; Craig had been asleep for two hours. "Yes, damn it!" he answered.

"Pasadena *Morning Dispatch* speaking. Is it true that you're responsible for the discovery that Quinn was poisoned."

"I have nothing to say," said Craig.

"We understand that you suggested analyzing the loz-enges in Quinn's pocket."

"Nothing to say," said Craig.

"Is it true that you solved a similar mystery several years ago at Earl College?"

"Similar?"

"And that you're now a professor of Oriental literature at Stanford?"

"Yes."

The reporter drew a deep breath. "Mr. Craig, we under-stand that President Radford has asked you to represent Western Tech in the search for Quinn's murderer."

Craig yawned.

"Then it's true that the chief of police has O.K.'d the President's request?"

"I have nothing to say."

"One more question," said the reporter. "Is President Radford interested in establishing a department of Orien-tal literature at Western Tech?"

"Have you asked President Radford?"

"He says no."

Craig laughed. "The Chinese philosopher, Ti Li, says: 'As there are times when the dice turn to seven, so are there times when even the most exalted of men speak the truth.'"

"Say that again, will you?"

"I never repeat myself," said Craig. "If that's all, I think we'd both better get some sleep. Good night."

3

Early Monday morning Craig received a call from police headquarters asking him to report at once to Quinn's hotel room. When he arrived there the two detectives appointed to the case were in the act of questioning Dr. Byrne. Detective Piper, the elder of the two, had a sharp, twinkling eye, ruffled white hair and the paunch of a beer-drinker. Detective Straight was a small, dapper man wearing rimless spectacles, a brisk reddish mustache and a scowl.

Of the two Craig thought he preferred Piper. He was, at least, easy to place. And Craig had at one time or another met up with enough of the police force to know that the veterans on it, a class to which Piper definitely belonged, indolent and complacent as they seemed, generally had it all over the younger men. Their old tricks, based on experience, generally worked; whereas all sorts of obstacles were raised by the psychological devices of the young experts. It was not their fault; it was simply that the mind and instincts of the average criminal were on a par with the methods of the unscientific detective. Both were unbelievably naive.

Craig remembered one case, a case which had appealed to his love of farce: any upset, he contended, any reversal of the expected, whether physical or mental, was farce. And this had in a minor way been an upset of scientific detection. A girl had been arrested. The police had nothing on her, but it was suspected that she belonged to a gang of counterfeiters. For days they worked on her; professors of psychology were called in; the lie detector was resorted to. All without result. The girl, though mystified to the point of hysteria, remained uncommunicative. They were about to give up and let her go when an old-timer on the force, a sentimental old Irishman who for thirty years had smoothed the way for dirty politics, said, "Let me see her." He went to her cell and came back with a full confession. "I didn't ask her a question," he reported. "But it was easy to see the poor girl was starved for a cigarette. And we both had a drink."

Whether Piper's twinkling eye was capable of a similar insight into human nature, Craig was not sure. But, at any rate, he looked more affable and less doggedly efficient than his colleague.

Dr. Byrne, having described Quinn's symptoms, explained with equanimity how he came to mistake them for the symptoms of coronary thrombosis. "Muscarin," he said, "is the name of the drug from whose effects Quinn died. It is found in the poisonous fly mushroom, and produces typical peripheral stimulation of the parasympathetic system: a greatly increased secretion of saliva and sweat; nausea, pupillary contraction, and palpitation. Death generally occurs by paralysis of the heart. The treatment is evacuation." He paused and cleared his throat.

"I treated the patient for coronary thrombosis, which is precisely what the symptoms of muscarin suggest. The treatment, in essence, is to ease the pain and protect the heart. Nothing is so effective for that as morphia. And that is what I gave Quinn. Any doctor would have done the same. Naturally, had I known he was suffering from an overdose of muscarin, I would have used the stomach pump. But to use a stomach pump on a thrombosis case would be fatal. You can see the predicament I was in—with no time to lose and no way to make tests. All the symptoms pointed to thrombosis; I've seen a hundred of those to one or two cases of mushroom poison; I prescribed for thrombosis and I was wrong. That's all there is to it."

Neither of the detectives made any comment on the ethical aspects of Byrne's testimony. "You referred to muscarin as a drug," said Straight. "Does that mean it's sometimes prescribed?"

"Yes. Wherever stimulation of the sweat glands is desired. It's extremely beneficial in the treatment of kidney disease although it was used more ten years ago than it is now. By increasing the secretion of sweat it secures functional rest to the kidneys and lowers blood-pressure."

Straight nodded. "I see."

"It must be powerful stuff," said Piper in his bass voice. "You can't put much poison on a fruit lozenge."

"You must remember that, in the course of the morning, the patient probably ate several lozenges," suggested the doctor suavely. "However, muscarin is exceedingly powerful. Especially the natural variety, which is ten times stronger on the heart than the artificial preparation."

"So it's prepared artificially too?"

"Yes. By the oxidation of cholin. I believe, though, that the drug administered to Quinn was undoubtedly prepared from the fresh fungus; its action points to that."

"You analyzed the lozenges found in Quinn's pocket?"

"I did," replied Byrne. "At Mr. Craig's suggestion."

"You're a doctor," said Straight. "You must have, at one time or another, prescribed muscarin. Yet it never occurred to you that the muscarin found in the patient's stomach was the drug rather than the poisoned mushroom?"

The doctor shook his head. Sitting back in his chair, with folded hands, his manners and voice were as impeccable as though at the bedside of his richest patient. "For obvious reasons, no! The poisonous substance found in the patient's stomach might have been either the extract or a constituent of the fly mushroom. It is impossible at that stage of digestion to differentiate between the two. But since the patient had eaten mushrooms for breakfast and since part of the contents of his stomach was the indigestible fiber of the mushrooms I naturally concluded that the poison was present in the fresh fungus. However," the doctor made a courteous gesture in Craig's direction, "when Mr. Craig suggested that I analyze the fruit lozenges on the person of the deceased I gladly cooperated with him."

"How many lozenges did you find poison on?" asked Piper gruffly.

"On one out of the four in the vest pocket."

"Was there enough on that one to kill a man?"

"Yes."

"How does muscarin taste?" inquired Straight.

"It is tasteless and odorless. And soluble," the doctor added as an afterthought. "In fact, when applied in powder form to the sugar coating of a fruit lozenge, it would be extremely difficult to detect."

"There was no chance of Quinn suspecting he was poisoned?"

"Almost none. The patient's first reaction, coming a few minutes after the taking of the poison, is an increased secretion of saliva and sweat and a stimulation of the motor centers, accompanied by an acute pain in the region of the heart. Paralysis follows shortly. The mind remains clear to the end. The action of muscarin, as a matter of fact, resembles very closely the action of the betel nut."

Straight nodded impatiently. "One more question, Doctor. Is it possible to purchase muscarin without a prescription?"

"I think not. In fact I'm certain that a prescription is necessary. Muscarin is toxic, and all toxic drugs—"

"Thank you, Doctor," Piper interrupted him.

"Not at all." Dr. Byrne arose. "If I can be of any further assistance—"

"We'll call on you," Straight assured him. "Murphy!" he called as the doctor left.

A large policeman appeared in the doorway.

"Murphy, have one of the men check up on every pharmacy and drugstore in Pasadena and Los Angeles. If any muscarin has been dispensed within the last year we want to know it. Here! I'll write down the name for you." He scribbled it down on a piece of paper which he handed to Murphy. "Probably a wild goose chase," he commented to Craig. "But it's part of the routine."

"A prospective murderer shouldn't buy his poison through the ordinary channels," agreed Craig.

The room provided by the hotel for the world's most celebrated astrophysicist was on the southwest corner of the sixteenth floor. Large, light, and conventionally furnished, it was unstamped by the personality of its most recent occupant. The bed was of metal painted to represent mahogany, and stood with its headboard against the west wall. It was covered by a spread of pale green rayon shot with silver. Above the bed hung an original oil of a Mexican woman in seductive mood. Two windows in the south wall led onto the iron balcony of the fire escape. Between them was an impractical Louis XVI desk with innumerable little drawers. The boudoir period was likewise represented by a low, flowered ottoman, delicate-legged tables, lamps, vases and tassels.

Craig had a good deal more respect for the bathroom. Highly-colored, economical of space and equipped with a superlative number of towels and soap cakes, it revealed to him sharply the ideal of American womanhood: voluptuous sanitation. Or sanitary voluptuousness. Magazine editors called it utilitarian beauty. Whatever it was, it sold

scented soaps, pastel toilet paper, lotions, disinfectants,
and bath salts in esthetic containers. It was a godsend to
manufacturers and a boon to housekeepers. Voluptuousness alone was immoral; sanitation alone was dull; the
combination was new, delightful, and virtuous.

On the other side of the bathroom was the valet's room,
smaller and with fewer lamps than Quinn's. But the Mexican lady biting a rose above the bed was equally arch.

Craig rejoined the detectives, who were going through
Quinn's closet. It revealed a precise row of coats, three
pairs of shoes toeing the base board and, on the shelf over-
head, a silk hat and a soft felt. Two of Quinn's suits, one
oxford gray and the other a lighter gray cloth of a her-
ring-bone weave, were for daily wear. In addition to these
were a Tuxedo, a pair of gray flannels, a tan Norfolk jacket,
a trench coat and a bathrobe.

"He was wearing a frock-coat, wasn't he?" asked Piper,
making a mental note of the contents of the closet. "How
about his overcoat?"

"Navy blue. And he wore a derby," answered Craig.

Straight glanced through the assortment of letters and
objects on the writing desk. All that had been found of
Quinn's correspondence was there, as well as the contents
of his various pockets and the objects he had been carrying
at the time of his death. The correspondence was divided
into two groups, personal and impersonal. After glancing
through the latter, which consisted largely of advertise-
ments, Straight slipped it, enclosed by a rubber band, into
the desk drawer. The personal letters he put into his portfolio for future reference. Quinn's check-book and nota-
tions, including a number of scientific papers, he left on
the desk along with a gold watch, keys, a leather wallet
containing sixty dollars, a box of matches and cigarettes,
a seal ring, a pencil and fountain pen.

His next concern was the bureau drawers. These, when opened, revealed a neat array of socks, shirts, collars, ties, pajamas and underwear; nothing more.

"Well," said Piper, "let's have the valet in."

"Wait a minute." Straight took several pipes from the ash tray on top of the bureau. "Good pipes," he said, handling them reverently.

"Give me a cigar," said Piper, pulling one from his vest pocket.

Craig strolled over to the bureau.

Straight took a round metal box lying beside the ash tray. "Tobacco, probably."

It contained, however, not tobacco, but a supply of the square, sugar-coated lozenges responsible for Quinn's death.

"Better have them analyzed," said Piper.

Straight called in a policeman and ordered him to take the candy to the city chemist for analysis. "And send in the valet," he added.

George Coburn, Quinn's valet, was a chubby, bow-legged little man with a pink face whose serenity, at present, was marred by a black eye just reaching the yellow-ish-green stage.

To questions concerning his nationality and background he replied in an accent that belied his cockney build that he was a Canadian, born in Montreal and by profession a jockey. In 1907, as a lad of seventeen, he had gone to England, where he had ridden up to the time of the war. His elaborations on the races in which he had placed and the stables whose colors he had worn were severely checked by Straight.

"And after the war," the detective interrupted a eulogy of a colt named Pillicoddy, "did you go back to racing?"

The former jockey shook his head sadly. "My racing days was over."

"Wounded?" asked Piper with a trace of sympathy.

"Worse than that." Coburn sighed. "I'd run to fat. Put on twenty-five pounds in four years. I was jolly well ruined, I was. Out of a job. That's what the war did to me."

Craig suppressed a smile.

"So the war made you fat," said Piper sarcastically. "Well, that's a new one."

"When did you start working for Quinn?" asked Straight.

"October, 1923," replied Coburn promptly. "His valet was an old buddy of mine, and when he quit service to go live on a ranch his aunt left him out in Australia, he says to me, 'Cobbie, you can have my job in settlement for that five quid I owes you.'"

"I see," said Straight. "And you've been working for Quinn ever since?"

"Yes, sir. And I can tell you anything you want to know about him. Intimate details and such."

"Not so fast, Mr. Coburn," said Straight. "There are still a few more things we want to know about you. How, for instance, did you come by that black eye?"

"Oh, that," said the valet fingering his eye gingerly. "Sir Arthur gave me that. And, if you don't mind, I'd just as soon you called me Cobbie. Sounds more natural."

"O.K., Cobbie," said Piper. "But how come you were sparring with your employer. Was that in your contract?"

Cobbie shook his head. "Can't say as how it was. But when you're working for a gentleman, especially a gentleman what's been knighted, you take things you wouldn't take from the lower classes." Walking over to the mirror he stood before it and experimented opening and closing his bruised eye.

"This time it's a pippin," he asserted proudly.

"This time," repeated Piper. "Was your employer in the habit of landing on you?"

Cobbie nodded cheerfully. "When he was feeling blue."

"And how often was that?"

"Every now and again. After scientific meetings or when he'd had a spot too much."

"Which was it this time?" asked Straight dryly.

"Well, it's hard to say, sir," said Cobbie with some embarrassment. "You see, it's one thing coming on top of another—"

"What came on top of what?"

"It sounds so piddling. If you know what I mean. But," Cobbie hesitated, then blurted out, "well, he caught me taking one of his blessed lozenges, that's what it was."

Straight repeated thoughtfully, "So he caught you taking a lozenge. When?"

Cobbie jumped at the sharpness of the question.

"When he came home to dress for the banquet. About six o'clock, I guess."

"You know you might have been poisoned."

"Golly!" Cobbie's hand flew to his mouth, and his eyes popped.

"So you did eat one?"

Cobbie nodded dumbly.

"Well, you weren't poisoned," Piper gruffly reassured him. "There may not even have been any poisoned lozenges in the box."

The valet looked puzzled. "You mean—"

"Don't strain your mind," said Straight quickly. "Your room's in there, is it?" With his elbow he indicated the door to his left.

"Yes, sir. On the other side of the bathroom."

"Oh," said Straight with a note of disappointment. "So you're on the other side of the bathroom. Then someone could have come in here Saturday afternoon without your knowing it."

Cobbie looked dubious. "I generally keep the doors between the rooms open. Especially when Sir Arthur's away.
That's on account of being in and out, pressing clothes
and the like."

"Let's see," said Piper, going and opening the door into
the bathroom. "Were you in there all day Saturday?" he
asked after a look into Cobbie's room.

"Most of the day. Yes, sir," answered Cobbie promptly. "I
was out to breakfast and lunch, but I had my tea sent up."

"What time did you go to lunch?"

"One o'clock. That's when Sir Arthur went to his luncheon. He had his breakfast here. About eleven that was."

"What time did you get back?"

"Not later than two. I had some work to do. We were
aiming to leave Monday. I mean today."

"How about your dinner?"

"It must have been around eight-thirty when I went
down. Sir Arthur wasn't out of the way until seven. And
I'd made a good tea, so I wasn't suffering any. When you're
working for gentlemen," he explained, "you jolly well get
used to their hours."

"Did you come straight back here from dinner?"

Cobbie nodded. "I was thinking of going to a movie,
but then, with my bad eye—"

"So you were here all afternoon and all evening?"

Cobbie nodded.

"What time did you go to bed?"

"Quarter of eleven. But I didn't sleep right off. I was
up bathing my eye most of the night. At least it seemed
that way."

"I see," said Piper perfunctorily. "Now while you were
on the job Saturday did you see or hear anyone in this
room? Anyone that had no business being here?"

Cobbie beamed. "Yes, sir!"

"Oh, you did?"

Cobbie's sense of importance increased visibly. "I wouldn't be surprised," he said, "if I could tell you a couple of things you don't know."

"What's holding you back?" asked Piper. "You've had twenty-four hours."

"Well, up to this morning I didn't know Sir Arthur was poisoned. First it's heart and then it's mushrooms and now it's poison. Downright confusing, that's what it is. And if the doctors say heart or mushrooms, how am I to know it ain't either one but something else again. And how am I to know anything I say'll cut any ice!"

"All right! All right!" exploded Piper.

Cobbie continued to wear an aggrieved expression.

"What have you got to tell?" Straight asked.

"Plenty!" replied the valet authoritatively. "There was a man in here Saturday that had no business being here. He sneaked up the fire escape, the little rat!"

"What time was that?"

"Seven o'clock. Sir Arthur had just gone down to dinner, and I was in the bathroom putting a cold towel to my shiner."

Piper tried the window leading onto the fire escape. "Locked."

"It wasn't locked Saturday," maintained Cobbie.

"What was he doing when you found him?"

"That's the funny part. He wasn't doing nothing to speak of. Just standing by the bureau turning the pages of the Bible." Cobbie shook his head and concluded philosophically, "Cuckoo, I guess."

"Was the lozenge box on the bureau?" asked Straight sharply.

Cobbie's good eye brightened. "Yes, by golly! I never thought of that. But where is the box?"

"We're taking care of it," Piper assured him.

Straight asked, "What sort of a looking man was he?"

Cobbie considered. "He wasn't so short. About my height," he added, making himself as tall as possible. "But skinny. Sort of a peewee, if you know what I mean. And he wore glasses, the kind that's cut like this all the way around." With his finger Cobbie described an octangle.

"How old was he?"

"Thirty, maybe. Maybe forty."

"That's definite. What was he wearing?"

"A brown suit."

"No hat or overcoat?"

Cobbie shook his head resolutely.

"What did he say when he saw you?"

"He said, 'Who are you?' Cool as a cucumber!"

"Go on."

"'I'm Sir Arthur's valet,' I says. 'Who are you?'" Cobbie, carried away by his recollection of the scene, assumed a belligerent attitude.

"Well?" demanded Piper impatiently.

Cobbie's hands dropped to his sides. "Then he called me Philip."

"Philip?"

Cobbie nodded. "'Have I been here so long and dost thou not know me, Philip?' he says. Honest!" Cobbie heaved a sigh. "I just looked at him."

"Philip?" repeated Straight in a puzzled voice.

Craig started to laugh. Piper and Straight, for the first time, regarded him with interest.

Cobbie smiled companionably. "Funny, ain't it?"

"It is funny," agreed Craig, arising. "I wonder if I could see the Bible in question. Where do you keep it?"

Cobbie hesitated. Then, with some embarrassment, he went to the small table beside the bed and opened the lower compartment. Taking out the Bible, he handed it to Craig. "It wasn't my doing," he explained. "Sir Arthur put it there Sunday morning. Before he went to church. I'd been telling him about this nut."

"What did he say?" asked Straight.

Cobbie shrugged his shoulders. "Nothing. He just pops the Bible in there. Sir Arthur never was one to talk much. He'd smile but he wouldn't talk. You'd never know what he was thinking."

Craig had been glancing through the Bible. "'Have I been so long time with you, and yet hast thou not known me, Philip?'" he read.

"That's it! That's it!" cried Cobbie.

"John 14:9," said Craig. "Whoever the man was, he evidently thought of himself as Jesus."

"I knew it," maintained Cobbie.

"Never mind what you knew," commanded Piper. "Go on with your account."

"Well," said Cobbie, frowning in a valiant effort to concentrate on facts, "there wasn't much more. 'My name isn't Philip,' I says, 'and you'd better clear out. If you don't I'll call the office.' That got him!" Cobbie nodded with satisfaction. "He says, 'I'll go. My business is with your master. Not with you.' Then he hands me the book and says he's marked a passage, and before you could say Jack Robinson he'd skinned through the window. That's when I locked the window."

"No idea what passage he marked?" asked Straight.

Cobbie shook his head.

"What's the difference?" said Piper.

Craig continued to glance through the last section of the Bible. "Considering his delusion," he remarked, "it's almost certain to be in the New Testament." A few minutes later he handed the open book to Straight.

"'For the wrath of God is revealed from heaven against all ungodliness and unrighteousness of men, who hold the truth in unrighteousness,'" read Straight slowly.

"It's the only marked passage I came across," said Craig.

4

"Could you recognize this man if you saw him again?" Piper asked the valet.

Cobbie nodded emphatically.

"Murphy!" shouted Piper.

The policeman entered from the hall.

"Murphy!" ordered Piper. "Take this man to headquarters. I want him to look through the rogues' gallery. When he's through bring him back."

"Yes, sir," said Murphy. "And we've got the night clerks waiting out here. Do you want them in?"

"Might as well see them next."

Straight nodded. "Send them in."

Cobbie, about to be led away, held back. Straight had his back turned, but Piper, who was lighting a cigar, asked, "What is it?"

"If you don't mind, sir . . . when's the funeral?" asked Cobbie.

Straight turned. "Whenever Lady Quinn gets here."

"Oh," said Cobbie with a curious inflection. He scratched his ear.

Piper's suspicions were instantly aroused. "Why the 'oh'?" he demanded.

"Know anything about her whereabouts?" asked Straight.

"All I know is that we left her in San Francisco visiting Mrs. Easterbrook."

"She isn't there now," growled Piper. "And she wasn't there yesterday morning when Radford tried to get hold of her."

"It's past me," said Cobbie, shaking his head disapprovingly. "She said she'd stay till we stopped there for her on our way back to England. Did you talk to Mrs. Easterbrook?"

"She said Lady Quinn went out early Saturday morning. Didn't take her suitcases or leave any word."

Cobbie stood for a moment, lost in thought. Murphy looked inquiringly at Piper, who replied, "O.K."

"Wait a minute," said Cobbie, pulling away from the policeman. "Maybe I was dreaming . . . I thought I was at the time . . . but now, according to what you say, maybe I wasn't." He paused and then, jabbing the air with his forefinger, he announced impressively, "She was in here Saturday night, she was. I'll swear it!"

"Lady Quinn?"

"Yes, sir. Lady Quinn! I'd know her voice in a million."

"You're sure of this, are you?"

Cobbie nodded so vigorously that his large head seemed about to topple off its inadequate neck. "I didn't mention it before," he explained, "because, being so sure as how Lady Quinn was in San Francisco . . . If you know what I mean. And I wouldn't mention it now only—"

"Only what?"

"If what you says is right," concluded Cobbie lamely, "she wasn't in San Francisco."

"What did you hear?" asked Straight.

"It wasn't so much what I heard," said Cobbie cautiously.

"What time was it?"

"Late-ish. The last time I wet the towel on my eye it was when I got up to answer the telephone. That was eleven-

thirty. Then I didn't fall right off. It must have been getting on toward morning."

"Could you hear what they were talking about?"

"No, sir. But, whatever it was, they was saying it jolly
loud. It woke me up."

"Were the doors closed?"

"The door between Sir Arthur's room and the bathroom
was closed. My door was half-way."

"I see," said Straight. "And you didn't get up?"

"Well, sir . . ." The admittance seemed to cause Cobbie
some chagrin. "As a matter of fact, I did. Some nights I
helped Sir Arthur off with his clothes," he added quickly.

"You went in the bathroom?" asked Straight.

"Yes, sir."

"You didn't get a look at the lady?"

"No, sir. The key was in the keyhole. On the other side
of the door. And I didn't dare open the door because . . .
well, I had one black eye."

Cobbie's discretion caused no comment. "How long did
they talk?" asked Straight.

"They stopped right away, sir. That's why I couldn't be
too sure it was Lady Quinn."

"A minute ago you said you'd know her voice in a million." Piper's eyes were accusing.

"I would," asserted Cobbie. "But the only word I really
caught clear was Arthur. And you can't go much by that."

"You said they stopped talking?" said Straight. "Did
the woman leave?"

"Yes, sir. I heard the door open and close hard. That's
all I heard. And then I skinned back to bed."

"You heard nothing more that night?"

Cobbie shook his head.

"All right," said Straight. "Go on with Murphy and see if
you can identify the man with the Bible. Send in the hotel
clerks, Murphy. But, first ask one of the boys to step in."

Murphy and Cobbie left.

"Search the valet's room!" Straight ordered the policeman sent in by Murphy. "With a fine-tooth comb!"

Johnson and Kravick, the two night clerks, were both fairly young men of the cosmopolitan class found in de luxe hotels. Johnson, who was on duty from four p.m. until midnight, had no significant information. Kravick reported that shortly after he came on duty Sir Arthur had come in. Neither man remembered answering any question in the course of Saturday night concerning Sir Arthur or his room number.

Straight, obviously disappointed by their lack of information, dismissed the two clerks.

"The valet must have been dreaming when he thought he heard Quinn's wife," said Piper. "She'd have had to get the room number at the desk."

"She might have gotten it from the elevator boy," said Straight. "Or Quinn might have written it to her."

"Or she might be psychic," scoffed Piper. "Well, I'm damned if I think she was here at all!"

"Where, then?" argued Straight. "She's not in San Francisco."

Piper pushed back his chair and stood up. At that moment the telephone rang violently. Piper strode over to it. "Hello," he shouted.

At the end of the conversation he put down the receiver more gently than he had taken it up. "Maybe she was here," he said, turning to Straight.

"Lady Quinn?"

"Yes. The San Francisco police are on her trail. When she didn't show up Saturday night her friend notified the police."

"Have they found her?" demanded Straight.

"No." Piper took a cigar from his pocket, bit off the end and spit it out. "But a woman answering to the description of Lady Quinn was on the *Patricia* when she sailed from San Pedro Sunday morning."

"She was here, then," said Straight. "Where is she now? Are they holding her in 'Frisco?"

Piper shook his head. "When the boat docked at 'Frisco this dame was missing. Not a sign of her: no luggage or anything. They checked up on her and found that the name she'd used was Lady Quinn's maiden name: Beryl Ashcroft."

"Missing," said Straight. "I'll be damned."

"It looks to me," announced Piper, "like the valet was right. Lady Quinn was here. She quarreled with her old man, left him some poisoned lozenges, and then pulls a fake suicide. What do you think, Mr. Craig?"

Craig smiled. "Why not? As the Chinese say: It is only the natural piety of females that allows any husband to reach old age."

The cross-examination of a number of other hotel employees—elevator boys, chambermaids, telephone girls, anyone in fact who might be able to verify Lady Quinn's presence in the hotel on Saturday night—was cut short by a telephone call. It was from police headquarters, and it was to the effect that Mrs. Easterbrook, Lady Quinn's hostess, had flown down from San Francisco and was on her way from the airport to the hotel.

A few minutes later she arrived. Ultramodern in dress, and possessed of an orchid corsage, a set of artificial teeth and a contralto voice, she made an entrance whose effectiveness was lost on the two detectives. Not until she drew off her gloves and loosened the collar of her caracul coat was it apparent that this radiant widow was within a short radius of fifty.

The preliminary introductions over, she lost no time in producing odds and ends of information. "We were going shopping Saturday," she began in her rich, drawling voice. "I'd told the chauffeur nine o'clock. I'd made an appointment with the hair-dresser. I'm going to make you over, darling, I told her. What if he is a few years younger? He wasn't so much younger than Beryl. She and I were at school together in Switzerland. Well, six or eight years younger. Have you a cigarette?"

Craig lighted a cigarette for her.

"My doctor said, 'Don't go; your blood pressure is two hundred now.' Of course I came. I shall live on carrots and rutabagas all next week, I promised, and strike me pink if I eat at Victor Hugo's. But, oh," she appealed to Craig, "have you tried their *poularde Strasbourgeoise?* Stuffed with *foie gras*. You can't imagine! And, think of it—I've never seen Sir Arthur! Whenever I was in London he was on the continent. I don't suppose it will be quite the same: seeing him now, I mean. Although the undertakers nowadays are real artists." She sighed. "He must have been very handsome. I told Beryl if she'd only let me take her in hand. . . . 'These women you're jealous of,' I said. 'Do you suppose God tinted their fingernails and plucked their eyebrows? At least you're tall and thin.' . . . 'Keep the whole day open,' I told Antoine. 'You must make her husband love her.' I think he could have."

Straight took advantage of the pause to inquire: "It was agreed, wasn't it, that Lady Quinn was to stay in San Francisco until her husband arrived there?"

Mrs. Easterbrook nodded. "I'd sent out invitations for a dinner for Tuesday night. The British Consul and his wife. . . . I'd sent to Portland for crayfish. Beryl seemed quite her old self. We'd been to a movie, and when we came home . . . well, you know what San Francisco fog can be . . . there's nothing like a highball. But don't tell my doctor, I said. I'd ordered champagne for the dinner. Magnums." Mrs. Easterbrook paused and shook her head in a puzzled manner. "I don't know what it could have been. We were sitting there reading the evening papers. Beryl liked the *Examiner* so much better than the London *Times*. I thought maybe the highball had gone to her head. People differ so. You'd never guess to look at me how much I can take. She turned so red. And tears in her eyes! 'What's the matter, darling?' I asked. But she insisted on going straight to bed, though just a minute before she said she'd love a game of dominoes."

"Was that the last time you saw her?" asked Straight.

"The last time. I wish I'd kissed her. But I did think it was the highball."

"What time Saturday morning did you discover Lady Quinn had left?"

Mrs. Easterbrook tucked her handkerchief back into her bag. "My maid discovered it. I sent her to ask Beryl if she wanted to come in and have breakfast with me. Naturally when Marie came back and said that Lady Quinn wasn't in her room I said, 'You silly girl! Look in the bathroom!' But she wasn't in the bathroom. I looked myself."

"Did anyone see her leave?"

"No." Mrs. Easterbrook turned to Craig. "Are there any more questions you want to ask me, or may I go now and look at Sir Arthur?"

Craig referred her question to Straight.

"You can go," replied Straight dryly. "I don't think there's anything else. Are you returning to San Francisco at once?"

Mrs. Easterbrook nodded. "But if you need me again, just wire and I'll fly straight down." She drew Craig aside. "If you're not too busy why not have lunch with me at Victor Hugo's? My doctor will never know."

Craig shook his head. "I'm sorry," he said with a smile that caused Mrs. Easterbrook to bridle with delight. "Interested as I am in *poularde Strasbourgeoise,* I'm more interested in discovering why Lady Quinn left San Francisco on such short notice."

"Did you say Victor Hugo's?" inquired Piper with obvious interest.

Mrs. Easterbrook regarded him haughtily. "Yes, I said Victor Hugo's. Good-by."

Piper, with forced nonchalance, puffed at his cigar.

"Murphy!" called Straight.

The policeman appeared instantly.

"How about that search of Cobbie's room? Anything to report?"

"Not a thing, sir. They made a thorough job of it, too."

Straight received the announcement with obvious disappointment.

Piper reached for his hat. "While you're looking for skeletons," he declared sarcastically, "and Craig is finding out why the old lady left San Francisco, I'm going out to lunch."

5

"I'm going to the public library," said Craig, finishing the sandwich and glass of milk that constituted his lunch. "Want to come along?"

"The public library!" Blake looked aghast, one of his theories being that indiscriminate education was a curse. "My Lord! What next?" Voicing his protestations against the schools that taught people how to read, the men who wrote books for them to read, and the publishers who printed the books, he followed Craig.

The reference room, toward which they directed their steps, was thronged as usual with vagrants of varying nationalities. There were very few women. Craig, with the expediency that characterized all his actions, found what he was after, the San Francisco *Examiner* for the previous Friday, and sat down at one of the long tables to read it. Blake dropped into a chair beside him.

At the same table were an Englishman with an active Adam's apple, studying a book on bird life, an Italian audibly puzzling over a Genoese newspaper, a Filipino devouring a book on thermodynamics, a sailor whose eyes wandered constantly from the travel book before him, and a school-boy taking notes on the Diet of Worms.

The surrounding tables presented much the same picture. Of all the men in the room, and there were at least

a hundred, Craig and Blake alone represented the upper
ten per cent of society—Craig, especially, with his narrow,
well-shaped head and his lean face, bronzed still from a
summer of tuna fishing and bathing, that might in one or
two more generations have become decadent. More sensitive or flexible lips, a slightly sharper nose, paler blue eyes,
and it would be the type of face possessed by the amiable
and worthless young men who are sent by their families to
rubber plantations, only to leave them on stretchers.

Craig, himself, was aware of this quality in his appearance and used it as an excuse for not marrying. Eugenical-
ly speaking, he claimed, I should marry a peasant: good
earthy stock. If I marry according to my inclinations our
children will look like Hollywood juveniles.

Whatever truth there was in this statement, as his blue
eyes roamed, item by item, over the pages of the San Francisco *Examiner*, and he pushed back now and then the lock
of straight blond hair that distracted them, Craig, even
without the contrast of the dilapidated men around him,
was vigorous and keen.

"Any news?" asked Blake after a long series of yawns.
"How many airplanes did the Japanese build on Friday?
Tell me if you find any nightgowns on sale."

Craig, ignoring his friend's interruptions, continued to
scan the newspaper. Finally, taking out his notebook, he
copied a paragraph into it.

"The look in your eye tells me you're ready to put the
screws on someone," said Blake. "Who is it this time?"

There was no smile on Craig's face as he replied, "The
usual *belle dame sans merci.*"

Straight, Piper and Cobbie, all looking exceedingly
bored, were in Quinn's room when Craig arrived there.

"I thought you were the copper what went after my
lunch," said Cobbie in an aggrieved tone. "I'm starved, I

am. Looking at mugs all morning. And then it was a waste of time."

"So your friend wasn't among the rogues?" asked Craig.

"We have a new line on him," explained Piper. "Some prof telephoned the sergeant. Said a Russian student tried to attack Quinn after his lecture Saturday afternoon."

"That's what was eating him," interrupted Cobbie, nursing his black eye. "He was taking out the Russian on me."

"He sounds like the same man," continued Piper. "Anyway, we sent for him. He ought to be here now."

A knock followed immediately on his statement. Straight opened the door to admit a policeman.

"The chemist's report, sir."

Straight glanced through it before dismissing the man. "No poisoned lozenges in this batch," he announced.

"That lets out the Russian," said Piper with obvious regret.

"How come?"

"I thought the dope was that he planted the poisoned lozenges in the box."

"Exactly," confirmed Straight. "He put them in the box and Quinn scooped them up Sunday morning before going to church. Did you ever put the lozenges in Quinn's vest pocket for him?" he asked Cobbie.

Cobbie shook his head. "I never touched them, not as a rule, that is. Sir Arthur took some from the box every morning. And sometimes he carried a few in his overcoat pocket."

Straight went to the closet. "None there now," he announced after an investigation. "Well, as I see it, there's no way of knowing whether the poisoned lozenges were put in the box or whether they were slipped into his vest pocket or his overcoat pocket."

Piper, with a look of disgust, spit into an ashtray. Cobbie sighed. "The porkers that furnishes the ham for ham sandwiches must've gone on a five-year plan."

A few minutes later two plain-clothes men brought in the Russian. Undersized and anemic, the disparity between his large head and narrow frame made him resemble a caricature. It was obvious that he was intelligent; his brown eyes, behind the octagonal spectacles that had so impressed Cobbie, were alert; and his features expressed a sensibility that was almost feminine. It was equally obvious that he was an egomaniac governed by the pride and determination and self-confidence that the misfit in society resorts to. Craig felt at once that it would be impossible to like him, since liking implied a feeling of kinship, and, between this Russian and any other man there must always be the unbridgeable gap of his distrust and self-consciousness. It was difficult even to pity him.

"That's him," Cobbie announced with great importance and without an instant's hesitation. "Hello, there!"

The Russian replied to his greeting with a contemptuous stare.

"You know why you've been summoned?" asked Straight.

"Yes."

"What's your name?"

"Victor Yenei."

"Nationality?"

"I am an American citizen."

"Born in Russia?"

"Yes."

"Age?"

"Twenty-nine."

"You're a student at Western Tech?"

"Yes."

"How do you make a living?"

"In the summer I work in canneries. I live on very little."

"That's no lie," said one of the plain-clothes men.

"Is it true that last Saturday afternoon you tried to at-tack Sir Arthur Quinn?"

"Yes."

"And that you entered this room Saturday evening by way of the fire-escape?"

"Yes."

Straight took the Bible from a drawer, opened it to a marker, and handed it to Yenei. "Did you mark this pas-sage?"

"Yes."

"Was it intended as a threat?"

"Naturally."

"Why did you threaten Quinn's life? What did you have against him?"

"He was an enemy of society and a discredit to sci-ence. He sneered at the Divine Plan and used his scientific knowledge as a weapon against the Creator."

Piper and Straight, rather taken aback by this calm ex-position, looked at one another.

"Under the guise of progress and rationalism, he preached skepticism. And because he was clever in manip-ulating scientific theory and because he denounced faith as naiveté, and belief as herd suggestion, the world be-lieved him. Scientific knowledge was the price he offered for human souls."

"I thought you were studying science," said Straight.

"That is why I am equipped to point out the fallacies in his devilish arguments," replied Yenei sternly. "It is my destiny to prove to mankind that science confirms God. It is my privilege to interpret in His Name the principle of Indeterminacy and the second law of thermodynamics. It is I who must rid the world of the teaching of such hereti-cal scientists as Sir Arthur Quinn."

"That's the way it is," said Piper.

Cobble's mouth hung open. The two plainclothes men were openly doubtful of Yenei's sanity.

"So you poisoned him," said Straight in a matter-of-fact tone.

"No," denied Yenei. "God saved me for His other missions. Another hand than mine silenced Sir Arthur Quinn's voice."

Straight nodded. "We'll see. Lock him up," he told his men. "I'll arrange about the charge later."

Yenei made no trouble. A moment after his departure, Murphy entered the room carrying a large paper bag. "The sandwiches, sir," he said, setting it down on the table.

Cobbie's face lighted up. "I could jolly well eat the rump steak of a race-horse," he announced, reaching eagerly for the bag. "You didn't forget the mustard?"

Murphy shook his head positively. "I did not."

Cobbie thrust his hand into the bag. His grin faded. "It don't feel like a ham sandwich," he exclaimed, pulling out a chicken head.

Piper roared with laughter.

"Playing practical jokes, Murphy?" asked Straight.

"No, sir," replied Murphy, the puzzled look on his face changing to consternation. "But, come to think of it, there was a woman next to me getting scraps for her dog. The waitress must have got fussed and switched the bags."

"Next time don't get her fussed," said Piper. Murphy blushed scarlet.

"And what isn't heads is feet," asserted Cobbie bitterly, hurling the bag to the floor.

Straight stood up. "For God's sake, Murphy," he said, "take him out and buy him some lunch."

Cobbie jumped up with alacrity.

"Yes, sir," said Murphy humbly.

"And take those chicken heads with you."

"Yes, sir," said Murphy, stooping over to pick up the paper bag.

"And don't get him drunk."

"No, sir," said Murphy with intense humility. Turning to Cobbie, he jerked his head in the direction of the door. "Come on, you!" he blustered.

"That Russian doesn't strike me as a killer," said Piper.

Straight shook his head. "You can't tell about that sort. Clever as hell, and trickier. The only way to get at them is to break them down."

"Give him the works," suggested Piper.

"That won't do it. I've seen a Russian hold out after a grilling that would raise a cold sweat on a clam. A few days in solitary may help, though."

"The more I think about it," said Piper, "the more I think it's the wife. What do you want to bet they never find the body?"

"But what brought her down here?" speculated Straight. "When a woman goes four hundred and seventy miles to kill her husband, she has a damned good reason."

"I've never seen them go that far for any reason but jealousy," commented Piper dryly.

"Jealousy," repeated Straight meditatively. "How about a look at Quinn's check-book?"

Lona Lang introduced Craig to her three protégées, who went under the names of Yolande, Mirande and Melisande. Attractive girls of three distinct and striking types, they nevertheless lacked the power to command interest that was possessed to such a large degree by the older dancer. It was not so much physical as a quality of mind and expression, for they were all three much prettier than she. Craig, in fact, was surprised that she should have chosen for her protégées three girls of such conventional prettiness.

Mirande was of the baby-doll type, small-boned, demure, and pastel in coloring; Yolande and Melisande gave the impression of being taller and more mature; they were both brunettes, one in a lustrous Hebraic way, the other more moderately so. All three were dressed uniformly in navy blue, and possessed the high-pitched voices that Craig had discovered were common among dancers.

"I'm looking forward to Wednesday night," said Craig. "The last time I had the pleasure of seeing you dance was two years ago in Prague."

"Prague," said Mirande with a grimace. "The State Theater. How I hate State Theaters. Tacks in the floor, and the performance started at six. I can still smell beer and oranges."

"Now you're smelling the Berlin Schauspielhaus," Craig corrected her.

"Berlin?" She laughed a dancer's quick, vivacious laugh. "Oranges . . . Berlin. Maybe."

"Go and do your shopping, girls," Lona told them. "Yolande," she addressed the grave brunette, "don't forget to stop at the jeweler's for my watch. See that Mirande mails the letter she wrote home last night. Did you write it, Mirande?"

Mirande's lashes closed over her china-blue eyes, and two panels of straight yellow hair fell forward over her cheeks.

"Write it before you go out," admonished Lona severely. "Melisande! Remember, no candy or ice cream!"

The three girls left the room. Lona Lang looked quietly at Craig. "You were with Sir Arthur Saturday night; in the lobby."

Craig nodded.

"He was my friend," said the dancer. "Twenty years ago, for one month, we were lovers. Is that what you want to know?"

"Why are you telling me?" asked Craig.

"Because it is the only way to make you realize how complete and real our friendship was. A man and a woman of our temperament cannot be friends without having been lovers, and while they are lovers they are not friends. Can you believe that?"

"About you and Sir Arthur, yes," said Craig.

"Why?"

"You're intelligent and you have outlets, other than the purely physical, for your emotions. Is that it?"

"Yes. You do see."

"But Lady Quinn didn't," said Craig.

The dancer arose and turned away. "Lady Quinn was older than her husband."

"I know."

"She was plain."

"Yes," said Craig.

"It was her uncle, Lord Ashcroft, who arranged for Sir Arthur to be knighted."

"I see."

The dancer turned and faced Craig. "Do you? Can you? I wonder."

"Is it complicated?" asked Craig. "A plain woman jealous of her celebrated husband."

"Complicated?" Her gray eyes were suddenly casual, and a sarcastic smile played on her thin lips. "For the woman and her husband, certainly. For you and me . . ." She shrugged her shoulders.

Craig took out his notebook, opened it and handed it to her. "This was in the Friday edition of the San Francisco *Examiner.*"

"But it's only a press notice," she said, glancing up. "It's quite true; I did cancel my Middle-West engagements in order to appear in Los Angeles on Wednesday."

"Lady Quinn read that story Friday evening," said Craig. "Saturday morning she left San Francisco."

"I've read the latest extra." The dancer lighted a cigarette.

"Was that your first intimation of Lady Quinn's visit to Pasadena?"

"No."

Craig felt suddenly that she was amused. Unaccountably amused. Was she so volatile, he wondered? Was she capable of swift changes of mood: sincerity, bitterness, amusement, all in the space of a few minutes? Or had he been mistaken in his first judgment? Meeting her hard, satirical glance, it was difficult to believe she had ever been genuinely candid and sincere.

"No," she repeated. "Your worst fears are confirmed: the social comedy has turned into farce, bedroom farce. Saturday night Lady Quinn found her husband in my room."

"And then?" asked Craig.

"My part was played. I went to bed. Alone." With a curious, slow smile at him, she turned away.

"One more question: Was Quinn wearing his overcoat when he arrived?"

The dancer shook her head.

Returning to Quinn's room, which was just around a bend in the hallway, Craig found it invaded by reporters. Straight and Piper, at one end of the room, were giving out stories. At the other end a pretty girl was smiling fixedly at the lens of a camera.

The photographer looked around. "He'll do for a customer," he announced. "Come on over and get in the picture. You're buying candy from this young lady. Understand?"

"Sorry," said Craig. "But I don't think I do."

"Hello, there," Piper's greeting was unexpectedly cordial. "What do you think?"

"I think," replied Craig, with an appreciative glance at the photographer's subject, "that she's pretty enough to sell Peruvian bonds. What do you think?"

The girl dimpled with pleasure.

Piper walked over to her. "This little lady," he said, pinching her affectionately, "has just come through with a great piece of detective work. She works in the candy store downstairs here. And when she read in the papers how Quinn was poisoned and that he was sitting between Radford and a Jap, she remembered that on Saturday evening she sold some fruit lozenges to a Jap."

"In a dress suit," added the girl, pulling her skirt an inch higher over her knees.

"In a dress suit," agreed Piper enthusiastically.

"By the way," asked Craig of Straight, who had finished with the reporter, "what was the result of the check you had made on the local pharmacies?"

"Not worth a damn. Only six sales within the last month, all O.K. I told Murphy to drop it."

"After all," said Craig thoughtfully, "Western Tech has a well-equipped pharmaceutical school."

"Have all the scientists access to its supplies?"

Craig nodded. "They're kept locked up, of course. On account of the students. But the faculty has access to them. And even though there's a boy in charge, it would be fairly easy, while his back was turned, to get away with something, I know Blake occasionally does."

"Find out how large a supply of muscarin they have," ordered Straight. "No! I'll send Murphy. If it's in a bottle there may be fingerprints."

6

The results of Murphy's visit to the pharmaceutical laboratory were disappointing. No fingerprints were found on the bottle containing muscarin; and the lad in charge was unable to say whether or not the supply had diminished.

Straight dismissed the policeman.

"I guess that angle's out," said Piper with a yawn.

"Mind if I look at this?" Craig indicated Quinn's checkbook, which was lying on the desk.

"Go ahead," said Straight. "You won't learn much. And there's no way of checking up on his balance because he and his wife had a joint checking account."

The book, issued on a New York bank, was more than half full of blank checks; the used stubs bore only neat entries of deposits and withdrawals. Craig, glancing through them, noted many more deposits than withdrawals, most of them an even thousand dollars. Quinn's bankbook and the receipts for deposits mailed by him to the bank testified to the accuracy of his entries in the checkbook. His first deposit, made evidently while he was in New York, for it was one of the three in the bank-book, had been for fifteen hundred dollars; his last, dated January third, for one thousand.

"One grand for a lecture," said Piper, looking over Craig's shoulder. "How do they get that way?"

"It's quite a lot, considering he didn't sing," remarked Craig placidly.

"Didn't sing," repeated Piper with a puzzled stare. "You don't mean sing?"

Craig shook his head. "Let it pass," he said, smiling. "I should have known better."

"I didn't think he was a singer," observed Piper agreeably.

Again glancing quickly through the stubs Craig noticed that the only large checks had been in payment for hotel bills; the smaller ones were mostly made out to cash.

"Think of never knowing what your balance is," exclaimed Piper. "You might be overdrawn and not know it."

"I think you'd find out eventually."

"Well, I'm damned if I'd have a joint account with my wife." Piper spoke with conviction.

Straight, who was playing solitaire at the other side of the room, looked around. "I thought you were a bachelor."

"I am," said Piper. "And at that I'm overdrawn. You couldn't lend me a fiver till pay-day, could you?"

"I could not."

There was a knock on the door and Straight shoved his cards off the table into the waste basket. "Here he is," he said. "For God's sake, Piper! Button up."

"Button up?" queried Piper, standing. "Oh? My collar."

Craig opened the door to admit Yozan Saijo in the custody of two policemen. Small and sleek as a terrier between two collies, he held himself with the same fastidious aloofness that Craig had marked Sunday morning as Saijo walked down the church aisle between Radford and Quinn. The tragedy, with its train of melodrama, did not seem to have altered him in any way. His face, less yellow than parchment-colored, was calm and unlined; and Craig wondered that, with such a gift for unexpressiveness, the Japanese were not better politicians.

With great formality the Japanese bowed. "Mr. Craig," he enunciated.

Craig introduced the two detectives.

"Now then, Mr. Saijo," said Straight, "let's get to the point. You bought twenty cents worth of fruit lozenges at the hotel candy shop on Saturday evening."

Saijo indicated his assent.

"Good. Now will you please tell us for what reason you wanted those lozenges."

"To eat."

"Oh?" said Piper. "To eat?"

"Are you in the habit of buying fruit lozenges?" asked Straight.

"No."

"I suppose seeing Quinn eat fruit lozenges made you think you'd like some. Is that it?"

His gentle acquiescence infuriated Piper. "If Quinn had been eating birdseed I suppose you'd have gone out and bought birdseed!"

Saijo nodded. "Yes."

"Listen," said Straight, "you're not helping yourself any by saying yes to everything."

Saijo raised his eyebrows. "But I mean yes."

"That doesn't make sense." Piper leaned forward pugnaciously. "He's not such a fool as he makes out," he argued in response to Straight's frown.

"Thank you," said Saijo.

"See here, Mr. Saijo," said Straight, "you might as well know right now that you're in a bad spot. We don't know anything about your relations with the deceased, but we do know that on Saturday night you bought some lozenges like Quinn's and that on Sunday morning you sat next to him in church. Those two items alone are enough to incriminate you."

"President Radford sat on the other side of the deceased," said Saijo.

"What's that got to do with it?"

Saijo shrugged his shoulders.

"Did you buy those lozenges with the intention of poisoning Quinn?" shot out Straight.

The faintest flicker of surprise disturbed the exquisite calm of Saijo's feature. His polite "No" contrasted dramatically with the detective's bluntness.

Straight leaned back in an attitude of exasperation. Piper scratched his head.

"Perhaps Mr. Saijo meant what he said," suggested Craig.

"All I've heard is yes and no," exclaimed Piper.

Craig turned to the Japanese. "Those gentlemen would like to know why you particularly wanted lozenges like Sir Arthur's."

"I think they will not understand."

"We'll understand," said Straight.

"At the banquet," said Saijo, "Sir Arthur made the statement that the Japanese are third-rate scientists. I was resentful. He had disparaged my people. I wished to disparage him. How will I do it? I thought. To take notice of his remark will deprive me of my dignity. I must not take notice of this remark." Saijo paused. The bland expression on his face did not alter as he looked from one to another of his three listeners.

"You are familiar with Japanese art," he continued in his modulated, unhurried voice.

Piper, though he looked deeply pained, made no reservations to this statement.

"You know our definition of painting: to so represent an object or scene as to express its essential attributes with the fewest possible number of strokes."

"Is this necessary?" asked Straight. "This . . . discourse on painting."

"I am answering your question. I am telling you why I bought lozenges like Sir Arthur's."

"I'd never have guessed it," said Piper.

"I wished," said Saijo, "to express his essential attributes with the fewest possible number of strokes."

Craig observed with delight the perplexity on the faces of the two detectives. "Will you forgive me, Mr. Saijo," he asked, "if I add a common analogy to your admirable explanation?"

The Japanese bowed his head.

"If Mr. Saijo had been a cartoonist," explained Craig, "he would have exposed Quinn to ridicule by drawing a cartoon of him. In short, by emphasizing his main characteristics. Like this." Whipping out his pencil, Craig quickly sketched a crude cartoon of Quinn.

"Damned good!" approved Piper. "Do one of me, will you?"

"As Mr. Saijo is not a cartoonist," Craig went on, "he intended to expose Quinn to ridicule by selecting and imitating his most individual mannerism: that of eating lozenges in public. Is that right, Mr. Saijo?"

Saijo again bowed his head.

"Eating a lozenge doesn't strike me as being much of a way to expose anyone to ridicule," observed Straight.

"Perhaps Mr. Saijo will give us a demonstration," suggested Craig.

"Certainly." With infinite restraint Saijo duplicated Quinn's gestures.

A broad smile spread over Piper's face. "Say! you ought to be on the stage."

"Pretty clever," admitted Straight, regarding Saijo with a calculating eye. "Pretty clever!"

Saijo received the compliment with a deprecatory gesture.

"When are you leaving Pasadena?" asked Piper. Before Saijo could answer, there was a knock on the door and a policeman put in his head. "President Radford's here."

"Just a minute," said Straight. "We're through with you for the present," he told the Japanese.

Bowing to each of the three men in turn, Saijo left.

"Check up on him," Straight ordered the policeman. "Get everything you can and report back to me this afternoon. Send Radford in."

"Wonder what the old boy wants?" speculated Piper.

"Good afternoon! Good afternoon!" Radford jauntily greeted Craig and the detectives. "Don't get up. Don't get up!"

But they were already on their feet. Radford put his derby on the table and sat down in an easy chair. "Just thought I'd see how you were getting along. No new developments?"

"Nothing conclusive," replied Straight. "We're working on several lines."

"Naturally, naturally!" Radford took a handful of cigars from his vest pocket. "The case is still young. Here! Have a cigar!"

Piper accepted with alacrity. Straight and Craig refused.

The President lighted up, and for a moment conversation lagged.

"What do you think of the political situation?" asked Piper sociably.

"The political situation?" Radford looked startled. "Is there something new?"

"I don't know," said Piper. "But I thought you might."

The President cleared his throat. "Of course, you men are aware," he began genially, "you don't need me to tell you that the eyes of the entire world are on us right now. Scotland Yard cabled to know if they could be of any assistance. Private detective bureaus have offered their services. And unless we can get this matter cleared up soon . . . Well, it's most important that we do."

Straight nodded. "We're doing our best."

"That goes without saying. And anything I can do . . . The facilities of Western Tech are yours for the asking."

"Thank you," said Straight.

"Not at all! Not at all! Tragedy binds men together. And this one, unless cleared up immediately, will be a permanent blot on the fair name of Pasadena. The murder of Sir Arthur Quinn, as long as it remains a mystery, will be laid at our doorstep. I beg you"—the President clasped his fat hands in a gesture of entreaty—"no step toward its solution must be left unturned; there must be no dissenting note."

Straight's eye was penetrating. "Have you any suggestions regarding our procedure in the case, President Radford?"

"No, no! Nothing like that." Casting off his formality, the President awkwardly draped one leg over the other. "The procedure is in your hands. Excellent hands, if I may say so. But I do have one request. And that is that you release the young man you jailed this afternoon. I refer, of course, to Victor Yenei."

"The Russian?" demanded Piper incredulously. "Why?"

"Now, mind you, I don't want to interfere. You're conducting this investigation and you have my hearty cooperation." The President smiled deferentially. "But, as it happens, I take a personal interest in Yenei. He's a sensitive fellow, and I don't like to see him suffer. If you'll release him I'm willing to guarantee that he'll be here when you want him."

Straight considered the President's request.

"He's absolutely harmless," said Radford. "And a brilliant student. I know a good many of the professors don't like him, and I've often felt that they treated him unjustly. After all, his religion doesn't interfere with his research. On every subject other than religion he's absolutely normal."

"As a matter of fact, President Radford," said Straight, "we haven't locked up Yenei for the reason you think. We're not afraid he'll escape."

"Why have you locked him up, then?"

"To break down his mental resistance," said Straight, harshly. "To get the truth out of him."

"The truth. What do you mean?"

"Frankly, that we're not sure he's as badly cracked as he makes out. Now you're probably right about him; maybe he is harmless. But there's been a murder committed and it's up to us to solve it. The evidence against Yenei is damned incriminating. If he can explain it away to our satisfaction, O.K.! He hasn't yet. So, if you don't mind, I think we'll keep him right where he is. In jail."

"But I do mind!" objected Radford, rising. "Surely my word—"

"Your word for what?"

"For his innocence, of course."

Straight shook his head.

Radford walked over to the desk and stood facing the detective. "If you keep that boy in jail, you'll ruin his entire future. And he has a future. Believe me! He is one of the finest research students we have at the Institute; his dexterity and delicacy in handling instruments are phenomenal. Right now he is working on an experiment that may revolutionize industry. By bombarding a mixture of aluminium and lithium with protons he hopes to release enormous stores of atomic energy. Do you know what that means? It means that, eventually, the energy of the entire world will be derived from the atom!"

"More unemployment," philosophized Piper.

"If he's destined to revolutionize industry, a few days in jail won't stop him," observed Straight.

"You don't know Victor as I do," said Radford. "He seems calm, but in reality he's nervous and excitable. As long as he stays within a certain routine he's perfectly normal; the instant that routine is disturbed or foreign elements are introduced—" Radford shook his head gravely.

"The foreign element got the worst of this deal," said Piper.

"I'm certain," said Radford, "that Victor had nothing to do with this tragedy."

"Have you talked with him?" asked Straight.

"They wouldn't let me."

"How did you know he was in the can?"

"He asked to have me notified."

"They're going soft on us down at the jail," said Piper. "We'd better look into that."

"So you won't release him?" said the President.

Straight shook his head. "Sorry."

"Very well." Nodding coldly to Craig, Radford took up his hat and left the room.

"He'll go to the mayor," said Piper.

"Let him!" answered Straight grimly. "It so happens that the mayor was once a councilman. I've got plenty on him."

And he, continued Craig mentally, has something on someone else who in turn . . . He smiled, for the cutthroat methods of modern politics aroused in him nothing stronger than amusement and a certain amount of admiration for the winning politician. It wasn't that the rather remote nature of his work had created in him a *laissez faire* attitude toward contemporary life; he was, on the contrary, vitally interested in economics. But his theory was that a good many reforms, unconscious reforms perhaps, had been put over by slippery deals, whereas, the general run of reforms concocted by pious men were unimportant, malicious, or economically unsound. There were times when Craig felt that all the esthetic and moral issues of the world could be resolved into economic terms. One's

standards of right and wrong, good and bad, false and true
depended wholly on which social stratum one inhabited.
As Ti Li said: "There are three circles in which man may
make his daily round: the copper, the silver and the gold.
And since the moral laws of each circle are determined by
its necessities, that which is proper in the gold is improper
in the copper." A maxim which Blake phrased as: "It's all
what you can get away with."

Craig didn't wholly agree with Blake, his interpretation
being rather more idealistic. A moral code, he thought Ti
Li had implied, was an informal agreement of the people
in a particular circle. And the code of one circle was no
less rigid, only different from the code of another.

His train of thought was interrupted by the opening of
the hall door.

"If you're not busy, sir," said a policeman looking into
the room, "I've got some information on the Jap."

Straight motioned him to enter.

"Let's have it."

"He registered here Saturday morning. Got in from
Seattle. He'd planned to check out tonight. But instead he
just telephoned to L. A. to cancel his reservation on the
Toyama Maru."

"Oh, he did?" said Piper. "After he left this room?"

"Yes, sir."

Piper frowned thoughtfully. "What do you make of
that?" he asked Straight. "Why didn't he say he was checking out tonight?"

Straight smiled expectantly. "Playing possum! He must
have figured if he didn't cancel the boat ride we would."
He leaned back in his chair, pulled out his handkerchief,
and blew his nose. "Well—"

He was interrupted by the entrance of a policeman. "A
radio message from Santa Barbara, sir," he reported, handing Straight a folded paper.

Straight glanced through it. "Lady Quinn's body was washed into shore two and a half miles south of Santa Barbara," he announced tersely. "Death was due to drowning. She was fully clothed but her purse and any other articles she was carrying are still missing."

Piper gave vent to a short whistle. "Suicide! Murder and suicide. Well, it looks like the Quinn case is in the bag."

Briskly, Straight stood up and lighted a cigarette. "Murphy! Radio Santa Barbara to send the body by car. And let me know when it gets here. If anything turns up in the meantime, I'm at the gym."

"So am I," said Piper. "Well," he announced jovially, slapping Craig on the shoulder, "it looks like a double funeral."

"That much at least is certain," replied Craig quizzically.

7

Craig stopped at the faculty club for Blake. It was a little after four and the daylight was fading as they entered the gate into Wechsel's garden.

Wechsel's house was small, cheap and uninspired; his garden covered two lots in area and three continents in variety. It was a wilderness of tropical and semitropical plants and trees shut off from the sidewalk by a bamboo hedge twelve feet high. Blake announced frankly that it was the only thing about Wechsel he had any use for, and, during the spring and summer when it was a mass of bloom, he spent a good deal of time in it, occasionally working but generally lying in a hammock. Wechsel didn't bother to do much weeding; he was content to water it and let plants spread and sow where they would so long as the paths were kept bare, and so long as no flowers he disliked found their way into it. These, Craig had discovered during his last visit to Pasadena, when the garden had been at its most magnificent, included all the flowers to which any sentimental significance was attached: pansies, forget-me-nots, roses, bleeding hearts, daffodils, and any others celebrated in mediocre verse. This curious aversion, combined with a love for luxuriant and exotic growths, determined the character of his garden. Twelve months of the year it was a theater of contrasts: desert shrubs and

tropical vines thriving alongside common Mediterranean
and Oriental species, for Wechsel had bought, begged and
stolen florae from the corners of the earth, and very few
of his colleagues returned to Western Tech from scientific
excursions without bringing him seeds or cuttings.

Now, in January, although many of Craig's favorites
were missing: the scarlet mallows and coral trees—the dark
blue flowers of the Iochrome and the yellow flowers of the
wild tobacco shrub, both in great bunches and shaped like
fire-crackers; brilliant blossoms of the thorny Palo Verde
tree, the orchid-like Bauhimia, the blue and pink loti, and
the tall bird-of-paradise flowers—the garden still presented an arbitrary beauty.

On every conceivable plane, in every degree and shape,
color was massed against a background of paler or more
intense color: lantanas, pink yellow and orange; kumquat,
pomegranate, lemon and loquat trees; orange to red bottle
brush; cacti of every shade but blue; and the large tubular
white flowers of the nightshade.

"Hello!" shouted Wechsel, rising up from behind a banana plant to wave a paint brush at them. "Come on over!"

Wearing corduroys and a sweat shirt, he was standing
on a circle of Japanese moss. On the easel before him was a
large canvas, still in its early stages, representing a desert
landscape inhabited only by horses. There were horses in
the foreground and background, horses galloping, horses
trotting, and horses grazing.

Blake and Craig stood contemplating it. After a moment
Blake turned to Wechsel, who was putting away his paint
tubes, "I always said you had an inferiority complex."

Wechsel dropped the paint tubes. "Why, you damned
neurotic!"

"Neurotic!" said Blake with a broad wink. "You should
have seen me ten years ago!"

Wechsel laughed ironically. "I'll bet you went so far as to grow a beard."

"Subtle, that's me." Blake started toward the house. "Mind if I look in on your wife?"

"Not at all!" replied Wechsel with exaggerated cordiality.

Blake vanished into the bamboo thicket, singing merrily: "There was a little man and he had a little can and he wanted to get it filled with lager. . . ."

"The damned fool," said Wechsel, returning to his task of putting away his paint things.

Lighting a cigarette, Craig wandered about, examining the more bizarre plants. For a few minutes neither man spoke. Then Wechsel said casually, "Well, Craig, I hear you've joined the local detective force."

"A silent partner," admitted Craig with a smile.

"Well, I hope when you find the murderer you hand him a bouquet for me." Wechsel self-consciously rearranged the tubes in his paint box. "Because, whoever he was and whatever his motives were, he certainly did me a good turn."

"It's true, then, that Quinn could have blasted your infra-red theory."

Wechsel nodded. "My paper's almost done. I've been working five years, working like a fool over it. There are a dozen, easy, spectacular experiments I could have been doing, experiments that would have gotten me publicity and raises in salary. You know of Radford's weakness for publicity."

Craig nodded.

"Well, I let all that slide. Why, when I got a bid from another college I didn't even tell Radford. I was afraid he'd say take it. I couldn't take it; I couldn't complete my experiment away from these laboratories."

"I've heard they're the best equipped in the country."

"They are," said Wechsel. "That's why I've slaved here for five years like a rat in a garret. Teaching undergraduates all day, working all night. Summer and winter. Never a vacation. And just when I was seeing the end of it, seeing the time when I'd be independent of Radford and his laboratories"—he smiled ironically—"along comes Quinn with his boast that nothing but a miracle can save my experiment from being still-born. Well, the miracle happened."

"But what's to certify that Quinn's boast would have come to anything?" asked Craig. "Surely, there's honor among scientists. If your conclusions were sound—"

Wechsel shook his head. "Quinn would have read his interpretation of the red shift before the May meeting of the Royal Astronomical Society. My paper, published a month or two later in some dinky journal, would stand as much chance as a snowball in hell. Oh, ten or fifteen years from now someone might rediscover it, might dig it out of the junk heap of relativity literature. . . . That sometimes happens." Wechsel's laugh was bitter. "Try and tell the public that there are fashions in science, that Quinn set the style in universes just as surely as the Prince of Wales does for haberdashery. They'd think you were being funny. But, by God, it's true!"

"And now, with Quinn out of the way?" asked Craig.

"With Quinn out of the way my explanation of the red shift stands a damned good chance. It's conservative, it's practical, and it's in step with Einstein's and de Sitter's cosmologies." Wechsel thrust his hands in his trouser pockets, and his pale eyes glittered. "Quinn's and Lemaitre's bubble universe has had its day. Unless I miss my guess it's due to be scrapped. Too damned fantastic. Philosophers were for it; it gave them a chance to quote from *Alice in Wonderland;* and the public likes any concept that reads like a Sunday-supplement feature." Wechsel laughed sarcastically.

"The bubble concept was popular long before there were Sunday supplements," observed Craig. "Buddha said, 'Look upon the world as a bubble. Look upon it as a mirage.'" He smiled. "Much the easiest way of looking at the world."

"By God!" said Wechsel, "Quinn knew what he was doing when he dressed up that theme in mathematical symbols and modern theories."

Craig nodded. "New words to old music."

"Popular science." Wechsel laughed ironically. "Well, by now Quinn is part of the cosmical constant." His eyes hardened. "And it looks as though I'd get my turn."

Polly Wechsel, having come down the path in time to hear her husband's last words, placed her hand on his shoulder. "What are you trying to do?" she asked. "Establish a motivation for having killed Quinn?"

Craig laughed.

But Wechsel turned furiously on her. "Shut up, Polly!"

Polly winked at Craig over Wechsel's head. "Isn't he a honey?" she remarked with sarcasm.

Wechsel calmed down sufficiently to light a cigarette.

"You know it burns me to be sneaked up on like that," he grumbled.

"He's very nervous today," explained Polly to Craig, "or he wouldn't be painting. He never paints unless he's under some sort of a strain."

"She's not only a shrew," said Wechsel, "she's a liar."

"You think of everything, don't you?" Polly patted his cheek. "Come on in and get some beer."

Craig spent the evening at the typewriter. At the end of several hours he handed Blake a sheaf of notes. "Want to look them over?" he asked.

Blake awoke, yawned, and stretched his arms. "Want to?" he said sleepily. "I'm on pins and needles."

The notes were as follows:

LADY QUINN

Description (compiled from data furnished inadver-
    tently by Cobbie and Mrs. Easterbrook)

1. Five years older than Quinn; *i.e.*, 51.
2. About 5 ft. 8 x 150 lbs.
3. Sexually passée, but interested.
4. Childlessness and flat breasts suggest subnormal
    ovarian gland.
5. Excellent health, hearty appetite, energetic.
6. Interest in charity points to sentimentality points
    to Victorian childhood. (Normal.)
7. Interest in charity points to sentimentality points
    to incomplete experience; *i.e.*, lack of mother-
    hood and halfhearted wifehood. (Abnormal)
8. Jealousy probably due to romantic tendencies.
9. Romantic tendencies based on sublimated idea of
    normal intercourse.
10. 6 plus 7 equals thought processes inhibited and
    warped by emotions (reverse of intellectual).
11. Intellectual inferiority likewise grounds for
    jealousy. See 8.
12. Sum total of psychological complexities: plain,
    pathetic, angular, timid, pleasant, kindly, naive,
    apologetic, puzzled, comic creation of tragic cir-
    cumstances. "A most unattractive old thing, tra-la,
    with a caricature for a face."

Evidence Against:

1. Avowed jealousy.
2. Suspicion, if not certainty, that dancer and Quinn
    once lovers.
3. Safe to infer that news story concerning dancer
    inspired trip to Pasadena.

4. Found Quinn with dancer.
5. Accompanied him to his room; ensuing scene matter of surmise.
6. Had opportunity to plant poisoned lozenges in box on bureau.
7. Suicide.

Evidence For (theoretical as opposed to circumstantial evidence against):

1. Natural inclination of jealous wife to poison other woman. Theory: half a husband better than no husband.
2. Hardly logical to wait twenty years to poison husband unfaithful for twenty years.
3. Murder motivated by jealousy, crime of passion. Lady Q. past age limit.

GEORGE COBURN
Description:

1. 43, 5 ft. x 140 lbs. or thereabouts. Canadian.
2. Good-natured, unscrupulous and selfish.
3. Calloused by combination of poverty and race-track life.
4. Uneducated, unmoral and unambitious.
5. A snob, *i.e.,* does not resent blows delivered by upper classes.
6. Probably a coward: held soft job in army.
7. Considers food, drink and comfort all important.
8. Virtues are surface virtues: sense of humor, philosophical outlook on life, geniality, sporting attitude; *i.e.,* the long chance.
9. Faults deep-seated: faults of character. See 2, 3, 4, 5, 6, & 7.

Evidence Against:

1. Opportunity to put lozenges either in Quinn's pocket or in box.
2. After 10 years' association with Quinn, regards his murder without emotion.

Evidence For:

1. No obvious motivation for murder.
2. Item 2 of Evidence Against can be interpreted as proof of innocence. Guilty man would affect grief.
3. Negative quality of Evidence Against.

VICTOR YENEI

Description:

1. 29, 5 ft. 6 x 130 lbs. Of Russian parentage.
2. Fancies himself as scientific savior: Christ of twentieth century.
3. Genius for research combined with fanatical hatred of scientists who use science to disprove God.
4. Complex, level-headed, and, with the one exception, normal: most dangerous type of fanatic.
5. Careless of personal safety; probably desires to follow pattern and die martyr.

Evidence Against:

1. Entire force of his fanaticism directed against Quinn, who was ringleader of heretical scientists.
2. Tried to attack Quinn immediately following lecture to effect that religion is naive, Creator sans *raison d'être,* and universe is running down.
3. Shortly after attempted attack in lecture hall, entered Quinn's room.

4. Marked threatening passage in Bible.
5. Had opportunity to place lozenges in box on bureau.

Evidence For:

1. Character of mania suggests lack of secrecy; *i.e.,* if he had killed Quinn, would admit murder, even take pride in it.

YOZAN SAIJO

Description:

1. Approximately 38, 5 ft. 5 x 135 lbs.
2. Character typical of aristocratic Japanese, proud, fearless, polite, whimsical, sensitive.

Evidence Against:

1. Admittedly insulted by Quinn's statement: Japanese are third-rate scientists.
2. Revenge a compelling force and a tradition.
3. Known to have purchased lozenges shortly after banquet.
4. More familiar with varieties of mushrooms than any other suspect.
5. Rode to church with Quinn and sat beside him; thus had opportunity to slip lozenges in Quinn's vest pocket.

Evidence For:

1. To one acquainted with Japanese mind, Saijo's explanation of his reason for buying lozenges is credible.
2. His motivation for murder inadequate to induce intelligent scientist with university position to risk consequences.

PAULA WECHSEL

Description:

1. 28, 5 ft. 7 x 130 lbs.
2. Hard, ambitious, vindictive, wilful; *i.e.*, an opportunist.
3. Governed wholly by love for and pride in Wechsel.
4. Not quite civilized, in that intellect is dominated by sensual instincts.
5. Kept at high pitch by incessant emotional warfare with Wechsel. Solution: motherhood and plenty of hard work.
6. Restless from effect of too much leisure and lacking the balance derived by Wechsel from intellectual interests and outside contacts.

Evidence Against:

1. Fact that she prompted T. F. to sound out Quinn on red shift betrayed vital concern over future of Wechsel's project.
2. Knowledge that Quinn stood in path of Wechsel's success a strong motivation for desperate action.
3. Left room directly after Quinn's statement that he had more lozenges in overcoat pocket.
4. 15 min. absence sufficient time to poison lozenges.
5. Wechsel's inexplicable nervousness might be traced to knowledge of wife's guilt.

Evidence For:

None.

DAVID RADFORD

Description:

1. Between 55 and 60, 5 ft. 6 x 170 lbs.
2. Pres. of Western Tech.

3. Sufferer from combined egomania and inferiority complex, indicated by:
a. Abnormal desire for publicity.
b. Repeated attempts to reap credit for experiments executed at Western Tech.
c. Consistent resentment toward successful scientists.
d. Emphasis on humility in others.
4. Hypersensitive to ridicule and completely wanting in humor.
5. Intellectually encumbered by religious tendencies.
6. Sentimental and unwittingly hypocritical.

Evidence Against:
1. Opportunity at church or on way to church to slip lozenges into Quinn's pocket.
2. Endeavor to protect Yenei suggests complicity.

Evidence For:
1. Position.
2. Weakness of character.

EVIDENCE AGAINST ALL 6 SUSPECTS:
1. Knowledge of Quinn's fondness for mushrooms.
2. Knowledge that since mushrooms were in season he would probably eat them at least once per day; *i.e.*, judgment of accidental death likely.
3. Knowledge that Quinn invariably carried lozenges loose in vest pocket.
4. Equal access at one time or another to pharmaceutical shelves.

Blake read the notes. Occasionally he gave vent to exclamations of surprise and delight. "Where's Wechsel?" he asked when he came to the end. "And the dancer. Where's she?"

"The murderer," said Craig, "had access to Quinn's overcoat, the vest he wore Sunday morning, or the box on his bureau. All six of the persons I've named share that qualification."

"Wechsel's as good a bet as his wife," insisted Blake. "I don't see why you have it in for Polly; she never did anything for you."

Craig smiled. "Concentrate, T. F.! Wechsel wasn't out of our sight Saturday evening; he didn't leave the room while Quinn was at his house; he had no opportunity to get the lozenges from Quinn's overcoat or to poison them."

"Too bad."

"As for Lona Lang—we're certain she hadn't access to his vest or overcoat. Quinn was wearing his Tuxedo when he went to her room and had evidently left his overcoat in his room."

"What's to have kept her from going to his room sometime Saturday night. It's just down the hall."

"Nothing," said Craig. "Except the fact that Quinn was there. She wouldn't have had a chance to take a lozenge, prepare it, and replace it in the box. Unless . . ."

"Unless?"

"Unless Quinn left his room after the scene with his wife. We have no way of proving he didn't go out again that night."

"The night clerk would have seen him go through the lobby," said Blake. "Or he'd have seen him on his way back to his room. There's not much lobby traffic around two and three a.m."

"Right," said Craig. "But the elevator boy is our best witness. I must see him."

"If Quinn went out again Saturday night," speculated Blake, "the dancer's alibi is ruined."

Craig nodded. "But, even so, she had no reason for poisoning Quinn."

"The next thing," Blake accused him, "you'll tell me theirs was a platonic love."

The ringing of the telephone cut off Craig's reply. He took up the receiver. Straight's voice at the other end said, "Craig? We've just had a batch of hotel employees down to the morgue for a look at Lady Quinn. One of the night clerks says she was at the hotel about one a.m. Sunday morning. He says she asked for the number of some woman's room. Wait a minute!" There was a slight pause and then Straight said. "Lang's the name. A dancer."

"Are you at the hotel now?" asked Craig.

"Yes. Can you come down?"

"Yes."

"I've never gone in for big game," said Blake plaintively, "but I used to be a son of a gun for rabbits. Can I come along?"

8

It was shortly after eleven p.m. when Craig and Blake arrived at the hotel. Straight's first words to Craig were: "Who's your friend?"

"A scientist from Tech," Craig explained. "His specialty is analysis."

"Analysis?" Piper looked up with a frown. "What does he analyze?"

"Light wines and beer," answered Blake promptly.

"We don't need you," said Straight.

Blake looked askance at him. "You never can tell."

"We don't need you, I said."

"Well, if you do," rejoined Blake pleasantly, "I'll be in the lobby."

"Now to get down to business!" said Straight gruffly as soon as the door had closed after Blake. "The first thing is to see this dancer; she may be able to shed some light on why Lady Quinn killed her husband."

"You're convinced that Lady Quinn did kill her husband?" asked Craig.

"Absolutely," said Piper. "You haven't seen that dame. She was a female Tarzan. Without the sex appeal."

"Aren't you convinced?" Straight's glance was sharp.

"I'm not sure," replied Craig. "I want to think about it a while longer."

Piper shook his head disapprovingly. "You thoughtful birds are O.K. in some lines, but you don't get far in the detective game. Murderers are men of action and it takes men of action to deal with them." He sat back in his chair, his chest expanded with importance. "Collect your evidence; make up your mind who did the job; and clap the handcuffs on them. That's all there is to it!"

Craig smiled. "Your method has its points, but don't you find that you sometimes hang the wrong man."

"Damned seldom."

"That's taken for granted," said Craig graciously. "But in any case, I think I shall stay with the Chinese theory."

"What's the Chinese theory?" asked Straight.

"'It is better that the hourglass of the executioner contain too many rather than too few grains of sand.'"

Piper looked puzzled.

"An hourglass," Straight sarcastically informed his confrère, "was a little gadget used by the ancients—"

"I know what an hourglass is," Piper interrupted.

"Oh, you do?"

"Yeah! We've got one in our kitchen. When half the sand is down your egg's soft-boiled and when—"

"What is this? Home hints for housekeepers?"

Piper wore an injured expression.

"Snap out of it!" ordered Straight, getting to his feet. "We're going to pay a call on this dancer."

"Maybe she's in bed," suggested Piper.

"Maybe you're a detective," observed Straight. "But you don't always act like it."

Piper ignored the insult. "If she saw Lady Quinn Saturday night why didn't she report it?" he meditated. "She might have known it'd come out sooner or later. I smell dirt."

"Probably your cigar," suggested Straight.

Piper indignantly relighted the dead cigar stub clenched tightly between his yellow teeth.

"Come on," said Straight. "We're going to put that dancer through a third degree that'll tie her up in knots."

"I hope she's a kootch dancer," said Piper.

Craig and the two detectives went down the hall to room number 1606. Piper knocked boldly on the door. There was no answer and he knocked again more energetically.

"This may be her sitting room," suggested Straight. "She has 2, 4, 6 and 8, but the clerk said he had orders to put her telephone calls through to 6. Let's try 8."

The first knock on door number 1608 brought no response. "There's still 2 and 4," suggested Piper. "What does she want so many rooms for, anyway? She can't use more than one at a time."

"Dancers are that way," said Craig with a twinkle of amusement. "They don't like to be cramped."

"Draw him a blue-print," suggested Straight.

"Never mind the blue-print." Piper winked suggestively. "I've got you."

Craig laughed. "I don't think you have."

His explanation of the dancer's use for four rooms was delayed by the opening of the door to 1608. One of the dancer's protégées—for the life of him Craig couldn't remember whether it was Mirande, Melisande or Yolande—stood in the lighted doorway. Her short blond hair was hastily combed, she was wearing blue silk pajamas, and a very sleepy and indignant expression. The two detectives gasped at the sight of this delectable child.

"What do you want?" she asked firmly. "Oh? Mr. Craig!" Her manner became instantly cordial. "I didn't see you."

"What the hell?" demanded Piper.

"We want to see Miss Lang," explained Craig to the girl. "We couldn't get any response from 1606, so we tried this door."

"Lona is out." Suspicion and a suggestion of fear lighted her blue eyes.

"Where can we get in touch with her?" asked Straight. "It's important."

The girl cast a glance of coquettish appeal at Craig.

"Please tell us if you know," he asked.

She hesitated a moment, then, with a winning smile at Craig, conceded, "She's at Mr. Cochran's house. Mr. John Cochran."

"Cochran!" exclaimed Piper. "The banker?"

The girl nodded.

"Thank you," said Craig. "And good night."

"Good night." With a bewitching smile intended for Craig alone, she closed the door.

"Looks like you knew the lady," observed Piper enviously.

Craig smiled. "Our acquaintance is a very casual one."

"If that look she gave you was casual I'd like to see her when she meant business!"

"Who is she?" asked Straight. "The maid?"

"A protégée of Miss Lang's," Craig informed him. "One of the three girls who dance with her."

"Do you know this Lang woman too?"

"I've met her," said Craig.

"Good! You can come along to Cochran's house. We'll use you as a decoy."

"Delighted," murmured Craig in a manner that was not quite convincing.

Cochran's residence was located in an exclusive district not far from the heart of the city. Dismissing their taxi at the entrance of the private driveway, the three men entered the spacious, landscaped grounds on foot. The house, set a hundred yards back from the street, was a dignified Georgian building of weathered red brick relieved by white window frames and cornices and a columned doorway. It impressed Craig as being conservative, restful, and self-sufficient. The rolling green lawn surrounding it

seemed to isolate it even further from the twentieth century and the hectic life of southern California. That there
were orange groves, picture studios and oil wells within
a radius of a few miles seemed absurd. Craig, strolling
up the gravel highway, felt transplanted to Warwickshire
or Boston or Victoria. Even the oaks, the holly trees, so
prized in California, and the box hedges arranged formal-
ly to increase the symmetry of the lawn, supported that
illusion, giving him a brief respite from the monotony of
palm and pepper and eucalyptus trees.

Approaching the house, the three men became gradually conscious of the music of an orchestra. Incongruous
as it seemed in so cloistered a setting, Craig was forced to
believe there was a dance in progress, evidently at the rear
of the house, for only a modicum of light issued from the
windows of the façade.

They reached the porch.

"It's a party," exclaimed Piper.

Straight regarded him scathingly.

The door was opened by a uniformed maid. "What do
you want?" she asked with a suspicious look at Piper.

Piper flashed his badge. "Is this Mr. Cochran's house?"

"The police!" The girl started back in alarm. "Good-
ness me! What's the matter?"

"Nothing," Straight reassured her. "We want to see
Miss Lona Lang. Is she here?"

The girl nodded; the color came back into her cheeks;
and she stepped aside to admit the three men.

They entered a wide, paneled hallway that occupied
the center third of the house. Into one of the rooms com-
pactly disposed on either side of it, the maid vanished. A
graceful stairway near the entrance mounted to the upper
story, while at the far end of the hall was a double doorway leading, apparently, to the salon, for it was from there
the music came.

The effect of the whole interior was one of simplicity and solidarity. And to Craig, who disliked intensely the cut-up architecture of so many modern houses, this exaggerated symmetry was imposing and beautiful. What was sacrificed in convenience or privacy by the thoroughfare system of planning was, he felt, glancing from the carved doorway at one end to the stairway with its stout newels at the other end, more than made up for in comfort and interest.

"Wonder if they're dancing?" said Piper, starting down the hall. He was on the point of opening the double door when it was opened from the other side by a Filipino boy carrying a tray. Piper jumped aside with alacrity. The boy passed him and entered one of the side rooms.

"Did you see what he had on that tray?" demanded Piper, returning to the end of the hall. "Champagne! Two quarts!"

"Trying to get launched?" asked Straight.

Piper's retort was curbed by the appearance of Lona Lang. The severe white gown she wore accentuated the pallor of her heart-shaped face, and there were dark circles beneath her eyes. Craig thought of Jocasta, the mother of Œdipus. All the requirements of the part; the depth of character, the haggard beauty, the implication of past joy and future tragedy seemed to him to be personified by the dancer.

At the same time he wondered if he were not, because of her glamorous reputation and the strange conditions of their first meeting, endowing her with a personality that was richer than the actuality. It was so easy, given a literary background, to mold new characters for the men and women of one's acquaintance. The less one knew about them and the more reserved they were, the quicker one was to label them as Hamlets, Candidas, or Peter Pans.

He had no assurance that Lona Lang was other than an adventuress or, apart from her dancing, other than commonplace and ambitious. Artistically, she was first-rate. In fact, thought Craig, so long as biographers insist with such diligence that good artists are bad citizens, the artist is obliged to be a bad citizen in order to be considered a good artist.

Putting aside momentarily that sensational postulate, he wondered if Lona Lang might not be in love with Cochran, might not, after all, be in love with the peace and solidarity represented by his house. It was possible to interpret the romantic and passionate episodes of her life as fitting, rather than disqualifying, her for a sincere affection for an American business man.

But, in that case, why had she allowed Quinn in her room? If she was weary of complications, as her manner and appearance implied, why had she incurred them? And why, Craig again asked himself, had she, half-way through their previous conversation, adopted an ironic tone?

Cochran, whom Craig recognized at once as her escort of Saturday night, followed the dancer into the hall.

"Miss Lang," said Straight, "may we have a few words with you? Alone."

Cochran stepped forward. "What's the meaning of this?"

"Sorry, Mr. Cochran," said Straight, "but we're investigating Quinn's death—"

"Please, John," interrupted the dancer, laying her hand on Cochran's arm. She looked at Craig. "Good evening, Mr. Craig. Shall we go in the study. I think there's no one in there."

"O.K.!" said Straight.

"Lona!" Cochran's voice rang with desperation.

The dancer, with a distressed, affectionate smile, looked up at him. "Leave me alone with them. Please."

Without another word Cochran left.

Lona Lang led the three men into Cochran's study, a room paneled in walnut and lighted indirectly by a single lamp. She seated herself in the swivel chair behind the desk. Piper and Straight pulled up leather chairs; Craig wandered over to a bookcase.

"Miss Lang!" said Straight severely. "You've been withholding information pertaining to Quinn's death. Why?"

The dancer regarded him quizzically. "What information?"

Straight leaned forward, a pugnacious look in his eye. "The law is not to be tampered with, Miss Lang. As a German citizen you should know that. I advise you to tell us everything of consequence."

"Certainly," answered the dancer gently. "I have no intention of concealing anything."

"Not much!" exclaimed Piper brutally.

"You don't believe me?"

"Why didn't you come to us, then, instead of waiting to be hunted out?"

The dancer toyed for a moment with the cabochon ruby ring on her finger before answering. "I have been withholding information," she acknowledged quietly. "I had my reasons."

"She had her reasons," repeated Piper with heavy sarcasm.

"Naturally, they were trivial. I think," she added with a deprecatory gesture, "they had something to do with my reputation."

"What happened Saturday night?" demanded Straight.

"Saturday night . . ." She smiled wearily. "Of course you know that Sir Arthur—"

Her sentence was interrupted by the sudden intrusion of Cochran. His face was flushed, and the cords on his neck stood out. "Detective Straight!" he announced sharply. "The chief of police is on the telephone. He wants to speak with you."

Straight went immediately to the desk and took up the telephone. "Hello," he said. "Yes, sir. Yes, sir." He hung up.

"What the hell?" said Piper.

Straight turned to Cochran. "It won't do any good. We're called off," he informed Piper. "Come on!"

Cochran made no comment on the situation, but the dancer, who had been regarding him with level eyes, said, "He's right: it won't do any good. You shouldn't have done that, John."

"When these gentlemen have left there'll be time enough to go into that," retorted Cochran brusquely.

"I don't agree with you." Lona Lang put down the magazine. "Wait!" she ordered the detectives.

Straight shook his head belligerently. "I'm going down and have a talk with the chief of police."

"That won't be necessary."

"Mr. Cochran's influence may be good for twenty-four hours," continued Straight, disregarding the dancer. "I wouldn't give it more than that. You'd better think up your alibi."

Cochran turned on him. "How dare you!"

"Please, John," implored the dancer wearily. "You're only complicating matters. I have nothing to conceal, not even for twenty-four hours."

"Precisely!" agreed Cochran.

Lona Lang shook her head. "Don't anticipate me, John."

"Well?" demanded Piper.

"Sir Arthur came to my room after midnight Saturday. His wife found him there."

"I don't believe it!" gasped Cochran.

Piper rubbed his hands together with satisfaction. "So that was why she killed him!"

"Take it easy," Straight advised Cochran, who was purple in the face.

Cochran waved him off. "Leave my house!" he shouted.

"You'll be ill," said the dancer.

Cochran turned his back on her and haltingly left the room.

"You'd better come back to the hotel with us, Miss Lang," said Straight.

"Very well. I'll get my wrap."

Piper went with her.

"Excuse me, sir," said the maid, meeting Craig and Straight as they entered the hallway, "but I'm afraid one of your men isn't feeling very well. He's in there"—she pointed to a door down the hall.

"One of our men," repeated Straight in amazement. "You must be mistaken."

"No, sir. He said he was a plain-clothes man. He came just a few minutes after you."

"Let's see him."

The maid led them to the dining room. On the table was a bottle of champagne three-quarters empty, a glass and a platter of hors d'oeuvres. In a chair beside the table sat Blake, clutching his throat and looking very pale.

Craig bent over him. "T. F.! What are you doing here?"

"I'm afraid he's going to be sick," said the maid confidentially.

"Going to be!" gasped Blake. "Hell! I am sick."

"Better get him outdoors," said Straight in disgust.

Craig telephoned for two cabs.

"I didn't know you were leaving, ma'am, or I'd have had the chauffeur here," the maid apologized to Lona Lang.

"It doesn't matter," said the dancer.

They left the house without seeing Cochran. Although it was 2 a.m. the orchestra continued to play softly, and no other guests seemed to be leaving.

"They're playing cards," explained the dancer in response to Piper's statement that it was more like a wake than a party. "Most of the games are upstairs."

The cabs arrived and Blake was put in one of them. Craig started to get in beside him.

"Piper can take him home," said Straight. "You come with us."

Piper complied, but not without a maximum of complaints. Craig, Straight and Lona Lang got into the second cab. For the first few minutes no one spoke. Then, as they passed a billboard advertising the dancer's performance, Straight uttered an exclamation of surprise. "Funny I never noticed your name before," he said. "So you're scheduled to dance Wednesday night!"

"Yes."

Craig regarded her left hand. The dancer slipped it inside her wrap.

"When were you to have been married?" he asked.

"Married?" repeated Straight with some surprise. "To Cochran?"

"Thursday," Lona Lang answered without emotion.

Straight looked with growing interest at Craig. "How did you know?"

"Up to a few minutes ago Miss Lang was wearing an uncut ruby on the second finger of her left hand."

The dancer smiled sadly. "Yes. Tonight Mr. Cochran announced our engagement to his friends. The ring was part of that ceremony."

"Where is it now?" asked Straight.

"I left it for him."

The remainder of the ride was completed in silence. As they entered the hotel lobby, a bus boy hurried toward them. "Miss Lang!" he said. "An important call has just come for you."

The dancer, followed by Straight and Craig, hurried to the telephone exchange. Unfolding the slip of paper handed to her, she read it.

"I must go back," she said dully. "He's very ill. A heart attack."

9

The dancer remained impassive. "I think I'll go to my room first," she said.

Straight and Craig stopped at Quinn's room, where two plain-clothes men were quartered for the night. Straight interrupted their game of rummy with an order for one of the men to accompany Lona Lang to Cochran's house.

As the three of them went down the hall toward the dancer's room, she came out to meet them. She seemed greatly perturbed.

"Anything wrong?" asked Straight.

"Mirande has disappeared."

"Mirande?" said Straight. "Who's she?"

"One of my girls." She turned to Craig. "You remember her. The very blonde one. The youngest."

Craig nodded. "The one we spoke to tonight," he informed Straight.

"You spoke to her tonight?" demanded the dancer anxiously.

"Just a few hours ago. We knocked at her door by mistake and woke her up. She told us where you were."

"Oh!" A look of distress darkened her eyes.

"Have you any idea where she could have gone?" asked Straight.

"No." She shook her head. "No. Unless she told the other girls. Wait!"

The men followed her into her sitting-room. She went quickly through her bedroom into the adjoining room, 1602. A moment later she reappeared. "They haven't seen her at all. I'm dreadfully worried."

"You go on to Cochran's," suggested Straight. "We'll find her."

The dancer pressed one hand to her forehead. "I'm all right," she told Craig, who made a move to steady her. "I'd better go. There's nothing I can do about Mirande. And she may come in any minute. Telephone me."

Craig nodded.

"Thank you." Accompanied by the plain-clothes man, she left.

"The first thing," said Straight, "is to account for the help. Someone would have seen her go out. After that I'll telephone headquarters and have them check up on the hospitals and police stations."

The elevator boy reported that a little blonde had gone down about an hour before but she hadn't come back up.

The men stepped from the elevator into the lobby. "By God!" exclaimed Straight. "Look who's talking to Piper!"

Across the deserted lobby before the florist's window stood Piper and Mirande. They were engaged in earnest conversation.

Straight and Craig went over to them.

"This little lady has something to tell us," said Piper. "What do you say we take her across the street for a glass of beer?"

"Where have you been?" Straight asked her.

Mirande lifted her engaging young face. She was wearing a polo coat and a tight, dark beret. "I had to see you," she said. "There's something I want to tell you. It's about me and Lona."

"We'll listen," said Straight.

"After you came and asked where Lona was I began to think I ought to tell you." She puckered up her white forehead. "I couldn't sleep. So I got up and walked to Mr. Cochran's house."

"Walked?"

"Yes. I couldn't make up my mind whether to tell you or not. I wanted time to think. And then, when I got there you'd just left. So I took a taxi back here."

"I was just coming in when she called me," elaborated Piper. He grinned. "I didn't know who the hell she was. Thought some baby was picking me up."

The girl blushed.

"Telephone Miss Lang she's been found," suggested Straight to Craig. "And then meet us at Joe's."

"No, don't," pleaded the girl. "She mustn't know I'm telling you."

"She won't stop you," said Straight. "She's at Cochran's bedside."

"What do you mean?"

"He's had a heart attack. She had to go right back."

"It's all my fault," Mirande was crying as Piper and Straight led her from the hotel.

Craig, after telephoning Cochran's house and leaving a message for the dancer, joined them at the rathskeller across the street.

"You tell me what Lona told you!" the girl demanded of Craig as he sat down in the booth. "They won't tell me."

"Why should we?" said Piper.

"Because I know she lied to you. And I've got to know what she told you. Don't you see?"

"Why do you think she lied to us?" asked Craig.

"To protect me. And I don't want to be protected. I won't be!"

"O.K. by me," observed Piper.

"I'm not a child. I know what I'm doing."

"Four beers," Straight told the waiter. "And some sand-wiches."

"And I'm glad I did what I did."

"What did you do?" asked Straight.

"I had an affair with Sir Arthur."

"You too?" Piper's eyes glistened.

Mirande shook her head emphatically. "Just me. Not Lona. I knew she'd tell you he'd been with her."

"Then he wasn't with her at all on Saturday night?" asked Straight, watching her narrowly.

"No!"

"Tell us the whole story."

"I want to." Mirande's voice was defiant. "That's what I've decided to do. Have you a cigarette?"

Craig supplied her with one. The waiter brought four steins of beer, hard-boiled eggs, and a plate of sandwiches.

"Sir Arthur started it," said Mirande. "Friday after-noon I was down in the coffee shop. He came and sat at my table."

"How long have you been with Miss Lang?" Craig in-terrupted her to inquire.

"Seven years. I went to her school in Munich when I was twelve."

"A school, eh?" said Piper.

"She started it during the war. Now someone else man-ages it. Although it's still called the Lang School of the Dance."

"Where are you from?" asked Straight.

"Boston. My father was an importer."

"What's your name?"

"Dorothy West."

"And the other two girls?" asked Craig.

"They're sisters," said Mirande. "Their name is Kahn."

"O.K.," said Straight. "Go on with your story."

Mirande sipped her beer. "I'd always thought of Sir Arthur as an old man," she said innocently. "Until Friday. Maybe it's because I've grown up since I saw him the last time. I remember he'd come to rehearsals in London and bring us candy. Lona used to scold him for it." She tilted her head slightly to one side and a puzzled look crept over her face. "But Friday he seemed so—so different. He wanted to go somewhere and dance, only I didn't have time. I had to go to rehearsal. Then, in the taxi he held my hand. He was sweet!"

Piper cleared his throat.

"Did you make an appointment for Saturday night?" asked Straight.

Mirande shook her head. "We didn't make any appointment. I thought I'd see him again in the hotel but I didn't. And then, Saturday evening Lona said he wouldn't be there for our show; he was leaving Monday. I didn't know he was leaving so soon."

"Go on," said Piper, reaching for a cheese sandwich.

"I had to see him again. He'd been so sweet. Saturday morning he sent us the most gorgeous roses. They were addressed to all of us, but I knew he meant them for me." She took a sip of beer. "I had to see him again. And I knew he wanted to see me. Only, I suppose he thought it wouldn't be fair because I was so young, and he was a friend of Lona's." She cast down her eyes.

"So what?" asked Piper.

"Well, Lona was out Saturday night. And Yolande and Melisande had gone to bed. I couldn't sleep—"

"Do you always have trouble sleeping?" asked Piper sarcastically.

Mirande blushed.

"Shut up!" said Straight.

"I knew he'd been at the banquet," she continued. "And they're always over early. So I telephoned his room."

"What time was that?"

"About half past eleven. He wasn't there, but his valet gave me a number to call."

"Oh, he did?"

"I didn't know whether to or not. But I knew it was my last chance to see him. Sunday night he might be busy or Lona would be home, or something. So I did call him."

"What did you say to him?" asked Straight.

"I just said I had to see him," replied Mirande. "I didn't say why. At first he said he couldn't come. Then I cried and he said all right, he would."

"Well?"

"Well, he came."

"And stayed?" asked Straight.

Mirande nodded. "He didn't want to but I made him. I mean, he did want to but—"

"We understand."

"And I'm glad I did. I always will be glad!"

"How did Lady Quinn happen to come to your room?" asked Craig.

"She didn't come to my room. She went to Lona's sitting-room. Sir Arthur and I heard her knocking on the door but we didn't know who it was. Then Lona got up and let her in. Lady Quinn was terribly excited; she thought my room was Lona's bedroom and she thought Sir Arthur was in there. Lona told her it wasn't, but Lady Quinn wouldn't even listen to her. She called Lona names."

"You could hear her pretty clearly, could you?"

Mirande nodded. "We were standing at the other side of the door listening. I was terribly frightened. I thought maybe she had a pistol."

"What did you do?" asked Piper intently.

"Sir Arthur got dressed the minute he heard his wife. I kept telling him to hurry. It was awful. Lady Quinn was trying to open the door, but of course I'd locked it from my side. Then Sir Arthur left, and just as he got into the hall, out rushed Lady Quinn from Lona's room."

Piper gave vent to a whistle.

"Sir Arthur wouldn't talk to her. He went right to his room. But Lona went out in the hall and told Lady Quinn that she'd been right; Sir Arthur had been in her bedroom."

"That was decent of her," said Straight.

"Then Lady Quinn left and Lona came into my room."

"And that's all, is it?"

Mirande looked slightly embarrassed by the question. "Not quite all," she murmured.

"Go on then."

"Lona lectured me. I can't bear being lectured."

Straight regarded her pouting face. "What did she say?"

"Oh, that it wasn't fair to Tom. Tom's my . . . I'm going to marry him some day."

"Well," asked Straight. "Was it fair to Tom?"

"That's none of her business," declared Mirande, suddenly rebellious. "And that wasn't why she minded, either. What does she care about Tom? She never liked him!"

"There are morals involved," Craig reminded her.

"Morals!" repeated Mirande disparagingly. "Lona's lived with plenty of men in her day. And one of them was—"

She caught herself.

"Quinn?" demanded Piper eagerly.

Mirande maintained a stubborn silence.

"Then it was Quinn!"

"Well, it was a long time ago," said Mirande slowly, turning her glass around and around. She looked up. "But even so she didn't like the idea of someone taking him from her. No woman would."

"I don't know," argued Straight. "Why should she care? She's engaged to another man."

"As though that made any difference!" Mirande's quick scorn turned to thoughtfulness. "Of course, if he'd been just any man. . . . But he's so"—she corrected herself—"he was famous and there was a certain cachet to being seen with him."

"A certain what?"

"Any woman would jump at the chance," explained Mirande importantly.

"I see," said Straight casually. "So you think Miss Lang was jealous."

"Naturally. And that's what I told her when she lectured me about Tom."

"What did she say?"

"She laughed."

"Oh? She laughed?"

Mirande nodded; her blue eyes were hard. "And she tried to talk me out of the idea. All about having my interests at heart! Well, maybe she has, but I can take care of myself. I don't need a guardian."

Straight dismissed that issue. "Do you think she was in love with Quinn?"

"She was awfully fond of him. She was always writing him long letters."

"Fonder of him than he was of her?" Never taking his eye off her, Straight cut short her slow comments with curt, decisive questions.

"He was fond of her."

"But he didn't love her?"

"She's too old."

Piper nodded wisely. "So he was a chicken chaser!"

"Men of forty don't want forty-year-old women," retorted Mirande haughtily.

"Or, as the Chinese sage, Ti Li, observed, 'Love maintains its own balance: years added to the age of a man are deducted from the age of his concubines.'"

Mirande's eyes flashed. "I'm not a concubine."

"Whatever word you use," observed Piper, "Quinn's wife didn't stand a chance. I know. I've seen her."

"I never have," said Mirande.

"You can. Down at the morgue," said Straight dryly. "I don't suppose you realize you put her there."

Mirande recoiled.

"If she killed Quinn, it was your fault. And it's a sure thing she committed suicide for one of two reasons: either because she killed Quinn or because he two-timed her. And they both come down to the same thing—" Straight leveled an accusing finger at her. "That's you!"

Mirande turned pale but her audacity didn't desert her. "She thought it was Lona."

"The facts are the same."

"Still glad you made him?" asked Piper.

"Yes!"

"For such a kid you're pretty hard-boiled, aren't you?"

Mirande did not deign to reply.

"So you think he loved you?"

"Yes, I do."

"And you think what's-her-name was jealous?"

"I said I did."

"You women take a lot for granted," said Straight.

"What do you mean?" demanded Mirande angrily.

"I mean that Quinn only stayed with you under protest. And was probably damned sorry he had stayed."

"So that's what you think?" A certain arrogance crept into the girl's manner.

Straight nodded. "I also think that Miss Lang knew both you and Quinn well enough to know that the whole affair didn't amount to that." He snapped his fingers.

Mirande leaned forward; there was a curiously smug look on her face. "You know so much," she said.

"That's our business," said Piper. "You foolish virgins—"

"Well, then," Mirande interrupted him, "it's your business to know that Sir Arthur wasn't damned sorry he'd stayed!"

"No?"

"No!" Mirande's voice rose higher. "If he had been, would he have come back? Would he?"

"Come back?" repeated Straight. "No."

"Well, he did come back!" announced Mirande triumphantly. "He left his wife in his room and came back to me."

Piper looked dubious. "Yeah?"

"You don't need to believe it if you don't want to."

"How long did he stay?" asked Straight.

"Until five o'clock. He only left then to go to mass with President Radford. He spent the whole night with me. Now do you think the whole affair amounted to that?" She snapped her fingers and cast an exultant look at Straight.

He shook his head. "No, I don't."

"What are you getting at?" Piper asked him.

"You know," said Straight. "There's a possibility that Quinn wasn't killed by his wife."

Mirande looked terrified. "You don't think I killed him."

"No."

"Who then?" she asked in a tone of relief.

"Lona Lang," replied Straight thoughtfully. "Perhaps you're right. Perhaps she was jealous."

Mirande's blue eyes were distended with horror. "No!" she cried. "Oh, no!"

Straight shrugged his shoulders.

Mirande started to cry. "What have I done?" she sobbed remorsefully. "Lona didn't kill him. Oh! you made me say those things. You tricked me into it!"

"Sure we tricked you," agreed Piper complacently. "That's our business, too."

10

"Where were you last night?" asked Blake. "Some female's been trying for the last eight hours to get you on the telephone."

The bathroom door was open. With one eye on the reflection of T. F.'s haggard countenance, Craig lathered his face. "So you did come to," he remarked casually.

"Not completely," replied Blake with a grin. "But I remember answering the telephone four times."

"Always the same woman?"

"So far as my befuddled senses could tell."

"I wonder who it could have been."

Blake gulped down some black coffee. "It's a mistake for a Scotchman to drink anything but hard liquor," he philosophized.

"If Lady Quinn didn't poison her husband," said Craig, shaving himself dexterously, "why did she commit suicide?"

"What are you talking about?"

"Did she, for instance, know that her husband was dead?"

"But she did poison him," argued Blake.

"The boat she was on left Los Angeles at ten a.m.," continued Craig calmly. "The newspaper extras announcing Quinn's death were on sale by nine a.m. She must have seen them."

"They'd have been sold on the boat," speculated Blake.

"That's right. She couldn't have missed them." Craig shaved his upper lip in silence.

"But you do think she poisoned Quinn," persisted Blake.

Craig turned and looked at him. "I'm trying my hardest right now not to think that."

"Where will that get you?"

"Nowhere probably."

Craig finished shaving, wrung out his washrag in cold water, and applied it to his face. Suddenly he turned. "T. F.!" he said. "You know what she thought?"

"You tell me," replied Blake lazily.

"She thought Quinn died of heart failure."

"What!"

"Dr. Byrne's diagnosis was heart failure, and that's the story the first extras carried. Remember?"

Blake nodded. "But if she didn't kill Quinn, if she thought he died of heart failure, why the hell did she jump overboard?"

"Sorrow," suggested Craig. "Remorse, perhaps, at having caused the scene that she thought resulted in his death by heart failure."

Blake considered the various possibilities. "Well, if she didn't poison Quinn," he concluded, "she was just a damned fool."

"Ti Li said, 'In her full-plum period woman is whimsical enough; in her autumn-leaf period she is totally unpredictable.'"

"How old was she?" inquired Blake. "About fifty?"

The sudden and peremptory ring of the telephone drew a wink from him. "There's your—" He cleared his throat.

Craig took up the instrument. A smile appeared on his face as the woman announced her name. "I'll stop in on my way downtown," he told her. The woman evidently objected, for he agreed to meet her in the hotel lobby in thirty minutes.

"The champagne did blunt your senses," he said to Blake, putting down the telephone.

"How come?"

"That was Paula Wechsel. She said she'd tried a dozen times to get me."

"Polly?" demanded Blake incredulously. "Well, I'll be damned! What does she want?"

Craig lighted a cigarette. "She wants to tell me who killed Sir Arthur Quinn," he announced carelessly.

Paula Wechsel was waiting in a corner of the hotel lobby when Craig arrived. Although very few people were about, she had taken the precaution of selecting a sofa concealed from public view by a pillar and two potted palms.

Craig, amused by her jaunty costume, a leopard-skin jaquette, a tight green skirt and green beret, greeted her cordially.

Paula, however, was in no mood for light talk. Her eyes, beneath the fringe of black bangs across her forehead, were bright, and there was a feverish intensity in her manner as she motioned Craig to sit down beside her.

"What makes you think you know who killed Quinn?" he asked lightly.

She regarded him with antagonism. "You think I don't know what I'm talking about."

"I don't think that at all." Craig smiled disarmingly. "Just what are you talking about?"

"You think that Lady Quinn killed him," announced Paula abruptly.

"Well?"

"I don't think she did. I made Fritz take me down to the morgue to see her." Paula's lip curled with scorn. "She wouldn't have hurt a fly."

"You could tell that?" inquired Craig interestedly.

"Those gawky sentimental women have no guts. She's pathetic."

"There I agree with you."

"I know women," said Paula. "She was probably in love with him. Sexless women always love their husbands. Just because they never find out what it's all about."

"It's quite true that they're never disillusioned," augmented Craig.

Paula smiled contemptuously. "They never find out how ridiculous, how childish a man can be. I suppose she thought Quinn was God."

"I couldn't say."

"Of course she did. And every time he smiled at another woman she died. Poor fool!" Paula's voice rang with a sort of passionate sincerity. "I feel sorry for her!"

"I think Quinn was kind to her," suggested Craig.

"Of course he was. That's the worst part, I'd like to see Fritz be kind to me. I'd kill him."

Craig found it impossible to suppress a smile.

"You don't know," she said.

"Yet you don't think Lady Quinn killed her husband. According to you she had cause."

"She didn't kill him. I would have, but she didn't."

Craig regarded her quizzically, her moist lips, her sensitive nostrils and lustrous, heavy-lidded eyes. "Who did, then?"

She was about to reply. Suddenly the words died on her lips. Craig, wondering what had inhibited her answer, looked up. Striding across the lobby toward them was Wechsel.

"Polly!" Before he was up to them his voice rang out angrily. "By God, Polly, when I tell you to stay home, you stay home!"

Craig arose. "Hello, Wechsel."

"Hello, Craig." Wechsel's manner was slightly milder. "What's she been telling you?"

"None of your business," said Polly.

Wechsel glared at her. "Of all the stubborn wenches! You know damned well—"

"A nice, gentlemanly thing to do: follow me here," Paula interrupted him sarcastically. "I suppose you listened on the telephone, too."

"You—"

"Go on," urged his wife with a mocking smile. "Say it!"

Wechsel sighed. "Don't pay any attention to her, Craig. She gets this way. My dear child"—he turned again to Paula—"you've got to learn that you can't go around accusing people of murder and get away with it."

Paula fidgeted impatiently. "Oh, go away!"

"I'm damned if I will!"

"Very well, then. I'll say what I've got to say with you here." Her eyes switched to Craig. "Fritz may not agree with me, but I think that—"

Wechsel swiftly and brutally clapped one hand over his wife's mouth. "No you don't, my dear!"

Paula, struggling violently to get free, pulled at her husband's hand and made strange, guttural sounds. A bell-hop approached rapidly from the desk.

"Let go, Wechsel," urged Craig. "You can't keep her from talking."

Wechsel unwillingly loosened his hold. Paula took her mirror from her purse and commenced improving her make-up.

"It's all right," Craig told the bell-hop, and slipped him a dollar.

Strangely undisturbed by her husband's behavior, Paula, when she had completed her operations, smiled at Craig. "As I was saying, when Fritz decided he was a caveman, I think that President Radford poisoned Quinn."

Wechsel, sulking in an armchair, made no comment.

"What makes you think that?" inquired Craig.

If Paula was disappointed at Craig's lack of enthusiasm she gave no evidence of it. "He was sitting beside Quinn in church, wasn't he?" she said. "He took Quinn to church; he had all the chance in the world."

Craig contemplated her through the smoke of his cigarette. "That alone won't hang him."

"I know. But he's a dangerous man. I've always thought so."

"In what way?"

"Paula thinks anyone who reads the Bible and goes to church regularly is unprincipled and insane," interpolated her husband.

"I think Radford is a religious maniac!"

"That, my dear, is because I married you when you were too young, too immature. Mentally, not physically. You weren't ready to be introduced to scientific circles; you hadn't the balance. It takes a mature mind to deal with modern theology and ethics." Wechsel shook his head. "I made a mistake, and now I'm paying for it."

Infuriated by her husband's irony, Paula could only glare at him.

"You, Craig, see my point," continued Wechsel. "I've made plenty of fantastic statements about Radford. Most of them have had a grain of truth: that he's an egomaniac, for instance. But, as for taking them seriously and acting on them—it takes a woman like Polly to do that."

Paula's face was set, and her eyes were hot with anger. "You'll be sorry for this," she said softly, "You wait and see."

"I know damned well I will," agreed Wechsel. "Women," he explained to Craig, "have a very simple and effective means of revenge. But I can't afford to lose my job. Not now, at any rate, when the end of my experiment is in sight. No, Polly, not even for your blandishments."

Paula turned from him.

"You can depend on my discretion," Craig assured him.

"Discretion! Discretion!" Paula's lip curled. "Why are men such cowards?"

"Civilization, Mrs. Wechsel."

"Polly's vocabulary doesn't include that word." Wechsel held out his hand to her. "Come, my dear. Come home where I can lecture you in a language you understand."

Paula stood up. "You won't get me home in a hurry." Haughtily, she walked through the lobby.

"Good-by, Craig. See you later." Wechsel hurried after his erring wife.

Craig was waiting for the elevator when President Radford tapped him on the shoulder. His flabby face glowed with benevolence and vitality, both so obviously hollow that Craig questioned their purpose. He knew the President didn't like him, and more than once he had wondered why Radford had been so anxious to have his assistance in ferreting out Quinn's murderer. It was barely possible, of course, that the reason he gave was the true one and that the embarrassment and disgrace threatening Western Tech were at the bottom of his faith in Craig. He was not a man to let his dislikes stand in the path of his interests. The fact that he never got rid of a scientist who might bring him publicity proved that. And possibly he hoped, if Craig solved the case, to reap the credit for it.

On the other hand, Craig felt that the President's motives for any action would be so numerous and so incredibly selfish that certain of them would remain forever veiled in secrecy. Radford's mind might be, simple, but his emotions were strong and complex; to follow his thought would be as difficult, Craig thought, as to follow the thoughts of a child who had been taken to too many picture shows.

"Good morning, Mr. Craig," said the President cheerily. "Lovely morning."

Craig nodded.

"It gets one out early, this sunshine. I just met Mr. Wechsel and his wife leaving. A charming girl. A charming couple, I should say. So much in love."

"Yes," replied Craig. "They are." He stepped aside to permit the President to enter the elevator.

Their arrival at Quinn's room interrupted a conversation between Cobbie and the two detectives. "Good morning, gentlemen," Radford greeted them. "I come bearing news. We have received word from relatives of the deceased, Lord and Lady Ashcroft, as to the disposition of the bodies. They were in Italy when Sir Arthur met with his death, and we had some difficulty in getting in touch with them."

"Mussolini," interpolated Cobbie.

The President ignored the interruption. "Naturally they returned at once to England to arrange details. They wish both bodies to be shipped at once to Reading. Sir Arthur's estate is, I believe, near there."

"Just off the downs," announced Cobbie enthusiastically. "The best training-ground in the world!"

"Training-ground?"

"For race-horses."

"Oh!" The President frowned impressively. "As I was saying, the bodies are to be shipped to England tomorrow. I have already arranged for a cortège, a public procession in which all of Pasadena may pay its last respects to a great man."

"A procession where?" asked Piper.

"To the train, naturally! The police force, the Boy Scouts, the National Guard have all expressed a desire to participate. And the mayor has ordered a public tribute in the form of one minute of silent prayer. That will come at a quarter to twelve—during the brief ceremony that precedes the procession."

"You must have been busy," observed Piper.

"I have indeed." The President stood for a moment, tapping his false teeth with his finger nail. "And there's still a good deal to be done. The floral tributes are arriving by dozens. There's one elegant piece sent by the Theosophists: a telescope done entirely in white roses. Well!" Rousing himself with an effort from contemplation of the ceremonies, he held up his hand in a gesture of farewell. "I must be off now. There's much to be done. By you as well as by me." He paused. "That reminds me, I haven't inquired yet as to your status quo. Any new discoveries?"

"Not yet, sir," replied Straight.

The President scratched his chin thoughtfully. "I had hoped that by the time of the ceremony . . . Well, there's still twenty-four hours."

"About noon tomorrow, is it?" asked Piper.

"The procession leaves the funeral parlors at noon. It will proceed through the business district to the city limits. There the greater part of the cortège—the Boy Scouts, the National Guard, all those on foot—will disband and return to Pasadena. The rest of us, conducted by a police guard, will go on to Alhambra where the bodies are to be put aboard the Southern Pacific"—drawing a card from his pocket, he refreshed his memory—"due there at 12:43," Returning the card to his pocket, he directed his glance at Cobbie. "And that reminds me: before I engage a person to accompany the bodies to England I should like to be quite certain as to whether or not this man will be available."

Cobbie's eyes popped. "You mean you want me to—"

Straight interrupted the valet. "We're not detaining any witnesses after tomorrow," he announced shortly.

"The Jap left yesterday," added Piper.

Radford ignored the latter statement. "Splendid!" He turned to Cobbie. "I take it for granted you wish to pay this last tribute to your master and mistress."

Cobbie's nod was conclusive.

"Then shall we regard the matter as settled? The ticket and berth are already arranged for. You hadn't, by the way, a round trip ticket?"

"No, sir. We were thinking of going home by way of the Canal."

"I see. Well, no matter. Aside from the saving, it is more fitting that the bodies be accompanied by Sir Arthur's personal valet than by a stranger." He cleared his throat. "You will pack up tonight. Tomorrow morning at eleven I will call for you here. I think that is all, unless you have any questions."

There was a brief silence. The President started in the direction of the door.

"If you don't mind, sir"—Cobbie spoke thoughtfully—"before you go, there's one question on my mind. A question of etiquette, you might say."

The President, with one hand on the doorknob, waited. "A question of etiquette?"

"Yes, sir. You know, when Sir Arthur died—passed on, I mean—he was wearing his frock-coat. Well, I thought, seeing as how he has a Tuxedo, perhaps he ought to wear that for the ceremony. It might be more genteel."

The President deliberated "More genteel? A Tuxedo. Nonsense!"

"It suits him better."

Radford shook his head. "The frock-coat is quite proper. I see no point in changing."

Cobbie shrugged his shoulders. "Just thought I'd mention it."

"If that's all, I'll be on my way." Radford opened the door before addressing Straight. "We hope for a report soon."

"So do we," replied Straight wearily.

The door closed after the President's impressive figure.

"Having the time of his life," observed Cobbie. "It ain't every day he has a double funeral to look to. That reminds me: have you heard the one about Pat's widow?"

"No? And we don't want to." Piper bit the end off a cigar and spit it into a distant wastebasket.

Craig had been observing the valet. "Where were you last night, Cobbie?" he asked.

"Asleep in my bed, so help me! I'm not like Sir Arthur. My salad days, as you might call them, are over. And I jolly well know it. Not that I ever was one for the bright lights. Horse-racing is my vice. And all I want now is a stable of blue bloods with maybe a neat little Berkshire estate on the side." He confirmed his statement with a nod. "Peace and quiet on the downs suits me."

"How are you going to get all that?" asked Piper.

"A man knows what he wants."

Straight regarded Craig critically. "Why did you ask where he'd been?"

"He looks as though he'd had a hard night."

"That's where looks is deceptive," remonstrated Cobbie cheerfully. "If it's my color you mean—that's my kidneys acting up. Riding the ponies did that. The bouncing. That and beer fixed my kidneys for good. But I'm not complaining. If it's not the kidneys it's the liver."

"What is this: a clinic?" demanded Piper. "Are we going to spend the morning on his kidneys or on Quinn's murder?"

"The murder by all means," replied Craig gently.

Straight sat down; his face was drawn and irritable. "It's the toughest case I've seen," he observed with a sigh. "It's a good thing the main witness doesn't always commit suicide."

"If Lady Quinn murdered her husband, why the hell didn't she leave a note saying so!" said Piper, savagely striking a match.

"Oh?" queried Cobbie with some surprise. "And here was me thinking it was a sure thing."

"You did?" asked Straight.

"Well . . ." Cobbie shrugged his shoulders. "Women don't jump overboard for nothing."

Piper nodded. "That's what I thought. Until these dancers spilled their—" Stung by a glance from Straight he broke off in the middle of his sentence. "Anyway," he continued lamely, "what's there to prove she killed him?"

"Dancers?" asked Cobbie interestedly. "You don't mean Lona Lang?"

"What do you know about her?" Straight fired at him.

"Well," said Cobbie. "I wasn't aiming to mix her up in it, but now you ask me"—he winked suggestively—"I'd say they was old buddies, she and Sir Arthur."

"Buddies. What do you mean by that?"

Cobbie seemed unembarrassed by the sharpness of Straight's attack. "Friends with all the fixings: flowers; telegrams; suppers."

"And that's all?"

"All I saw?"

"You surely have some opinion."

"Opinion?" Cobbie shook his head. "No, sir. You couldn't tell about Sir Arthur. He was the sort of man who might. And then again he mightn't."

"You're sure you're not just being loyal to his memory. Because, if you are . . ."

"Loyal?" Cobbie interrupted him. "Oh, no, sir!"

"I believe him," said Piper.

Straight stood up and walked over to the window. As he did so the hall door was opened and President Radford entered carrying a newspaper. He was greatly excited.

"What does this mean?" he demanded, thrusting the paper under Craig's nose. "What does this mean?"

Craig read the headlines aloud: "QUINN'S AFFAIR WITH DANCER REVEALED. WIFE FINDS QUINN IN DANCER'S ROOM."

"Go on!" urged Radford wildly. "Go on!"

"'The motives for Lady Quinn's mysterious suicide were revealed last night when Lona Lang confessed that on Saturday night Sir Arthur Quinn was discovered in her hotel room by his wife. . . .'" Craig skipped to the end of the story. "'Whether this is conclusive proof that Sir Arthur Quinn was poisoned by his wife's hand the police have so far refused to disclose.'"

President Radford paced the room. "Well?" he demanded agitatedly. "Well? What have you to say?"

Straight had taken the paper from Craig's hands. "I don't know how this could have gotten out," he said, glancing down the page.

"Good heavens! It's not true?" Radford's eyes bulged.

"Not exactly." Straight turned to Craig. "Do you know how this got out?"

Craig shook his head.

"Piper! Do you?"

"I was wondering," said Piper with some hesitation. "You see, I was just down taking a Turkish bath. There was a man next to me, a nice young fellow—"

"You damned fool. He was a reporter!"

Piper nodded regretfully. "I guess he must have been."

"This is terrible!" said Radford. "Terrible! A common love affair. With a dancer! If we could only have hushed it up until after tomorrow!"

"If it were only one dancer!" said Straight ironically.

Radford's mouth fell open. "Is there more than one?"

"It's rather complicated," explained Craig.

Radford was wild-eyed, and his hands were clasped as though in prayer. "Dancers!" he exclaimed almost tearfully.

"Hotel rooms! Scandal! How could such a thing have happened here! In Pasadena!"

11

"How is Mr. Cochran?" asked Craig.

Lona Lang was resting on a chaise longue. Her whole attitude was one of listlessness. In response to Craig's knock she had called, "Come in," and now she lay just as she had been lying when he entered. In her right hand she held a burning cigarette; her left hand, ringless now, almost touched the floor. Only the movement of her beautifully arched feet, partially encased in satin mules, gave any indication of restlessness. She answered without looking up.

"The doctor says, if he's careful, this needn't make a great deal of difference."

"I'm very glad to hear that."

"Yes. So am I. It isn't pleasant to feel like a murderess."

"But if his heart was bad—" remonstrated Craig.

"Of course," replied the dancer impatiently, as though, having thought out all the answers in advance, she was bored rather than comforted by them.

"You're no more responsible for this than you were for Quinn's death," said Craig.

Lona Lang flicked the ashes from her cigarette onto the floor. "According to a newspaper I saw on my way home, I'm very much responsible for Quinn's death. As well as Lady Quinn's."

"Oh, that." Craig dismissed the sensational headlines with a nod.

"I shall probably do very well tomorrow night. A great many people with no interest at all in the dance will come to see the woman with whom Sir Arthur spent his last night."

"And, without suspecting it, see the woman with whom he spent his last night," Craig completed her sentence.

Lona Lang regarded him quizzically. "What do you mean?"

"Mirande is dancing."

"The little fool told you."

"Yes," said Craig.

"But it won't come out! The newspapers mustn't get hold of it!"

"Not now at any rate. If there's a trial—"

"Whose trial?"

"That," replied Craig, "is a matter of conjecture."

"Then . . . you don't think that Lady Quinn . . ." Her voice trailed off into silence.

"Frankly, I don't."

For a moment neither spoke. When Lona Lang spoke it was casually, as though she were discussing the weather, "She was unhappy enough to," she said. "And desperate enough. No one else in the world, much less here, had reason to kill him. What do the police think?"

"That you may have," replied Craig. "Motive: jealous of the girl."

"Mirande?"

"Yes."

Lona Lang smiled. "I had no idea public officials had so much imagination."

"You inspire them," said Craig. "As you inspired Lady Quinn, and John Cochran—to think the worst of you."

"And you?"

"I," replied Craig, "find you the victim of a perverse desire for martyrdom."

Lona Lang's indifference dropped from her. "You are insulting."

Craig shrugged his shoulders.

"Please leave my room."

"May I suggest," added Craig, rising, "that you apply to your private life a little of the wit and irony that illuminate your dancing. Contrary to the opinion of your Hebraic ancestors, we are not born into a vale of tears. Good-by."

"Wait!" Lona Lang stopped him at the door. "I'll stand for a good deal. I have to. My life hasn't been exactly virtuous. You may call me anything you like; question my habits, my friends or my character. But I will not permit it to be said that I have no sense of humor."

Craig's hand dropped from the door knob; his eyes expressed admiration and pleasure. "I withdraw the statement."

The dancer shook her head. "No. I wonder if you're right. Have I been noble and smug?" She smiled ironically. "And after all I've said of the Isadora Duncans and Ruth St. Denises!"

"What have you said?" inquired Craig with interest.

"I suppose you know what started Ruth St. Denis on her career," declared Lona Lang irrelevantly.

Craig shook his head.

"She saw a cigarette poster in a drug-store window. Of the Egyptian goddess Isis. 'That,' she said, and has been saying ever since, 'is what I want to be. Not a biting, scratching, petty, evil-motivated female, but a peaceful, powerful goddess, a symbol of infinity, the soul of a people.'" Lona Lang smiled again. "You see, I memorized it."

"Why?"

"Because I want to remember that I am a biting, scratching, petty, evil-motivated female. Because I want to be honest with myself. Because I want my girls to be honest with themselves. Have you read Isadora Duncan's autobiography?"

Craig nodded.

"Then you know how she sanctified every cheap liaison. Whether it was with d'Annunzio or an alley rat, it was beautiful and fine and necessary to her art. Even after she was too fat to dance; even after she smelled of depravity!"

Craig's eyes were understanding.

"I've been cheap, too," continued the dancer intensely. "Although I've never let myself go physically as she did. That and her pretense were both unforgivable. But"—her tone was passionately sincere—"whatever my life has been, I've never let it interfere with my work. And I've never made my work an apology for my life."

"Miss Lang," said Craig, "I wish you'd broadcast that statement. The public ought to know that it is possible for a great dancer to be intelligent."

"It hasn't done me much good."

Craig regarded her shrewdly. "Why were you going to marry Cochran?"

"Because I'm tired, I suppose. And poor."

"But you've made money."

She smiled apathetically. "A little."

"Why not retire?"

"I've never learned how to knit. And I dread boredom. More than death."

"What could Cochran give you?"

"The social existence I've never had. Do you know, for years I've been in bed by ten-thirty, I've dieted and exercised. Now I should like to dispense with that routine."

"A social existence might bore you," suggested Craig.

"No. For all over the world there are interesting people I've never had time to meet. And interesting things I've never had time to do. I want to go back to cities I've danced in and never seen. I want to travel in a style to which I'm not accustomed. I want—that is, I wanted to be Mrs. John Cochran."

"And what is there to prevent it?" asked Craig. "His doctor's report was certainly encouraging."

Lona Lang smiled. "A year ago when we met in Cannes he asked me to marry him. I refused. Cannes is a romantic setting; it does something to a man's sense of values. Then he followed me to Paris. I refused him again. I told him I'd had lovers; I think I even exaggerated the number; but he said it didn't matter."

Craig regarded her steadfastly.

"Then he came home. I didn't write to him. I didn't answer his letters. He never stopped asking me to marry him. But I got bored with the Middle-West; I felt suddenly that I couldn't stand another moment of the life I'd been leading. And I knew Sir Arthur would be here and I could ask his advice. So I canceled my Middle-West tour, wired my agent to arrange for this Los Angeles recital, and came to Pasadena. With tragic results."

"Did you consult Quinn before agreeing to marry Cochran?"

She nodded. "He agreed that I'd earned luxury. But he never believed—it was impossible to make him believe that I could be happy married to John."

"Because of his own married life?"

"No. Not that. Sir Arthur wasn't unhappy. He would have been far more unhappy married to a woman who made demands on him or took his mind off his work. As it was, when he wanted recreation he took it, with some child who could be so impressed and dazzled that she would make no trouble for him afterwards. Mirande, for instance."

There was a knock on the door. Melisande came in. "Aren't we rehearsing this morning?" she asked.

The dancer sprang to her feet. "Good heavens, yes! I didn't know it was so late. Will you come back later? This afternoon?" she asked Craig.

He nodded.

She did love Cochran, he realized intuitively, and, with the perversity that characterized her dancing, had excluded love from her motives for marrying him. The reasons she had given were selfish ones: her own boredom, her own fatigue and restlessness; but Craig was suddenly certain, more certain than if she had proclaimed it, of her admiration and affection for the banker. Perhaps it was a reaction against hypocrisy and righteousness that caused her to clothe her honest emotions in shoddy terms, or, more likely still, it was shyness, a natural modesty common to interesting and public characters. Craig had come up against it before. Literary men it generally made sarcastic and difficult; in actors it was often difficult to dissociate from conceit; while in politicians and economists an overcorrection of the same reserve was apt to result in pomposity and dogmatism. This, of course, was a trite axiom. Craig felt that too often in analyzing its heroes, the public was overgenerous in attributing to sensitivity their unadmirable qualities. And, conscious as he was of the warping effect of publicity and success, he had met enough important men who were likeable to suspect those who were not.

Lona Lang's perversity, whether it was due to shyness, to an impulse toward martyrdom, or to both, Craig found intensely feminine and rather childish. At first, he remembered, she had impressed and puzzled him. He had thought her complex. Now he realized that her exotic appearance masked simple feminine instincts. She was no more a

Jocasta than a Lady Macbeth; she was a normal, idealistic, perverse woman who wanted to marry John Cochran.

Craig returned to Quinn's room.

"Where have you been?" demanded Piper. "We had you paged downstairs."

"We've just had word from the jail," Straight interrupted. "Yenei is sick. Starved himself into a breakdown. They've moved him to a hospital. We're going down now and see him. You can come if you want to."

"Will they let you question him?" inquired Craig.

"We'll question him," asserted Piper.

Straight frowned. "I don't know. Depends on how bad he is. Radford talked the warden into having him moved. Anyway, we'll take a look at him."

"I don't think I will come," said Craig after a moment's deliberation. "But, if you're going now, you can drop me off at Cochran's house on your way."

"Cochran's house?" There was a note of suspicion in Piper's voice. "What are you going to do there?"

"How is he?" asked Straight.

Craig opened the hall door. "If you don't mind, I'd rather answer your questions after I've seen him."

Parting company with the two detectives before Cochran's house, Craig approached the front door. The maid who answered his ring looked askance at him. "Oh, it's you?" she said.

"How is Mr. Cochran?" asked Craig.

"Not so well as he was before you and your policemen friends called on him."

"I'm sorry," said Craig. "But, honestly, how is he?"

"He's sitting up," answered the girl grudgingly. "And I took him up an eggnog not so long ago. He doesn't look sick. But I guess he is."

Craig smiled at her dismal expression. "Do you think I could see him?"

"No, I don't."

"Ask him."

The girl shook her head. "I wouldn't dare. He has a trained nurse."

"Let me ask her, then," pleaded Craig. "Where is she?"

"Upstairs. The first door on your right."

Craig started up the stairs.

"Don't say I said you could go up," she called after him.

Craig knocked gently on the door specified. A crisp voice called, "Come in!"

"How do you do?" he said, entering the small sitting-room.

The nurse, who was sitting in a rocking-chair, knitting, glanced at him over her spectacles. "I suppose you're Mr. Cochran's secretary," she said. "Well, you can go in. But don't stay long, and don't tell him anything to worry him."

"I won't," Craig assured her solemnly.

"Business! business! business! They won't rest; they won't go a day without answering their correspondence. And then they wonder why they have heart attacks." She sighed. "Well, go on in."

Craig entered the adjoining room, quickly closing the door after him so that she wouldn't hear Cochran's brusque, "Hello! Who are you?"

Craig introduced himself.

Cochran, who was sitting up in bed, frowned. "What do you want? And how did you get in? Doctor's orders I'm not to see anyone."

"I know." Craig pulled a chair up to the bed. "But I've some information that may do you good."

"What is it?" Cochran's glance was skeptical.

"Quinn wasn't in Miss Lang's room Saturday night."

Cochran sat bolt upright. "What?" he bellowed. "You're lying. She said he was."

"She said that to protect Mirande, one of her girls."

"Mr. Cochran"—the nurse peered through the door-way—"I'm afraid you're exciting yourself."

"Get out!" shouted Cochran.

The nurse hesitated.

"Get out!"

Her bewildered face vanished.

Cochran leveled his eyes at Craig. "How do you know?" he demanded.

"Mirande told me and later Miss Lang herself acknowledged it."

The banker's expression shifted from incredulity to reflection and suddenly to suspicion. "What business is it of yours?"

"It has something to do with Quinn's murder."

Cochran accepted the explanation with a grunt. "Why did she tell me Quinn was in her room?"

"She told the police. You were there. You remember she wanted to see them alone."

"The girl isn't worth it."

"I agree with you," said Craig. "She's frivolous, vain, and selfish. But, then, as Ti Li said: 'The pious child is commended; the impious one is loved.'"

Cochran gave a brief, cynical nod. "Did Miss Lang know you were coming?"

"No."

"Good!" The banker's sharp eyes appraised Craig. "Don't tell her you were here."

"I won't," Craig promised. He got up to go. "Good-by."

Cochran shook hands with him. "Good-by. Glad you came," he added reluctantly. With a sigh of boredom he relaxed against his pillow. "There's a humidor on the table there. Help yourself to a cigar. And you might hand me one."

Craig complied with the latter half of the request and departed, taking with him a picture of one of Pasadena's

most prominent bankers, slightly paler than usual but un-
impaired in spirit, sitting up in a Queen Anne bed, smoking a cigar. Generally philosophic toward the inevitable,
Craig found himself more sensible than he had thought to
the minor tragedies of life. Cochran was so keen, so reso-
lute, and proud; to see him a victim of ill-health, one of
the few antagonists he couldn't fight back, like a bad work
of art, was depressing and unwarranted.

Craig had an enormous respect for men like Cochran.
Faced daily with large-scale problems and responsibilities,
they were taciturn, untiring, impersonal in their relations,
and unassuming in manner. Pettiness, malice, jealousy—
feminine traits that were apt to crop up in the professional and academic men of Craig's acquaintance—were foreign to them. They were completely virile. And therefore,
Craig reasoned, at the mercy of women. Lona Lang would
undoubtedly complicate his life. Craig hoped there would
be compensations in the marriage for Cochran.

Leaving the house, Craig walked slowly down the
driveway. The lawn, newly mowed, smelled sweet, the air
was damp and mild, and the sky overcast. It looked like
rain. Quickening his pace, Craig left Cochran's estate and
turned toward the hotel. Odd, he thought, that of all the
characters in this case the least eccentric and the one least
implicated should command his sympathy. Cochran had
character and solidarity—commonplace qualities, it would
seem, beside the brilliance of Quinn or the originality of
Lona Lang. His house, too, substantial and comfortable
as its owner, was no more extraordinary. The world would
always have its Georgian houses and captains of industry.
Then why, Craig asked himself, did Cochran so impress
him. Was it an ironic comment on his own associates that
geniality and dependability should seem more rare than
brilliance? Or, more significant still, was it a comment on
the times?

Craig was in a position to be surfeited with brilliance; students, faculty members, journalists and critics each had a particular brand; and it occurred to him that Blake was right in his statement that popular education was a curse. Already, combined with a maximum of leisure, it had produced a standardized type, physically lazy, astringent and theoretical. In short, brilliant.

Craig thought of Wechsel: he was that sort—level-headed and indefatigable so far as his work was concerned, otherwise capable of the maddest fantasy. And yet, was he? Craig, remembering his garden, the canvas he had been painting, and the apparent fantasy of his private life, was conscious of a certain deliberate and calculated disorder. He was a complex man; fundamentally, Craig felt, a logical man; and, therefore, not to be trusted.

It would have been quite logical for him to have killed Quinn. But when and how on Saturday evening could he have taken lozenges from Quinn's private supply, poisoned, and replaced them? Moral evidence was against Wechsel; Craig, walking slowly in a pouring rain he was scarcely aware of, searched his memory for circumstantial evidence.

A few minutes later a taxi driver, prowling the watery streets for passengers, drew up beside him with a sanguine, "Taxi, Mister?" And Craig, suddenly aware that he was caught a good six blocks from the hotel in a rainstorm that showed no signs of abating, climbed in.

Arriving, wet and still thoughtful, at the hotel, he was pounced on as soon as he entered the lobby by a bus boy evidently posted to watch for him. "They want you on sixteen," said the lad importantly.

Craig went up. He found Quinn's room the scene of a search conducted with feverish activity by Piper and one perspiring policeman. Rugs were rolled up, cushions were out of chairs, the bed mattress was humped over the baseboard; and Quinn's shoes, collected in a heap in the center

of the room, were the object of a systematic examination
by the detective, which consisted mainly of prying at the
sole and seams with a pocket-knife. Quinn's other wearing
apparel, shirts, socks, neckties and underwear, evidently
next in line, were dumped beside them, while his suits
were being hauled in wholesale quantities from the closet
and thrown onto the bed-springs by the policeman.

Craig made no effort to conceal his amazement at this
procedure. "I thought you'd already been over the room
quite thoroughly," he commented, remembering the search
conducted with the assistance of vacuum cleaners, mag-
nifying glasses, and fingerprint experts at the start of the
investigation.

Piper paused in his ravage of the shoes to greet Craig
with an uninformative. "Hello. You here? We telephoned
Cochran's but you'd left."

Craig's eyes, seeking to communicate some interpretation of this activity to his brain, roved once more over
the room. "I gather that Yenei wasn't too ill to talk," he
ventured dryly.

"Oh, we didn't even see Yenei. He's in a coma." Piper,
taking obvious pleasure in Craig's mystification, nodded
in the direction of Cobbie's room. "Straight'll give you the
lowdown. I'm too busy. Everything out of the closet?" he
demanded of the stolid policeman.

Craig, on his way to the adjoining room, stopped to
examine a trunk partially concealed by the open closet
door. It was a large, metal wardrobe trunk, scarred by
travel, and bearing the initials *A. Q.* Clean and completely
empty, it had, apparently, just been brought up from stor-
age, for Craig had never seen it before.

Straight and a second policeman were in Cobbie's room,
making with rather less effort and disorder than Piper, an
equally detailed examination of its effects. Cobbie, himself, stretched out comfortably on the bed with a copy of

Western Romances beside him, watched them through half-closed eyes.

"Hello, Craig." Straight, who was dismantling Cobbie's partially packed trunk, looked up. "Did Piper give you the dope?"

Craig made a gesture of negation.

"Radford was at the hospital," said Straight, forcibly pulling the pockets of a salt-and-pepper tweed coat inside out. "We were talking to him about Yenei; he's in bad shape, I'm afraid. We didn't see him. Anyway, Radford came through with a piece of news. The damned fool hadn't thought to tell us before."

"I'm rather curious," admitted Craig.

Straight deposited the coat he was holding on top of the trunk. "I took it for granted," he said, "that we'd accounted for Quinn's cash. There was sixty dollars in his wallet. Now it seems there should have been one thousand and sixty."

"You mean he was paid in advance for his lectures?"

Straight nodded grimly. "By check. What's more, the check was cashed. Cashed Monday, the day it was paid."

"Did you know it?" Craig demanded of the valet.

"Not me," replied Cobbie, sucking meditatively at the cigarette between his lips. "I wasn't a party to his finances."

"Perhaps he sent the money East for deposit without noting it in his check-book," suggested Craig.

Straight shook his head. "We wired his bank and got an answer back. The balance in his account is nine thousand, three hundred and sixty-eight dollars. And his last deposit was made over two weeks ago from Chicago. No. . . ." Methodically, and with the calm crispness that served as an index to his character, Straight reviewed the facts: "Quinn cashed the check. He didn't deposit the cash, and he couldn't very well have spent it. It wasn't on him, and I'm damned if it can be in either of these two rooms.

There's a thousand dollars to account for. Now, where the hell is it?"

"What do you think, Cobbie?" asked Craig.

Cobbie knit his brow. After a moment he observed: "Sir Arthur couldn't have spent it without me knowing. You're right there. And he wasn't the gambling sort; never'd put a nickel on the ponies, or on anything else that looked like a long shot. He shied at stocks, though the old lady took a flier or two in her day—"

"This isn't getting us very far," cut in Straight.

"I was just thinking," continued Cobbie dreamily. "What's to have prevented him from giving the money away?"

"Giving it away?"

"To that blond dancer. What's her name?"

"Mirande?" Craig smiled. "I don't think so."

"He slept with her, didn't he?"

"She might have taken it from his wallet," suggested Straight.

Cobbie looked pleased.

"On the other hand," added Straight. "If the money had been stolen prior to his death, he certainly would have missed it. Men aren't careless where a thousand dollars is concerned; it's not even likely he'd carry that big a sum in his bill case."

Craig nodded. "I agree with you. Either he disposed of the money of his own free will, and I can't believe he did; or it was stolen after his death; or . . ." He hesitated.

"Or what?" demanded Cobbie and Straight almost simultaneously.

"Or Lady Quinn, finding it in his room Saturday night, took it for safe keeping."

Straight looked dubious.

"Took it?" echoed Cobbie. "You mean it went overboard with her?"

Craig smiled at the anxiety in Cobbie's voice. "Why not?" he speculated. "Suicides can afford to be improvident. And she had no heirs."

"She had no heirs," said Straight. "But we don't know she poisoned him. If she jumped overboard because of his love affairs, if she didn't know he was dead, I'm damned if I think she'd have taken his thousand dollars over with her." He paused before concluding impatiently, "I'm damned if I even think she got her hands on the money in the first place."

A brief silence followed this statement. It was broken by a lengthy yawn from Cobbie, the intricacies of the problem having proved too much for a mind attuned to race-track tips and *Western Romances*.

Craig glanced toward the bed. Hands folded on his stomach, face sagging drowsily, his heavy brogues marking the clean pink coverlet, and two plump pillows behind his head, Cobbie presented a picture of complete inertia.

"I'm not convinced that Lady Quinn poisoned her husband," asserted Craig, turning back to Straight. "But I am convinced that she knew he was dead."

"You are?"

"Yes. I don't believe if he'd been alive that she'd have taken her own life. He'd been unfaithful to her before."

Straight accepted the argument with reluctance.

"What's more," continued Craig, "I've satisfied myself that she had every opportunity to see a newspaper announcing his death from heart failure." To prove his point he went on to reiterate for Straight the hour of Quinn's death, the hour the first extra had appeared on the streets, the hour when Dr. Byrne's original verdict of heart failure had been first disputed; and the hour that the boat, boarded by Lady Quinn at San Pedro, had sailed.

Straight listened with growing interest.

"I don't say her motives for suicide are of any real importance in solving the case," suggested Craig. "Unless

they should lead to proof that she poisoned him. So far
they haven't. As for the money: the murderer may have
taken it; it may have been concealed beyond all hope of
recovery by Quinn—not probable, I admit—or it's quite
logical, whoever killed Quinn, that Cobbie found and kept
the thousand dollars."

The figure on the bed stirred and raised up on his
elbows.

"You're accusing me?" expostulated Cobbie. "After I let
you go through my belongings even to ripping open the
coat on my back and the linings in my shoes? Did I make
any fuss, did I?"

"It wouldn't have mattered if you had," pointed out
Straight.

"Well, I didn't make any fuss and I never took the money, much less saw it. So you can jolly well look till dooms-
day and think what you like. And that's that!" Resentfully,
he sank back against the pillows.

"We've looked damned thoroughly," admitted Straight.
"We've been over everything he has, not to mention
Quinn's stuff. Logic or no logic, if he did take the money
I don't know where he could have put it. This man here"—
he indicated the policeman—"is a whizz. He's an x-ray! He
does a lot of work for the customs, and he can feel money
or dope through a brick wall. About through?" he asked
the policeman.

"Yes, sir. Just about."

"When you are," Straight instructed him, "I have another job for you. There's an outfit of dancers down the
hall here in 1606. The first chance you have, I want their
rooms searched. All their rooms. How many have they?"
he asked Craig.

"Three bedrooms and a sitting-room."

"For the money?" inquired the policeman.

"For the money. Pass up everything else. I don't know what denomination the bills are in; I don't know their serial numbers; all I know is that if that thousand dollars of Quinn's isn't in a purse at the bottom of the Pacific it stands a damned good chance of being in this hotel."

"Yes, sir," replied the policeman, holding the copy of *Western Romances* upside down and shaking it in the hope that bank-notes would flutter from between its pages.

"Straight! Craig!" Flushed with excitement as well as with the exertion of his labors, Piper burst in on his confrères. He was waving a letter.

With a terse, "What's this?" Straight took it from him. Cobbie sat bolt upright on the bed.

"It's from her uncle," explained Piper, beaming with pride at his discovery. "Lord Ashcroft. Radford was saying he's been named executor for Quinn's estate. I found it in with a stack of ads in the desk drawer. Quinn must have thrown away the envelope by mistake and then slipped it into one of the others that came in the same mail. It was in an envelope from a real estate firm in Florida."

Craig thought he had never heard Piper resort to so elaborate an induction.

"What does the old bird say?" asked Cobbie with reviving interest.

Straight made no reply. Intently, and with difficulty, for Craig observed that his eyes several times retraced the same line or remained fixed for some seconds on one word, he read Lord Ashcroft's letter.

"I couldn't make it all out," confessed Piper. "And there's a lot of talk about nothing. But there's one part that's got something to do with the way Quinn treated his wife." He sighed deprecatingly. "Why the hell can't people use typewriters!"

"If you'd ever seen Lord Ashcroft you wouldn't ask that," protested Cobbie. "He's one of the sort what spends

his forenoons writing letters to the papers about the kind
of bird he spotted with his field glasses yesterday. After-
noons he raises hell with the farmers what shoot foxes.
Hasn't missed a ride to hounds in thirty years. Lived ten
miles off the downs, but do you think he keeps racehors-
es?" Cobbie expressed his disgust and disillusionment in a
sigh. "Not him! The old devil hasn't an ounce of sporting
blood in him; thinks a horse is something to hunt foxes
on. And I've heard him say myself that he hates to admit
it but motor cars is the coming thing."

Craig burst into laughter.

"He ought to get a peep at the U. S.," exclaimed Piper.
"It'd be the death of him!"

"Here you are." Straight handed the letter to Craig.
Written on a full-sized sheet of thin, lightly-ruled blue
paper in a cramped, minute hand, it was headed:

> Ticehurst Hall, Little
> Twitchett, near Reading,
> Berkshire, England.
> January 6.

Dear Nephew [Craig deciphered],
A genial reference to you in a wireless talk by
the Hon. Worthington Hogge brings me sharply to the consciousness that I haven't replied to
yours of—heavens!—Dec. 15! But Dec. 15th
was precisely the date when, telling myself I
could ill afford it, I decided to have some im-
provements made on the estate (by way of a
Xmas present)—the chimneys repaired, water
laid on in the servants' quarters (Simpson, by
the way, took to bed last week. A bad case of
liver, the doctors say. But we think he is going to cheat the undertaker) and an American

bathtub for your aunt. I tell her she will not want to go to Italy this winter.

Liking America? I rather fancy, though Beryl writes me not, that the life over there—the noise and their constant high spirits, not to mention the difficulties of accustoming oneself to foreign menus—would prove a bit of a strain. Does it? Or are you so traveled that like (who was it said it?) you can be as bored in Timbuctoo as London, and at less expense.

However, I trust you are happy and that Beryl does not regret having returned to you. I told her at the time your separation appeared to be final that I felt no good could come of it and that, should you have another try at a reconciliation, its success would depend as much upon her as upon you. She is one of the best. As a girl I remember her as a charming mixture of innocence and French boarding-school sophistication. And I like to think that if you stick it a bit the two of you will win out.

Fine weather; December has been a good 'un. No fog but a fairest bit of frost. Roses in the garden.

You recall Dr. Beaver? I met him only last week at a parish meeting. He asked for you. . . .

Craig glanced through the remainder of the letter which related, for the most part, political and neighborhood gossip. "Very interesting," he said.

"Interesting!" repeated Piper. "I'll tell the world!"

Straight took the letter from Craig and put it in his brief-case. "You must have known Quinn was separated from his wife," he asserted, focusing his sharp eyes on Cobbie.

Cobbie shrugged his shoulders. "It all depends when a separation's a separation," he replied plaintively. "Lots of times Lady Quinn was down at her uncle's, or Sir Arthur and me was off lecturing on the continent. But I never heard no talk about separation."

"You mean to say you never gossiped about your employers with the other servants?"

"There wasn't no other servants except a housekeeper," retorted Cobbie scornfully. "And besides, it ain't my nature to gossip. Oh, if I know a body well enough I don't mind indulging in a bit of small talk. But between traveling around and changing housekeepers, we never got past discussing the weather."

"I see," said Straight, seemingly satisfied with the explanation. "All right. You can go on with your packing. And you check up on the dancers," he instructed the policeman. "I want that job done today."

Cobbie, with a groan, swung his brogues over the side of the bed; the policeman left by way of the hall; and Craig accompanied the two detectives through the bathroom into Quinn's room.

"Well?" demanded Piper. "What's the next move?"

"Damned if I know," said Straight with a distraught glance about the room. "It's a two-to-one shot he was poisoned by his wife. You can say what you like about that," he shot at Craig. Restlessly, running his fingers through his neatly brushed hair, he paced the floor. "It's a three-to-one shot," he asserted. "But the thousand dollars! By God! where is—"

The telephone rang. Straight, with the eagerness of a drowning man after a life preserver, reached for it. "Yes," he snapped at the mouthpiece. "Detective Straight speaking . . . yes . . . yes . . . yes . . . yes . . . yes . . . O.K.!"

Calmly replacing the telephone on the table, he turned to his companions. "Quinn's will just came through from

Scotland Yard," he announced. "Nothing to his wife even if she'd survived him; she had her own income. A couple of minor bequests to distant relatives, and the bulk of the estate to Lona Lang."

"To Lona Lang?" gasped Piper.

Straight made a gesture of affirmation. "Provided that, at the time of Quinn's death, she was not married."

"And, by God, she wasn't!"

"In case, for any reason, she forfeits her claim," continued Straight, "the money's to go to the department of astrophysical research at Cambridge University."

"I'll be damned," meditated Piper. "Do you think we ought to tell her?"

"No objection so far as I can see, so long as it isn't made public. Get her on the phone," Straight suggested to Craig. "Have her come here."

Craig, complying with the request, took up the telephone. "1606 please."

"Why not go to her room?" asked Piper.

Straight's glance was cynical. "One dancer at a time's enough for me."

"Is Miss Lang there?" Craig asked. "Yes, this is Mr. Craig. . . ." A moment later he turned, with an ironic smile, to the two detectives. "Miss Lang left the hotel half an hour ago on her way to Cochran's house. They're to be married at four o'clock." Piper looked at his watch. "It's five to four now. Shall we stop her?"

"Why stop her?" asked Straight. "Her marriage now doesn't cut any ice. She'll still get the money. The will says: provided she wasn't married at the time of his death."

12

The well-oiled gears of the funeral coach slipped into high. Suavely, on clean tires, it withdrew from the station, leaving behind an odor of antiseptics and roses.

On the station platform a group of portly men in frock-coats and top hats stood at respectful attention before a baggage car, while, from a window in the adjoining Pullman, a few yards to the right of President Radford's committee, Cobbie, wearing a bowler hat, a boutonnière, and a solemn expression, winked at Craig and Blake.

Porters along the line drawled, "All aboard!" With a crash of couplings the Apache jerked into action. It was a signal for general relaxation. The faces of the memorial committee slackened and Cobbie, having popped a stick of chewing gum into his mouth, waved a buoyant farewell to California as the train, bearing the bodies of the world's most celebrated astrophysicist and his wife, rolled from the Alhambra station.

Blake and Craig, declining the President's invitation to return to Pasadena in his limousine, left the platform. "You're not going to brood over this case?" Blake cast a solicitous glance at his companion. "Good heavens, Craig! What's it to you who murdered Quinn? Straight and Piper have a right to bellyache; this may mean a cut in salary for them. But you're a philosopher, in case you've forgotten.

Unsolved mysteries are right in your line. By the way," he
added in a rather less sardonic tone, "you've never told me
what Polly wanted with you yesterday morning."

The memory of the scene between Wechsel and his wife
brought a smile to Craig's lips. "Oh, she wanted to tell me
that Radford poisoned Quinn," he replied airily.

Blake whistled. "If he only had!" he exclaimed hopeful-
ly. "What a stink that would make!" Gradually, however,
as he considered the possibility, the gleam of joy faded
from his face. He shook his head disconsolately. "Damn it!
I'm afraid he didn't," he announced. "Radford hasn't got
what it takes."

"Pessimistic as ever," commented Craig with some
amusement.

"What do you think?"

Craig's deep-set eyes sharpened. His frown emphasized
the Satanic arch of his blond eyebrows. "I think Radford
has got what it takes," he said, thrusting his hands into
the pockets of his navy blue overcoat. "Egomaniacs are
fearless and they have a genius for conspiracy. As diplo-
mats they're unbeatable." He nodded, a curious smile on
his lips. "I think he was capable of it, all right."

Blake stopped short. "You do?" he demanded incredulously. He studied the expression on Craig's face. "Damn
it! you do!" He exclaimed joyfully. "Well, then, why not
do something about it? Tell Straight! Arrest Radford—"

Craig, with a look, quenched his companion's enthusiasm. "I don't think Radford poisoned Quinn," he announced
briefly. "I merely give him credit for being capable of such
an act."

"Why the hell—" commenced Blake.

Craig anticipated his question. "Murder," he said slowly, as though thinking out his theory, "isn't an intellectual
form of revenge; and I'm inclined to think that the motives
for it aren't often intellectual. Think of the sensational

murders of the past ten years. What, actually, has been the motive for most of them?"

"Love," responded Blake glibly.

Craig nodded and stroked his clean-cut jaw. "Or money," he added. "Once in a while sadism; but that's beside the point."

"Why?" inquired Blake.

"Murder by poison isn't the act of a sadist," pointed out Craig, leveling his keen blue eyes at his companion. "It's a means to an end."

"Not brutal enough," agreed Blake.

"Not brutal at all. In fact, as far as I can see, Quinn's murder was the work of an efficient and completely normal person."

"That doesn't sound like Radford," said Blake.

Craig laughed.

"Damn it, Craig, there aren't any normal people around here. And what's more"—stopping short, Blake gestured aggressively—"normal people don't commit murder."

"I know," Craig lighted a cigarette. "Those are just two of the flaws in my argument. But, to return to my original thesis—"

"Love or money?" said Blake thoughtfully. "The love angle's strong. There's the dancer, Quinn's wife, Polly. . . . Everyone of those damned women had an ax to grind."

"Quite a trio of *femmes fatales.*"

"Fatal as hell, any one of them," agreed Blake seriously. "Yes, I can see where the poor devil might have been a martyr to love. The money angle, though . . ." He shook his head. "I guess that's out."

"Hardly," said Craig. "At least not until the thousand-dollar check Quinn cashed Monday is accounted for?"

"The thousand-dollar check?" At the mention of so impressive a sum Blake's Scotch ears pricked up.

"What's this about a thousand dollars? It's the first I've heard of it. You're not holding out on me?"

With a laugh at Blake's quick revival of interest in the case, Craig denied that there was any malice in his neglect to report the new development.

Blake listened impatiently to the simple facts concerning the check and, at the end of the brief recital, started in a sudden burst of speed through the waiting-room.

Craig hastened after him. "What's your hurry?" he asked.

"Do you want some chambermaid to get away with that money?" demanded Blake without breaking his long stride. "Come on! We're going back to the hotel." He jerked his head toward Craig, adding, "In a taxi!"

It was the first time in their long acquaintance that Blake had suggested a taxi. The idea of paying more than a dime for transportation, or of paying even that when it was possible to walk, was painful to him. Craig, greatly amused by this singular and impulsive reaction, followed him to the street, where two cabs, day in and day out, waited forlornly before the station. One of them the men engaged to take them back to Pasadena.

"Although there's nothing to be gained by hurrying," suggested Craig practically. "The room's already been searched half a dozen times. As a matter of fact, Lady Quinn may have taken the money."

Blake knit his brows. "You don't mean to say she took her purse with her when she jumped?" he demanded.

"She must have. Or else it was stolen before the ship docked at San Francisco. It's never turned up."

"I don't believe she took the money," declared Blake optimistically. "If it's true, as you said, that they had a joint checking account with a good deal more than a thousand dollars in it, why would she want cash?"

"Precisely!" Craig's blue eyes, fixed on the passing landscape, were thoughtful. "With access to a checking account containing nine thousand, three hundred and sixty-eight dollars, why would she want cash?"

"On the other hand, women have been going through their husband's pockets for a long, long time," philosophized Blake gloomily.

"A possible factor, all right." Craig's voice was grave but there was a twinkle in his eye as he contemplated his companion. "And we have evidence that Lady Quinn was alone for some minutes in Quinn's room. Theoretically, a wife might take money merely to keep her husband from spending it on some other woman."

"Theoretically, then," concluded Blake, "there's a thousand dollars in bills in a purse at the bottom of the ocean."

"Granting that Quinn didn't have the money on his person and hadn't already disposed of it, yes."

Blake heaved a sigh of futility. "Too involved for my simple mathematical mind," he complained. "My Lord, Craig! I'd rather explain the theory of recurrent decimals to a platinum blonde than try to follow your lousy reservations."

Craig burst into laughter.

Reaching Pasadena, the cab turned toward the heart of the business district. Its normal routine, held in check for some minutes by the funeral procession, was again in full swing. Women shoppers hurried from one clearance sale to another; and clerks let down awnings to protect displays of artificial silk dresses, veneer furniture and artificial jewelry from the mild, but unflattering sunshine.

It was shortly after one o'clock. ALL PASADENA MOURNS SCIENTIST AND WIFE, proclaimed sixth-edition headlines; and newsboys, with a healthy emphasis on "big," commanded passers-by to "read all about the big funeral!"

Craig bought a paper. Before he had more than glanced at it the seventh edition, bearing a new banner concerning an airplane crash in Azusa, was on the streets.

Reaching the hotel, the two men went immediately to the room on the sixteenth floor, which they still persisted in referring to as Quinn's. Straight and Piper were there, conversing with the manager who, now that the funeral was over, was patently eager for their departure in order that the room might be aired and re-rented. The whole episode, he implied, whatever its effect on civilization, had been a poor advertisement for the hotel, since there would always be people who secretly believed that Quinn was poisoned by the mushroom omelet served him for breakfast.

Straight's remonstrances were in vain; the manager persisted in clinging to a grudge scattered indeterminately over science, the police force, melodrama and mushrooms.

While the detectives were engaged in replying to these polite recriminations Blake, with an attempt at casualness, made the rounds of the room, pulling open drawers and peering into their empty recesses, thrusting his arm under the bed mattress, ruffling the pages of the telephone book, standing on tiptoe to examine the closet shelf, and finally disappearing into the bathroom.

The manager, distracted by his behavior, cast suspicious glances in his direction, and Piper, seeing that the manager's attention was straying from the matters in hand, broke off in the middle of a sentence to growl at Craig, "What's he up to?"

Craig, with some amusement, explained his friend's motives.

Piper shook his head. "He won't find anything here," he declared summarily. "We've been over every inch." He turned to Straight. "Let's go."

The manager, wearing a hopeful expression, started for the windows.

Straight picked up his bulging brief-case. "You can send the bill for the room rent to Lord Ashcroft," he remarked coldly over his shoulder. "President Radford's office will give you the address."

"It went out in this morning's mail," replied the manager suavely as he threw open a window.

Craig started toward the bathroom in search of Blake. As he reached the door, Blake issued from the valet's former room, a light of suppressed excitement in his eyes.

"Find anything?" demanded Craig.

Blake, in portentous silence, brushed past him, at the same time pressing something into the palm of Craig's right hand. "We missed you in the funeral procession, Piper," he called loudly, hastening after the detectives. "I hope you at least observed the moment of silent prayer: your tribute to science."

"What's science ever done for me?" Craig, lingering behind to examine the card in his hand, heard Piper scornfully exclaim; and Blake's quick reply as he joined the detectives: "Not very much, I'm afraid."

A second later, having ascertained that the card was neither more nor less than a lottery ticket for the Mexican Grand National Sweepstakes, Craig followed them into the hall.

Blake gave him a cautious high-sign which, had not Craig known him so well, would have seemed to indicate that he had won a prize in the lottery rather than merely found a ticket; and, suddenly voluble, he announced gaily as the four men waited for the elevator that Quinn had made a fine corpse.

"He did?" said Piper with a surprising show of interest. "Well, he had a close shave last night."

"Insistent little things, whiskers."

Straight came very near to smiling.

"Not that sort of a shave, you fool!" Piper corrected Blake. "I mean some bird tried to get at the corpse."

Craig pricked up his ears. "How do you know?" he inquired.

"The night watchman telephoned for the police," explained Straight. "No harm had been done. The lid had been pried off Quinn's coffin, that's all."

Piper nodded and continued, "Whatever the bird was after, he didn't get it. He must have just gotten the lid off when he heard the watchman coming and beat it. A good thing, too. There'd have been hell to pay if he'd gotten at the corpse."

"And there'll be more hell to pay if you start shooting off your face about it around Turkish baths," Straight warned him as the elevator door shot open.

The four men filed into the elevator. "Don't worry about me," snapped Piper explosively. "I'm onto those dirty journalists." He turned confidentially to Craig. "The undertaker wants it hushed up," he explained *sotto voce*. "Afraid it will hurt business. So, whatever you do, don't let on."

"I won't," Craig assured him, aware of an intense curiosity on the part of the operator.

Stepping from the elevator into the lobby, they strolled in a desultory manner toward the main exit. Their business in the hotel was concluded and, despite the relatively brief period during which it had been their headquarters, Craig and the two detectives had the air of men suddenly evicted from their homes and jobs.

Blake paused beside the travel bureau, his eye on a folder picturing the rising sun, cherry blossoms and Mount Fujiyama. "I wish you hadn't let that Jap go," he said fervently. "I've always thought he knew more than he told."

"Yeah?" Piper regarded him contemptuously. "Another day and he'd have had the Japanese consul on us."

They strolled on in silence. A few yards short of the entrance Straight stopped, lighted a cigarette, and turned decisively to Craig. "Well," he said, "unless some new evidence turns up, and I don't see how it can, I guess this case is closed."

"You can take it from me," volunteered Piper, "it was closed the day his old lady was salvaged. Except for the money angle," he added. "That still has me guessing."

"She probably poisoned him," agreed Straight. "But we'll never pin it on her. There isn't the evidence. No!" He frowned. "This case is just another question mark."

"And question marks don't help a man's record any." Piper's tone was bitter. "Well, so long, Craig—Blake."

Craig, who had been plunged in thought, looked up. "Oh! Good-by, Piper."

"Good-by," said Blake.

Straight held out his hand. "Good-by, Craig. Thanks for the assistance."

Absorbed again in retrospection, Craig ignored the outstretched hand.

"Good-by," repeated Straight with a trace of impatience. Piper started down the steps.

"Oh! Good-by, Straight." Craig, in the act of extending his hand, hesitated. "Have the trunks gone?" he inquired in a tone whose casualness implied that the talk had for some time been along those lines.

"The trunks? Quinn's and Cobbie's? Yes, of course." There was a touch of annoyance in Straight's answer. "Why?"

Craig ignored the question. "I suppose they went to the station early this morning."

"The porter tended to that," said Straight. "All I know is that I left instructions with Murphy to see that the trunks were checked through to San Pedro. The steamship company will pick them up there and route them to England via the Canal."

"But you don't know whether they were packed in time to go out last night or this morning?" persisted Craig.

"Yes, of course I know." Straight, already harassed by the insolubility of the case, spoke irritably. "They went out sometime today. I don't know whether they were taken to the station early this morning or late. I don't see that it matters. But Murphy had orders to stay around last night until the trunks were packed and taken downstairs. The manager wanted everything out of the rooms by this morning."

"In that case they were in the trunk room over night," said Craig, seemingly pleased.

"Naturally." Straight, more puzzled by Craig's apparent pleasure over this answer than by his questions, voiced his perplexity. "But why the hell does that matter? And where do the trunks come in? We went through the damned things once. You were there at the time."

"I know," replied Craig easily. "And it happens that the trunks don't matter. I thought they might. Just a minute." He turned and walked in the direction of the information desk, leaving Straight and Piper, who had returned to the landing, looking after him with some annoyance.

"What the devil?" muttered Piper, throwing the butt of his cigar onto the marble steps.

Straight shook his head despairingly.

"He knows what he's doing. That's a cinch." Blake's pride in his friend was evident. He chuckled at the predicament of the two detectives, whose curiosity would not allow them to follow their natural impulse to leave Craig flat. "You don't find that son-of-a-gun barking up the wrong tree."

"No?" Piper's tone was insulting.

Blake merely grinned.

Several minutes later Craig returned from his brief conference with the young lady at the travel desk. To the three men, awaiting him with ill-concealed expectation, he announced as he lighted a cigarette that the Apache reached Palm Springs at 3:45.

"Who the devil is the Apache?" asked Piper.

Craig explained gently that he alluded to the Southern Pacific train which at 12:43 had whisked Cobbie from their lives.

Straight lost no time in getting to the point. "What have you got on Cobbie?" he demanded.

"And why didn't you break it at 12:42?" queried Blake, even he seeming for the moment to have lost faith in Craig's sagacity. He glanced at the lobby clock. "1:45; no lunch; and you want to start for Palm Springs."

"Start for Palm Springs?" Piper repeated incredulously, regarding both Craig and Blake with astonishment and a certain amount of commiseration. "You're not that crazy."

"You can't hope to catch up with the Apache," indicated Straight practically. "Not if it's due at Palm Springs at 3:45. That would give you exactly two hours to make over a hundred and twenty miles."

Craig received the information in silence.

"If you have anything on Cobbie," added Straight reasonably, "we'll wire ahead to the police at Phoenix, Arizona, to either hold him there or send him back here."

"That's sensible," commended Piper.

Straight was busy figuring. "She ought to get in to Phoenix about midnight. I don't believe there's much of a stop before that. Palm Springs, I happen to know, is only a flag stop."

"Give him the dope, Craig," urged Blake. "Let him wire ahead to Phoenix. That's the right idea."

Craig shook his head. "I have no evidence on which to detain Cobbie," he remarked pleasantly.

"Then, what the hell?" exploded Piper.

"No," meditated Craig. "Your suggestion, practical as it is, doesn't appeal to me. I think I will go to Palm Springs."

"Don't you see you can't make it in time!" pleaded Blake. "You'll drive like hell and get there an hour late.

For the love of Mike, Craig, use your head. This isn't like
you."

Piper lighted a fresh cigar. "I guess I'll get some lunch,"
he announced restlessly.

Craig calmly surveyed his three companions. "You seem
to forget," he observed with a smile, "that this is an age of
miracles. It's even possible to get to Palm Springs in two
hours."

"By plane," acknowledged Piper.

"And you say you have nothing on Cobbie!" Straight's
glance was shrewd.

"Nothing," replied Craig.

"Then you're nuts!" exclaimed Blake. "If you go to the
expense of chartering a plane to take you clear to Palm
Springs, you're nuts!" He thrust his hands emphatically
into his trouser pockets. "And that's final. I'm going to
lunch."

"Au revoir, gentlemen." Craig started down the steps.

Blake waited until sure of the sincerity of Craig's
intentions before starting after him. The two detectives
watched a taxi, hailed by the doorman, roll up to the hotel
entrance. Craig directed the driver and climbed in, followed by Blake. The taxi drove off.

"He meant it," said Piper simply.

Straight made for the door. "Where did that taxi go?"
he demanded, revealing his star to the doorman.

"The Glendale airport, sir."

"Taxi." A second cab rolled up to the entrance and
stopped. "The Glendale airport. In a hurry!" was Straight's
terse direction to the driver as Piper, obeying a signal,
hurried from the Hotel and climbed in.

Twenty-five minutes later, arriving at the airport,
Straight and Piper dismissed their taxi and made with
considerable speed for the depot. Their search for the
professors, as Piper insisted on calling Craig and Blake,

was brief. Blake, at the lunch counter, was hurriedly con-
suming a glass of beer while Craig made arrangements for
chartering a plane.

To Piper's chagrin no surprise was evidenced at his
and Straight's appearance. Blake, calmly spreading a ham
sandwich with mustard, jerked his elbow in the direction
of the office. "You'll find the general over there. I told
him he'd better make it a four-passenger in case you two
showed up. By the way," he called after Straight, "how
about charging it up to crime?"

But Straight, wasting no time in repartee, was already
on his way to the office. Piper, planting his foot on the
rail, replied for him, "It won't come out of my pocket.
That's a cinch!" "Draw one," he instructed the waitress,
helping himself to a hard-boiled egg.

"Come on, you two," Craig called to them a moment
later. Hastily draining their glasses and laying down the
money for two more sandwiches apiece which they took
with them, the ill-assorted pair—Piper hearty and pro-
vincial, Blake sardonic and lean—started after their confrères.

The four-passenger plane that was to transport them
made its appearance; the men climbed in and, a moment
later—2:38 by the airport clock—were on their way to
Palm Springs.

Above the noise of the engines Straight leaned forward
to shout one inquiry to Craig: "Think he's got the money
on him?"

Craig, gazing down on the dark patches of the walnut
groves, rapidly giving way to the waxier green of orange
acreage, nodded.

"Yeah?" shouted Piper. "Well, where was it last night
when we searched him? And if he has got it on him why
wouldn't the Phoenix police stand as much chance as us to
find it?"

Receiving no answer, he settled back into a comfortable doze. Blake occupied his time in jotting down figures on the back of an envelope which, later, as the plane flew over the pleasant green and brick-red panorama of Redlands, he passed on to Craig. The sum underlined at one corner of the envelope represented the compound interest on a thousand dollars put out at three and one-half per cent over a period of thirty-two years.

"Why thirty-two years?" asked Craig with a good deal of amusement.

"Cobbie's forty-three now," explained Blake, cupping his hands to form a megaphone. "If he lives out his life's span he has thirty-two years to go—"

A scant ten minutes later they sighted and outdistanced the Apache and, shortly afterwards, the plane dropped to a neat landing near the Palm Springs station.

Swiftly descending and ordering the plane to wait, the four men covered the distance to the tracks. The train, not yet in sight when they arrived, steamed toward them several minutes later and slowed down in response to Straight's signal.

Having ascertained that the next stop was Indio at 4:29, they climbed aboard the Pullman supposedly containing Cobbie.

It was far from full. And though they quickly enough found the berth belonging to the valet, he was not there. After settling with the conductor for their brief ride, they entered the smoking compartment. Cobbie was not in evidence. Nor was he in the observation car.

"He must be in the dining-car," observed Straight. Retracing their steps through the train, the four men again passed Cobbie's berth on their way to the diner.

Piper looked at his watch. "Four o'clock. Funny time to be eating."

"Not for an Englishman," said Blake. "Afternoon tea."

"Oh? Tea!" Piper's tone expressed a vast condescension toward the entire British nation.

Entering the dining car, they found Cobbie, with the exception of a half dozen Negro waiters, its sole occupant. A pot of tea and a plate of bread and butter and listless cake before him, he had his cup to his lips as he read a Southern Pacific time table.

Craig took command. "Hello, Cobbie." Casually, he dropped into a chair across from the valet. "We've come for the money."

Cobbie looked from Craig to the familiar faces of the three men standing over him. He put down his tea-cup. "The money," he said slowly. "Well, I'll be blowed! What money?"

"Stand up!" ordered Straight. "Take off your coat."

"You've been through this coat once," argued Cobbie, removing the coat of the salt-and-pepper tweed suit he was wearing.

Piper helped himself to a piece of cake. The Negro waiters looked on with interest, and Blake whistled a hymn.

"Nothing in the pockets." Straight passed the coat to Craig for examination. "Rip open the lining if you want to, although I'll swear there was nothing there last night."

"I spent half the night sewing up linings," complained Cobbie, turning to allow Straight to examine his hip pocket. "But go ahead."

Craig felt the wrong side of the coat, inch by inch, with sensitive fingers. Then, taking out a pocket knife and opening it, he carefully cut a stitch and pulled apart two sections of the lining. It revealed nothing more extraordinary than a thin layer of padding. "Shouldn't think you'd need padding, Cobbie," he remarked, cutting another stitch.

"I'm round-shouldered; the riding did it," rejoined the valet.

Craig loosened and lifted out the padding; then, non-chalantly, while the group about him looked on with increasing boredom, he repeated the operation on the other shoulder. A moment later, as unaffectedly as though it were padding, he handed to Straight three limp thousand-dollar bills.

"Well, that's that. Good work, Craig." Straight pocketed the money, while Blake, with a broad grin on his face, wrung Craig's hand, and Cobbie, standing beside the table in his shirt sleeves, shook his head. "Jolly bad luck," he muttered sadly.

Piper alone seemed nonplused by the performance. When he regained his speech it was to demand: "Where the hell was that money last night?"

"Sewed into Quinn's frock-coat," replied Craig promptly. "Wasn't it, Cobbie?"

Cobbie nodded. "But what put you onto it?"

"So you're the bird that was prowling around the undertaker's!"

"Partly your suggestion to President Radford that Sir Arthur be buried in his dinner jacket," Craig answered Cobbie's question. "The frock-coat, as you know, was more suitable."

"So that was the bloomer!"

"When I heard that Quinn's coffin had been tampered with," continued Craig, "I wondered what business anyone could have with a corpse. That is, until I thought of your anxiety to change the frock-coat for a dinner jacket, I wondered."

"Simple," commented Piper with some sarcasm and more envy. "And there's something else I wouldn't mind knowing: how do you make one grand turn into three grand?"

Cobbie answered that question himself. "Sir Arthur's orders to press them damp—that softened them up—and sew them in his frock-coat. He liked to keep a little cash on hand. That way when he put out a hundred quid on something he shouldn't, no one knew the difference. I sewed in five since we've been in the States. Three was all that was left."

"What do you mean: no one would know the difference?" queried Straight. "Who cared how he spent his money?"

"Who do you think? Lady Quinn!" rejoined Cobbie with unintentional disrespect. "He lived off her and her uncle before the easy money came along. How do you think she liked to see him blowing chippies to wrist-watches and champagne? The joint banking was a jolly good idea, but it didn't work."

Straight handed Cobbie his rather shapeless coat. "Better put this on. We're due at the next stop."

Cobbie complied with the suggestion. "Never thought I'd see Pasadena again," he commented cheerfully. "Jolly bad luck."

"Speaking of luck"—Craig, disregarding a lowering glance from Blake, took from his pocket the Mexican lottery ticket and handed it to Cobbie—"perhaps this will help pay your lawyer."

"Thanks." Coolly, the valet pocketed the ticket. "It would be just my luck to draw a winner now."

"You'll be out in five or ten years," Piper reassured him.

"Five or ten years?" repeated Craig questioningly.

"Sure. The term for grand larceny."

Craig shook his head. "Personally," he argued, "I don't think Cobbie will ever serve that sentence."

"Why the hell not?"

Straight, though he offered no criticism of the statement, appraised Craig's intelligently passive face.

"Because," said Craig, "I think he'll be serving a much longer sentence."

As he spoke he watched Cobbie. The valet's small, puffy eyes gazed back, undaunted, at him. "Got a cigarette, anyone?" he inquired jocularly.

What was he thinking, Craig wondered, and was it possible he had poisoned as well as robbed Quinn? The atmosphere of the race-track was indeed toughening if it enabled a man to kill and face the consequences with apparent serenity.

"Who was it, Cobbie, that first prescribed for your kidney trouble?" asked Craig. "An army doctor?"

Cobbie, puffing at a cigarette, made no answer.

"Answer when you're spoken to," ordered Straight curtly.

"That's right," muttered the valet.

"Ten to fifteen years ago, in other words."

"Well?" demanded Piper.

"If you remember," said Craig negligently, "Dr. Byrne said something to the effect that muscarin, though it's been supplanted since, was popular as a kidney remedy about ten years ago."

Cobbie gave no sign of having heard. Straight and Piper exchanged glances, and a slow smile of admiration spread over Blake's face. "I'll be damned!" he exclaimed, his gratitude for mathematical precision bubbling over. "You're a genius, Craig. It fits together like a jigsaw puzzle."

Craig nodded. "It fits together. But until the picture is completed don't put too much faith in my conclusions."

"Why not?" asked Piper.

"Have you ever done a jigsaw puzzle?"

"Who hasn't?"

"Then you know how deceptive they are. The field of corn can as easily as not turn out to be a sunset over Venice, and the white clouds in a blue sky, once you've found the boat, become a marine view."

Piper, much to Craig's amusement, was thoroughly impressed by this sophistry. He agreed earnestly.

"Tell me, Cobbie"—Craig resumed lightly his former conversation—"when did you find out that muscarin was identical with mushroom poison? Recently?"

"I didn't find out."

"Come now, it surely wasn't a coincidence that you poisoned Quinn with synthetic mushroom poison on the very day he'd eaten mushrooms for breakfast."

Cobbie's slightly puffy eyes regarded his inquisitor steadfastly. "I never poisoned him," he maintained. "I took the money all right, but I never poisoned him. Why would I after working for him ten years? It ain't reasonable."

"'For all men kill the things they love,'" murmured Craig. "You might have gone to Reading Gaol, Cobbie," he said. "A friendly jail inhabited by friendly ghosts. You must have passed it often on your way to the downs. Why didn't you poison Quinn in England and go to Reading Gaol for it?"

"That's right," agreed Piper, "why didn't you? And save the State of California some money! You know what it costs here to try and execute a man?"

Cobbie swallowed nervously.

"Plenty," continued Piper. "You're an Englishman. You kill another Englishman. And just because you do it on California soil it's up to our taxpayers to see you don't kill any more Englishmen." He glared resentfully at Cobbie. "I tell you something's got to be done about it. Dagos, Japs, Frogs, and now Englishmen: you all come over here to commit your crimes. It's not fair."

"Of course, when you come to think of it, Cobbie was wise to wait," observed Craig thoughtfully.

This unexpected tribute to his sagacity drew a sidewise glance from Cobbie. He learned nothing. Craig's blue eyes were as impersonal as though he were theorizing on a philosophical, not a flesh-and-blood, affair. "Quinn probably was carrying more cash than usual; there were no friends or relatives about to complicate matters; the coast was clear. What were you planning to do with the money, Cobbie?" he inquired casually. "Invest it in a stable on the downs?"

Reassured by Craig's easiness, the valet nodded. "That was the idea," he agreed amicably. "A stable on the downs. For twenty years I've had my heart on it. I couldn't seem to get the money any other way. If I could have . . ." He shrugged his shoulders. "But it wasn't my *forte,* you might say, to pick the winners."

"Then robbery was your last, not your first resort," commented Craig with a smile. "I suppose that's something in your favor. The real difficulty was that once you'd robbed Quinn, in order not to be found out, you had to kill him. Too bad."

"I never said I killed him."

"Quite right. I apologize for jumping at conclusions."

"A damned sound conclusion if you ask me," interpolated Blake. "Quinn treated you like hell. The day before he kicked off he blacked your eye."

Cobbie's face, so puffy as to be almost expressionless, darkened. "He treated me well enough," he muttered.

"Yes?" inquired Straight sarcastically. "That's what you say now."

"If he'd treated you better, if he hadn't blacked your eye, maybe he'd still be alive," suggested Piper importantly.

Cobbie shot a surly glance at him. "I stayed with Sir Arthur ten years," he maintained stoutly. "If he hadn't been done in I'd be with him yet. You can say what you like, but there it is. Sure he blacked my eye. It wasn't the first time either. But I never thought any the worse of him for that. Why"—glowering at the detectives, he announced emphatically—"murder Sir Arthur? I'd as soon have murdered my own father!"

"Exactly!" Craig's comment, delivered crisply, elicited a look of surprise from his companions. "You're just the sort of man who would as soon murder his own father. You were through the war; you saw thousands of men die; human life can't mean very much to you. And to people like you, without imagination, death means nothing."

Cobbie opened his mouth to expostulate. Craig, however, didn't give him the chance. "You were with Quinn ten years," he continued. "That doesn't mean you were loyal to him; it only means that it was to your advantage to stay with him."

"There's something in that," agreed Piper heartily.

"I doubt if you have any capacity for loyalty," Craig regarded the valet coolly. "Why should you have? You've never been treated with any consideration; as a boy you were no doubt kicked around; consequently you're out to get what you can however you can. If you were educated, as you're not, or idealistic, as you're certainly not, you'd never have killed Quinn. No matter how good your reasons, you'd have considered the possible results of such an act, as well as the loss to science. Naturally, such considerations never entered your head. To you Quinn wasn't a scientist; he was merely your employer, the man you'd robbed, so you got rid of him. Isn't that right?"

"No!" growled Cobbie.

"Robbery's a damned simple motive for the murder of a man like Quinn," suggested Blake.

Craig nodded and lighted a cigarette. "It is. But then, as I think I pointed out once before, the motives for practically all murders are elemental. And it's certainly a mistake to suppose, merely because the victim was profound or intellectual that the motives for his murder were on the same plane. They never are. Quinn was intellectual, Quinn was important; but when it came to murdering him, Cobbie didn't need any motive other than fear, and possibly hatred."

He paused and contemplated the valet who stared back at him with an expression of sullen contempt.

"Cobbie's a weak character," explained Craig. "He gives in to his instincts. When he's hungry he eats and when he's in danger he takes the easiest way out. Strong characters require greater provocation when it comes to doing wrong. And when it comes to committing murder—well—" Craig shrugged his shoulders and leaned back in his chair, an expression of rather weary repose on his handsome face. "One might almost generalize that the degree of motivation depends solely on circumstances and the actor."

"We're coming into Indio," announced Straight, turning from the desert landscape of sand and cactus. "Put on your coat," he ordered Cobbie.

The valet complacently picked up his coat. Then, with an agility that took all four of his captors completely by surprise, he made a dash for the corridor.

Luck was against him; the narrow corridor was already filled by the broad figure of a conductor; and before Cobbie could get through to the platform Straight was on him.

Followed by the startled conductor he dragged the valet back into the dining-car.

Piper sighed with relief. "Not a pistol or a pair of handcuffs on us," he commented. "He'd have gotten across the Mexican border and that's the last we'd have seen of him."

"We're taking him off at Indio," Straight explained to the conductor.

"Isn't he riding East with two bodies?" The conductor glanced through the tickets in his hand. "They can't travel alone. If he gets off they get off too."

"My God!" said Straight. "You can't do that."

"Orders of the railroad. No bodies without a man to look after them."

The train slowed down. "Indio?" asked Piper.

The conductor nodded. "If he's got to go back, why don't one of you men go on to New York on his ticket?"

Straight considered the suggestion. "All right," he announced decisively. "Blake, you'll have to stay on to New York. I'll wire the New York police to take charge of the bodies from there on. We'll send you a return ticket, care of the police."

The train came to an abrupt stop.

"Why me?" demanded Blake wildly.

"Because none of us can be spared. It's got to be you. How long's this stop?" he asked the conductor.

"Thirty seconds."

"Hurry up!" Hustling Cobbie along with them, the four men squeezed through the corridor out onto the platform.

"Better get back on," Piper cautioned Blake.

Blake unwillingly climbed onto the first step. "But I haven't any clothes."

"Buy anything you need at Phoenix. You'll have fifteen minutes there."

"Yeah, at midnight!" added Piper with a grin.

The train gave a jerk, preparatory to starting.

"A free trip to New York, T. F." Craig reminded him, a twinkle in his eye, as the porter, climbing onto the slowly moving train, forced Blake up the remaining two steps to the platform. "Good luck!"

Blake looked less forlorn, and a malicious smile lightened his Scotch countenance as he called back to the group receding more and more quickly from him, "I'll get even with you crooks! Wait till you see the expense account I pile up for you. I'll stuff on caviar. So long, Craig! See you in jail, Cobbie— unless you give them the slip . . ." His voice faded into the mechanical symphony of the train.

As that, too, faded out, leaving only the petty silence of a desert town, Cobbie turned to Craig. "I won't give you the slip," he promised in a startlingly good replica of his former brazen manner. "I poisoned Sir Arthur all right; he jolly well had it coming, too. But I won't hang for it. Not here in America, I won't. I'll hire a lawyer who'll prove I was insane—one of my uncles is in a nut house now—and what do you want to bet I'm not out at grass again in five years?"

Craig smiled, but his smile was tempered by admiration for the man's nerve. "You don't think much of the institutions of this country, do you, Cobbie?" he observed.

"Can't say I do. I've read up on too many of your murder cases. You never get anywhere with them over here." Cobbie's tone was scornful. "Now in England . . ." radiating a curious pride, he snapped his fingers. "If I'd been such a bloody fool as to kill him in England, I'd hang like that."

He jerked his head in the direction of Pasadena. "Come on," he ordered the astounded detectives. "Get busy! Take me back! No lawyers around here. How about some action!"

"Drive you anywhere you want to go, mister," drawled the owner of a nineteen-twenty Ford.

"Palm Springs?"

"One hour: five dollars."

"Four dollars," bargained Straight.

"Climb in!"

Craig's lazy smile approved the suggestion. "Excellent! The atheist turns out to have been a victim to his money, not his morals, and"—his blue eyes closed in on the reality of his watch dial—"I shall get back to Pasadena in time to see Lona Lang dance."

About the Author

Helen Babette Plechner (1905-1982) was born in Seattle, Washington. She met playwright Glenn Hughes while a student at the University of Washington and they married in 1924. While her husband became professor of English at UW, Babette published 15 one-act plays and two mystery novels. The Hughes divorced in the 1940s, and she relocated to New York City, where she married public relations executive Benn Hall in 1947 (and eventually took over his firm after his death).

COACHWHIP PUBLICATIONS
ALSO AVAILABLE

SULTAN'S HAREM MYSTERY

Drink the Green Water
The Milkmaid's Millions

HUGH AUSTIN

COACHWHIPBOOKS.COM (PRINT)
COACHWHIP.COM (EPUB)

*Death Has
Seven Faces*

HUGH AUSTIN

COACHWHIPBOOKS.COM (PRINT)
COACHWHIP.COM (EPUB)

The Adventures of the
Brave Baron von Kaz
in the Northern States of America

1 THE TICKING TERROR MURDERS
THE FEATHER CLOAK MURDERS

DARWIN AND HILDEGARDE TEILHET

COACHWHIPBOOKS.COM (PRINT)
COACHWHIP.COM (EPUB)

DEATH
ON THE CAMPUS
ADDISON
SIMMONS

THE SPECTRUM OF
ENGLISH MURDER

The Detective Fiction of
Henry Lancelot Aubrey-Fletcher
and G. D. H. and Margaret Cole

CURTIS EVANS

COACHWHIP PUBLICATIONS
ALSO AVAILABLE

MURDER TAKES
THE VEIL

MURDER AT
ST. DENNIS

SISTER SIMON'S
MURDER CASE

THE MARGARET ANN HUBBARD
MYSTERY OMNIBUS

COACHWHIPBOOKS.COM (PRINT)
COACHWHIP.COM (EPUB)

LAVERNE RICE
WELL DRESSED
FOR MURDER

www.ingramcontent.com/pod-product-compliance
Lightning Source LLC
Chambersburg PA
CBHW022144010726
47493CB00002B/328